THE BLUE

D1056178

THE BLUE

Charles Bartholomay

VANTAGE PRESS
New York

This is a work of fiction. Any similarity between the
characters appearing herein and any real persons,
living or dead, is purely coincidental.

Cover design by Lucy Bartholomay
Cover design element/photo by *fantaSeas* of Palm City, Florida

First Edition

All rights reserved, including the right of
reproduction in whole or in part in any form.

Copyright © 2001 by Charles Bartholomay

Published by Vantage Press, Inc.
516 West 34th Street, New York, New York 10001

Manufactured in the United States of America
ISBN: 0-533-13665-2

Library of Congress Catalog Card No.: 00-91597

0 9 8 7 6 5 4 3 2

To all who love the sea and her creatures

THE BLUE

Prologue

The tall man surveyed the slick calm tropical sea for a time as he drew frantically on his cigar. He pulled the fine Cuban from his mouth in disgust, pitched it overboard and watched as the ashes descended with the light rays into the sea's 2000-foot depth. He shook his head slowly as he resumed his scan of the flat ocean, taking in all of the horizon for an unknown sign of life. The only disturbance atop the peaceful sea was the wake behind his boat. He began to pace nervously as he fired up another cigar.

"Where the hell is he, Houghton?"

"Under the boat, boss, down there," the Captain replied from the bridge, gesturing with his index finger.

The man walked to the corner of the boat's cockpit, opened the drink cooler and reached for a beer. Slamming the brew in his coolie, he decided to climb the bridge ladder to have a 'conference' with his Captain. When he arrived up top, he found his man staring into the display screen of the vessel's color depth sounder.

"We've pretty much pounded this place to death, don't you think, Houghton? I need a blue marlin and you haven't so much as had the bite of a barracuda. What the hell are you trying to prove out here?"

The man's eyes did not leave the viewing screen.

"Pretty dead today, Frank . . . not happening anywhere. Most of the boats are fishing inshore on the drop, and all you hear is an occasional 'cuda, . . . a wahoo. The water's cold and green all the way in, and I've not marked that much bait in there all week. Seems to me like we're working with just a few resident fish, Boss.

1

No migratory push goin' on here now. I—"

"Guess what, Houghton, you're biteless. I haven't seen a damn thing here all morning! Give me one reason for your being here."

"Frank, fifty boats and nobody's even had a sighting since lines in. I wouldn't be taking this personal so soon. At least we have some good conditions here."

"Screw your conditions, Chad. I'm more a structure fisherman, and I need a shot at a marlin! How about doing something up here besides steering the boat around."

"As I was saying, Boss . . . in working the break of this canyon wall, ebbtide and opposing current have provided us a sharp edge with warm blue water on the offshore side. I've seen plenty of tuna ducks, petrels and shearwaters flyin' around out here, too. So the fish aren't in the go mode right now, Frank, I mean the ocean is flat as a parkin' lot. When and if they get serious, I believe we'll get our chances here."

"Chad, are we hunting a marlin, or are we out here bird watching? Tell Billy to change out the lures. Find me a fish, Houghton, or start thinking about finding another ride." Conference over.

Chad about bit his lip clean through as his boss, Frank Whitman, went back down the ladder. The experienced captain shook his head as he witnessed his owner's mood swing back to cordiality, when he gave the slow fishing report to his angling partner, Senator Jack Hamm.

First Mate Billy Amis looked up to his captain as Chad pointed to all four lines, two outriggers and two flat, indicating a complete changeout of the spread. The mate opened the lure bags and produced two new offerings knowing Whitman wouldn't detect the switch of his own choices over to the other side of the boat.

Amis moved to the left side of the fighting chair and cranked the eighty-pound class reel until he could reach the rubber band

2

connecting fishing line with tag line. He broke the elastic from a pre-measured dacron loop, whipped on the fishing line, and started retrieving the condemned lure. Carefully packing and leveling the line on the spool with thumb and index finger, Billy cranked to and past the splice of his wind-on leader, leaving the final terminal swivel a few feet below the rod's roller tip.

"Billy, find me one in that bag of tricks that works."

"Tryin' Mr. Whitman, but it doesn't sound like anyone's seen one today."

"We're not anyone, Amis," Whitman snapped back. "You and Chad haven't raised shit all week behind this boat. You must not be doing something right."

The young mate didn't look up as he quietly snipped the 500-pound test leader from the swivel. With machine press, he quietly crimped the new selection in its place. Billy picked up the lure and eyed it a final time, checking the double hookset for bind as he straightened the skirt.

"Maybe we ought to throw some natural bait out there, Whit," the freshman senator from North Carolina suggested walking back out on deck from the cabin.

"Lures, Jack, are the only way to go anymore. They account for more tournament victories than any natural bait. Ask anyone on the dock tonight," Whitman evenly stated as he pulled hard on his fresh cigar.

"More boats pull lures here for many different reasons, Sir, but I don't agree with that last statement at all," Billy observed while he carefully laid the lure back in the water and free-spooled it back out to its original position. Reaching for the dacron loop, now a few feet in front of the rod tip, he inserted a new rubber band securing it to the tag line with a couple of half-hitches. Resuming his free spool, Billy watched the tag line attached to the outer eye of the outrigger, as it quickly arced the rubber band out and away from the boat until it reached the end of its tether.

Satisfied that the lure was pulling well without tumbling, Billy completed his presentation by putting the reel in gear, positioning the drag lever just behind the 'strike' button on the reel housing. All four fishing lines were now held by the rubber bands at the ends of the tag lines. The initial strike by the fish would snap the elastic, releasing the lure to the fish, and finally to the rod and angler.

Billy had total respect and confidence in his captain, Chad Houghton, to find the fish and provide the precious few opportunities. They had caught more than a few marlin over the years in many different locales, in many different conditions and circumstances.

Chad accepted that in the business of big game fishing, it was hard to be at the top of your game every time. There were many others with matching skills and experience. But the patrons of the sport not only demanded success, they expected it.

If cream rises to the top, a huge portion of luck certainly helps it along. Over the course of many seasons, however, there emerges a far smaller field of consistent producers. Better to be lucky than good any day, but being lucky is a tall order if you don't spend most of your fishing time around what little there is out there.

Whitman's cell phone now chirped from the corner of the boat's cockpit. "Damn thing is such a nuisance . . . Frank here. Hold on, Brenda, let me get inside. Be right back, Jack, the cockpit is yours," instructed the CEO of Whitman Technologies as he closed the cabin door behind him.

"If I was one of you tall dogs, I damn sure wouldn't want to be found if I was out here enjoying the day, I swear," Billy laughed as he took a long pull on his Coke.

"Goes with the territory I'm afraid, Billy. If you're Mr. America of the computer world, you're not going to be left alone for very long."

"Yeah, that's right," was all Amis could provide to fuel the discussion, as he drifted off into another afternoon in Key Largo. He and Chad had agreed at the outset of the Bahamas Blue Marlin Championship that an 'all lure' presentation was the only way they could fish Frank Whitman. He was an inexperienced angler and certainly not up to the needed finesse required in bait fishing. Nor was he the kind of angler to spend hours in the fighting chair after 'lines in,' a necessity in natural presentations. An aggressive fish will eat in the blink of an eye and waits for no man.

As the crew, they were willing to concede numbers of shots for getting the 'right' kind of bite—the kind of bite that a high speed lure with two clearly exposed 11/0 hooks can give you. Besides, with the exception of Chub Cay in the Berry Islands, most sites for the Championship required a lot of area to be worked. Higher trolling speeds required for lure fishing would widen the coverage and possibly offset other concessions. Through it all, however, they both knew Frank Whitman was reasonably green in the sport of big game fishing.

It was late afternoon before a northeast breeze finally came up, rippling the surface of the smooth cobalt water. Houghton felt it was just too pretty out here in the deep to leave and go back inshore. There were still no runs, no hits, no errors, not even a sighting, at least by the talk on the radio. It was pretty out here and it felt right.

Throughout the day, Chad had observed the 'right' birds on fly by, the flyers that usually put you on the meat. Where were they going...hunting...leaving from...he wondered. He had to believe there were tuna working somewhere along this color change.

He took an offshore tack into the pretty water side of the current edge, where the two water masses pressed up against one another, never blending together. Chad turned the bow of his sixty-five-foot sportfisherman directly into the current that he already knew was pushing him to the east. He scanned his GPS, LORAN and sumlog, comparing speed through the water with the slower speed over ground, and validated what he had already suspected. The easterly current was far stronger than yesterday, resulting in the sharper and steeper appearance of the current rip. It was time to make a move.

"Crank 'em in, Billy, we're gonna pick up and run down to the eastern' and fish that other canyon."

"Done, Cap." Billy sprang to life and in no wasted motion had everything down and in the cockpit in less than a minute. The *Byte Her* was now powering up on plane out of a trail of black smoke left from the air-starved turbos of her sixteen-cylinder diesel engines. It would take twelve minutes to cover the five miles hooked up and running at cruising speed.

As Houghton neared within a mile and a half of his destination, the larger of the birds came into view. Circling higher than the smaller chickens and tuna ducks, the shearwaters and petrels always sensed first where the bait would next be forced to the surface by the feeding tuna below.

Chad pulled the boat back off-plane well short of the surface frenzy, slowing his rig to nine-and-a-half knots. Amis made ready the trolling spread of four lures and two hookless teasers. Staying off the fish until all were deployed, Houghton now began his approach to the perimeter of the circling and diving birds.

Occasionally, he would observe feeding yellowfin tuna away from the boat cutting and showering the bait. But each pass he made on the spot tended to push the bait and feeding tuna down. The fishes' wariness did not surprise him, such as conditions were, and Chad suspected his lures probably wouldn't even elicit the bite of a tuna.

No matter. Like the marlin cruising in the deep blue below, he was only looking for one shot. He knew the great fish was eyeing all the activity up above. The Big Blue was merely waiting for a tuna to falter, which would create the opening for its own kill. The huge predator would then take the hunting tuna as *his* quarry.

Chad might be invited to enter this timeless drama of creation, if he could only blend in with its rhythm for a few seconds. Everything had to be set right. Amidst a great deal of life and death, the two watched and waited patiently for their moment.

Minutes passed and there were still no sightings behind the boat. The feeding frenzy had only intensified as there were now hundreds more birds circling the area. Surface activity covered a square mile. Chad took his eyes off his lure spread to watch a couple of decent fifty-pound-class yellowfin tuna cutting through the indigo blue sea scattering the dense pods of bait across its surface. The color sounder's monitor was continually marking the thick balls of the smaller bait, displaying them as subsurface yellow globes, showing red centers of even greater density.

"It'd be nice to at least get a tuna interested," Billy lamented, calling up from the cockpit.

I hear ya' real fine Billy, Chad thought to himself. He motioned for his mate to come upstairs.

"Tell ya' what, man, you got the right idea in pullin' a couple of tuna into the spread. Pull your 'riggers in short, and move your teasers in the same distance. Got any small ballyhoo or finger mullet rigged up?"

"Both."

"Pull 'em on the flat lines. Get 'em back there . . . not quite long 'rigger distance. We'll draw everything in, throw in a little natural look, and maybe we can convince a tuna or two to drop what they should be doin' and take an interest in us."

"You and Whitman have a nice chat, Cap?"

"I wouldn't dignify it by calling it a conversation, Billy."

"Nobody done squat, have they?"

"I've not heard of one being seen."

"Up till now, Chatsworth," the mate replied quickly, going down the bridge ladder.

Amis had finished his rigging and alterations and was just pinning down the second bait when the other flat line snapped out of the pin on the covering board. Watching the rod tip slowly bow over and start jerking he yelled, "fish on the left flat, probably a tuna." No response.

Billy stomped the cockpit floor a few times until the salon door opened and Whitman appeared with his cell phone in hand. "You got a small tuna on the left flat, Boss, shall I crank it in? Billy knew the program.

"Let Jack take it, he could use a little practice," Whitman replied as he passed the senator on his way back into the salon.

"Not much fight to these," the senator observed as he skipped the fifteen-pound tuna to the boat, "nothing to it."

"Agreed, Senator. A small skippy is no match for an eighty with twenty-two pounds of striking drag. It's not exactly what we're huntin' for, but its a—"

"Left rigger, he's under the left rigger, Billy!" Chad bellowed from the bridge loud enough to rouse his boss from the inside of the boat.

Billy flashed immediately to the left outrigger where the black and orange lure was dutifully diving down the face of the wave created by the wake of the turning boat. The offset head imparted a slight wobble to the lure's tracking leaving an air trail of white 'smoke', each time it barely broke the water's surface. He also saw the huge dark silhouette behind and below the lure a few yards.

"I don't see a thing," the senator said, lifting his hand to his brow to create a visor.

Showing uncharacteristic speed, Frank had already gotten himself into the fighting chair and half into his bucket harness when Chad droned, "He faded off."

Chad turned the boat to starboard into the fish, never ceasing his scan of the spread. Seeing nothing for a minute or two, and now moving away from the surface activity, he carved a long slow turn to port. He put a couple of hundred rpm on the engines, and with a counter turn, created a figure eight that would return him to the same location and position coordinates. The presentation would now be recreated exactly.

As he entered to the sighting position, he stole a glance at the color sounder and noted the bottom break where the ocean floor first rose up two hundred feet. Then it plummeted five hundred feet in less than a quarter mile, profiling the wall of the deep sea canyon.

The marlin had been cruising about one hundred and fifty feet offshore the current edge Chad was working in the cleaner, warmer blue water. All the feeding activity he had observed since his arrival here, had been on the offshore side of that rip. He was now coming back into the zone . . . 1700 . . . 1800 . . . 1900 . . . 2000 . . . 1800 . . . 2000 . . . 2250 feet of water.

"What do you see up there Houghton?" Whitman's distractions were all but ignored.

Chad straightened up to resume scanning the spread and immediately picked up the fish on the same lure. "There he is again on the left long . . . hold on, Billy!"

"Picked him up?" Amis yelled from the cockpit deck.

"I got him, he's movin' over to the right side, Billy, he's still down there!" This time when Chad turned into the fish he reappeared under the other outrigger. "Right rigger!" Chad screamed, "He's there, he's comin' on it!"

The blue marlin had by now made his five hundred pounds quite public to all but the bewildered senator. The marlin's huge tail was all 'lit up' in neon blue, breaking the water as the fish began to kick harder. The creature's face, pectoral fins and lateral bars, were aglow in electric hues of blue, unlike the very dark, ebony color he had shown just seconds before.

"He's fired up Billy! Keep an eye on your flat line baits!"

Chad screamed from the bridge.

The huge creature was suddenly in the middle of the bait spread, directly behind the small ballyhoo, its glowing tail quivering and kicking uncontrollably. In the next second, the Big Blue spun on the right outrigger lure, crashing the bait from the side in a burst of speed exceeding 50 mph. But for all the show, the fish had only made a slight contact with the lure with the tip of its three-foot bill. He never found either of two hooks, nor struck it hard enough to break the rubber band.

At least we saw one, Chad thought as he set up for another tack over the spot. It wasn't much of a chance for his boss, to be fair, but that was a given when pulling plastics. In essence, it was no more than a glorified gaff bite on the fish, a controlled crash. It required little finesse or feel on the hookup, as in the dropback process of feeding a billfish a natural bait. Chad knew the challenges for the angler after a fish gets on the line may be considerable, whether a lure or a bait is involved. As for the hookup on a lure, a chimpanzee would fare very well, as the rod holder often does. "What the hell is going on, Houghton?"

"Wouldn't do business, Frank! Be ready and don't go nowhere. Keep your eyes on the spread and quit your yackin'!"

Houghton looked back at the lure and bait array, then at the right flat line not swimming, but now skipping on the water.

"Right flat must have popped out, Billy."

As Amis went to repin the mullet, Chad saw an indistinct dark form down deep under the two flat lines streak back and forth from bait to bait. "Another fish down there, Billy, screwin' with the flat lines. I don't believe it's the same fish, not as big, could be a small blue or a white . . . here he comes. It's a blue one!"

And willing that fish was, all over the ballyhoo trying his best to eat and put the bait deep inside its belly. Whitman held the rod with his left hand on the butt and the right hand on the foregrip above the reel. Each time the marlin tried to seize the

10

bait between bill and lower jaw, Frank would rear back with both hands and try to hook the fish, dragging [scaling] the bait from its mouth.

"It's not a tug 'o war, Frank, let him eat it!" Amis felt like ripping the rod from Whitman's hands.

"What?"

"Drop it back to him, Boss!"

After a couple more swings and misses, the mangled bait popped up in corkscrew spin. Bent on suicide, the fish returned a third time seizing the bait entirely, taking it to the side in one frenzied motion. Feeling the steel of a not so small 9/0 hook, the Blue initiated a blistering surface run, windshield wiping on his left side. The marlin peeled off a quick hundred yards of line as it beat the water into a white froth.

Fortunately for the fish, and less so for the crew, Frank had elected to put the reel into an unguided free spool when he saw the marlin make his move to the side. The sudden burst of speed by the fish had caught the inexperienced Whitman off guard. The rapidly accelerating spool had not only severely burnt the man's thumb, but created a bird's nest in the line, so complete that it would have to be entirely stripped and repacked at the dock. When the ball of mono jammed in the reel casing, the loud crack of the snapping 100-pound test line, could be heard by all on board.

Amis looked over at his angler whose jaw had dropped wide open, "Think you'll find any eggs in that nest, Chief?"

"What the hell are you doing to me, Amis! You set this reel up with way too much heat, the drag is all screwed up," Whitman barked as he tried to throw the rod into the nearby holder on the side of the fighting chair. He missed, however, and the heavy eighty-pound rod and reel took a sizable chip out of the teak deck as it crashed to the floor of the cockpit. Big Frank looked out a hundred yards at his broken-off blue marlin, still jumping and quivering as it tried to throw the hook. Game over.

"Shit," Whitman screamed at the top of his lungs as he made his retreat inside.

Chad looked down at his friend and mate who had become still and speechless. "They just called lines out, Billy, let's go home." When Billy had gathered everything in, Chad pointed her south for the ten mile run back to Walker's Cay.

1

It was late afternoon on a beautiful October day in south Florida, temperature in the low eighties, blue skies and light cumulus clouds. The bait runs had been underway for some time and Captain Louis Gladding was on the search for silver mullet of assorted sizes. The smaller finger mullet would be deboned and gutted from the top for use as a fine trolling bait for sailfish and dolphin. The larger specimens used to troll for marlin, could be deboned by tube, and/or split-tailed and could also be employed as hookless teasers in chains or umbrella rigs. Louis needed to catch and prepare his bait stash for the coming sailfish season in addition to needing some fresh bait for the charter he had booked for the morning.

Louis loaded the old Ford 150 with two coolers of ice, a few knives, salt, baking soda, a heavily leaded ten foot cast net, and headed for the Indian River.

Crossing the first causeway he glanced at the backwaters for signs of activity. Maybe birds, boils, tarpon rolling, bottlenose dolphins, you never knew what the huge bait schools running up river might bring into the estuary from the inlet. He was driving on the inner island now, heading for the mosquito bridge just this side of the next causeway leading out to the barrier island and coastal beaches. Here on the western shore of the Indian River, with its maze of grass and sugar sand flats, is where Louis would do his hunting.

As he slowly drove by the small mosquito bridge, he observed a number of budding cast netters tossing, hurling, flipping, heaving, dropping their nets to the few terrified mullet below. Louis scratched his head for a moment as he watched the 'wannabees' deliver the monofilament mesh in every possible way except open, circular, and ready to do business.

Louis eased the truck off the road and parked on the shoulder a few yards down from the bridge. Looking north along the river's western edge, he began a long scan of the mangroves lining the beach edge. He saw a few bait pods, a couple of blue herons, and then he focused on a lone snowy egret about a third of a mile up from the bridge.

Louis took off his topsiders, threw them into the truck along with his wallet and locked it. He grabbed his cast net laid neatly in a couple of stacked buckets, and proceeded to walk down to the river's edge. From there he would wade around, through and under the protruding mangroves ever closing in on his white bird.

When Louis had approached within forty yards of the egret, he could see the huge school of silver mullet mudding on the sandbar in front of the bird's perch fifteen feet high up on the mangroves. Louis set everything down, unfolded his net and soaked it in the water, straightening it out as he did so. He returned his gaze to the snowy egret who had been absolutely still ever since he had first sighted it.

Louis had few equals in the art of throwing a cast net. Because he had developed an underhand delivery, he consistently achieved maximum distance and surprise at the net's opening. Making his final approach in a crouch, Louis cautiously waded to within thirty feet of the mullet school. All hunched over, he and the egret made for a great still life together, both motionless, patient, and suspended in time. Louis knew he needed to close in on the quarry another five feet, but with the sun at his back and behind a cloud, he remained motionless. When the sun popped back out he would take two heel and toe soft steps on the sand bottom and launch.

Five minutes passed, and although his back was tingling sore, he knew any movement by him or the bird would scatter the bait school in a heartbeat. When the rays pounded the water once more, the old man took his steps and launched the monofilament net from his hip in one fluid motion. With a slight roll of hands and wrists, he released his snare on its way steering it like he might have been bowling.

The ball of net remained low to the water casting no shadow of its own upon the target. As it reached the end of its tether line, nearly over the school of bait, it began to level and open. Aided by a twitch from Louis, it neatly exploded into a complete circle as it dropped over the school of mullet. In an instant, a frenzy of fish found net, their silver undersides exploding like firecrackers.

The large white bird began to flap its wings as Louis began to tuck the net's leaded perimeter into its center. As he pulled the outer drawstrings attached to the tether line through the center horn, the net began choking its catch into a ball. In one throw he had enough bait to keep him cutting well into the night.

The smaller bait fish were now leaving the net through the 3/4 inch mesh as he drew it to him. Once gathered into a ball, he grabbed the horn and raised it high over head, thus opening and releasing the mass of mullet into the awaiting buckets. Louis now picked out of the net the remainder caught by their gills, and pitched them onto the beach in the direction of the egret.

Eagerly, the bird flew down to devour his feast as he had done often with the old fisherman. Louis gave thanks, whistled gently at the bird, and headed back to get his catch in a salt brine. It would take two trips to haul his mullet from the single throw.

When he neared his truck, Louis found he had company. He noticed a man of around twenty-five years getting out of a convertible Mercedes, and the stranger was now walking toward him.

"Excuse me, sir, but I wonder if you could direct me to where I might find a Capt. Louis Gladding? I was told he might be catching bait in this area."

"I'm Gladding," Louis answered after a brief eye contact

with the stranger. "What can I do for you?"

The young man fell out of sync for a moment as he studied the old fisherman before him; blond hair now streaked white, deeply tanned skin where creases and wrinkles had given way to larger folds of leather, powerful hands that were scarred and wrinkled showing signs of skin cancer, and of course the eyes, the cobalt eyes, clear and blue as the Gulf Stream, cutting right through him from behind the man's permanent squint and crowsfeet.

"Scott Byrd, glad to meet you," he offered his hand, "call me Scoot, everyone does."

Louis shook the man's hand, "Louie."

Again distracted the younger man studied the old captain in his rolled up jeans, madras shirt, and Busch beer cap tilted 20 degrees to starboard, and wondered if he had the man Whitman was looking for.

"Maybe you were expecting sportif shorts and gold marlins around the neck," Louis observed, keenly aware of the man's uncertainty in his mission. "So what does a stranger in a fancy car want with an old charter boat captain?" Louie continued on, speaking rather slowly.

"I work for a man named Frank Whitman, who shares the same passion for big game fishing as yourself. He is most interested in retaining your skills and experience for some tournament fishing here and overseas."

"I haven't fished a tournament in twenty years, what does Mr. Whitman want with me?"

"I'm not prepared to say any more at this time, but between you and me, he wants you and he'll definitely make it worth your while. Here's my card, mull it over tonight and let me know in the morning."

"I'm booked for charter tomorrow, all day."

"Ah . . . call me when you get in, it's important. I would give this some thought, Capt. Gladding." The young man went back to his Mercedes without another word, and took off in a cloud of dust.

When Louis had finished cutting his mullet and had them soaking in an overnight ice brine of salt water, he hung up his net and jumped in the shower. The day's encounter with the stranger had him thinking overtime, and it had unsettled him. He would have a little piece of fresh dolphin for dinner and wait for his daughter to come home from the junior college.

Louis had lost his wife to the recklessness of a drunk driver seventeen years ago. Since that tragedy, he had been living with his only offspring, his daughter Julie. She worked part-time, and went to college part-time. Truly, she was the only reason Louie had given any consideration to Whitman's offer. A big hit right now could help her into the university next fall.

Louis knew his health was suspect from a recent Coast Guard physical. Blood work indicated changes going on inside, and the doctors insisted on a biopsy and further tests. He had forgotten to make that appointment months ago. Now, here was a shot at some real bucks, he conceded. There may never come another one that I'd be healthy enough to take advantage of.

Then he reminded himself of his growing disfavor with marlin kill tournaments. Competitive fishing in general had become a turnoff to him, and he had grown weary of the senseless slaughter of brood stocks in bringing to the dock the larger female marlin. Louis had come to believe there were enough challenges in blue water fishing competing with one's self and mother nature—the journey being far more important than the destination.

What is there in great weight he would say to himself, other than the traveled life and nobility of the fish itself. They might all be blue marlin, but they were all unique. He had seen big fish lay at the gaff like a puppy after twenty minutes of light battle. Too, he had fought granders well into the night. And, of course, there were 'those' creatures that could never be stopped.

Probably the worst mauling he could remember at the hands of a Blue, came from a fish weighing no more than 500 pounds. He would argue often that if competition was necessary to enjoy your fishing, it might as well be in numbers not size. Show the folks you know what you're doin'. Catch more, not bigger, and you won't have to kill any of them for a senseless reward. Such thoughts had caused Louis to fall through the cracks of his trade.

As far as Louis was concerned fishing had become a lost art, obscured by the onslaught of hi-tech electronics and satellite imagery. Over time, technological parity had supplanted hands-on experience. Reputations were helpful, but like loyalty, no longer that necessary. Egos, personalities and screen tests had invaded the natural order of things It was more a 'bite or be bit' world where individual dominance reigned supreme, usually at the fishes' expense.

As a young man he could remember speaking of the deeds of great fish. He admired their beauty and integrity and cherished the purity of their actions. Fishing was more fun then if, for nothing else, it held far greater mysteries. Things had become just a little too much bottom line these days.

Now a modest charter boat owner/operator, Louis enjoyed the day-to-day sharing of the deep blue with his clients. The love of the ocean and her creatures was surely genuine to them. Catching fish was a bonus not a given. Just being there on the blue sea, moment to moment, interacting with mother ocean, was the reason for it all. Better to have seen and not caught, than not to have seen at all.

Louis disengaged himself from his wandering thoughts and realized he was no closer to a decision. He picked up his book and began reading until he was asleep in his chair. Tonight, he would dream of his younger days fishing the waters off Cuba, not realizing that his answer was already being given.

"Scott Byrd."

"Mr. Byrd, Louis Gladding calling. I have decided to at least meet with your Mr. Whitman and see what he has to say."

"Fantastic, Captain, I'll pick you up at 7:00 A.M. and we'll take it from there."

"So be it."

2

A cold front's passing in the night had left the early morning in patchy fog. When the Mercedes pulled up to the cracker house in an older part of town, Louis was already getting a bad vibe from all this. He had awakened as usual at around 4:30, not quite believing the turn of events and this new-found interest in his abilities. He had decided to call a few old captain friends in Palm Beach to do a little checking of his own on Mr. Frank Whitman. At precisely 7:00 A.M. he saw the headlights of the Mercedes pulling into his dirt driveway.

"I'll get back to 'ya Crafty when I get home, and let 'ya know what's going on." Louis hung up the phone, grabbed his faded blue windbreaker and was out the door. Scoot flew out of his ride and opened the passenger side door—a first in Louis' world.

Now rolling down I-95 at about 85 mph, Scoot felt compelled to break what had been virtually twenty minutes of dead air. "I'll have you back before dinner, Captain. We're just going to take a little trip up to Mr. Whitman's office so the two of you can meet and map out strategies."

Louis slowly turned to Byrd and replied dryly, "If we get that far."

Scoot exited at Belvedere Road and headed to the private hangars at the south side of Palm Beach International. Once cleared at the security gate, he proceeded to a parking area adjacent the customs office. They got out and walked through another gate and onto the tarmac towards the Whitman Technologies' Gulfstream IV jet parked a couple hundred feet away. The pilot emerged from the cabin and walked down the gangway to meet them.

He looked too young to be flying this thing, Louis thought to himself, much too young. But he seemed friendly when he extended his hand, and it appeared as though he was having a hard time hiding his amusement at all of this. Louis shook the pilot's hand enthusiastically as he introduced himself.

In minutes they were airborne, being served breakfast on their way to Charlotte, North Carolina, for an 11:00 appointment with the CEO of Whitman Technologies. Byrd occasionally looked over at the old man, and wondered what impact all this fanfare was having on him. Gladding had spoken little during the trip, asked no questions, and appeared relatively unaffected by it all. Byrd surmised that if the old captain lived up to his reputation, he had fished some very famous and wealthy clients over the years. He had probably felt their money many times before.

The jet touched down at around 9:45 A.M. concluding what had been a flawless and most comfortable flight. After securing the plane, the pilot emerged to help with the unloading, and once again offered his hand to Louis, "I hope your flight was enjoyable, sir."

"It was," Louis answered, "you're a fine pilot, son, that was very pretty work."

"There's the limo," Byrd interjected not allowing the moment to linger any further, "gotta keep moving, Captain."

The two men entered through double oak doors into a reception area where Louis was invited to take a seat on a giant leather couch. Byrd made inaudible small talk to a pair of secretaries, each seated at her own desk behind an impressive array of computers and VDTs. Byrd then disappeared through another door and emerged with a striking redhead, whom he introduced as Mr. Whitman's personal aide.

"Hi, Captain Gladding, Brenda Holloway. Frank has told me so much about you and your fishing, I feel as though I have known you for years. It must be quite a thrill pulling in one of those big ones." Louis could feel the distance between them but she was trying hard to make him feel comfortable, professionally speaking.

"How about some coffee, Louis?"

"Louie, coffee sounds good, thank you Brenda."

Louis waited undisturbed for the next hour, until precisely at 11 o'clock, Ms. Holloway returned to escort him through her outside office. The pair entered through a final set of double oak doors to the inner chambers of Frank Whitman. Louis took a chair immediately in front of Whitman's desk, and waited as the business man finished his phone call.

He could not see Whitman as the man had turned the high-backed leather chair so the back was facing him. Louis took the opportunity to take a look around the dignified setting. Oak bookcases, plush beige carpeting, banker's green everywhere, a separate desk just for computers. Business rewards and accolades adorned the rear walls. A picture of Whitman in the White House with the President. A few fishing photographs dotted the landscape.

Suddenly, the chair spun around to reveal Whitman in the act of chasing down some paperwork. He quickly glanced and smiled at Gladding before looking away. He repeated this ritual a few more times as if to get a handle on where to begin with the old Captain. Louie simply held his gaze on Whitman, smiling in return when the situation required it.

"Let me hear from you when the road is smooth and you receive the units . . . Sounds good . . . I won't be in town . . . Brenda will take care of you if you hit a snag, she is well briefed on the matter." Whitman signed off on the speaker phone when his side of the conversation subsided. He spun around to face Louis Gladding, set both hands on the desk in traditional executive repose, then extended the right hand, "Frank Whitman."

The Captain reached forward and firmly shook the man's hand never leaving full eye contact, "Louie Gladding." He sat back and waited for Whitman.

Frank peeled off his reading glasses and began to rub his eyes as he began speaking. "Captain, my people tell me you're a doer, a man who can get the job done. Your reputation definitely precedes you, at least with some of the older, more experienced fishing captains I know. I like catching big fish. It has become an obsession of mine, one that I intend to excel at. In order to attain that success and gain the respect of others, I need opportunities and exposure to the sport. I require a crew with the drive and experience to put me on the fish and make them bite."

For the first time Whitman left his chair to initiate a 360 degree walkaround of Louis seated before his desk. Louis knew the man wanted to look him over, and he held his gaze straight ahead while Whitman continued on.

"Louie, we both know you've caught more blue marlin than any man alive, and then some. We also know that you dropped out of sight years ago, a generation, in fact. I know you are still actively fishing in Florida and the Bahamas, and I know that the financial strains of putting a daughter through college as a single parent, are real and understandable. I feel we can be of help to one another. Are we on the same page, Captain?"

"Why the big splash, sir? I mean fly me all the way up here, you could have phoned me. You appear to know all about my situation, therefore, you must know that I have acquired a strong dislike for 'kill' tournaments. I've not fished one in many years."

"I heard that," replied Whitman now standing directly behind Louis, as the Captain kept his focus straight ahead. "Perhaps I wanted to impress upon you just how important this matter is to me by bringing you here in person to discuss it. You see, Cap, I am a man who has grown accustomed to winning. If I commit to something, I intend to succeed at it. Not overnight always, but I will succeed. I hope you appreciate my being direct."

"Why me, Mr. Whitman? There are many out there more

visible than I, fully capable of leading you to your glory. You even hit a big one last spring in the Abacos with Houghton and Amis. The word is they showed you plenty of fish, and I'd be curious to know where they have wandered off to. It would seem that you are an owner with a tendency to go through a lot of crew."

"Louie," Whitman paused to refocus, "... we simply agreed to disagree, and everyone went their own way. They were well taken care of, I can assure you of that. But I do appreciate your checking up on me, in fact, I welcome it. We're more alike than you think."

"What do you really want from me other than to run your boat in a few tournaments?"

"You're a man with too much savvy to talk around the issue any longer. I need a favor done and you are probably the only one who can handle it for me. Louie, I want to fish the Cuban Hemingway Blue Marlin Tournament this spring. It's by special invitation only, just a handful of boats from this country will get the nod and I want to be one of them. You have fished many days with the Premier, whom we both know to be a fishing nut. At one time he considered you to be a great personal friend."

"Hmmm," entered Louis Gladding. "You want me to secure your place in Havana next spring for the purpose of adding to your fishing notoriety. That was years ago, I can't guarantee that I would even be remembered. What's the other reason?"

"Yes, it is a special tournament and it would wear well for me. Cuba, on the other hand, is a land soon to undergo many political changes. New markets are going to open up when these changes begin to occur, especially in your line of work. What will be good for Cuba will be good for the States, good for the Yucatan, good for everybody. I see no reason why Whitman Technologies cannot emerge as a leading trade partner when things begin to loosen up down there. You do see why I need your help?"

"Yup."

"I am prepared to pay you a salary of $2,000 a week, and any winnings you and the mate each get 25% off the top. I believe the Calcutta last year was somewhere around $400,000 if I'm not mistaken. Get me in the Hemingway, Captain Louie, and you've got a $20,000 bonus paid before we untie the lines. Am I talking dirty, Captain?"

Louis sat quietly a moment more, and then rose from his chair extending his hand. "Mr. Whitman, thank you for your time and making the offer available. The financial part of it is more than fair, but now I must leave and return home. I will have an answer for you in a few days."

"Take all the time you need, Captain Gladding. It's a few months away, but arrangements will have to be initiated by the first of the year. Brenda will show you out, have a nice trip back to Florida."

Whitman remained standing until the doors closed behind Louis, and then summoned Scott Byrd via intercom as he took his chair.

"That dog will hunt, eh Boss," Scoot prophesized as he entered the room with a wry grin.

"You should have more respect for age, Byrd, it can be a great teacher."

"You ever heard a man speak so slowly as our Cuban Louie? I wonder if it's congenital."

"He was rather deliberate in his conversation wasn't he, although he was quite lucid without any extra words. Ah . . . he's just a typical conch head from Marathon, set in his ways and on the back nine of his life. I will tell you this, Scoot, he can help our situation, and he is going to take me up on my offer."

"Based on—"

"Based on the fact that I know Louis Gladding, his character and his vulnerability. In my world, I make it my business to know people, it's why I'm sitting at this desk today. Louis Gladding will, with much reservation, assent to our plans. Meanwhile, you are to learn all you can about the boat's systems and propulsion. I doubt if Mr. Gladding is up to speed on some of the refinements present in a modern day sportfishing boat. I want you down at the yard starting next week so I can have Houghton pack your brains as much as possible before I fire him."

"About time, Frank."

"Really, Scoot, I thought you might be sad to see him go."

"Right."

"Everything in good time, now get out of here."

"Yes sir, I'm on me way."

3

Louis was nearly at the end of his agonizing. The situation with Whitman and his offer had consumed his thoughts for days, and he knew he had to make a decision. His personal discomfort with the whole scheme was undeniable, yet his daughter was the only important person here. Lord willing, he was going to Cuba. He reached for the phone.

Louis immediately recognized his old friend, "Alfie, . . . Louie."

"Luis, how you be, I not see you for while, still fishing hard?"

"Yeah, Alfie, I am. Got a little charter operation in town, go to the islands once in a while. What's up with you, still got that pretty 53-foot Whiticar?"

"Yes, my friend, I still have her. She is the only one of my wives who still loves me. She is mad at me now; I not fishing too much, and I not going to Cuba this spring. I am old fart, Luis, I catch more fish in my dreams."

"As do I, Alfie, it's not that bad a place to go anymore."

"It was more fun back then eh, amigo? Why you call, Luis?"

"Alfie, I have a sponsor for the Hemingway if he can get in. It will mean a good deal of money for me if I get him an invite, enough that I can almost get Julie through college. This is important to me, I am asking for a favor."

"I not call back yet on my inbitation, I put you and your boss name on my reply, so Premier know it is you, Cuban Louie, who want to fish. He still talk about you."

"It would mean everything to me, Alfie, how can I ever repay you?"

"De nada, Luis. What is heffe's name?"

"Frank Whitman, Whit-man, got that Alfie?"

"'Ees done. You come down here when you get home and take me yellowtail fishing. 'Ees good?"

"A done deal. You're sure old friend?"

"I sure. Your word is good, son, we go fish. Adios."

"Okay, Alfie."

Louis gave thanks for his life-long friend and already felt a sense of relief in the way things were falling together. There was just one more thing he needed to nail down before calling Frank Whitman, he reached for the phone.

"Hey Crafty, it's Louie. What's your book look like for May?"

"Supposed to fish the BBC at Treasure with T-bone, but I can off it, what'ya got ol' boy?"

"Got a guy on the line who wants to fish the Hemingway in Havana, provided the invitation goes through. I need 'ya in the pit on this one, Crafty. If we're going to win this thing I'm sure we'll be spendin' some time in the 'bowl.'"

"Ah huh."

"We've done this before, and it would be the business to have you runnin' the cockpit. It'd be a nice payday for y'all as well. You and I split half of the winnings. Interested?"

"No other place I'd rather be. I'm in. I'll off this other ride to Squeeky and Boy Roy tomorrow. He'll be over there anyway for the first leg, it'll fill him out nice. You've done it again, Louis. A constant source of inspiration."

"Thanks, buddy, I be grateful. We'll get together for a couple of Busch sometime soon and I'll fill you in. See ya."

Louis cradled the phone in a big yawn. He stared blankly into the fading afternoon light, letting his mind wander until he was barely grasping of anything, except for her.

Louis took a deep breath as he scanned the entire sand and grass flat, looking for any subtle changes in color or surface interference that might betray the cautious movement of fish working in the shallows. His eyes slowly followed the white sugar sand on which he was wading, as it expanded out for a half mile from his position. He noted the various grass patches and darker, deeper channels of brilliant aquamarine water, as they meandered towards the outer drop-off.

It was a fresh spring morning, a bluebird sky with only a few high clouds that seemed to rise up forever. He could see the mountains of Cuba to the north, standing tall, clean of all haze. The beautiful green grazing lands of the ranches stretched before him, with many horses and colts playing and running down the hillside.

His friend Alfie could be seen on the far side of the flat wading slowly along. He was hunched over slightly as he readied himself for a careful presentation of his conch-tipped jig to a very skittish bonefish.

Louis stared at his Cuban friend for some time and wondered if he was ever going to make that cast. They were young and they were brothers now. Louis looked down and saw his feet in the sand. He saw, too, the small coral that occasionally dotted out of the grass. He moved his gaze to a small flat area of hard coral bottom where a leopard ray swam along its perimeter. Some parrotfish had entered the coral flat from the field of bulbous coralheads that separated flat from the barrier reef that lay beyond. They were swimming on their side picking at the generous supply of hermit crabs that lay for the taking in the fifteen inches of water.

Gentle two-foot waves caressed the barrier reef from time to time, their breaking, the only interruption in the thick warm silence. The brilliant white shorebirds would fly by, their underwings a brilliant sapphire from the reflection off the crystalline water.

Beyond the reef, lay the endless miles of the deep blue, her water more purple than he could ever remember. A lone man-o-war bird circled endlessly offshore riding up on the thermals with ease.

Louis felt warm, but not uncomfortable. The ocean's twelve knot tradewinds touched every part of him to his core. He felt held in her hand, with no other moment more important than this one. His heart was grateful, and he felt at home.

His eyes steadied at a point of land directly across the flat, and settled on a young woman playing with a small child at the water's edge. Her long dark hair was waving in the gentle breeze, in perfect sync with the coconut palms behind her. She stood up and began waving to Louis, beckoning her husband to come in for awhile.

Louis' heart was aglow as he began to wade toward her. But the water was getting a little deeper and his legs were beginning to tire. He waved back to her and she was smiling now, but she remained on shore. He was starting to feel weary as each step seemed to sap his strength a little more until he saw that he was not getting any closer to her. She was now standing and receding toward the tree line. Louis could barely make her out as she vanished into the palms.

"Daddy . . . daddy." The young woman gently stirred the man into an easy awakening. "It's midnight, Dad, why don't you go to bed and get some sleep." She had done this for her father many times, and never once told him he had been dreaming.

"Whitman Technologies how may I direct your call?"

"This is Louis Gladding calling, I wish to speak with Mr. Whitman."

"One moment please."

"This is Ms. Holloway, Mr. Whitman's personal aide, how may I help you?"

"Hello Ms. Holloway, this is Captain Louie, I just wanted to speak with Mr. Whitman briefly if that's possible."

"Captain how are you? Frank is on another line, I can have him return your call when he is free; or you can hold for a bit."

"I'll wait I'm in no hurry."

"Okay. It shouldn't be too long, Louie. Stand by."

Louis heard the click and then the muzak let go with brass renditions of old rock hits. A few minutes later another click, and the serenade came to an untimely halt.

"Captain Louie how goes it? Are we ready to go catch some blue marlin."

"Yessir. We're pretty much set to go down here. I've lined up the mate and gone over a few things. We got the bait and tackle and all other provisions lined up for the trip. We need only to go through the boat and take a little sea trial to see how she's running and all."

"I can assure you, Louie, that the boat has been impeccably maintained and cared for. There shouldn't be any surprises. Ah, Louie . . . I was under the impression that my man Byrd would go along as the mate. He is familiar with the boat and should be a great help to you in finding your way around."

"Ah huh." Louis had a feeling that Whitman was going to go this way. "Well, sir, I'm used to pickin' the men that I fish with, and what with all that's at stake, I feel very strongly on this point. I hope this doesn't kill the deal for me," replied Louis essentially taking the decision out of Whitman's hands. He did not break the following silence.

"No, of course not. You're the Captain. We'll give him 200 a day and his expenses, and I will honor our agreement in regard to any winnings. Satisfactory?"

"That'll work fine, sir. I would be happy to have Mr. Byrd along as a second mate. We can always use another pair of hands, you know. I just want to know who's in charge of the cockpit."

"Splendid. I appreciate your calling, I prefer to clear up these loose ends before we untie the lines. I shall be arriving in

31

Florida on Saturday the 29th of April. That should give us all time to meet and get reacquainted. I wouldn't mind going along on the shakedown cruise myself. I'll see you then."

4

Louis arrived at the boat promptly at 9:00 Sunday morning. Scott Byrd began the new captain's tour of Whitman's 65-foot *Hatteras* at the main control panel in the salon, the main living area of the vessel. He opened two wide teak panel doors that were a section of a well integrated teak interior wrapping around the entire salon as a whole.

"Here's the business end, Louie, DC on this side, 12 volt here, 32 volt here," Byrd amplifying his droning with occasional hand reference to the maze of circuit breakers, selector switches, meters and indicator lights. "The bridge and engine room also have their own service panels as does the galley. Over here the AC panel for the ship. The air conditioning has its own service panel down here, units 1, 2, 3, and 4, and the sea pump, the rest back up here divided into A&B circuits. Questions?"

"Looks okay to me."

Byrd closed the two panels and exited the salon through a solid lexan door leading out to the cockpit and lifted a hatch that appeared to be part of a built-in fishing station. A small pneumatic ram held the hatch up as he unlatched the frontal door to reveal stairs leading down into the engine room. Before entering, Byrd hit the lights by lifting up on a red throw switch mounted on the side of the gangway. Louis followed him down.

"These 1692s have given us perfect service, Louie. We just spent a great deal of money on interval maintenance, cleaning the entire air system from turbo to aftercooler, and refitting all new premium grade injectors."

"Why?"

33

"The old captain was somewhat of a fanatic on this kind of thing. Personally, I think he just liked the high of spending Frank's money."

From his visual inspection, it took Louis very little time to recognize the professionalism of his predecessor. It was an engine room in bristol shape. The maze of wiring and hoses encapsulating the pair of diesels was orderly and well clamped, everything spray painted in awl-grip, no rusty hose clamps or green oxidations from salt water leaks, parts and tools organized into waterproof containers. The sea strainers, responsible for filtering the incoming salt water that would eventually be used for cooling purposes, were clear and free of particles and sediment. The engines and generator were fresh water cooled in closed systems, and were outfitted with 'heat exchangers.' Here, coolant would travel through a core element, continually bathed in circulating cooler ocean water drawn through the hull near the keel, and passed out of the boat through the exhausts.

Louis had also noticed the addition of mechanical gauges mounted on the bulkhead or rear wall of the room. He assumed the former captain had also pushed for this as most builders do not consider them standard equipment. Louis also felt they were an indispensable redundancy, adding reliability and aiding greatly in troubleshooting.

Louis' scan stopped at the hour meters and noted the engine's age at 544 hours. He was all for preventative maintenance, but that did seem a little early for the extensive air system cleaning and injector exchange just completed. He did not doubt the integrity of the former captain, and wondered what he might have been sensing. Something must not have been completely right down here. Louis felt someone step on the boat.

". . . working perfectly, turning up under load at 2300 rpm. At 2000 she's burning 144 gallons an hour. The cruising speed . . ."

"Yo, Byrd, slow down a might. I know about sixty-five hatts.

34

Besides, it's bad luck to brag too much on your engines."

"Sorry. If you have no questions let's take a quick look at the bridge." Let the old fart make his own mistakes, an offended Byrd considered as he led the way out.

When they emerged from the engine room, they found Crafty going through fishing tackle in the corner of the cockpit. He had all the drawers out on the deck, and it appeared that he was taking inventory and making a shopping list while straightening up .

"Who the hell are you, and what do you think you're doing on this boat?" Scoot was beet red and beginning to vibrate.

"Meet Crafty, Scott, our new first mate. He's in charge of the cockpit and all that pertains to the tackle," a familiar voice from the bridge replied, "now apologize and introduce yourself."

"Sorry, Frank. Scott Byrd, Crafty, I . . . ah . . . work for Mr. Whitman on different projects, good to meet you. I've been managing the boat and fishing with Frank." Byrd was not totally broke, but very badly bent.

"Crafty, just call me Crafty." When they shook hands the older man held up Byrd's hand for a moment, turned it over and looked at it, and finally let go before going back to his spring cleaning.

"Scoot, see if Crafty has anything for you to do while I show Capt. Louie this bridge that I'm so proud of. Come on up Louie."

Frank had everything open and all the electronics running when Louis arrived on the bridge. "I deal with Scoot on a need to know basis. That is, I don't tell him what he doesn't need to know." Whitman looked down at a glaring Byrd and did curtail his laughter somewhat. "What do you think of her so far?"

"All right, good boat going into a sea, I reckon. She has been kept nice, though." Louis knew his remarks had devalued Whitman's pride, but accepted that he could not be frank with Frank. For all the bells and whistles and appliances the *Byte Her* had built into her, she was still a fishing boat, and that's how Louis viewed her. She would do well running into a big head sea. But for fishability and maneuvering, presentation and raising the fish, he very much preferred his old wooden forty-six-foot Whiticar, as good a sea boat as was ever built.

"Yes, indeed, Louie. As you can see if it runs on electricity, I've got it on the boat. For your navigation, state of the art Trimble GPS and laser plotter, great for working an area. Every possible chart on CD, with zoom and scale for the entire South Atlantic. Top of the line Furuno color sounder, here, 48-mile Simrad color radar, Stevens Single side band, ICOM VHF, Apelco ADF for painting the enemy. Robertson auto pilot up in the overhead, here, there's a remote behind this door with about 20 feet of lead. Dual action electronic controls. Trim tabs, here.

Over in front you have sumlog, water temp gauge, and digital depth sounder. This right overhead, compartment has a backup Northstar 800dx Loran C, with a Northstar GPS next to it. And here, another ICOM VHF. Finally, my little toy, one of my prototype PCs works directly on satellite feed. Better than any service you can buy, the very latest satellite weather and oceanographic information from my network at home. Can be faxed to me directly each morning. Well?"

"You seem to have it all covered, sir. Do you have anything up here to make a fish bite?"

"We're working on it, Louie," a now beaming Whitman grinned. "Thank you for appreciating my thoroughness in rigging the electronics."

Having turned off all the bridge electronics Louis turned to his boss, "Ready to go for a boat ride, Mr. Whitman?"

"She's all yours, Captain."

Louis went down the bridge ladder and into the salon. Opening the two doors hiding the electrical panel he reached for the on/off/on toggle switch marked preheat/stop and held it on for about fifteen seconds before flipping the start toggle switch next to it. When the generator caught fuel and began to run he released both and switched the engine breakers on.

Louis went back outside and informed Crafty they were getting ready to go, and proceeded back to the bridge. Turning the port ignition key on, Louis activated the alarm system and pushed the start button. She started right up and settled into her idling at 600 rpm. Louis watched the port exhaust until the initial gray smoke, caused by partially burnt fuel, cleared the area. He then shut down the engine and turned the starboard key on. After a couple of seconds the engine started and chugged slowly up to its idling speed amidst a small cloud of gray and blue smoke. *Hmmm*, Louis thought quietly. After about thirty seconds, all the smoke cleared and he restarted the port engine and they were ready to go.

Louis idled the rig out of the condo channel, pulling the engines out of gear to ease over a spoil bar, and proceeded from the waterway out into the north end of Lake Worth. He slowly brought the boat up on plane and settled her into her cruise of 2000 rpm.

He pulled the boat off plane as he passed under the sixty-five-foot span of the Singer Island Bridge, making a hard left to follow the deep channel east on a parallel course with the bridge. The channel curved back to the south following the shoreline of the barrier island, and Louis continued his idle past the row of marinas.

He heard a shout from the charter dock at Sailfish Marina, and focused on a pair of waving arms belonging to a couple of friends. They were younger captains, two of the many he had helped along in the business. They were smiling and calling his name, and when he passed by them, they pointed at the boat and gave Louis a questioning look and gesture. He answered in like body language and shrugged his shoulders. It had been years since anyone had seen him on any boat other than his own.

At the southern tip of the island, Louis made his left and got the boat up on plane again, and proceeded out Lake Worth Inlet. By now, Frank had everything electrical running on the bridge, and Louis kept heading to the east. There was very little traffic, and Louis was able to devote most of his time scanning the gauges and instruments. When the engines had reached normal cruising temperature, he powered up to full throttle, and watched the slow climb of the tachometers as the pair of 1692s strained to reach their full load performance of 2300 rpm. They leveled off at 2295 and after thirty or so seconds of full load, Louis pulled the throttles back to fifty percent power, and turned off the synchronizer. When the starboard slave returned the positive control of the throttle to the cable, he manually synched the engines at cruise for a couple of minutes. When temperatures had settled, he once again went to full load, requiring each engine to do its job independent of the yoke of the synchronizer.

He yelled down to Crafty and motioned for him to put the head phones on, and go into the engine room and make a check. He also made a gesture with his hand as if he was pushing the throttles as far as they would go.

When the tachs leveled off Louis read the port at 2325 and the starboard at 2275. Hmmm. The starboard engine was also running a couple of needle points hotter than the port. He looked back at the wake against the windless rolling sea, and could see no signs of smoke or hazing. That was good, but with a perfectly clean air system, both engines should have loaded out at over 2300 rpm, assuming of course that the boat's wheels, (props) were properly formulated.

"What do you think, Captain?"

"It's acceptable, Frank."

"Acceptable? She's running strong and not a lick of smoke."

"The starboard engine is pulling the port down, and running a little hotter than its partner. Somewhere it's deciding to trade a little horsepower for heat. But like I said, it's acceptable."

Crafty came up on the bridge and stood by his boss. "Everything looks fairly normal down there. Stuffing boxes were drippin' right, no leaks. You were definitely dead racked on both sides, I guess you know the starboard runs a little hotter than the other one."

"Yeah. It's pullin' the other one down."

"What do you mean dead-racked," Frank interjected.

"Simply that the fuel delivery was at its maximum."

"Oh."

Louis brought the boat back to cruise, and began a check of all the electronics. He set the boat on auto pilot, operating the dodger and course selector, and the interfacing with the nav aids. He worked the trim system up and down, painted the radar, and roughly checked the compass deviation by lining up on some land ranges.

Having done all he had wanted with the boat's systems, he slowed down to a stop, and went into reverse to start backing down. Louis proceeded to throttle the boat until water broke over her transom. He pivoted her in a series of commands, various combinations of throttle and power flow [for'd and rev], simulating potential maneuverings that a hot fish might require of her. The electronic controls would add lack of response time to what Louis already perceived as a sluggish boat. Their electrical/solenoid operation of extension and retraction operated at a fixed rate and he knew he wouldn't be able to impart a sense of urgency to them. He would have to fly way ahead of himself on a tough fish.

This part of the sea trial now over, Louis put the vessel in neutral. All was quiet and peaceful, and the old captain took a long stretch. He reset the Busch cap on his head and turned to his employer.

"Let's go fishin', Mr. Whitman."

"Why not, Captain Louie."

5

"Wendt Productions, Mr. Wendt's office, Ms. Winfield."

"Hi Beth, Frank Whitman. Is the big guy available?"

"Hello, Mr. Whitman, good to hear from you. Adam is just about through with his meeting with the NBC people. He's trying to schedule his *Tonight Show* appearance as soon as can be done to conclude his talk show circuit. I'm worried for him Mr. Whitman, this last tour and book promotion has left him really fatigued. It's starting to show a little."

"I have just the tonic for him, a couple of weeks in the warm Caribbean, with nothing more to do than relax and play."

"I'd like to buy into a little of that, sir." A clicking could be heard on the connection. "That's Adam, Mr. Whitman, I'll put you through."

"Thanks, Beth."

" . . . .Whit, how's your gigabyte hanging?

"In need, Adam. When are you going to give it a rest, and stop practicing to be a workaholic?"

"Very soon. I just penciled in for Friday night, and that should just about wrap it up for awhile."

"Beth was bringing me up to speed. Our talks of last month concerning the Caribbean markets have come full circle, and I have excellent news. I'm going to the Hemingway in Havana with a new crew, and have the prospect of an excellent entrée into the area down there. I need a fishing partner and you need a couple weeks vacation. Get down here, and join me on the boat. I won't accept anything but a 'yes.' Understood?"

"Sounds mighty tempting, Whitman. Can I bring a friend

or is it load as we go?"

"Which starlet are you doing now?"

"Hey. I'd like you to know that I am very involved with a heady high fashion model who has a talent for keeping me quite honest. Cheryl Luria, know her?"

"Who wouldn't. Must keep you rather busy, Adam. I'll have Cami along, you met her last year, so what's it going to be? Those four walls or blue water, palm trees, and warm sun?"

"You have me at a clear disadvantage, Frank. I really could use the break. My answer is an emphatic 'yes.' When should I book our flights?"

"I won't have any of that. I'll send my pilot out to pick you up Monday morning around seven-thirty. We'll catch up with you in Palm Beach around three or so. You'll love the new jet, she's half again as big as the old one. Enjoy yourself."

"You're the boss."

"I'll have Scoot tag along to take care of your personal needs if you run into any problems."

"You're sure, Whit?"

"Absolutely! I look forward to seeing you, now that we're ready to proceed with our marketing plans for our southern friends."

"Can't thank you enough, Frank. Take care."

Whitman's jet touched down at LAX at exactly 6:30 A.M. the following Monday morning. It was directed to the private hangars that stabled the most impressive collection of corporate aircraft in the world.

The Scoot had arranged for a private limo to meet him and run him over to Wendt's Beverly Hills home to arrive at precisely 7:30 A.M. He was surprised to see so much activity at that time of day in the private terminal, even more so when he had to pick his driver out of a crowd of chauffeurs, each holding an ID sign. He cued the one holding 'Whitman Tech.' and

41

the neat young man came quickly forward stripping Byrd of his carry-on bag.

The stretch Lincoln was soon heading north on I-5 giving the jet-lagged Byrd a chance for a quick nap. The voice of the driver gaining clearance through the front gate of the Wendt residence was the next sound he heard.

The limo pulled into the turnaround of the huge Tudor mansion, where another man was in the process of bringing much luggage to the end of a canopied walk.

Adam Wendt briskly stepped through the open door and waved at Byrd as he was exiting the rear of the limo. "Scott, how the hell are you doing? You look good, things must be on an even keel between you and the Whit."

"Hey, Adam, been awhile hasn't it. Is this everyone or . . . "

"Cheryl will be right along." As Wendt passed by Scott to get in the car, he spoke quietly in the young man's ear, "We'll talk on the plane." Wendt sat down in the rear seat, opened his briefcase and pulled the cell phone from his coat pocket.

The tall brunette soon made her appearance in the doorway, covering the distance between her and Byrd like she was in grand view on a runway. As she neared the door Byrd was holding for her, she held her hand out for further assistance befitting a royal.

"How do you do, Miss, Scott Byrd at your assistance. Looking forward to a little island getaway?"

"All this . . . so grown men can return to their adolescence. And you are?"

"Scott Byrd, I just introduced—"

"Oh yes," was all the brunette could say before she slammed the car door in the Byrd's face.

Scoot quickly climbed in the front seat of the limo, pointing and nodding to the driver. He turned to face his two charges in the back, the woman still had her sunglasses on.

"Thank you, Scott," a smiling Wendt offered as he raised the electric divider between the compartments.

They had been airborne for nearly two hours. Whitman's guests had been served a gourmet breakfast of filet mignon and omelets, all the way from Bloody Marys to the fresh danish they were now sampling with their coffee.

Byrd and the plane's steward studied the couple for their cue to clear the table of the meal set before them. Wendt finally signaled over to Byrd as he rose to his feet and stretched.

"Everything to your liking Adam?"

"First cabin, Scott, delicious. I think Cheryl is going to try and catch a nap. We should be fine until we land," replied Wendt to the two men as he made for a seat at the other end of the cabin.

Byrd phoned ahead to his boss to be sure things were on time in Florida, while he supervised the steward/co-pilot in his cleanup duties. When all had been stowed away, the steward walked forward to the cockpit door, entering and closing it behind him. Scoot took a window seat in the rear of the plane, staring out at the sky until sleep overtook him. He soon became aware of movement in the seat next to him.

"Well, Scott, tell me what you've learned."

"Not much to tell yet Adam, it's just starting to take form. He's got the engineers working overtime back at the shop and he won't stop talking about Cuba. How big is this thing?"

"You have no idea. It's not just Cuba, it's the whole Latin potential of networking down there. Virgin markets are emerging everywhere."

"Whatever, Adam. I'm sure others are aware of that fact too."

"You ignorant son of a bitch! Do you really think I planted you into Whitman's world as a favor from one friend to another? Please. There is a hundred million dollars at stake here! Quite probably a great deal more."

"I heard that."

"Then don't be so thick in the head. Your boss is not just the CEO of Whitman Technologies, he's an institution with an army of experts and engineers cranking on these needed systems. He's not one step ahead of his competition, he's a hundred. Your job is to be a fly on the wall and follow my lead only. Got that?"

"Look, I know you brokered this project, and I'm comfortable with the arrangement we've agreed to. I don't need nor do I want, to know anything more, But check this out," Byrd spoke quietly as he met Adam Wendt's gaze head on, "I'm the man in the middle down there, the one that's going to make it happen at the precise time and place to insure success. We have been over this many times, Wendt. You know damn well he is insulated to the max and impossible to get at in his world. On the boat, he is not well secured, he has chosen this vulnerability for himself. I want it done surgically clean with a trail as cold as a whore's heart. In the end, it will always be my call."

"I don't have a problem with that, otherwise, I wouldn't have selected you."

"Good. Hold on to that understanding," Byrd replied looking back out the window.

"You mentioned yet another crew change, Scott. How does this square with your planning?"

"That's the best part, Adam," a grinning Byrd replied, turning back to Wendt. "Not only did this Florida cracker get us where we want to go, but he'll be far less a factor than the bastard we just got rid of."

"Very well." Adam Wendt rose up out of his seat and again sat down next to the sleeping brunette.

6

Chub Cay lay at the southern end of the Berry Island chain, about fifty miles northwest of Nassau. Situated on the northeast corner of the Tongue of the Ocean, it had through the years established itself as a good marlin fishery. It was by design, a glorified fish trap moving migratory fishes into a deadend known as the pocket, around to the east and back out around Whale Cay.

A relatively small area, it could be fished in a single day, running across fifteen miles to Morgan's Bluff, working north to Joulter's Cay, towards the pocket, easterly to the Yellow Bar, and then Rum Cay.

The Chub Cay Club had originally been established by a group from the original Key Largo Club as a semi-private island, offering the cruising public fuel and dockage, fresh water, a restaurant and small motel. To the west of the marina were private docks and residences off-limits to the rest of the island.

Chub had made remarkable progress since being razed by 200+ mph winds of a level five hurricane a year and a half ago. The signs were still there, a bent radio tower, piles of rubble, a fish scale tower of steel folded on the ground like a pretzel. Swaths cut through the Australian pines, the result of many tornadoes as the eye of the great storm passed directly over the island.

Louis remembered his last trip here a year ago. He had walked into the remains of the old bar, where many had once laughed and drank. The hub of the island, it was a place where fishing was spoken and lies further along. In here, women were circled and fought over, and blowboaters were generally run out.

Unless, of course, they held some entertainment value.

He remembered entering the place seeing sunlight baking the interior, as the roof had been completely torn away. The old bar top itself had been completely lifted off its structure, and the tables, chairs and stools were in a heap in the middle of the room in a pile of bits and pieces. Then he recalled the walls, where all the old fish mounts hung and where the aerial picture of the island chain was displayed.

In that photograph the Berrys resembled very much the image of a queen conch—the islands dotted against the sand flats of their backside. What amazed Louis was the pristine condition of that framed picture, and that it remained in its usual resting place. In fact, all the mounted fish and creatures of the sea were unmarred, resting comfortably in their original locations. An eeriness had so overtaken Louis that he had to leave the old watering hole, never to return.

Now fighting the effects of the Gulf Stream's strong northerly current, Louis corrected the boat's heading a few more degrees southerly. The water was a brilliant, shiny, indigo where current rips periodically created lines of interference in the tranquil sea. Some rips trapped free-floating sargassum creating weed lines where a sublife of minnows and other baitfish sought haven. He had seen some small skipjack tuna busting on the surface, and the many birds flying by would stop and investigate these areas passed. He usually took a look under most floating debris if not out of the way, and he had noted some dolphin and baitfish working under a few pieces. He was on a schedule this trip and would not have the luxury of flipping a spinning rod at them.

The captain needed a spell to take a look around down below and he called the mate to come up. Briefing Crafty quickly, he turned over his command and made his way down to the cockpit. He put the headphones on as he opened the engine room door, flicking on the lights as he proceeded in.

Louis made a good scan of all three power plants, noted a couple of oil drips, and saw nothing in the way of fuel or water leaks. He inspected his risers and exhausts as he listened to the main engines straining through the muffled headset. The mechanical gauges agreed with his electrical instruments up above and were holding steady. The only adjustment to be made at this point, were the stuffing boxes, the sealed, packed points of entry where propeller shafts came through the hull. Having been repacked recently, they would need a little retightening from the 'true' run now being put upon her.

By the time Louis had reappeared on the bridge, Great Isaac's Light could barely be seen on the horizon over the vessel's bow. Louis checked the GPS unit's steering window and noted that the "Distance to Waypoint" indicated twelve miles.

"Makin' pretty fair time, Crafty, I guess the current wasn't that strong today," Louis mumbled to himself.

"How's everything lookin' down there, Cap?"

"All right, I guess. I don't know, Crafty, I just got a feeling about that starboard engine. Not a vibration really, but it just don't seem to want to sync with its soul mate, kinda like a surge or something. I can't find anything wrong. I got a feelin' that's all."

"She's only got to make it for a few weeks, she'll do all right."

"That's right. But if it's man-made, you know it's going to break sooner or later," Louis added with a chuckle.

When they arrived at Great Isaac Light, the tide was on the flood. The clean, offshore water had pushed up on the shallows of the bank resulting in a calm, gin-clear view of the reefs and ocean floor. Both men gazed quietly into the turquoise and aquamarine waters. Coral and coralheads, red fans and staghorns of wheat color permeated the undulating bottom against the white sand.

Louis eyed the old lighthouse as he carved a long, slow port turn around its southwest quarter. He could see that the old structure was in some need of attention, and he wondered if there would ever be a time when lighthouses were no longer needed. He had his own history with Great Isaac as he knew every sailor did whoever plied these waters over the years. It had given many a seaman a haven from all kinds of dangers.

A couple of sportfisherman caught Louis' eye a few miles to the southwest. Probably out of Bimini fishing the Hens and Chickens. His color machine was aglow, marking many stands of bottom fish and balls of bait. Flying fish and ballyhoo were periodically busting out of the water away from the boat, often a sign of predatory fish below. As it was near flat calm, the boat appeared almost to be suspended over the bottom. The two men did not speak as they continued to peer quietly into mother nature's aquarium.

Continuing east southeast, they left the reef bottom at the dropoff, and were now traveling over the undersea desert of flats, occasional coralhead and mud patch typical of the Great Bahamian Bank. When he had passed the old light on his port side a while back, Louis punched in his second waypoint on the lat-lon GPS, and on the Loran C using the next pair of TD numbers. The target was a buoy about five miles west of Northwest Providence Light.

Northwest light marked a safe lane running nearly due east and west from which to enter the deep blue waters of the Tongue of the Ocean. To attempt passage too far north or south of the light spelled trouble for the mariner in the form of shallow and dangerous reefs. Most experienced pilots used the buoy to line up on the light at the appropriate angle. Many had found trouble when approaching Northwest Light from too steep an angle relative to the east-west line.

After a couple of hours of traversing the 10-15 foot deep bank, the *Byte Her* passed the red buoy that had been her second waypoint. Louis was now free to enter Northwest Light as the next target. The water shoaled up even shallower in this area, to as little as eight feet in spots, primarily sandy in nature. Twelve minutes later Louis found himself just north of the light about fifty yards, proceeding to enter the deep blue dropoff.

Only a couple of boats could be seen fishing the 'pocket' this afternoon, as Louis scanned the deepwater edge working down to the west and south. Chub lay only a few more miles about 115 degrees.

"Beautiful day ol' boy, makes you feel just glad to be around."

"You're right about that, Crafty. All we need is a windshift into the southeast and a few fish for the boss to work on. For whatever reason the water up in here is a bit dull don't ya think?"

"Yeah, not the condition for findin' 'em tight up in here. Damn bank-water spilled out over the edge of the dropoff."

"Reckon we'll drive over a few anyhow, but I'd like to see the man get enough practice at feeding some marlin. It's got to come together in a short time."

"The kid could use it, too, Cap, he's a real load. If those hands ever done any fishin' it was for compliments."

"Yup. I noticed that from the get go—more baggage. He does seem to know the boat some, and I figured as long as you were here, we could get some work out of him. Take her, man, I'm going down below to fill out our paperwork for Remedy.

"Still here?"

"That's right, a fixture the hurricane couldn't blow away."

When Louis returned to the bridge, Chub Cay lay a mile on the bow. Carving a turn around Mamarouta Rock leaving the rock islet to port, he headed for Chub Point where he would pick up a pair of range markers marking the channel into the island. He followed the range on idle, leaving the top marker directly over the bottom one, a situation made by staying the course on a narrow line. He turned off the range at the mouth of the cut and headed in directly to the fuel dock. Crafty made ready with the lines and hoisted the yellow quarantine flag on the right outrigger. They were met by a young Bahamian.

49

"Hey, Cop, been lookin' for you, mon. You be Mr. Whitman's new drivah?"

"That's me, Louie Gladding. This here's Crafty, glad to meet ya. I guess we'll top her off while we're waiting for customs," continued Louis after the handshaking was over.

"No probe'lem. Customs, he be comin' down the rood, now. You slip be right dere, mon, on d'en by dat big Merritt. My name be Godfrey. You need it, I get it for you." Louis continued nodding and smiling.

When the older man in black pants, white shirt and epaulets arrived, all became quiet as Louis turned to face the man. The customs officer's business face melted into a broad grin as Louis began speaking, "Remedy, you must really like this place to be hangin' 'round here all these years."

"Coptin' Louis, don't keep yourself from heah so long. Too much time go, you not be 'round, mon. You bring dat pirate wit you, too." Crafty stuck up an index finger, and then began a big belly laugh. The three men exchanged handshakes and back slappings.

"Louis, how it be you Whitman's new drivah, and all dat?"

"Just for a little while, Remedy. A week or two here, and a week in Cuba for a tournament. He's payin me well."

"Dat mon mus haffa pay his crew a lot. How is Alfie, Louis? Still like pumpin' on big blue? Oh dat las' fish, I ting it kill him."

"He's fine, Remedy, still lives in the Keys and still has that Whiticar boat, though he doesn't fish much for marlin now."

"I miss hem like de ol days, Louis. When you see Mr. Silva, tell him Remedy want to see hem bock soon. Dat man and dat fish. I tell you."

"I will, friend. Hey, come on board and have a cool drink." Louis and the customs man went below while Crafty finished fueling the boat. After a few minutes of stamping and signing, Louis was officially cleared into the Bahamas at the Berry

Islands, Chub Cay. With the purchase of a fishing license, the boat was good to go.

"Louis, I ride ova to slip wit you, I got boat dere' now to do."

"Sure, hang Remedy, lemme sign for the fuel and we'll put her away for the day." Louis rotated off the fuel dock and quickly backed the boat across the basin to his slip on the member side of the harbor. A slight turn at the mouth, and he backed her right in smoothly to within a few feet of the dock. Crafty sprung her off, tied the stern, and lassoed the two bow pilings to complete his setting of the lines. Shore electrical was hooked up, then dockside water. Louis shut down the main engines and closed the bridge and its electronic boxes. He went down into the salon to switch from generator power to dock power and all was quiet.

The salon door opened and Remedy emerged with his briefcase and proceeded off the boat. "Good see you bock, Cop, dem marlin all run for covah now. Dey know Cuban Louie be lookin' all oba for dem. Catch 'em up, mon."

"Thanks, Remedy. Does your brother still have that taxi?"

"Ortnell be pipin' down the rood in dat taxi as we speakin."

"We need to meet the boss and his guests at the airport later this afternoon. If Ortnell can be here around 4:30, that would be perfect."

"Fo' tirty, I tell him. Latah . . ."

It was a still, hot and sticky afternoon. The only relief was a slight breeze coming from the open windows of the old Jeep Wagoneer as it sped down the dirt road leading out to the airport. The three mile road was a jungle tour of sorts, weaving through the palms and vegetation like a serpent. It passed by a few houses, where gardens and plantains grew among the flowers. It took the highest elevation possible where it ran among some tidal pools. There were a few small, dirt turnoffs along the way, and the tourists always asked where they led to. They were always told 'nowhere.'

51

Chub Cay has always had a fairly well-maintained airstrip, quite long for the size of the island, and able to accommodate jets as large as some airliners. For that reason, many different things have been found over the years at the ends of those mysterious roads, from trash and abandoned cars to drug caches and such. People that didn't need to know, didn't want to, and those that wanted to know probably shouldn't. Everyone could live with that.

The old jeep busted into the airport clearing in a cloud of coral dust, and proceeded to the small concrete block terminal. Things were quiet and there didn't appear to be any sign of life at all. A windsock hung limp at the runway's edge, a half dozen private planes rested on their mooring chocks. A message radioed ahead, stated that Whitman's plane was running a half hour late, but that it was in route.

Louis got out of the Jeep, and decided to take a stroll down to the water's edge, which paralleled the runway. The backside of the island offered a different, though no less beautiful panorama. While the marina looked out over the deep blue of the Tongue of the Ocean, the airport vista took in miles and miles of pristine shallows and flats. A man could wade forever. Louis had already observed many houndfish and small barracuda darting over the clear pearl shallows and the darker, deeper channels.

He took off his khakis and began to wade out to an aquamarine stretch of water that connected two different flats. A few small bonefish were working toward him down the edge of the flat, and even though he was motionless, they eventually found the sand he was kicking up and spooked. He shrugged and looked into the trough as he walked along. When he found what he was looking for, he bent over and reached down into the water, coming up with a nice specimen of queen conch. When he had recovered a few for a salad, he went back to shore and suited up.

By the time he got back to the Jeep and stashed his catch,

the sound of the decelerating jet could be heard. He picked up the aircraft behind the Australian pines at the east end of the runway and watched as the plane made her steep approach. Not a second after the wheels touched down, he heard the power back off, and then suddenly surge louder than before as the pilot had the thrust reversers pinned.

The Gulfstream taxied to within 100 feet of the small concrete building and immediately shut down. In a couple of minutes the airplane door opened and the boarding ladder automatically extended. Byrd was the first one out, and when he set foot on the deck, he turned and offered his hand to the woman who followed him out. Louis did not recognize the next man, but assumed he came with her.

Whitman finally emerged from the cabin having to duck his head going through the door, leading a second woman behind him. Brother Louis' eyes rolled skyward at the realization of his enlisting in what was rapidly becoming a beach party. Think positive old goat, you've been paid. Time to deliver.

When he got to the group Ortnell was calling his brother on the radio, announcing the arrival of the Whitman party, and the need for customs and immigration.

"Well, we made it after all eh, Captain Louie."

"Welcome to Chub Cay, Mr. Whitman, let me get some of them bags."

"They can wait. Louie, I'd like you to meet a good friend, Adam Wendt. Adam, shake hands with the famous Cuban Louie, one hell of a marlin fisherman."

"Louie Gladding, Mr. Wendt."

"Pleasure's mine, Louie, call me Adam. My friend, Cheryl."

"Ma'am." The woman did not offer a hand nor speak a sound, but even with her sunglasses on, Louie could see she was high maintenance. She had a lot of other things going for her.

"Hi, Louie, Camille. I'm Frank's girlfriend for the week,

53

isn't that right sweetie," replied the pretty blonde as she winked and grabbed Whitman's manhood most irreverently.

"Nice to meet you, Camille," responded Louis with a smile, genuinely unruffled by the woman's sporting gesture.

"It's been a tremendously long afternoon, Captain. I believe the four of us are going to head to the house, and kick off our shoes. We'll touch base tomorrow."

"Fine, Mr. Whitman."

The captain, the baggage and the conch would make the second trip.

7

Louis was up at his usual hour, about forty-five minutes before sunrise. When he walked outside the boat he found the early morning still and cool. The flags on the yardarm hung limp, only occasionally stirred by a puff of west wind. Better get the engine room stuff done early, Louis considered. From the look of things the day's heat will come early.

He looked around the marina and saw a fair number of boats even for May. Quite a few sportfishermen, a half dozen motor sailors, and a couple of big motor yachts both on the public and members side.

Louis jumped onto the finger pier from the covering board that ran the perimeter of the boat's cockpit. He walked over and lifted the lids of two ice chests that lay on the outside end of the dock. He took almost as much pride in Crafty's work as the mate himself. He had prepared thoroughly for the day's fishing by rigging about six dozen skipping and swimming ballyhoo, a dozen Spanish mackerel, and a dozen split-tailed mullet—all pretty and perfect laid in rows, bellies tilted up and lightly salted. Aesthetics ruled, the mate gave evidence of his name one more time, and the captain gave thanks for having the best he could have down in the pit.

"How's your coffee, Cap, need a bump?"

"That would be nice, Good morning."

Radford Kraft ducked back in the salon for a few seconds and reappeared with a fresh pot taking the distance between him and his captain in about three leaps. He was after all, a man in remarkably good shape considering his years. The blue water

55

had kept him youthful and strong, at forty-five he'd pass for his early thirties.

The product of a Cape Hatteras upbringing, Rad had taken to the water at a very early age along with the other boys. By his early teens, he had commercially fished and netted and already had his own boat paid for. He was marked and recognized by all in town as a gifted fisherman who surely was destined for greatness.

When he began to hire himself into the sportfishing business of blue water big game fishing, he was addicted from the beginning. It took no more than a year for Radford Kraft to launch himself into notoriety in a labor of love that would carry him far away from the Outer Banks of North Carolina.

He would fish every ocean, every specie, every season, from Australia to Africa, Madeira to Venezuela, Prince Edward Island to St. Thomas in the Virgins.

Along the way he would at some point earn his license, and move up to the bridge. Only for a brief time would he play captain, however. He would return to his true love, the cockpit. He liked holdin' 'em about as much as catchin' 'em. He so loved the fish, the interaction and the connection.

"You know that guy Wendt, Whitman's buddy, he was on the *Tonight Show* last night, couldn't believe it. Our guy, what a small world! I knew I'd seen him before somewhere. He's some kind of shrink or sports motivator. Got a bunch of books and videos. The rich and famous hire him on to be their psychic trainer. Can you imagine, Louie? Captain Louis."

"Sorry ol' boy, I was just driftin' back to another time. What'd ya say, we got another VIP aboard?"

"That guy Wendt is fairly big time, his ladyfriend is a model who probably pulls in as much as him."

"You know, Crafty, I don't figure on this wind coming around for us today," Louis intoned as he stared at the high cirrus clouds aloft. "Mares' tails still hangin' right over the top of us."

"They'll bite when they want to."

"They will," Louis broke out into laughter.

It was almost noon when the boss and Camille showed up with picnic basket and videocam in hand. Louis had disconnected the shore power and had the generator and main engines running at the first sight of Whitman walking down the coral path from the house.

"What say we give it a few hours, Louie? Adam and Cheryl took the plane to Nassau to see some friends at Lyford Cay."

"All ready to go, Mr. Whitman," Louis responded for the crew as he lent a hand to the lady. "How's Miss Camille today?"

"Louie, we're fine, and would you please call me Cami."

"Done."

"I see you have the fifties out, are we going to warm up on dolphin today, Louie?" Frank began inspecting the four Penn 50 Internationals, one in each of the four rod holders of the fighting chair.

"It's a fifty-pound tournament, Mr. Whitman, I thought you knew. In fact, it used to be a thirty-pound deal, but it was bumped up this year."

"Well, no I didn't. They look like pea shooters next to the eighty-pound outfits I'm used to using for marlin. Can they hold up?"

"Oh yeah."

"How does it affect the lures?"

"Lures come in all sizes, sir, but you'll not have to worry about it."

"How's that?"

"You won't be pulling lures in Havana, that is unless you want to be laughed at up and down the dock."

"I'm not following you, Gladding, I'm used to catching Blue Marlin on plastics. I don't think I've even caught one on a bait."

"I know, and thank you for being honest, Mr. Whitman. But the marlin down there are used to an environment not unlike the

57

one here at Chub. Tight against the dropoff in relatively shallow water. These fish have a tremendous amount of bait to work with, and it is natural bait that accounts for nearly all the catchin' down there, like at Chub here."

"There have been marlin caught on lures here."

"It happens as anything is possible out there. But when the fish are on the 'go' here, the baits will outfish lures every time. We'll be fishing a smaller area than you are probably used to in your Bahamian tournament fishing. It's less of a search and more of a presentation. We ain't gonna be wanderin' around waiting to drive into an accident."

"I don't know, Captain, I might differ on opinion with you."

"Mr. Whitman, you hired me to help you improve your angling skills and make a stab at winning this thing. This a necessary step in that direction."

Whitman left the conversation dangling and went into the salon as if the discussion had never taken place. Louis climbed up the flybridge ladder sensing he had held the battle line, . . . at least for the moment.

Louis idled the boat out of the marina into the cut that lead to the range markers. Once lined up on the range, he proceeded to Chub Point passing by the many sailboats at anchor where they would ordinarily be in the lee from the surge of southeasterly breezes.

Today it was again slick, calm and hot, and all were relieved when Louis put the power to her. He decided to run across to Joulter's Cay to at least assess the situation over there. He was not that optimistic, as three days of westerlies usually create deteriorating conditions for Joulter's. However, he needed a first hand look at the place he would most like to fish when things were at their optimum. He was pleased to find good clean blue water in the middle, and it held quality all the way into the 300 fathom depths on the other side.

Louis set down for fishing offshore of the 'edge,' a term

generally used to refer to water depths ranging from 100 to 600 feet. It is the area where shallow reef structures of the continental shelf drop off into the deeper oceanic water. Considerable marine life inhabits these depths, bait and predators alike. Unfortunately today, even offshore the edge in 1200 feet, the water quality exhibited a dull slate color. Sargassum weed, eel grass and other plant life were liberally scattered everywhere.

"Crafty, put a few skipping 'hoos out while I take a brief drive through the park."

Louis had the color machine dialed in to his liking, and he began trolling a stretch of his most productive areas. Beautiful reef structure and fields of coralheads inshore lead to a field of mountain top pinnacles off the edge. As the boat tracked over the spiked ocean floor at a speed of a little over six knots, the color machine continually charted the area to be a target-rich environment. Various bait schools subsurface to fifty feet, stands and trees of the bottom varieties such as grouper and snapper, and blue singular targets of larger creatures all emblazoned Louis' color sounder.

After an hour of no bites, omitting barracudas, Louis decided to push south for Morgan's Bluff. Under some of the highest elevations in the Bahamas the descending ocean floor plummeted steeply down. You could be in 1800 feet of water only a couple of miles off the bluffs. When conditions were tough on this side of the Tongue, this area at least held onto a little bit of quality water. Today, it had drawn the bulk of the fleet fishing out of the island.

The radio had been silent for some time, and the old captain looked up to see if he was on the right channel. Unfortunately he was. He could see the remnants of the fleet ahead of his position as most of the boats had long given up the chase and headed back across to Chub.

Those pulling lures stood out amongst the rest of the boats with their higher trolling speeds creating higher wakes and wave patterns against the flat ocean. In stark contrast, those pulling baits appeared to be dogging it ever so slowly, their boat wakes showing no white water, just a little turbulence.

"It would be the big luck to get a bite of anything today save a fish box full of barracudas. Louis silently laughed to himself as he envisioned the ubiquitous schools of the toothy critters as Pavlovian dogs donning their bibs at the familiar sound of diesel engines. How many hundreds of thousands of dollars of bait had been bitten off short since people first started fishing chub. They had burned up over a hundred today all ready.

Louis left his chair for a stretch and walked to the edge of the bridge overlooking the cockpit. The boss was fidgeting with everything he could find or pull out of the tackle drawers, rearranging things to his own liking, even though he would never have need to go into them for anything. Whitman already had everything stowed in the side compartments out on the teak deck for inspection, and was now in the process of looking under two deck hatches where, among other things, the spare wheels were stored.

Crafty appeared tired and hot from the constant changing of baits and whole spread patterns due to the bumper crop of barracuda bites. He watched in amazement at Whitman's exercise in absurdity, imperceptibly shaking his head from side to side. If they were jumped by a fish now, they would be completely helpless and unprepared. Their preoccupied angler was distracted and away from his post at the rods, his only true responsibility. More importantly, a dangerous situation had been created in littering the cockpit deck with many sharp and potentially harmful objects. Crafty viewed the scene with disdain, amazed at how the CEO of one of the world's leading corporate empires could be so lacking in presence of mind.

The captain decided to give everyone on board some relief and turned the boat offshore on a return course to the island. He walked around to the front of the bridge and informed a topless

Cami that they were going to be heading back and that she might prefer riding home someplace other than the foredeck. Smiling, she cut short her sunbathing, gathered up her gear, and walked to the rear of the boat.

When everything had been taken in and put away the mate waved his hand in a circle. After raising the outriggers and seating them against the boat in their holders, Louis put the starboard engine in gear and engaged the synchronizer. He slowly brought the power up until the boat settled up on plane heading to the northeast back across toward the island.

"Thanks, Louie, for a beautiful day. You two guys worked pretty hard to get Frankie a marlin," a tan and flushed Cami offered as she joined Louis on the bridge. "He's down there pouting, talking to a friend coming up from Nassau. They were one for a doubleheader pulling plugs all the way."

Louis turned to Camille with a soft smile. She had donned a white T-shirt that had only accentuated her gifts. She had a warm natural smile, an enduring beauty, freckles under her blue eyes. "You've done this before," Louis half stated, half questioned.

"Grew up in Lauderdale. My dad had his own charterboat at Bahia Mar. Whatever you do, don't tell Frankie," the blonde answered knowing full well that she had told Louis all he needed to know.

Louis peered over his sunglasses and gave her a wink before returning to his scan of the horizon. Something in the distance caught his gaze, a bit of white water in the nearly flat sea. He turned the boat toward the sighting to take a look. The second sighting made it clear to Louis that it was a pod of pilot whales, ranging in size from a newborn calf to the bull leader of over twenty feet. In all, about a dozen whales lay calmly on the surface poking their heads out of the water as if to take a look around.

"Louie, do other fish ever travel with whales?"

"It's not uncommon to find marlin around pilot whales, and dolphin for that matter, although they're not usually embedded within 'em. I like what I see though, their bein' here supports a notion that other pelagic species might be around."

Louis pulled the power back and turned the color machine back on. "These larger blue objects are most likely the whales, and this," Louis zoomed and blew up some smaller targets at a certain depth to encompass the whole viewing screen, "looks a lot like squid the way they are kinda' draped."

"Beautiful." Her eyes wandered from screen to sea and back.

Louis shut down the Furuno and began idling away from the whales all the while staring into the water, his back to the sun. There goes another one, he mumbled under his breath.

"Hey, Crafty."

"Hello," came the reply as the mate stood at the transom to sight his captain in his reply. Louis held up two fingers in a victory symbol. The mate quickly removed two rods from the chair, setting each in the outside rod holder port and starboard. He then grabbed two small rigged ballyhoo, snapping the baits on the rods and proceeded to let them back as flat lines. Louis made his turn into the pair of dolphin and could not get them to bite for the folks.

"What are we doing, Louie?" Frank called up emerging from the salon. He was shrugging his shoulders and pointing to his watch.

"Trying to catch a dolphin."

Whitman turned to the stern and just now realized they were fishing once again. Louis' return pass brought more success as he fanned the two skipping baits in front of the dolphin in a sharp turn. The larger bull went for the trailing bait of the two, pushing water with his high square brow in full kick. As the fish seized the bait, Whitman lunged for the rod grabbing the line as well. When the fish got tight and bent the pole, he customarily reared back with great force only to snatch the hook from the fishes' mouth. The released hook, under great pressure, became a missile as it zinged back into the stern of the boat with enough force to take a chip out of her transom.

"Really murdered that one, sir. Bout as ugly as it gets, huh Cap!" Crafty tried his best to conceal his laughter.

"Who the hell you think you're talking to, Mate! You want to check out early on the plane tonight. Huh?" Whitman was livid and beet red. He was in no position to notice that he had simply hurt the feelings of the big-hearted mate, not angered him. Crafty's life at sea had shown him the value in eliminating formalities, to produce a more exacting message. Too, the mate had not expected the inexperienced Whitman to cut so easily.

Cami had quietly descended the ladder and was now hastening to the rod on the other side. In unhurried motion she lifted the rod from its holder placing her left thumb lightly on the spool of line, while her right hand pulled the drag lever all the way back towards her effectively taking the reel out of gear. She raised the tip of the rod twitching it a little imparting even more movement on the bait attached to it.

The bull took notice and rammed the bait head on repeatedly, doing everything but putting his lips over it. She would let the fish pull the rod tip down, only to have him drop the bait every time. She quickly put the reel back in gear and took a couple of cranks taking the bait away and ahead of the fish. This time when the brilliant green, blue and yellow fish grabbed hold, she felt his weight to the bottom of the rod tip's arc, and when the rod tip was pointed nearly at the fish she free spooled him as he turned to the side. She knew he had taken it from the feel of line pressure beneath her left thumb as it barely caressed the accelerating spool. She threw the drag lever to the strike button, and the fish took to the air.

She enjoyed playing with the dolphin, not horsing him in too fast, but simply making easy light pumps. She would slowly raise the rod and began her cranking a moment before she would lower the tip, taking in the line gained as the tip lowered. When the fish went airborne she would immediately crank slack as she lowered the rod, so as to have the reserve of raising the rod if all the line cleared the water at once creating instant slack. Through it all she kept a steady bend in the rod, a most important factor in tiring the fish.

"Nice work, Cami. She might have done this before eh, Louie," noted Crafty trying in vain to keep a straight face. She had the fish positioned about ten feet off the starboard quarter [corner] of the moving boat when she slowly stepped back a few feet so the leader was presented perfectly for the mate. Crafty gathered in the leader with open hands and took a single wrap with his left hand to take control of the fish. She set the rod gently in the holder and walked to the side to see her catch swimming along side the boat.

"Maybe twenty, darlin'," Crafty guestimated as he reached for the gaff.

She gently laid her hand on his glove and shook her head. "There's not enough filet on him for everyone, let him go. Besides, his girlfriend misses him already." She pointed out the cow who had followed her hooked mate all the way into the propwash and was now swimming away from the boat.

"Not a problem," replied Crafty reaching for his bait knife.

The blonde looked at a somewhat stunned Whitman and then up at the smiling Captain leaning on the bridge rail. "Beginner's luck," was all she could say before darting into the cabin.

Louis continued on home, knowing she was already getting into him without really trying. Better watch yourself and be careful old man, you might trip and stumble.

8

It was nearly four o'clock by the time Louis had completed docking the boat and plugging in the shore connections. Up and down the line crews were performing the wash and shammy ritual of their boat's daily cleanup—the time of day, when owners and crews would mingle, gather fishing reports, ogle each other's vessels, and map out the new day's game plans. And drink. Maybe drink a little more.

Louis was carrying plenty of fuel and nothing else required his attention at this time. Being one of the later arrivals from the day's fishing, he and Crafty were just beginning their cleanup as the majority of crews were winding down. They would get an early punchout. He and Crafty would fare better on the water pressure.

The boss was now making his exit, Cami in one hand, the picnic basket in the other. As he stepped off the boat he turned to Louis. "Louie, why don't you and Crafty join us all for dinner, we'll look for you around 6:30 for cocktails up at the house."

"That sounds good, Mr. Whitman, thank you. 6:30 then." It was not an invitation but a request. "That doesn't give us much time to clean her properly and rig up for tomorrow, sir. If Mr. Byrd is available we could use another man down here to help out."

"Absolutely. I love my girl and I want her to be kept clean. I'll send him down."

Whitman entered his home on the hill, the largest on the

island, through the portico overlooking the point. They took their sandals off and rinsed their bare feet with the foot shower before entering the open sliding doors that lead into the living area. There they found the other couple and Byrd enjoying a bottle of wine as they munched on some crackers and caviar. Both men stood.

"There they are." Adam announced, "Tell us a fish story, Frank."

"Not a very good day, Adam, there's nothing to tell."

"Oh, no. Sorry to hear that."

"It was a beautiful day, though, wasn't it, Frank?" Cami offered. "We saw a whole school of whales that looked like they were guarding a newborn. They stayed on the surface for a long time. It was fantastic. And we did catch a nice dolphin."

"You caught a nice dolphin, I caught a boat ride. Hell, Jack Hamm trolled lures coming up from Nassau and caught one out of the two he raised. We were obviously in the wrong place."

"Senator Jack Hamm?" Adam's attention was perked.

"Yes, Adam, he's an old fishing buddy of mine."

"It would seem our fabled Cuban Louie didn't live up to his billing, eh Boss," Byrd observed seeking to commiserate with his boss.

"Scoot, get your butt down to the boat and help with the cleanup so we can all make dinner on time tonight. I want to be ready to fish in the morning."

"I just jumped out of the shower, I thought that was his mate's—"

"You want to be around tomorrow?" Frank began to rekindle his anger. "You're low man here this week, you're nothing more than a piece of equipment. Now!"

The Byrd's usually pale face was now beet red as he charged out of the room and down the path to the docks.

Whitman turned to his company and forced a thin smile as he shook his head. Everyone appeared to be rather scarred from the whole episode as the silence lingered uncomfortably.

Whitman walked over to his humidor and pulled out a fresh Cohiba. He gave it the traditional licking, snipped the end, and lit it as he settled back into his chair. He blew out a puff as he stared out into space waiting for someone else to break the silence.

"I understand completely, Frank. When someone works for you there is nothing to be gained by blurring the lines of duty and professionalism. It's best kept that way, don't you think?" Adam offered trying to provide a little healing.

Whitman agreed quietly, slowly nodding his head staring into nowhere as he puffed away. Adam and the two women resumed their conversation about Nassau and Lyford Cay, and who was there, and how the shopping was, and all that weighty stuff.

Byrd hit the docks still hunting for his composure. As he walked pass the row of boats and crews, he felt a familiar sense of isolation. For in a business that was small enough for everybody to know or know of nearly everybody else, he knew nobody, and nobody knew him. It really confused him more than it saddened him.

When he arrived at the back of the boat he found Crafty seated on an upside down five-gallon bucket facing a couple of ice chests. On the top of one lay the tools of his trade: wirecutters, pliers, file, bait knife, sharpened hooks, pre-cut leader material, rigging wire, sewing needles and threads, as well as a large tupperware bin with numerous pre-made ballyhoo rigs. Two other buckets set on both sides of him. One was a salt brine containing freshly rigged baits, the other merely for rinsing and thawing.

"I'm here, Crafty, what do you need me to do?"

"Better check with Louie," he replied gesturing with his right thumb.

"Quite the office you have set up here."

"Gotta do what ya gotta do."

"Why do you cut the eyes out of those ballyhoo, won't that make them appear less real?"

"Nah . . . you see here," he picked one up, "they got a socket between the eyes. Once they been in the water swimming for awhile, the water pressure forces their eyes to bug out causing 'em to swim funny, This eliminates that, and helps 'em swim perfectly from the get go. Sort of Skip and dip."

"I see. I'd like to learn some of your tricks sometime when you have the chance."

"There are no tricks, Scoot but yea, anytime." Crafty answered earnestly.

Byrd jumped on the boat and seeing that the engine room door was opened, stuck his head inside and saw Louis pumping some oil into the starboard engine via the oil change system.

"Hey, Cap, how can I help?"

"Byrd man, how 'ya doin'? How are things down in New Providence?"

"New Providence?"

"Nassau."

"Oh."

"Just puttin' a little oil in the girl to top her off."

"Burning a little extra on this side?"

"Yes we are, have been right along. We didn't take any spray today bein' a flat ocean and all, so just give her a good squirt from the overhead on down. Soap and rinse her from the bridge deck on down, cockpit, and transom. I'll follow you around with the shammy and three of us will knockout what's left when Crafty's done riggin' up. Questions?"

"Got you good."

"Well have at her, we don't want to be late for dinner."

68

Byrd climbed back out of the engine room feeling a little better than when he went in. His captain was showing himself to be a man of character, who at least knew how to treat others. *Yeah, so what*, the Byrd thought to himself.

9

Louis wrapped the towel around his waist as he made his way back to his stateroom. Opening the closet door, he gave thoughtful consideration to making a selection for his evening attire. Standard working uniform by day consisted of tan dickies, white T-shirt, and topsider sneakers. Evening wear required two modifications, loose white cotton knit shirt worn untucked, and a swap of leather deck shoes for the sneakers.

Crafty was contemporary nautique opting for sportif shorts, aftco print fishing shirt, and non-slip reef rider sandals. Walking the path to the house they looked more like father and son, than the brothers they truly were from the skin on in.

Cami heard them talking as they approached the house so she went outside and waved at them from the patio. From there she led the pair through the open sliding doors into the enclosed living area where a bar had been set up. The four of them had already had a round and were into their second cocktail. Some hors d'oeuvres had been set about, and everyone appeared festive and animated.

"Come on in boys," said Cami walking between the two men, an arm around each of their waists.

Frank walked up and shook each of their hands, "What would you like, we've got about everything here?"

"Beer in a bottle would be fine," answered Louis.

"Crafty?"

"Bacardi and Coke, no lime."

"Roland, how about a clear Becks for the captain and a Bacardi and Coke for the mate, no lime.

The young Bahamian dressed in a flower shirt and black pants nodded, and within a minute walked over to the new arrivals and presented them their drinks on a tray.

"Roland, this is my crew on the boat—Captain Louis Gladding and his mate . . . Crafty." Whitman had a private laugh as he suddenly realized that he still did not know the man's full name.

"Roland. Hi Roland, how's it going?"

As Roland grabbed Louis' hand his face lit up in a big smile, "I know Capin' Louie for long time, mebe he not remembah me, I only be dis big." The young man indicated a height about up to his belt. "I be Ortnell's youngiss boy. Cop and me, we go bun' fishing all de time. I alwes' get conch for you."

Louis smiled fondly at the polite young man, "I can't believe it, Roland, you are a man now. My memory is like the tide, it comes and goes." Louis put his hands on Roland's shoulders, and then drew him to him in a hug.

"Captain, is there anyone on this island that you don't know?"

"Sure."

"Well now that everyone has met, why don't we go out on the patio, there's a nice breeze coming up, and the bugs haven't come out yet" Cami prodded the group grabbing Frank by the hand.

Louis walked to the edge of the small hillside that overlooked the point and anchorage and the sea beyond. He could see all the way across, the late afternoon almost gone with the sun waning behind a cloud line rising up over Andros Island. The light was saturated in color, pinks, orange, reds, and magenta, blended in reflected richness off the dark gray clouds. It was another magnificent sunset, crafted uniquely for the day.

The breeze had come up from the east southeast at about twelve to fifteen knots. It swept the island clean of all lethargy and oppressiveness, and the more natural rhythm of the tradewinds was returning once again. The wind caressed the skin and awakened the nerves and heart. Noise carried so much farther in still air. Louis always felt it was quieter and more peaceful in the gentle breezes.

He remembered the day and its events, and what he had seen and not seen in his search. When the morning would come it would be a different ocean and a new day. He felt renewed and grateful that he was led to this life, for he could think of no other more beautiful that could have been given to him.

Louis' mind continued to wander as it always did at this time of day and for the moment no one sought him out. He looked out into the fading colors as he drew a deep breath, and he began to see into the looking glass.

He was in his first memories of his youth spent in the orphanage. These fragmented images soon gave way to a clearer memory of an uncomfortable and isolated adolescence, spent mostly in truancy and crime. He surely must have been saved from the clutches of his own will, and an early and untimely death. From here he could easily see his demise, most likely at the wrong end of a gun.

The sea and all that was in it, was Louis' first true salvation. From the moment Alfie Silva 'adopted' him and welcomed him into his family after he fled Florida, to the time they had to flee Cuba barely escaping with their lives, he knew the road had been laid out for him. The good Lord had searched his heart and had given him His word. He had provided a life of beauty and peace and one of great reward. His word was as perfect and true as the creation that now stood before him.

"One out there with your name on it, Captain?"

"Truthfully, no, Mr. Wendt. There isn't anything out there with my name on it."

"Come now, Captain, your reputation precedes you. You are a predator on the high seas as much as any other are you not?"

"Only if I kill for the wrong reason, sir. Life requires life, we have to eat. Though to answer your question, I was a senseless killer for a long time. But not anymore, I just like being there, sharing the day with the fishes. They are there for us to enjoy as a gift. But one must fish for them to engage and experience them, as they have no use for us."

Wendt forced a smile, "Captain, man is in charge of nature, he is the most rational being around. With each new day, science and technology convince us of our superiority. Our brain is truly 'our' weapon isn't it?"

"I wouldn't argue with that, Mr. Wendt. But even if mankind has been given dominion over the creatures, he does not have sovereignty over them. They do not belong to him. He must govern with love, wisdom and respect, much like a good father. You're a psychologist, Mr. Wendt?"

"Please, call me Adam."

"Did you know that the bottlenose dolphin has a greater ratio of brain mass to spinal cord than even man?"

"No, I didn't. So they can perform a few tricks and have constructed a minimal language, I wouldn't call that a cultural phenomenon."

"They have a rather complex language and a far ranging, superior perceptual skill. Their culture has endured far longer than ours, lacking only the undesirables of war, hunger, and self-predation. What is our boast against that simple observation?"

"They have remained in the water by choice, as you would say, Captain. Compare what they've achieved in the sea with what we have been able to build in our world."

"Mr. Wendt, that would be so foolish as to prove nothing."

"Yes, well . . . I would say that in the end, it is rather a level playing field. Evolutionary theory plays no favorites, we are all evolving together, don't you quite agree?"

"I'm not much on evolutionary thinking, sir."

"Survival of the fittest, Captain, do you not see it every day you are out on the water?"

"Would you say, Mr. Wendt, that we are a specie where the strong and superior members survive and dominate?"

"Absolutely!"

"Or, in other words, the best of us never die young before our time."

"I didn't say that."

"Oh?"

"You know what I'm referring to, Captain."

"Not really. I believe your evolutionary theory makes the false assumption that the creation was not already perfect in its origin. Out on the sea, I do see a natural selection of predation upon the weak without conscience, and that is in keeping with a perfect harmony. But your Darwin assumed he was going to get scientific help somewhere down the line, and he hasn't."

"How do you mean, Captain?"

"There has never been found a form or fossil in transition. Or, as far as you are concerned, your 'missing link.' What has been found, however, are fossilized remains of fish in the act of eating other fish. Wouldn't that suggest something sudden and cataclysmic?"

"I'm not so sure about that."

"Many scientists are. In fact, one of the biggest scientific defections going on today, is from evolutionary theory over to the truths of creation. That is where the evidence lies."

"I didn't realize boat captains were so well informed on the damn subject."

"I can read, sir. The truth favors no university, but enters the soul through the heart."

"A noble thought, indeed, Captain Louie," Wendt dryly observed.

"If as you say, Mr. Wendt, that we are all derived from a single cell, I would suggest that you ask Mr. Whitman about a computation made last year by one of his super computers out in San Diego. Go 'head."

"I'm right here, Louie, I vaguely remember that study."

"Please, Frank, do shed some light on the matter," Wendt jokingly urged.

"Some anthropologists from UCSD out there programmed our super computer with the latest technological data on the carbon dating of our fossil remains, our age in years. They plugged in the data base stored on a single strand of DNA and all available lab data on induced mutation on a chronological timeline, you know viruses, antigens, etc., etc.

"Yes, Frank."

"Well, it spit out two conclusions. One, that a single strand of DNA holds enough information to fill a set of Encyclopedia Brittanicas. Second, even more peculiar, that given our oldest age in terms of carbon dating that is verifiable, the chances of us being at this stage of development from random evolution from a single cell . . . would be one in 485 trillion."

"In other words, . . . " Adam quizzed Whitman.

"In other words, it was saying that everything exists now as it pretty much always has. Breeding can influence size and traits, but not structure. At least that's what our 'puter said. Some species have not survived, obviously."

"Fascinating. We should continue this dialogue at another time, Captain, I find your views quite stimulating."

Actually, I hope we don't, Louis reflected silently.

"What's the game plan for tomorrow, Louie?" Whitman continued on, Wendt taking full advantage and exiting to the bar.

"Mr. Whitman, I'd like to get an earlier jump on the day, I feel like we're in for a good day of fishing."

"No, I mean where should we be going? Come over here for a second."

The pair walked back inside over to the corner of the living room, where Whitman snapped on a desk lamp that lit up the large scale chart laid out on the desk.

"Here, take a look at my satellite reports, they show a fairly wide body of warm water working west from Spanish Wells off the north tip of Eleuthera."

"Looks interesting, might be a sixty mile run."

"I'm not the least bit concerned about the fuel bill. We could run around to Little Harbour and pull artificials from there over to here," exclaimed Whitman indicating a position on the chart.

"I really appreciate the input, Mr. Whitman, but I don't think I'll make any such decisions until the morning when we untie the lines. That has always been my way."

"Surely, you're not going to drag us back to where we were today?"

"I liked what I saw over there, the chain of life was definitely in full bloom."

"Captain, we didn't get a shot. I don't think there are any fish over there right now."

"I eyeballed a few fish."

"Where, when?"

"In the water, all day long."

"I'm serious, Louie. I didn't see one bill behind the boat all day."

"Nor did I. They were off the edge down deep, they just weren't in the biting mood. This run of calm weather and moon-lit nights might have made them a little horny, hard to say. It really doesn't matter anyway, but we did have a couple of sail-fish trail our outriggers for a good long while. They faded off as well, it was that kind of day."

"You saw all this, why didn't you alert the rest of us?"

"It wasn't necessary, besides you were busy."

"Doing what?"

"Taking inventory in the cockpit."

"I do whatever I deem necessary on my boat!"

"Mr. Whitman, I mean no disrespect here. But the things I

am telling you are for improving your angling ability, assuming you were legit in your desire to become a better fisherman. When a blue marlin comes knocking on our door, you had better be at the rods when he makes his move. The last thing we need with the mate going crazy trying to clear the pit, is a deck littered with hooks, knives, fly gaff heads, ice picks, and beer bottles. You know a good doctor on the island?"

The boss man gave Louis a good hard stare for a few long seconds, time enough to concede to the wisdom of his captain's statement. "Your point is well taken, Louie."

"If my guess doesn't work out tomorrow, we'll go with your plan B, fair enough."

"I can live with that. Let's go eat, I'm starving."

The Whitman party made the walk to the restaurant by way of the salt water pool, passing by a few cabanas and down through a covered walkway to the main path leading to the only two public structures within the club. As the hurricane had leveled the public dining area a couple of years ago, all dining had been redirected to the restaurant on the members' side. Directly across the eatery was the ship's store, which was usually quite well stocked due to the islands proximity to Nassau. There was a patio separating the two buildings used for tournaments and social functions.

Inside the main entrance there was a dining area to the right and one to the left where it adjoined a bar open to the public. Quiet dining was preferably to the right, and tonight the Whitman party would be dining there.

Louis brought up the rear of the group as they entered, and a quick scan of the populace told him that not one pair of eyes failed to notice the two women as they came through. He was hardly surprised as they would have turned all heads in any joint they ever happened into. Over here they were a real life fantasy, carving up deprived crews and owners alike.

77

Frank took a seat at one end of the table, while Cami seated everyone from the other end. She put Louis on her right, Adam on her left, a mute Byrd to Frank's right, Crafty next to Louis with Cheryl at Frank's left. A young Bahamian, dripping with gold chain, arrived almost immediately to begin taking their drink orders.

"Ya folks my nem be Jeremy, ah we drinkin' dis evnin'? Lay-deez."

"Jeremy, why don't you bring me one of those heavenly Goombay Smashes. Cheryl?"

"Do you have any bottled water? Evian?" She still had not removed her dark glasses.

"Evian far you."

"Come on, Cheryl, loosen up for cryin' out loud, and join me in an island drink. She'll have what I'm having," Cami insisted as she waved her off.

Jeremy moved to the other end, "For de gentlemon."

"Absolut martini on the rocks with a twist. You're a vodka and tonic right, Adam?"

"Please."

"Bacardi and Coke, no lime," pointing at Crafty. "Clear Becks, Louie?"

"Noo Becks, Kalik?"

"Fine, Jeremy."

"Al' ret den," and he was gone.

"What's good, Frank?"

"Everything, Adam. The food is wonderful here."

Silence fell as everyone began scanning the balanced but not overly extensive menu. Jeremy returned with the drinks before the conversation had resumed, and when everything was set in place he grabbed his pad to take the dinner order.

"Is the lobster fresh?" Adam asked without taking his eyes off the menu. He did not see the subtle shoulder shrug of his waiter.

"Fresh frozin'."

"You know, Frank, you'd think over here it would not be that hard to get fresh lobster."

"It isn't. They're out of season . . . to all but a couple of Bahamian divers," he replied with a slight wink of his eye.

"The lobster tail then," requested Adam leading the way.

"What are you having, Louie, help me out?"

Louis leaned over and pointed to his selection on Cami's menu. "Hmmm, Jeremy that cracked conch and grouper combo sounds hot."

"Crack conch cumbo for de lady, and fer you, too, cop?"

"Great and throw some peas and rice on there, too, would ya, Jeremy."

"No probe'lem."

"I'll have the same, man," Crafty inserted.

"Just the grouper for me," requested Cheryl.

"I think . . . I'll . . . have . . . the pork chops and throw some peas and rice on mine, Jeremy, if you will."

"Very good, sah."

"I'll have the same, Jeremy," Byrd concluded.

"I'm not sure if I have ever had grouper," observed Cheryl, beginning to uncoil from the Goombay and its completely undetectable proof. The glasses come off.

"It's a wonderful sweet and light fish, and it was probably caught today," Louis explained, "freezer space is at a premium."

"Isn't there something you have to watch out for with the grouper, something about some toxin or parasite?" Wendt posed the question as he continued to scan the menu.

"It's not all that common, it's called ciguetera. A few reef dwellers get it from eating the wrong kind of diet," Crafty clarified for the group. "Besides, the locals can usually cull 'em right out, and they know which areas from which not to take fish."

"Oh, how's that, Crafty," a curious Whitman asked.

"Simple. As the filets are laid out in cleaning, they check

'em to see if any flies will light on the meat."

"How uncivilized," Cheryl replied, "having flies land all over your fish."

Frank and Adam shared a chuckle believing it to be a joke.

"Actually, you have it backwards. If the flies won't land on the meat, it is more than likely holdin' the toxin and will be thrown out. Believe me, it works. The Bahamians are excellent cooks, I'll be happy to finish what you don't want."

Cheryl straightened her back and craned her neck in anticipation of whether her luck was running hot or cold, "That's comforting to know, Crafty."

"I think everyone wants to try a little fishing tomorrow, Louie, you really think the bastards will bite?"

"I think so, Mr. Whitman, things seem to be in our favor. We've finally got the wind where we want it and we're just about comin' on the full moon. Been talkin' to some of the boys on the dock, and it's been a few days since anything has really been happening."

"What is it about the moon that seems to get the marlin biting?" Frank seemed to throw out the question for a toss up. "You read about that all the time as it pertains to different fishing locales, it seems like a consistent factor on good 'bite' days just about everywhere."

"I'm not sure, Mr. Whitman, but it would appear to have something to do with 'grouping' fish populations rather than distributing them. Might have something to do with reproduction."

"How big can they get?" Cheryl enters the conversation.

"The biggest on a rod and reel was caught in Hawaii, a little over 1800 pounds. When the fish was landed, it was reported to have had a 150 pound yellowfin tuna lodged in its throat. Bigger specimens have been seen over the years by longliners and other ocean fishermen."

"Oh my." The sultry brunette had become quite wide-eyed.

"Captain Louie, Frank tells me you once fished with Ernest

Hemingway, is that true?" asked Wendt moving on to newer territory.

"That's true, Mr. Wendt. I fished with the man many times when I was a teenager living in Cuba. I knew his captain, Gregorio, and worked his cockpit for him."

"He was quite a legend, and probably a hell of a fisherman," Adam stated enthusiastically. "He must have been a dominant force in every tournament."

"He was a fine fisherman, and a true pioneer in the sport."

Louis laughed briefly, "Not that he didn't desire to dominate things, Mr. Wendt, but he had little appetite for tournaments."

"I find that hard to believe, Captain. He was a highly competitive man, certainly worthy of displaying his mastery over nature."

"I believe his fishing filled him up completely, something even his writing could not do."

"Whatever do you mean, Captain?"

"It was a heart-driven thing, Mr. Wendt, something beyond the intellect."

"You're losing me again, Captain."

"The spiritual experience, sir. He loved the fish for what they were."

"Oh that word, so misunderstood . . . Frank, thanks so much for the use of the jet today. I know the girls had a highly successful shopping adventure in town."

"Anytime, Adam. Gives my pilot something to do besides waiting on me. Looks like our dinner is on the way."

"Jeremy, when you get a chance, how about bringing us two bottles of your best Chardonnay."

"Certainly, sah."

The plates were piled high with delicately battered filet and thin ribbons of conch, steaming hot, with a pile of peas and rice. A house salad was placed at everyone's left. Nobody waited for the wine, not even Cheryl. It became quite silent at the table.

"Forget it, Crafty you're out of luck on the fish," a transformed Cheryl declared as she devoured what was left of the grouper. "I've eaten in some pretty trendy places in this world, but I don't think I have ever had a better piece of fish. I don't think I'll crap for a week."

In mid-swill of his drink, Crafty had to manage his laughter as it upwelled within him. He gave her a wide smile, "I knew you'd like it, once you tried it."

Adam continued to pick at his lobster tail, only once looking over to his girl with pursed lips. His quiet disapproval of her new-found candor was evident. Crafty was beginning to feel in the middle.

"Saw you on the *Tonight Show* the other night, Mr. Wendt, I imagine you must be pretty good at what you do to be on the tube all the time."

"Glad you saw the spot, Crafty, it's nice to know you're getting out to people. It was the culmination of my book tour, the end of the line of ten very hectic weeks of travel. This week has certainly arrived as a needed change of pace."

"Are you a psychiatrist?"

"Not at all," Adam grinned, "more of a personal motivator and trainer. My work involves helping people to maximize their inner resources, and get in touch with their deeper, underlying dynamics. Most people have yet to utilize the full potential within themselves. Everyone needs redirection at some point in their life."

"Adam is being modest, Crafty," Frank interjected. "He has worked with some of the most noted and gifted people of our time. Professional sports figures, actors, politicians, artists and businessmen all come to him for consultation, advice, and direction when they feel they're slipping in some fashion."

"You're too kind, Whitman," Adam replied.

"Well, your track record speaks for itself. Best sellers, testimonials, videos, television. Adam is very much in demand and has helped great numbers of well-known people."

More like leading the lemmings off the cliffs, Louis quietly observed. He was beginning to see Wendt's role in Whitman's assessment of things. Certainly, these men had the right to their views, and Louis felt it proper not to place himself in the middle of things. He knew in his gut, however, that this new man would be an obstacle to his boss becoming a better angler, and that was really all Louis cared about.

"Would you call yourself a guru?" asked Crafty dropping the bait back a little.

"No, but you could," replied Wendt. He wouldn't eat.

"I feel wonderful, but a little sleepy. Anybody else?" Cheryl's face had radically softened with the weight of her eyelids causing them to droop. It only enhanced her allure.

"I'd be happy to walk you back," Crafty offered.

"Nonsense, Scoot can escort the girls back to the house while the men have a whiskey and cigar."

"Appreciate the invite, Frank, but I'm caving in a little myself," countered Adam rising from the table. "Wonderful dinner, please excuse the two of us."

"It would seem that everybody is comfortably settling into the island rhythm, which pleases me immensely. The morning will come soon enough, let's all get a good night sleep. I think we're going to need it, eh Captain Louie?"

"I believe we will."

10

Louis awoke at his customary hour and immediately made a pot of coffee. With mug in hand, he opened the salon door and stepped out into the cockpit, taking a seat on the covering board at the transom. He was pleased that the breeze had persisted through the night and the morning was cool.

He listened to the grating serenade of laughing gulls pierce the quiet lapping of the water on the boat hulls. It reminded him of dogs barking in a country town at the change of light. They were always there.

Louis looked down into the water and saw schools of mangrove snapper and sergeant majors swimming under the boat. Small barracuda and needlefish also darted around subsurface over the other fish looking for a morning meal to seize in their canines. He tipped his coffee mug so a few drops fell in the water, the circles rippling out on impact. Immediately, the three foot 'cuda turned to the source of the disturbance before resuming his constant search. *No wonder you get all my bait*, thought Louis, *I have been teasing you from an early age.*

The only other soul out and about at 5:30 A.M., was a young captain sitting in his helm chair on the bridge of his sportfisherman two slips over. He appeared to be receiving a weatherfax or some kind of satellite data and was scanning the paper with a flashlight as it was being spit from the unit. A minute had passed and he tore it off the constant feed roll and closed the compartment housing the receiver. He descended the ladder into the cockpit and then stepped off the boat, taking a seat on his dock box where he had set his coffee mug.

Louis went inside to fetch another cup and when he returned he saw the young man walking his way, examining the transom of the boat in between.

"Morning, Cap, going to be out there today?"

"Oh yeah. We're gonna try it when the boss gets here about nine," came Louis' reply.

"Yeah, we raised a couple of blues yesterday, and let one go. Hit a green and black Schneider doorknob on the right flat line. Decent fish about 300."

"Glad ya got him."

"That's all we seen, though. Out in the middle of nowhere halfway between here and New Providence."

"Lay your eyes on any tunas out there?"

"Didn't see a one. You fish yesterday?"

"We gave it a few hours in the afternoon."

"Do anything?"

"A dolphin."

"Yeah, it's been slow, ain't it? Jimmy Donato."

"Louie Gladding."

"I think the boss wants to try it around Whale this mornin'. Where you headed?"

"Joulter's. It looked good over there for not catchin' much."

"Gotcha good. Gonna be on 71?"

"Rogo."

"I'll give ya a check about noon. Nice talkin' with ya."

"Good Luck, Jimmy."

"Same to ya, Louie, catch 'em up."

"Hey, what's the name of your boat?"

"*Reel Job.*"

"Okay, Jimmy."

Louis was nearly half way across when he decided to make a slight course correction. He had been running at the south end of Joulter's Cay, but considering it would be high tide within the half hour, he elected to set a course three miles south of his original heading. The new target was an area where the edge of the shelf took a westerly turn inshore, creating a canyon break in an otherwise linear stretch of bottom.

He was willing to gamble that tide and wind pushing west together, would act to drive the deeper, cleaner water with great force into the mouth of the indented canyon. If such were the case, it would create a significant amount of upwelling currents as the tidal flow made an impact on the walls of the canyon. As the plankton layers would compress and escalate upward to attract the bait fish, the bait in turn would bring in the larger predators. It would make for a nice ambush, if, Louis conceded, he was guessing a'rightly.

He scanned the forward horizon, and had noticed many 'good' birds flying with him. The sea conditions were ideal at a comfortable two- to three-feet, fringed with a few light white caps. Today's choppy sea conditions might aid in pulling more bait to the ocean's surface. The turbulence would infuse more oxygen into the water in addition to providing a little more camouflage. Sheets of flying fish were frequently breaking the surface, where yesterday he saw only a few large ones busting out of the slick calm ocean.

When he was within a mile of his destination, Louis unlatched the bracket arms holding his outriggers against the boat, and lowered them into their forty-five degree fishing position. He backed off the drag on his teaser reels, which deployed the various combinations of artificial and natural chains of hookless attractors. Today he would pull a chain of squid on the left side, and a large pink neoprene softhead on the right as one faced the rear in the direction of the trolling spread.

Crafty had his four bait selections snapped to the rods laying in wait on the deck—two swimmers and two skipping baits. Each side of the bait pattern would present one of each and the long right outrigger would spend nearly all of its time subsurface.

Louis never second guessed Crafty's selections.

Louis brought the boat down to a six-and-a-half knot trolling speed, taking dead aim on the center of the canyon mouth. His first tack down sea would lead him right in.

Crafty hurled the daisy chain of five pearl-colored squid over the side and it began to slide back as the first element in the spread pattern. Louis tightened the drag on that reel when it was a distance of fifty feet behind the boat. Having let the outrigger bait out behind the boat a selected distance of around 150 feet, Crafty set the free line into the clip and was now hoisting it out and away, four feet from the tip of the left rigger. That done, he put the reel back in gear and fined-tuned the distance one more time.

He moved to the number two rod, and took the reel out of gear as he flung the bait over the side. He dropped the Spanish mackerel to a distance nearly twenty feet behind the end of the squid chain, and clipped the line to a second pin as part of a shorter halliard that would terminate about two-thirds the way up the outrigger. In place, he locked the second reel up.

The number three bally was fed back to a like distance with the left short rigger, locked in gear and clipped to a release pin mounted on the transom on the outside rub rail. The clips were all identical and had been preset to release the fishing line at sufficient impact of a fish's strike. The lines were not pinned but ran through the clips, and could be easily adjusted for distance from the boat. The skipping and/or swimming action of each bait could be dialed in by raising or lowering the clip on the rigger line that held the suspended line. It was a simple, time-tested system for presenting natural trolling baits; there were no rubber bands or tag lines.

Out went the right teaser to its appointed distance behind the boat where Louis locked it into position from the teaser reel upstairs. Nicknamed a 'trashcan,' this large skirted neoprene softhead pushed copius amounts of water, chugging and foaming a frothy mess in its wake. It mimicked quite well the look of a fair-sized fish crashing a bait.

For those fishing aboard the *Byte Her*, the first encounter of the day would not be long in coming. As Crafty was in the process of letting out the last right rigger bait, he saw the dorsal fin cutting the water in a quivering motion behind the chain of skipping squids.

"Left teaser, white marlin!" Louis bellowed from up top as he took hold of the teaser line with his hands.

"White marlin on the teaser, Boss, he's all over it!"

"Yeah, so. What do I do?"

"Huh? Knock the short left out and bring it up along side. Let's go!"

Whitman left the chair and reached for the number two rod, picked it up and pulled the suspended line through the pin. It did not release.

"Knock it out, man! Jerk the tip down and away."

This time the pin let go the line and it dropped from the outrigger until the slack was gone and it was again being pulled from the rod tip.

Louis leaned over the bridge and spoke quietly to his mate, "We got another on the right flat."

"Crank it up to the teaser, Frank, c'mon!" Crafty yelled as he put on the clicker on number four reel still dropping its bait back behind the boat. Whitman was slow in bringing his bait alongside. "Frank, get your frickin' mackerel up there man, and stick your rod tip out over the side!" Crafty's improprieties of yesterday had all but been forgotten.

The marlin was now intent on killing every squid in the chain, beating them with repeated swipes of his bill, knocking them clear out of the water.

"Try and lead your bait next to the teaser by sticking your tip out over the side. Take it out of gear and give him a rod tip and a second when you feel the bite." Crafty had settled himself and was now coaching and walking his angler through the hookup in an even monotone. Louis took one hand off the teaser line and aided his angler by turning off the fish causing the bait to track to the left nearly alongside the chain of squid.

The fish would not get off the teaser, however, for it was now in emotional overdrive, purely focused on the squids. His large pectoral fins now fully extended, he was lit up in electric hues of turquoise from head to tail.

"Give it a twitch, Frank, get your bait skippin' up top a little."

Instantly, the fish leaped across the few feet to the bait and took it on the run, again causing Whitman to rear back with the rod. Whitman won the tug of war with the marlin and was once again left holding the free-swimming but mangled bait.

On the right flat line, the second white marlin had committed itself, crashing the ballyhoo and bending the pole over as he danced straight up on his tail.

Louis had detected a third fish swimming away from the boat in the vicinity of the still free-spooling right long bait, "Long right, Crafty!"

"Here he comes again, Frank, don't snatch him, give him a rod tip," barked the mate as he reached behind his back and lightly thumbed the free-spooling reel.

Once again, Frank's fish seized the bait from the side, only to have it elude him from the angler's premature yanking. The mackerel had been damaged beyond function as it corkscrewed erratically through the water. Strike two.

The airborne marlin on the right flat line had gotten his bill wrapped up in the leader, as billfish often do, and was only moments away from ridding himself of its encumbrance. Hearing the clicker surge and feeling the spool of the reel behind him suddenly accelerate under his light touch, Crafty threw the drag lever into strike putting the reel in gear, never taking his eyes off Frank's fish.

Of the three fish in the encounter, only the one on the long right had managed to find hook, as the pole in the rod holder was now beginning to bow over.

"That was an angry mob," Louis chuckled to himself as he began to simultaneously crank in his teasers and maneuver the boat's stern to face the lone marlin now greyhounding away from the boat. With the spread now cleared down below, Louis easily closed on the fish, backing down sparingly with only one engine at a time. He wanted to see his angler work a fish, to observe his timing and angling sensibilities. He was pretty good, Louis judged from what he was seeing—well-timed pumps, aggressive when the fish let him be. He showed patience when the situation dictated, like now when the marlin was making a long deliberate run to the deep.

The white proved to be a good 'swimmer,' not burning himself out in rapid fire aerial tactics. Thirty minutes later when Crafty took control of the leader, the reason for his durability was made clear. He had been foul-hooked on his back behind the dorsal fin and had maintained free movement at the head throughout the fight. Big luck, a foul hooked fish in a tough place, hooked 'blind' by the mate. No matter, Frank had done a nice job playing the fish. Take one out of three.

"Did a good job with him, Mr. Whitman. Hook was in a tough place. Let's get another," spoke Louis calmly leaning over the bridge rail.

"That's more like it, Captain." Frank yelled up. "First time I ever got one on a bait! I'll do better on the next one."

As Crafty was in the midst of putting out a new spread, he paused to examine the remnants of Frank's mackerel, most of which had been scaled from the hook. He appreciated the shots, but secretly hoped they would come up one at a time for awhile. From the first sighting to the lone eventual hookup, the whole event took no more than twenty seconds. He hoped that Whitman at least learned the need for speed.

With his fresh spread now deployed, Louis set up for

another down sea tack into the break of the canyon wall. When he had gone far enough in to a depth of 120 feet without any bites, he hung a U-turn and headed back offshore. Engaging the other engine ahead, he bumped his speed up to a crisper seven-and-a-half knots going into the sea.

Louis turned on the power to the color machine, setting the depth range at zero to 150 fathoms. The bottom immediately came into view as it descended sharply as the boat worked its way offshore the 'edge.' There were some bait markings sixty feet below the surface where the deepening slope of the canyon hit about 120 fathoms—720 feet of water. He studied the deep ledges and occasional pinnacles of sub surface mountain peaks where he also marked stands of bottom fish he guessed to be grouper or yellow eye snapper. They appeared as little chartreuse trees ascending upward from the sharp bottom.

Louis suddenly looked back at the spread and settled his scan on the dark silhouette of a billfish trailing far back of his right outrigger bait. "We got one on the right 'rigger, boys, but he don't look like he's gonna eat." Louis goosed the speed and action of the swimming mullet by turning off the fish a bit, placing the mullet on the outside of the turn causing it to briefly pop from the water. The marlin's high scythe-like tail imperceptably broke the water as he, too, picked up his speed with a slight kick. The extended pectoral fins of the awakening predator were beginning to light up in a day-glo greenish blue. Just when it looked as though he were going to make his move, he faded back and off, and was lost in Louis' field of vision.

Immediately, the old captain reversed his course turning back into the fish, carving a sharp turn to port. As the leaded split-tailed mullet slowed, it began to sink beneath the choppy sea as the boat continued her hard turn.

"Be ready, Frank, we might get eaten up in this turn," Crafty warned as he and Louis gazed back and forth from the rod tip to the outrigger pin.

91

The dangling line running off the pin, billowing in the breeze suddenly became taut and free of slack. The clip strained towards the fish taking all slack out of the outrigger halyard. But because they were turning with the fish on an axis, there was insufficient pressure on the line to cause the clip to release it. Whitman did not readily grasp the scene beneath the waves.

"He's got it, Frank, crank to him!"

"Huh?"

"Crank till I tell you to stop!"

And he did. The gathering tension finally tore the line from the clip, picking up the slack from the water as in the tightening of a loop, until the angler became 'straight to,' the fish under the right 'rigger directly off the boat's portside.

"There he is," Whitman screamed as the rod bent over in his hands. The white marlin popped up and began shaking his head until he decided to motor off taking a hundred yards of line in a matter of seconds. Louis cranked in his right teaser till it dangled straight down from the outrigger eye, harmlessly out of the way, while Crafty knocked the right flat line out of its pin and cleared it quickly into the boat. Again, Louis initiated an unhurried backing down, reversing his starboard engine only as he cranked in his other teaser. His mate was gathering the left short as the boat continued its backing nearly on top of it. The left long was of no immediate concern as the boat passed it by, letting it trail off beyond the bow.

At the end of its blistering run, the maniacal fish did a 180-degree turn, getting on its tail in a showering spray. It jumped again, clearing the water entirely by six or eight feet in a forward somersault. Again it jumped in a frantic quivering and shaking, its beautifully formed tail kicking as if it were trying to 'swim' in the unresponsive air.

On his belly now, the creature made a turn toward the pursuing boat, instantly throwing slack into the line. The fish kept coming, pectoral fins lit up, bill and body quivering from side to side, trying in vain to rid himself of the hook that was so alien to him.

Louis had instinctively put both engines ahead at the first sign of the fish's charge at the boat. And now, seeing that his angler was not keeping up with the fish in his cranking up the slack, Louis increased the power to the engines to put a little distance between boat and fish. As Whitman regained a little of his rod bend, the marlin continued to charge the stern still on its belly. When the black cloud of smoke cleared and the noise of the surging engines died down, Crafty had the leader in hand cutting it immediately with his bait knife.

"He's alive," an admiring Crafty laughed as he watched the now freed marlin still tearing up the surface trying to shake the hook. "Didn't feel like over-handling that one, might have hurt him. A maniac wasn't he?"

"You should have held him by the bill so I could get a good close up picture," Wendt countered, "Frank might have appreciated that."

"Did ya get some of the fish workin' out, Mr. Wendt?"

"Most of it I believe."

"Well, then?"

"It's all right Adam, it was a legal release, I had my fun with him."

Crafty peeled off his cotton gloves and chucked them into his rigging bucket while stealing a glance at his captain upstairs. Louis knew his exact thoughts and gave him an okay sign. The two men went back to work.

They'd been back on the troll for about an hour when the blonde made her appearance on the bridge. "Louie Gladding, you are on the meat today," she said giving him a big hug.

"It's nice to be lucky isn't it."

"That was an incredible fish, I don't think he spent all of thirty seconds in the water."

"They are pretty like that, ain't they?"

"Somethin' else."

"The *Byte Her*, are ya on there Capn' Louie?" came the voice over the radio, "*Reel Job* tryin.'"

"Yeah, go ahead, Jimmy."

"Whatcha done for 'em, Louie?"

"Go to seventy-four."

"Seventy-four."

Louis turned the channel select dial till 74 appeared in the LCD window. "I'm here if you're there."

"Back to ya, tell me a fish story."

"Seen a few white marlin here this mornin' and had a few chances, Jimmy. Let a couple of 'em go, jumped a bill wrapped fish off. Hadn't had a bite for awhile, though, workin' my way up towards Joulter's."

"That where ya seein' the fish?"

"Coupla miles south of there."

"Oh yeah, got ya real fine."

"What's happenin' round the corner, there?"

"Not much to it, caught a few dolphin on the edge, have not seen a billfish."

"Yeah. Well, there's a few here, I heard one boat off Morgan's let a small blue go. Few boats up at the pocket, been a sighting or two up there. That's 'bout all I heard."

"Sounds better your way, Louie, I'm thinkin of pickin' up and running back to y'all. I'm getting into worse lookin' water the farther up the line I get."

"I'm just zig-zaggin' my way up the edge now. Maybe I'll bump into 'ya this afternoon."

"I think so."

"All right then, appreciate the check and I'm gone."

"See ya."

Louis switched back to channel 71, and set the mike in its holder. Cami had brought him up a fat turkey sandwich and the

Coke that he had asked for, and he was enjoying it immensely.

"Everyone all right down below, Cami?"

"Just fine, everybody's having a good time, even Cheryl."

"That's good. Maybe if we stumble onto a few dolphin, some of the other guests can do a little catchin'. What is Mr. Byrd up to?"

"Just got through making our lunches, otherwise, he's been inside the salon all day reading fishing magazines."

"Probably wouldn't hurt, but I need to get him involved somehow with the team, you know. Would 'ya send him up here when you go back down. I mean don't go yet, I like havin' you up here, aah, . . . I like havin' your company . . . "

"I know what you mean, Cap," she said with that smile. "Here, give me your plate, I'll tell him to come up."

She was sweet, the old man thought to himself, and she had awakened a part of his biology that he thought had been put to sleep forever. He was not an old fifty-eight, but fifty-eight nonetheless, old enough to be her father. *Enough, old man,* he thought to himself, *stay clear and get out of the way. There's only trouble in it for you.*

"What's going on, Louie, you need me to do something for you?" Byrd asked sticking his head over the top of the bridge ladder.

"Hello, Scott, enjoying your day?"

"If the boss is happy, Scoot is happy. But I'm really not that eaten up with fishing. Hunting is more my game."

"You like to scope 'em, I prefer to let the creatures make the first move. Anyhow, it's time to begin your training as our gaff man."

"Gaff man?"

"That's right, the Hemingway is an all 'kill' tournament, nothing is released. Sails, whites and blues all 'on the dock' a point a pound. You're the man. You get to stroke the fish. Ever use a flying gaff before?"

"Sure. A few times with Frank."

"Good. There is always room for more practice. When you go down tell Crafty to load the tagsticks, so you can begin looking at your targets. He'll tell ya what to do."

"Get right on it."

Louis no more liked tagging fish than bringing them into the boat to photograph. He was convinced that it did them absolutely no good at all. But he was not one to let Byrd shoot live trap by killing where it wasn't needed. At least here at Chub, tagging would make Byrd get up close and personal with the fish. He knew full well that the man had never used a fly gaff in all his life.

Louis had briefly considered the use of wind-on leaders to free up Crafty's hands, but chucked the whole idea for a good reason. Being a fifty-pound line restricted tournament, only a limited amount of drag could be utilized in the fight. Lacking the heat to sufficiently tire the fish, would mean getting the marlin quickly to the boat—more than a little on the 'green' side. It demanded that Crafty, arguably one of *the* best 'wire man' in the game, be on every leader. Case closed.

It was one in the afternoon when Louis arrived at the southern end of Joulter's Cay. He was working in and out from the edge in a typical ground covering 'Z' pattern. He would troll directly down-sea going inshore and fish the 'trough' between the waves as he worked back out to 150 fathoms and back in. He was concentrating on his ranges that were etched in his memory, contouring across and around the various sea mounts and structures that had provided him with the most productive sightings over the years. If any fisherman knew the area better than Louis, he would be the first one to say so.

The tide had begun to ebb, but the water quality had remained clean, holding its deep indigo shine. A tropic bird, pure white in coloration with a very long tail, was working the place along with him. Not only were they pretty, but they usually were a good bird for the fisherman.

He came to an old familiar piece of bottom, and hooked around the submerged peak, heading west and inshore to a depth of no more than eighty feet. *'Bout time for a 'cuda,* he mused, *might break the spell anyhow.* He literally fanned his spread over the edge of a tremendously rich field of coral heads as the clear aquamarine water revealed the white sandy bottom between them, ninety feet down.

The first sailfish rose up directly behind the swimming ballyhoo on the right flat line and took a whack at it, releasing the line from the clip. Crafty had seen it coming and alerted Frank to tend to the rod. In his excitement, Whitman had grabbed the outrigger instead, just as it had been knocked down by a second sailfish.

"That's a sailfish on you, Mr. Whitman," Louis hollered from his post. But the more slender of the billfishes, with its huge high dorsal nearly extended, had not truly taken hold of the mullet. "Crank it back on top out in front of him, get the bait skipping where you can see it. When you feel him take it, drop it back for a few seconds."

A little quicker in this encounter, Whitman was still awkward in his handling of the tackle. To execute the commands given him by his crew, he had to take his eyes off the fish to visually aid himself in manipulating the reel, drag lever, and crank. With a little 'outside' help, he was finally able to 'set up' on the fish; left thumb on spool, reel out of gear ready to 'drop back,' rod tip held high leading mullet and trailing sailfish.

"He's comin' on ya, let him have it!" Crafty remained fairly calm at his right side.

"I don't feel a thing."

"He's got hold of it, drop it back!"

Crafty grabbed hold of Whitman's shirt, and slowly tugged at the sleeve, "He's not going to rip it from your hands in a jolt, it's really more of a soft tug or resistance when he grabs it, kinda like snagging a towel."

"There he is again, Frank, just drop it back," a resigned Louis calmly instructed him from the bridge.

"There, I think I feel something . . . "

"Then let him have it!" Crafty was now running his hands through his hair.

"Frank, I'm coming underneath you to get this other rod out of your way," Cami quietly spoke, grabbing number three rod and trailing flat line bait, walking to the other side of the cockpit. A focused Whitman took absolutely no notice of her.

"Frank, when I say 'now,' just point the rod at the fish and let the line go out. Okay, here he comes again. NOW!"

Whitman did lower the rod, and began periodically letting the line go out, occasionally stopping the line all together.

"Crank it back up, Frank, until you pick up the bait on the surface," a steadfast Crafty coached from the side. "Ya see him back there a few feet following your bait, [and what a tough bait, thank you, Louie] we have a very willing creature here. One more time, he's got it!"

Miraculously, the rod tip went down under the weight of the retreating sailfish, as the spool really began to pick up RPMs even under the excessive pressure of Whitman's thumb.

"Ya feel him now don't ya Frank?" the mate inquired.

"I don't know, dammit, how the hell can you tell?"

"Just put it in gear," was all Crafty could say after about a 'ten Mississippi' count of dropback.

The line had become quite light when Frank began to crank, and when the end of the rig busted water, all that could be seen was egg sinker [lead], hook, and a few inches of dacron thread streaming back from the wire twist. "San cocho!" Crafty lamented as he took a much needed stretch. "Well, he gave ya half a dozen shots, anyway, boss. That's how we learn," Crafty conceded as he stole a glance at his smiling captain.

"I've got one on here," came the feminine voice from the other corner, "but he's got the better part of the spool out there. Want him, Frank?"

"Don't be ridiculous, I'm having a beer," replied the chief as he slammed his rod into the holder on the covering board.

Cami started packing line, as Louis helped her with the boat. It was a juvenile fish that had been hooked in the soft triangle underneath the base of its bill and did not take to jumping very much. She led him in for the mate who took a single wrap, and called for Byrd to poke the tag in the shoulder meat just under the front of the large dorsal. Tag and release, right now for Cami. There was less jubilation at this juncture.

As the early afternoon had progressed with no more sightings, so the tide continued to ebb against the wind. Although conditions still seemed favorable to Louis, the water quality on the 'edge' had lost its shine, giving way to an acceptable clean blue green. He had covered the break from the south end of Joulter's Cay to his current position on its northern boundary fairly much to his own satisfaction.

For the past few minutes, he had been working around another break in the fairly straight linear dropoff that ran north and south. But the retreating tide had slowly given way to the less attractive bank water and scattered eel grass that was moving in all around him.

He had heard of a few sightings at the north end toward the 'pocket,' but already he could see a fair-sized fleet of boats beginning to collect up there. More than likely it would get even more crowded as the afternoon wore on. Louis preferred not to fish in a fleet situation if at all possible. He liked to work his own little piece of ocean where he felt he had a better chance of making or breaking his own luck.

Feeling a little stiff, he rose from his chair, engaged the autopilot, and walked to the outside of the bridge for a stretch. *I need to take a tack offshore where I can pick up that pretty water color change again*, Louis decided quietly.

He initiated a very long, thorough scan of the water to his east from the bow to the stern. He saw nothing unusual at the water's surface, so he stuck his head up and out from under the overhead and repeated the scan looking skyward. He might have seen a high flyer, but his aging eyes weren't completely convinced. They were still far better than average at a mile, and lethal within the trolling range.

He peeled off his polaroids and cleaned them off with his T-shirt, rubbing and massaging his eyes as well. When he put them back on, he forced his gaze into a hard squint, and went back to his target. Yeah . . . could be . . . yes, a high circling frigate bird in the distance. Might be on something. They were a good bird, though for the most part, it usually meant dolphin. Louis laughed out loud. The ocean is a place with no conscience, and even less rules. I do not know what the man-o-war is seeing.

He went back to the helm, and turned the course selector on the autopilot till the boat's starboard turn brought the bow in line with the high circling bird. He then went back to the side of the bridge to observe the graceful black hunter with the large wingspan and long forked tail. He was flying lower now, in tighter circles, flapping more and gliding less. He has picked them up again, and is planning his dive for food. The wide wings tucked and he swooped down flapping them to brake his descent as he picked up a piece of baitfish with his talons.

Louis arrived to see sheets of small flying fish shower from the indigo water some distance away from the boat. Beneath their flight the brilliant yellow and green dolphin, fins fringed with powder blue, gave chase as they ran hard through the face of the waves. There were many fish in the school, for he saw they were without pattern, dodging one another like exploding fireworks.

"Should I trade in the big baits for a coupla' hoos, Cap?"

"Yeah, let's catch a few for dinner, and give the guests a little fun," replied Louis as he slowly encircled the feeding activities.

With only three baits in the water, Louis watched the purple water between his flat lines suddenly transform into a mass of green. One could almost walk across the water as the huge school covered them up on the first pass. The lone outrigger came down with a leaping fish right out of the clip, while the pair of flat lines each held a tail-walking dolphin in the process of crossing lines with one another.

As the Captain slowed the boat's forward motion to a crawl, Crafty snatched up the right side rod and lowered the tip, leading it under the left rod whose leaping fish just cleared the top of it.

"One for you," Crafty handed the rod to Cami. "One for you," reaching back to hand the left side rod to Adam, "and one for Cheryl" as he lifted the outrigger pole from its holder, "the tan and terrific dark haired lady. If you two can play 'em from over there, we'll let Cheryl play hers from the left corner. Probably bring your two in first. Are we eatin' dorado for dinner tonight?"

"Yes, mahi mahi" was the chant.

"Anybody want a belt?"

"Please. Okay." Cheryl and Adam chimed in together.

The fish all appeared to be around eighteen to twenty pounds, a nice eating size, and the trio was having a lot of fun doing a little weaving and dodging of their own. Cami had hers alongside first despite the fact that Wendt had been non-stop cranking since first being handed his rod. She and Louis, by his slight turn to port, presented the fish off the port quarter [stern] of the boat. Crafty gently half-wrapped the leader, and without lifting the fishes' head from the flow of water made a sure stroke with the gaff behind and over its eye. In one motion the dolphin was hoisted up and slid into the open fish box, steered by the gaff handle and the mate's other hand on its tail. The mate then dislodged and withdrew his weapon, quickly closing the lid of the box sealing the dying fishes' fate.

Adam's fish was taken in similar fashion, doubling up the

thumping and quivering sound of death coming from the fish box. Adam and Cami went into a little impromptu reggae in time with the dolphin, hoppin' all around the cockpit.

"Mine is coming in, too, Crafty."

"Take your time, darlin', we'll get him," Crafty reassured her as he joined in with the 'rasta' fish dance.

"Crafty!" Louis bellowed from up top.

Cheryl let out a genuine scream of terror just as the mate was beginning to react in spinning around to face the rear of the boat.

As the four-foot dolphin lay suspended in midair, at the top of the arc of his most desparate leap to stay alive, there appeared beneath him the unmistakable black shape of a huge blue marlin. He was charging through the propwash just under the surface, pushing so much water with its high head that only the dark silhouette of the great fish could be discerned. With only a few inches of his bill's tip and tail actually breaking the surface, specific features of eye, pectorals, and dorsal, remained concealed. His presence had, for the moment, robbed everyone on board of their speech.

Suddenly, the fifteen foot fish came aglow in the familiar trademark hues of electric blue and platinum, clear back to his tail, higher than his quarry was long. The killer measured his prey for only an instant, as the dolphin would soon re-enter the uninviting sea.

The great fish exploded in a fury, showering the cockpit with spray, unable to lift its great weight fully from the water. He seemed to coil his head and bill to one side, his eye the size of a tennis ball, rotating in its socket as it tracked the doomed dolphin only a few feet away. Just as the prey skimmed the surface to set up for another frenzied leap, the Blue uncoiled his contorted body to the opposite side as he descended upon the target. With perfect accuracy and timing, the bill had struck the dolphin behind the gill plate, severing the fishes' backbone instantly.

102

As the dying fish lay twitching on the surface, the marlin circled back around seizing his kill between bill and lower jaw, flinging it away from the boat twenty feet in the air. Louis was hypnotized as he put the boat back in gear, slipping the trashcan teaser back to its boiling posture.

In one kick of it's great high tail the marlin was on that teaser, seizing it in similar fashion as it twisted to the left away from the stern. The 300-pound test-line snapped instantly with a loud crack, slightly whipping around the huge bill. The noble creature with no natural enemies made two kicks and was gone.

Cheryl was holding her rod that had once held the dead dolphin like a rifle across her front. She was dazed and her slender legs had begun to quake just a little. She slowly set herself down on the covering board.

The scene played out before her had lasted only a few seconds. Perhaps, it was the tremendous size of the fish that had slowed her perceptions down to an almost unreal slow motion. In unhurried grace, the creature had displayed for her the perfection of death and dying in the natural order of the blue expanse. Did the mammoth Blue lack heart in not eating that which he had killed. She thought not, only conscience.

Crafty put his hand lightly on her shoulder as he slowly coaxed the rod from her grasp. "Aren't they beautiful?"

"Yes . . . they certainly are."

"Had to have been a grander, don't ya think, Cap?"

"Comfortable."

"Captain, why would a fish like that kill something and not eat it?" Wendt was now standing on the bridge ladder his head poking over the upper deck.

Louis, himself a little dazed, was not immediate in his answer. It had been a long time since he spent a moment with such a fish.

"I don't think he felt like sharing his food with anybody. They can become right territorial, you know. They kill a whole lot more than they eat." Louis began to laugh a little out loud before quietly talking to himself, "Shouldn't have tried to tease him with that big softhead, I guess."

"But why do you suppose that is?"

"Why what is Mr. Wendt?"

"That they kill without always eating."

"Mr. Wendt, I'm quite sure we're not equipped to know that."

"I see, Captain Gladding," Adam replied in a frown. Unsatisfied with the fisherman's well-meaning answer, he went back down below.

Louis put the boat ahead to trolling speed once more, electing to give the area some coverage, although he doubted that he would see that one again. That was okay with him. He was thankful just to have encountered such a great fish and for the awesome display of beauty and power it provided his people.

An hour had passed without incident. Even the dolphins' feeding had subsided, although the area still showed ample supplies of bait on the color machine. Louis and Crafty continued their diligent scan of bait spread and sea for signs of anything happening behind or away from the boat.

The radio was quiet, the wind had persisted, moving into the southeast a little more. The boat's gentle roll had subdued the women into restful naps, and Louis watched as Frank's head began to droop on a mission of its own as he sat back in the fighting chair. He assumed Wendt and Bryd were in the salon, when the final bite of the day came.

"Watch the right rigger, Crafty," Louis hollered down, "something back there!" Louis squinted hard into the blaze and glare of the afternoon sun that was dancing on every wave like a crystal chandelier. He had only seen a slight streak of something cutting through the water well behind the bait. As Louis steadied his gaze on number four right outrigger, he heard the clip on the left rigger free the line. He instantly drew a bead on a big boil that had left a sizable hole in the water where the horse ballyhoo had once been skipping.

The line came down tight and immediately bent the pole over as the reel began to scream, straining from the forces of fish and drag. Whitman snapped out of his catnap, grabbed the rod and put the butt in the gimbal of the fighting chair. Holding the rod steady at about a forty-five-degree angle, Frank let the fish have his way with the line he was burning off the reel.

"He's haulin' ass, he's got a third of a spool already," Frank screamed.

"Clear the flats, I'm coming through!" shouted the old man from the bridge. Crafty leaped at the right flat nearest him, speed cranking it to the boat before slinging it on the deck, before ducking under Frank's line to grab onto the left. He did not make it in time, however, as Louis had just backed over it both engines screaming in reverse growling and vibrating the entire rear of the boat mercilessly. The left flat line had now been grabbed by the reversing starboard prop which had become a reel in its own right packing the line around its hub. Crafty cut the line off the left flat rod releasing the bow that had been imparted to it.

"He's goin' up sea and to the right. If I have to spin on him, we'll go that way!"

"Gotcha, Louie," shouted Crafty as he went back across to the right rigger line which was now well out in front of the bow. The poor girl was hammered down in a hard reverse as the stern of the boat was being pelted by head seas breaking over the covering board at the stern's transom. Whitman was getting a good dunking, and the cockpit had a foot of seawater in it in only a matter of seconds.

"Still going, Louie he's gettin' us, dammit!" Frank was hanging in there, however, and he still had not laid a hand on the crank.

"Let me know when you see the gold of the spool," Louie

hollered as he continued to crank in his teasers, also trailing behind the backing boat.

"I can see it now, I can see it!" Whitman's plea was frantic. "He's got to have 500 yards out there by now!"

"Here we go, Crafty," was the warning from up top.

Louis powered off the starboard engine, and through it into full forward. He knew the rpms would have to fully back down, before the electronic shifter would give him the transfer and eventual forward power. *Come on, come on,* Louis pleaded with the solenoids in charge of governing the system. When he felt the starboard engine rev back up in forward, it began to lurch the boat into a stationary 180-degree rotation to port, and he readied himself on the port side control. There was black smoke everywhere, a lot of cavitation and window-shaking vibration, but the boat was doing her thing.

When the rotation had moved beyond 120 degrees, Louis took the port engine out of gear letting the forward drive of the starboard engine push her more toward the fish and away from Frank's line. When Louis eyeballed the bow to be nearly on a course with the rapidly escaping fish, he put the power to the port side, and the boat was now up and running and giving chase on a plane.

The fish was now in a direction underneath the port side outrigger and Frank was still facing astern.

"Your fish is over there, Mr. Whitman," Crafty yelled pointing toward the bow. "We have put a big loop in your line. Hopefully when we overtake him, you gotta crank up the slack as fast as you can. Do it!" As the boat would gain a little, the line would lift from the created arc in the water. If Whitman fell behind, Crafty would wave him slightly off the course away from the fish. If the fight created more rod bend, he would motion his captain more on top of him. It was working. Frank had become a winding fool, and the boat was steadily draining its cockpit full of water through the scuppers.

When they recovered more than three-quarters of the spool, Louis rotated the boat till the stern again faced the line going into the water, this time reversing a little less dramatically. He slowly backed as his angler continued to pack line. Louis knew they were near the fish, but a magician he was not. The fish could have looped him in any direction down there, and he was determined to be cautious until the angle of line in the water, and the rod bend gave some indication as to the fishes' whereabouts. He looked down and followed Franks line as far as he could see it penetrate into the blue sea.

Suddenly, it was a standoff. Cami was in the pit urging Frank on, Adam and Cheryl appeared on the bridge videocam in hand.

"What have we got on, Captain?"

"Can't be certain, Mr. Wendt, with the lighter drag we're fishing. I know it's fast and of size, and judging by the relatively shallow angle of the line goin' in, it doesn't look too deep—acting more like a billfish than a tuna. When you see that line begin to raise up, follow it on out and you'll have your pictures."

A few minutes had passed, and they were able to keep with the fish with just a gentle backing. Frank had maintained a good rod bend, was gaining line, removing loop and getting straighter to the fish with every crank. The angle of the line was becoming more shallow, as its entrance point moved away from the boat, nearly dead astern.

"He's comin' up, everybody ready! Be ready Mr. Wendt."

The blue marlin leaped from the sea almost fully vertical, thrashing and shaking his head from side to side, trying to throw the hook. But rather than sink back in, his powerful tail maintained his upright posture, causing the great fish to continue his 'windshield wiping' in a full 360-degree circle, throwing massive sheets of spray fifty feet across. Behind his gill plate, a good flow of blood was now streaming down his silver belly.

"Leakin' some oil now he is, Cap."

"Yeah I know," answered Louis loudly with a troubled look on his face, "He's got it in there deep, let's try and get him quick, Crafty."

With that, Louis put the power to the starboard engine, and then the port, steering stern of the boat simply by surging or backing off the power of each to force the transom to the left or right. *It had been a very lucky day*, thought Louis, and it appeared as though their luck was still with them, and the fish.

For as the 'blue one' continued jumping away from the boat, Louis was able to overtake him, allowing Crafty to quickly dispatch him by cutting the leader, giving the marlin his best chance for survival. The sudden lightening of pressure within his stomach settled the stout fish down. He swam into the depths below with deliberation and good color, albeit, trailing a stream of maroon. The hoots and hollers began for a few minutes.

"If he had been hooked fairer, we'd handled him a little for 'ya Mr. Wendt, but as you could see, he was gut hooked and bleedin' pretty good. He'll be all right, we have had a fine day."

"Discretion is the better part of valor isn't it, Captain. However, you're certainly not letting your angler enjoy his conquest."

"I heard that, Mr. Wendt, but the decision was an easy one."

"I'm not sure you gathered my meaning," the man stated as he started down the ladder. "You need to learn how to handle your angler."

I do not like this man, the old captain thought to himself. If he wasn't so stupid, I'd probably let him get to me.

"You on this one, Louie, the *Reel Job*."

"Back to you, Jimmy, g'ahead."

"I think I'm looking right at ya, if that's you blowin' all that smoke up there."

"Been real lucky today, Jimmy, just let about a 350-pound blue go right here."

"Pretty work, Cap. That just about slams it up for ya, don't it?"

"That's right."

"Finest kind, Louie, give the boss my congrats."

"Yessir, I'll do that. Saw a fish here an hour ago that took my breath away, Jimmy—biggest one I've seen in a few years. Listen, we're pickin' 'em up now, I'll see you to the dock."

"Please."

"Catch ya in there."

Captain Louis idled her into the marina basin about 4:30 that afternoon. A majority of the boats were still out hoping for a shot or two, for late afternoon was a good time of day for the blues to be out and about. But when the dealing was done, the flags flapping from the fleet's outriggers would indicate a sprinkling of caught fish. A blue here, a white there, maybe a sail or two. There would be but one boat with a grand slam with a white marlin left over. The old man would sleep well tonight, for he was grateful and had done what he could do.

The group was gathering up their things after having a drink on the boat, and they were all pretty much ready to jump off and head for the shower. Crafty was returning from the fishhouse with the filleted dolphin which was the unanimous choice for dinner.

"A great day, Captain, first grand slam for me," a beaming Whitman offered his hand before stepping off the boat.

"We were very lucky today, Mr. Whitman, everything kind of went our way."

"Except the big one got away," Adam noted with some concern.

"They will a lot of the time, Mr. Wendt."

"It doesn't always have to be that way."

Louis looked the man squarely in the eye for an eternity of seconds and felt the weight of the enmity between them, and wished truly that it wasn't there.

"Adam, you just don't catch a slam everyday," Cami

109

exclaimed with great affection and a wink for Louis.

"She's right, Adam, we've had a good go of it, and I have another notch in the old gun Louie, Crafty . . . please enjoy the dolphin with us tonight at the house, and see if you can get one of the dock boys to find us a few conch for fritters and salad."

"Thank you Mr. Whitman."

"Thank you, Captain."

Cheryl was the last to leave the boat, and as she grabbed Crafty's hand for a help off she turned and said quietly, "Really fun."

11

Just a beautiful evening, Louis thought to himself as he took a seat on the dock box set on the concrete bulkhead behind the boat's slip. It was nearly sunset, and the moon was hanging low in the eastern sky, but with a slight tint of ochre. The moderate breeze was soothing and refreshing. It always seemed to especially enrich the evenings in the islands. Louis gazed all around and studied the high cirrus clouds overhead still white with the setting sun. He thanked the good Lord for this day.

Crafty was putting the finishing touches on his editing and rerigging of the bait boxes as the good light was going and soon it would be the bugs' time to be out. With the bait slime blanketing him, he would be a primary target.

"Louis, you're a good man and a fair boat captain. It was quite a day."

"Quite."

"I think we're pretty much ready to rock and roll. I re-iced and did a quick editing job, and rigged enough to get us back to where we started this morning."

"Take a shower you bilge rat, we're headed for the house for dolphin remember. Besides, I can't imagine going three days in a row with this group if it's not required."

"Heard that, I'm done. Why don't you go on ahead, I'll catch up in a few."

"I'm just waitin' on Roland's boy to get here with the conch. The folks up the hill were asking for fritters and salad tonight. I see him over there, he's just finishing his cleaning up

"Ah, t'will be another fine fare. I'll sees ya, I'm going below."

111

The boy was only eleven, but he was capable and had been well-loved and disciplined. He came at a brisk walk down the dock, with everything Louis had asked for.

"Cop, I bring you de conch you as' for, and de bird peppers, too."

"Thank you, Rollie. You are a good man and a good hunter who knows how to prepare conch." Louis reached into his wallet and gave the boy ten dollars. He pointed to where the house was and explained to him how to find the door to the kitchen. "When you get there call out for your father or the cook, I think her name is Rosie, and give them what you have brought to me. Thank you."

"I go now. You catch 'nuddah slam in mornin, eh mon?"

"We'll sure try, Rollie, if we get the chance. I am sure of that. Go now."

Louis watched the boy race up the hill on the coral path, and he wondered how his life might have been had he a son of his own. He had a beautiful daughter, and she looked like her mother he thought gratefully. She was his treasure. There hadn't been enough time to have any more children. *Perhaps, I was the wrong man to have had a son,* he thought to himself. *I know many men with many sons, am I not worthy?* He bristled and immediately dismissed the thought as it made him uncomfortable inside. He took a slow long stretch and made his way up the hill.

"Come on in, Louie, and join in the celebration. Roland, bring the good captain a cold Becks." Frank was still walking on air.

"Thank you, sir, we were blessed with much luck, today."

"Better to be lucky than good any day, but you really kept us on the fish all day. I apologize for second-guessing your strategy last night."

"Not necessary. I appreciate your input, and you have always been a man of your word with me. But sir, every dog has his day. Let the team get the credit it deserves."

"True enough, Captain, and quit calling me 'sir' and 'Mr.' all the damn time. Frank will do just fine."

"Hello, everybody." Adam emerged from the other room, "Roland, how about a nice tall Absolut and tonic, I believe I'm ready."

"Sah."

"Frank, I hope I've served you well as your photographer today, I think we've got some interesting footage to view."

"Great, Adam, we'll take a look after dinner. Here, have at some of these conch fritters. They are truly artful."

Adam took a couple of fritters and chased them down with half his cocktail. "On the money, Frank, delecti. Fritter, Captain Gladding?"

"Please." Louis reached for the bowl not allowing Wendt to get up. "What time do you want to head out tomorrow, Frank?"

"Louie, as much as I would love to fish tomorrow, Adam has convinced me that we have unfinished business to take care of, and of course, there is much preparation to be done for Cuba. Adam will be accompanying us to Havana I am delighted to add."

"I see." Louis reached for another fritter.

"Unfortunately, all my software and modems are set up for the boat, I really have nothing to work with here at the house. So, we'll be tying up the boat all day with our boring business activities. Say, why don't you and Crafty take the little boat and show the girls the back side of the island, they would enjoy that no end."

"I believe Cheryl mentioned something about shopping in Nassau, Frank."

"Nonsense, they've done enough of that. Whatever, they can decide."

"Be happy to do that, Frank. We could do a little bonefishing or shellin', maybe snorkel around the corner for awhile. We'll make a nice day for 'em."

"Really, Cheryl is not much of an outdoor girl, I think she was definitely counting on Nassau," Adam asserted.

"Speak for yourself, Adam. You're the bore that wants to crunch numbers all day," came the husky voice of the brunette as she entered the room. "I would like nothing more than the guys to give us a little island tour, sounds relaxing to me."

"Well it's a done deal then. Who's ready?" Frank pointed and surveyed the room for the next round. Cami entered with a fresh batch of conch, and it appeared as though the cocktail hour would be extended a might.

Dinner was served promptly at 8:30. The dolphin arrived on a huge platter done three different ways: blackened, coconut fried tempura, and Nassau style, a hot roasting with tomatoes, peppers and onions. On the side, a huge bowl of conch salad and fresh green beans brought in by the plane.

Crafty had arrived a little late but made up for lost time at the drinking hour, power gulping a few rum and cocas. All ate up to capacity and then some, before finally pushing away from the table.

The girls helped clear everything off, and excused themselves early. The day had taken just about everything out of them, and the fine dinner had finished the job.

"Before you retire, Cami, how about bringing me a bottle of Crown and a box of cigars. Roland, grab four of those glasses would you please," requested Frank pointing to a wall cabinet. Frank poured a generous measure in each glass and passed them to the four men present.

"To Havana."

"Havana."

Whitman pointed to all four in a circle as he looked at Roland, indicating another round for the group. He opened the humidor and pulled out four cigars, tossing one in front of each man.

"If ya don't mind, Frank, I'll pass on the smoke." Louis was the lone dissenter.

"Here, Roland, would you like a fine Cuban cigar?"

"Yessah."

Relax, pour yourself a shot to take with you."

"Sah."

"That'll be all for tonight."

Those that were smoking followed the ritual displayed by Whitman, and in a manner of seconds, clouds of smoke were being led out the room by ceiling fan and the night's breezes.

"Fine cigar, Frank. Really hits the spot once in awhile."

"It ought to be, Adam, at three hundred a box even over here."

"Oh . . . ah, Mr. Wendt. As I was cleaning the fly bridge this evening I found something I think is yours." Crafty stood and groped at his many pocketed shorts to locate what turned out to be a vial of pills. "Yes, it's got your name on it, here sir."

"Thank you, Crafty," an anxious Wendt replied quickly grabbing the vial and stuffing it in his pocket.

"It looked important, sir, I thought you might need it," Crafty continued intending to prolong the man's discomfort.

"Just medication, not life threatening. Frank, you really did a fine job on those fish today, let's take a quick look shall we?" Wendt stood and walked out to retrieve the tape.

"Where's Scoot, Mr. Whitman, haven't seen him all evening?" Crafty looked at Frank.

"He went back to Miami with the plane, said he had some personal details to attend to. They'll be back in the morning."

"I got 'ya. Ready for another day tomorrow, sir?"

"Crafty, the consensus is that you and the good captain are taking the girls out on the little boat tomorrow for a little excursion and an island picnic. That all right with you?"

"Love to." Crafty appeared well pleased with the plan.

"We need to tie up the big boat for the day with business."

115

Louis, in tune with his mate's new-found innerglow, threw him a look of caution. He'd much preferred to have gone fishing, but the thought of spending the day with the ladies was undeniably stirring up his own insides as well.

"Here we are, gentlemen, the goods." Wendt moved to the VCR and loaded the cassette before returning to his seat. The others adjusted their position to get a better look at the monitor. "You gentlemen will have to bear with me, I'm not exactly a born cinematographer."

After a few seconds of snow, the picture came in to reveal a quick, jerky pan of the horizon, moving into close-ups of all aboard. A splice breaks the peace, and there is Frank pumping away on his first white marlin. He is looking good, and not looking at the camera which is shooting up at him from the cockpit deck. There is an off camera scream, he sets the rod down, smiles and claps his hands.

The second fish is apparently taking a little line, but the angler is holding to, pumping away. Off camera, there are shouts and orders, somewhat unclear against the constant wind and drone of the engines. A brief splice and Frank is again smiling and clapping, a brief shot of the second white shaking its head on the surface.

There is another interlude of panning and zooming, cameos of all present, some aware of the camera's eye, some not. Suddenly, there is Whitman holding a rod with the mate at his side providing a running commentary for his tyro. And suddenly it is lost.

The last section of footage is taken from the bridge shooting down at the man in the chair. He is getting a good dunking as wave after wave is breaking into the cockpit over the stern, the boat reversing hard against the sea. This time, the shouts from crew and angler are heard clearly, black smoke is everywhere. More static and snow. Finally, a quick pic of a thrashing blue marlin half out of the water, blood streaming

116

down his side from the gill plate.

"He was bleeding pretty bad," Whitman observed loudly, having his first real look at his quarry up close and personal.

"He had it in there, real deep," Louis reiterated.

The show ended with a final disordered pan, sky, outriggers, and finally, a smiling angler rising from his chair, claiming victory with a raised fist.

"It won't win any academy awards, but you looked pretty good there, Frank. I suppose I could use a little help with my panning."

"Adam, it's not easy shooting a videocam on a bumpy ocean. It appears much easier than it really is."

"A fair statement, Mr. Whitman." Crafty's eyes rolled slightly skyward as he blew out a big cloud of cigar smoke.

"Crafty, without you standing at my side and coaching me, I don't think I would be much use at all. How do you know when . . . to set the hook I mean?"

"It's an acquired 'feel,' Mr. Whitman. Umm . . . like a golf swing maybe. The more you think, the more things get in your way. An angler's gotta take things to a certain unconscious level to get that feel, and make quick, sound, judgments as to the type of fish he has up before him."

"I couldn't agree with you more on that point, Crafty," Adam stated passionately, "we humans are such a repressed lot. One has to fully explore his internal workings all the way to the core, to bring himself up to his peak. That awareness can only come from within, but it must be first recognized to be truly utilized. Fortunately, there are ways to enhance that ability," Wendt spoke glibly, talking with his hands in a most telegenic manner.

"I think . . . Mr. Wendt, you misunderstood my point altogether. I simply meant that a good angler is one who can rely on split second eye-to-hand coordination, unconsciously. In so doing, he can minimalize himself to the max, allowing him to devote his total attention and senses to the fish before him."

"Nonsense! The one hooking the fish must use his intellectual edge over his prey, that is always his trump card."

"You mean like tricking him?" Whitman probed.

"I'll be truthful with ya, Mr. Wendt, the angler doesn't hook the fish, the fish hooks himself," Crafty calmy observed.

"The fish hooks himself . . . you're telling me that the fish hooks himself? Maybe if he has the mind to he puts it in a place where it won't stay," Wendt replied now laughing and looking around the table. Whitman reinserted the fine Cuban cigar and began to gnaw on its end.

"I'm not saying the man holding the rod is not important."

"What are you saying," Adam pressed on as he blew a big stream of smoke right at the mate's face.

"He's saying, Mr. Wendt," Louis forcefully interjected, "that even you aren't going to outsmart something that doesn't think."

"Come now, Captain Gladding, your boss has raised an important issue here. Are you so dull and obtuse in your thinking that you have nothing to offer him?" Wendt sat back in his chair as he gave the captain a hard stare. "Give us something!"

"Drop back," Whitman sought to redirect, "you hear it all the time with regard to billfishing technique. Drop it back, give it to him, let him have it! I heard that shit at least a half dozen times today. What is the best way to go for hooking success?"

Crafty started grinning and took the cigar from his lips, moving it over to Louis as if it were a mike, "Cuban Louie, your thoughts on dropback technique."

"Well . . . there are only three kinds of drop back, yunno. Too long . . . too short . . . and . . . 'just right.' Yup, I guess that covers it."

Wendt was really shaking his head now, and he drained the shot glass before him. "Define 'drop back' for me will you please, Captain."

"Free spool."

"When you are done free spooling, don't you then hook the fish?"

"We covered that, Mr. Wendt, as Crafty has already noted. Your closed-mindedness has hidden the answer from you. Your wisdom might only be as good as the questions you ask."

"Now you're in my ball park, Gladding, and I demand an answer. Isn't it the angler who puts the hook into the fish after free spooling him for a period of time."

Louis sighed, "The fish hooks himself, sir."

"And how is that achieved, Gladding?"

"By leaving the hook with the fish, Mr. Wendt. The angler only sets that which is already in place."

"A ridiculous argument."

"Louie, I think I now see where you are going, but how do you know when and for how long?"

"You have to know the kind of fish that you're workin' with. They are all different and unique, and can be aggressive and/or just hungry, Frank. You just have to go out and meet up with as many of them as you possibly can, by experiencing them. There is no other way, there are no shortcuts. Maybe you can leap over the backs of your competitors and adversaries in your world, Mr. Wendt, but that is merely a man-made notion. Whatever you might have learned back there, you can't bring it along with you. Out here, you'll start in the same place as everyone else, and more than likely, will make the same mistakes."

"That's it, that's all there is to it?"

"I never said it was easy, Mr. Wendt. But it sure is simple."

"You seem a little 'out' there to me, Captain, but you're entitled to your opinions."

"You may call them that if you want, but I call it learning. If you expect to work with nature, the first thing you must do is downplay self. Oh there are things a fisherman must learn: tides, currents, temperatures, baits and tackle, hunting tactics, birds and such. Senses have to be learned and sharpened, eyes trained.

119

But the greatest of all fishermen will always fish with their hearts. Their minds will be laid open to experience and learn from that which is far greater than their puny selves. Out of the sea itself, they will come to recognize it as the bounteous gift it truly is."

Louis suddenly felt the need to pull himself back. Whitman was getting just what he wanted in this little game of confrontation he laid out after dinner. Louis knew he had drunk more than he was used to, and although not really in his cups, he was more loose-lipped than he wanted to be.

"Not to change the subject, Captain, I could not help but notice that you had most of your electronics shut down today on the bridge. Do you think you are using all the resources available to you in putting Frank on the fish? That is what you are being paid to do, isn't it?"

"Yes, that's right, Mr. Wendt. I have running what I need to have running."

"You have all kinds of computer plotting and imaging available to you and it just idly sits by."

"Out here on the ocean, the computer game is much like your inexact science, Mr. Wendt, in that it explains everything and predicts absolutely nothing."

"Oh? Just what do you mean by that?"

"The machine hasn't been built that can direct the fisherman where to take the boat in the next moment."

"But how do you know where you are, where you have been?"

"I know where I am before I get there. I am lucky over here, in that this computer," Louis pointed to his ear, "doesn't need to be told what it already knows."

"I'm sorry, I just don't follow you, Captain."

"This old man is starting to rattle on, if you all will excuse me, I'm goin' to bed."

"It's early Louie, stick around I'm finding this conversation stimulating and most helpful," Whitman pleaded. "No early jump on the day needed, sleep in tomorrow."

"Nah, it's time to put it to bed. But Mr. Whitman, take a walk for a couple of minutes if it's not a bother?"

"Be delighted."

The two men got up from the table and made their way out onto the veranda and down the path. Crafty and Wendt puffed on their smokes, and continued sipping the good Canadian whiskey. When he had drained his glass the final time, Adam rose and was the first to speak.

"Your captain is rather an odd sort, Crafty."

"Sir, Louis knows every mountain, rock, pinnacle and coral head in that stretch of ocean out there. Why should he engage in regress and waste his fishing time on someone else's theory on the day. That would be unprofessional and counterproductive. Computers, after all, are not greater than the sum of their parts, are they Mr. Wendt?"

"I appreciate you returning my medication, Crafty, although you could have shown a little tact and done it privately."

"I'm sorry, sir, I didn't really give it a second thought. Was there something you didn't want known?"

"Right." Wendt eyes glared intensely at Crafty. "I trust that you will be responsible with the ladies tomorrow."

"Of course, sir. It is my duty."

The man walked closer and stood over the mate. "I think you know where I'm coming from. Watch yourself." He then started out of the room.

"Mr. Wendt, one more thing."

"Yes."

"The fish, next time don't forget the fish."

"The fish? Be specific, your not making sense."

"When you create a fishing video, you are supposed to have pictures of the fish. It's not an anatomical study of the angler. Unless, of course . . . you find that more stimulating."

Crafty smiled broadly at Adam and downed his shot glass

before rising and heading out into the night.

The two older men had undertaken a brisk walk out towards the point. They had engaged in small talk, reviewing the day's locations, time of bites and water quality conditions in the area.

The moon was now overhead and quite bright. The illuminated Tongue of the Ocean was tranquil, the silence occasionally broken by small schools of bait fish feeding on her surface.

"Mr. Whitman . . . "

"Frank."

"Frank . . . all this out here is what it's really all about," Louis started in, gesturing with a broad sweep of his outstretched arm, "This place, this sea, is a whole lot bigger than you and I."

Louis again waved his arm across the horizon.

"I've spent most of my adult days out there, and I'm still learning and unlearning. Truly, I am as 'green' as the next guy. Your knowledge will only grow when you plug into that rhythm of life out there. Turn away from relying so much on that self laying within that armor plate. If you don't, not only will you be frustrated with your fishing, you will be shortchanged in your enjoyment of it."

"That's why I have invited Adam along into the thick of it, Louie. He can do us both some good. Why don't you just ease off him a little and hear what he has to say. He's the best."

"Mr. Wendt may have a talent for business and promotion, but as it relates to what we are trying to do here and next week in Cuba, it is of no use to you." Louis chuckled briefly. "We all would like more bites, more action, more fish. But, Frank, truth and knowledge of this beautiful world, come but from one place, one source. Believe me when I tell you, it does not originate from another one of the mortals walking around. No matter what the claim."

"Captain, I really do want to pull this all together. I admit that I don't have all the answers, but damn it, Louie, what do you want from me! Look here, I'll share a secret with you. When I started my company, I didn't know a byte from a hard drive. What I really know how to do is build a company, and I'm always more than happy to pick the brains of the people I have placed around me."

"Frank, when I'm out there I don't pull the strings, and I can't truly make it happen. It happens 'to me' if you will—when I have been paying attention and interacting well with the sea. I'm not the one in charge, and I certainly don't scope the fish except on rare occasion. It's faith that keeps me around, faith that this is where it will happen when the one in charge decides that it will happen. Yes, I have to pay attention to all that's going on around me at every moment. I have to pull a pretty spread, and I must like the water in which I'm investing my fishing time. But . . . in the end, it's not up to me."

"Louie, Adam has—"

"A real life example, Frank. There are 200 boats in a fifty mile stretch of ocean. None have raised a sailfish to their baits all morning, from north to south. All at once, everybody up and down the line, is starting to hook up at precisely 10:30 in the morning. Would this be properly called an act of individual effort?"

"Nature will have her way, Louie."

"Always, Frank. You can learn far more from the ocean by scaling back your head, experiencing her with open heart and mind. Or, you can remain bound within your ego and all its limitations, protections and traps. You'd better get this personal motivator, shrink, psychic trainer, shaman, astrologer or whatever you choose to call him, off your back. Just be his friend. Take a good long look at the beauty out there as if you were a child seeing it for the first time. That's the best advice an old man can give you. You have kept your word, and I must do the same. I really mean no disrespect, and I'm sorry I've talked your ear off tonight. Sleep well, Frank, and dream of the fishes."

The old man turned and made his way back down the beach path, looking back once, before he slipped through the Australian Pines. The tall man had taken a seat on a piece of coral rock, and was seen enjoying the bright moon and that cigar.

12

Another beautiful morning had unfolded on the Cay. Many people were out and about strolling the dock, tending to their vessels as they socialized along the way. The marina was somewhat barren this morning, with far more boats out fishing on the reports of yesterday's good catch.

Louis and Crafty had re-iced all their coolers and were finishing the straightening up of their dock area. They had spoken to several crews earlier in the morning, who had seen fit to pick their brains a little on their fishing successes of the day before; their location, depth, water quality and time of bites, in that order. The crew had just finished splashing the flats boat off the davit, when the boss's party began to make its way down the hill.

"What a beautiful morning, Cap, it's a shame we aren't out there enjoying it."

"You're certainly right about that, Frank."

"Duty calls I'm afraid, Louie. We have much to get done before next week," Adam remarked as he handed down briefcases and satchels to Louis and Crafty. "Hopefully, this will all be history by tomorrow."

Louis carried the precious cargo into the salon and carefully laid it out on the dinette and teak table. Frank immediately opened two small cases that contained an LCD monitor and keyboard, plugging each into a phone connection jack on a nearby wall.

"Whatcha got there, Frank?"

"Rather cute aren't they, Louie. Lap top computers, my newest toys the boys back home have built for me. Get used to seeing them, Cap, they'll be everywhere in a couple of years. Why you'll probably have one along side you on the bridge!"

"Might be a while on that one, Frank. Everything all set, any thing missing you might need?"

"Looks in order, Louie, you guys go ahead and have a nice day. The girls brought a picnic basket, so you're all set."

"Okay, Frank. Hope your day is productive."

When no more was said, Louis closed the salon door quietly, and stepped off the boat. He had provisioned the trip earlier in the morning with four sets of snorkeling gear, four light spinning outfits and about a dozen and a half 1/8 oz. Phillips jigs, tan and pink in color.

The girls clad in their bikinis and T-shirts were tearing up the remainder of the dock population, growing by the minute in the vicinity of *Byte Her*'s slip. Crafty took everything as Louis passed it down, and finally, the remaining three members of the expedition hopped in the fifteen-foot skiff as Crafty started up the outboard.

"Where are we headed today, Cap? I don't wanna do any steerin'," Louis drilled his driver.

"We'll top off the fuel first sir, and then head for the backside as the tide is still floodin'," Crafty evenly stated.

As the group headed out the cut, they made a right turn at the range markers instead of the usual left that would have led them out to sea. Up on plane now, they followed a channel, carrying four feet of water, that separated Chub Cay from the private Crab Cay. They cruised around the land head to a bay that dramatically opened up to reveal miles and miles of light emerald and pearl-white sand flats, with veins of darker, deeper water networking throughout as far as the eye could see.

"Cap, pull over by the airport so I can grab a conch for a little scent."

"Yes, sir."

"All right, all right."

Crafty brought the boat to a stop adjacent a shallow sand flat, where a dark green hole could be seen about fifty feet away. He shut off the outboard, and it was silent. Louis hopped over the side and began his short hike to the hole where he would snag a conch to cut up and tip his jigs with. *We ought to catch a few bones today, we're catching the tide perfect,* he thought.

"It's so beautiful and peaceful out here," Cheryl noted as she made a slow 360-degree scan, drinking in the gemlike appearance of the waters. "Look at the underside of those birds, Cami, they are positively lit up like emeralds from the reflection off the water."

"I know, girl, the flat is a very pretty place."

Louis was already returning with his conch, and as he neared the side of the boat he asked Crafty for a screwdriver and the diving knife. Turning the knife around to use the handle as a hammer, he drove the screwdriver into the conch's shell at a point slightly off-center, the spiral on its top. When he had opened a hole about the size of a quarter, he inserted the blade of the knife and severed a tendonlike appendage that held the animal to the inner shell. He seized the fringe of the creature from where it entered its hardshell case, and slipped it neatly right out of its home. He scraped the gelatinous 'snot' off the conch, and cut the rest of the meat into popcorn size pieces. He poured his fresh bait into a zip lock bag, and they were off.

"Ya know if we're going bonefishing we ought to do it soon, tide's only got another hour to flood. Crafty, in that little cove around that point east of the airport, there is a channel that connects about three different flats. They ought to be thick in there workin' against this current for the next hour or so. Let's give it a shot."

"Let's go." The mate put her right up on top and headed in that direction, favoring the subtle, darker water of the wide and shallow flats. Tiny coral stubs and starfish on the bottom went fly-

127

ing by as the four rode and looked. Once in a while a houndfish would wheelstand out of the water, riding on his tail over the surface at great speed, until it finally settled back in to resume its swimming. Sea urchins, rays, small sharks and all the other players were continually being pointed out by the crew, the ladies were fully enjoying themselves.

"You two bring enough sunscreen, you can get cooked out here?"

"Yes, Dad," replied Cheryl.

Neither of them appeared to have much need for it though, as both women were well tanned. But, Crafty reminded himself, *I said I would be responsible.*

The boat rounded the point and headed to the southeast. They were only a few hundred yards off the beach at the eastern end of the airstrip, and Whitman's jet could be seen parked just off the runway.

"Right about there ol' boy, ya see that little dark 'Y' in the water?"

"Gotcha good, Louis."

Crafty spun the boat a little to the northeast and pulled the power back a moment later. He slowly idled into the flat until the bow made contact with the sand, and he shut the engine off.

"Who needs a rod?" asked Louie once again hopping over the side stuffing his bait bag in the pocket of his shorts.

"Tell you what, you two," replied Cheryl speaking to Louie and Cami just now entering the water, "why don't you give it a whirl here for an hour, and Crafty can take me for a little boatride up the line. I just like looking around, and I'd probably be in the way."

"No you wouldn't, Cheryl, come on."

"I can fish later. Really, I wouldn't mind trying to hunt for a few quality shells. Sound okay to you, Crafty?"

"Sure, whatever you want to do."

"You keep the hand held radio, Crafty, we can always wade

in to the airport if we have to for some reason."

"That'll work, thanks, Louis."

Louis took a couple of spinning rods out of the boat and gave his mate one last eye contact. He checked his watch, "It's nearly eleven now, how 'bout pickin' us back up at say, 12:30."

"Done."

"See yah."

Louis proceeded to tie a pink jig to one rod and a tan jig to the other, tipping each with a piece of conch. They watched as the skiff meandered around in its heading off, hearing the outboard for just about as long a time as they could see it. Soon they were alone, and Louis was a little uncomfortable.

"See how this channel works up there about 200 yards and then splits off, Cami?"

"Sure do."

"That's where we want to be. The sun will be behind us, and the fish should be pushin' the tide movin' down the edge of those two flats, right against the deeper water."

"Sounds good to me," as she smiled at Louis and gave him a pat on the back. "Let me borrow the backside of your shirt to clean my glasses with, mine's all full of salt."

Louis turned to let her grab a hank of his tee.

"Your shirt's wetter than mine," Cami chuckled as she removed her shirt and top, wrapping them around her waist.

"You had to do that." Louis flushed.

"You mind, Cap?"

"Here," Louis divided the conch pieces into a another small bag and gave one to Cami, "stick this in your T-shirt where it won't slip out. Let's stay about fifty feet apart as we work up that way, you take that side."

"Roger that."

The pair fanned out to either side of the deeper green channel, staying about thirty feet off the break in the knee deep water. As they carefully stepped their way across the bottom, they could see the craters and mounds created by the burrowing or 'muddy-ing' activities of feeding bonefish in recent tides. Out here, mangroves were not a problem as snags, but they could see that the little green twigs dotted around would serve pretty much the same purpose. A good amount of bladed sea grass all around provided the greatest camouflage for the bonefish. Their nickname, 'Gray ghost of the flat', was justly deserved.

Louis ceased his careful heel and toe stepping and went into a slight crouch. He looked over at Cami, and waited for her to look back before pointing to an area about seventy yards in front of her. She shook her head and shrugged, she hadn't yet picked up the target, nothing was breaking the surface. Louis held his hand steady, pointing to the lead fish in the school as it cautiously worked towards the girl.

"I'm blind, I can't make them out."

"They're there."

She raised her rod to make a cast, and let fly in the general vicinity of where Louis was pointing. As soon as the jig impacted the water, the whole school panicked, bunched, and took off in all different directions. It was quite a sight seeing fifty or so turbo bonefish frantically vacating the area.

"I'm sorry, Louie, that was pretty pathetic wasn't it?"

"Don't worry about it," Louis replied, trying to suppress his laughter. "There's plenty more out here. Stay right there. I've got a bunch way up the line, but there movin' on us fast."

"Go get 'em, Cap."

Louis inched his way along another twenty feet and then went down into a deep crouch. To the untrained eye, the eight or ten fish in this school would be impossible to detect. But Louis stared and focused on the bottom texture and shading of the total picture, the interplay between light and shadow. At this distance he did not see fish per se, just movement—movement of light, and an interference in the ripple pattern at the surface.

Confident in sensing their path of travel, he keyed on a

spot twenty-five feet in front of the lead fish, and ten feet to the left and made his cast. The jig found the mark, settling into the shallow water quietly, mostly due to the low trajectory Louis had given it. But for the moment, Louis had merely closed the bail putting the spinning reel in gear. He had begun a waiting game with the approaching fish, for they had slowed their movement towards him.

Still as a rock, he waited until the lead fish entered an intercept zone with his jig, and he began to gingerly retrieve his offering to within a few feet of the fish's nose. He could see the bones clearly now as they disturbed and worked over the bottom to reveal the buffet that lay hidden underneath.

His pink jig lay but two feet in front of the lead fish's mouth, and Louis gave a slight twitch to the lure in a slack loop as not to actually move it from its position. The fish was on it, and quivered slightly from the dorsal fin to the tail, and the old man could no longer see his pink jig. The bonefish made a quick lateral movement, and Louis set the hook. Ignition!

The seven-pound 'bone' made a confused circle, and once pushing against the reel's drag, turned on the afterburner taking out 300 feet of line in a manner of seconds. He truly looked the picture of a torpedo being shot out of a submarine, pushing water like a bullet in the shallows.

Louis held the rod and reel high over his head to try to avoid snags as the fish fired off. He felt the heat rising in the spinning reel, and hoped that the fish would not 'spool' him. *He might very well*, Louis thought to himself, *he is a nice sized fish and the reel continues to scream at its unraveling.*

But this fish eased up on Louis and soon slowed to allow the fisherman to gather back some of his line. When he reeled the bonefish within sight of his wading feet, the speedster spooked and was burning off-line once again.

"Whoa," his fishing partner screamed from across the way, "check that out!"

131

Louis was smiling, and shook his head from side to side as he stole a quick glance at Cami. The fish would yield once again until he was cranked into where Louis' kicking up sand sent him off for the last time. A weary bonefish now finally came into his captor's hands without a struggle.

Louis gently cradled the fish from its back, holding the bonefish in an upside down position, while he removed the jig from its mouth. He showed Cami, now at his side, the grinders in the fishes' mouth that enabled it to crush and pulverize the crabs, shrimp, and other crustaceans that bonefish feed on.

"They are so unbelievably fast, Louie, it's awesome."

"Look here, Cami, see how the fins are all oversized, and this pair underneath, he has got an extra one. Built for speed they are, make a pretty good marlin bait as well."

"Can you eat them?"

"Some do, they can be a little work. I can think of other stuff I'd rather chew on, anyway." Louis laid the fish back in the water and turned him over, moving him forward and back to get the water going through the gills again. Feeling the fish swimming harder in his grasp, he let him go. The fish darted off and was out of sight in a few seconds.

"That was fun. Pretty good fish too, around seven maybe."

"My turn, Louie."

"So it is. Stay right here on this side of the channel. That other school by you held quite a few fish, but they were small. Their behavior can be so integral, they spook real easy. That school was smaller but the fish were feeding more aggressively, and they gave me a fair chance there."

"Sounds good to me."

So they continued on their way to the split in the channel up ahead, and before ten minutes were up they had another opportunity. Louis stood behind her quietly, and coached her as to what she should be looking for, moving her head for her, rather than pointing at the fishes' position.

"Ya got 'em in sight yet?"

"No, this is frustrating!" She stared and stared. "I . . . got them now! Right there about fifty feet, one o'clock."

"You are on the meat, darlin," replied a calm Louis with restrained enthusiasm as he stepped back out of her way to give her the casting room she needed. "Put your jig three feet to the right and fifteen feet in front of the closest fish you can see."

Nice. She could do that, Louis thought to himself. "Just pull the jig slowly along the bottom to intercept that fish, so he can swim up on it."

"I understand. I think he's got it."

"Still see your jig?"

"No. But I don't feel anything."

"Take another crank."

"I can't even feel my jig."

"Set the hook!"

She whipped the tip to the side as if she might have been standing in a boat. With the rod bend came the surface explosion, and the reel started to sing. She screamed.

"Man!"

"Hold on. Get your rod as high as you can, hold it over your head and let him take the line. He's going to anyway."

She was doing all right as the fish was still burning line toward the darker water 100 yards away. She looked over and smiled to him, "There's nothing I can do, I think he's going to get all my line."

"You're doin' all you can, he just might."

She looked back at her fish as it had made its way into the current of the deeper channel. It continued to strip the line from the reel until all at once the line went limp, and Cami felt herself tied to nothing. She began to reel in the limp slack until she got to the parted end, and then waded over to Louis to show him the reel nearly empty of its line. "What did I do wrong?"

"Not a thing. Fish wrapped himself around a piece of coral

or somethin' and cut your line. You'll have that."

"I did all I could do."

"Course ya did. Did ya enjoy that?"

"Yeah," she said with that beautiful smile.

"We'll get the next one, then. Take my rig."

"No."

"Yes. I got one and you don't have enough line left to do battle. Here." They swapped and continued on their way until they arrived at the spot they had been targeting for the last half hour.

"We'll camp right here and let them come to us. No point really going any further, all we're gonna do is kick up a lot sand and marl which the current will take on down. Might spook 'em. Besides, the biggest fish always seem to be the last up on the flats at the top of the tide."

They cleaned their polaroids and waited comfortably for fifteen minutes, seeing nothing. Louis could see that the tide was nearly high, and the current had slowed to almost slack. *How 'bout one more for Cami*, he thought.

"Louie, look up there. What are those small sharks?"

Louis turned his attention back to the flat from his wandering, and immediately drew a bead on the pair of three-foot dark silhouettes slowly working their way into the channel junction.

"Good Lord, look at the size of 'em."

"What are they?"

"Bonefish, darlin'. Remember everything we covered, and good luck." Louis now retreated away from her to give her some space, and slowly he found a position twenty feet at her right on the other side of the darker water the two loners were working in. He looked in front of him and studied the pair of adjacent flats—a quarter mile square—that lay before him. He decided that the one on her left side looked like the clearest with the most sand. If he could, he would try to take it that way. It was up to her now. He waited in stillness for her to make her connection.

The two bonefish had taken on a dark leadish color, even

against the backdrop of the greener, deeper water of the channel. He had fished the virgin waters off the Bay Islands of Honduras many times, an area noted for its ten-pound-plus fish. Almost always the larger fish swam in pairs, electing to enter the flat from the closest, deepest water available, sometimes from the barrier reefs themselves.

Louis saw the cast, and he knew it was true. He was just waiting for her to feel the fish, and do her business in setting the hook. Any moment now . . . she remained motionless. Suddenly, she quickly cranked the loop out of her line and raised the tip over head with a scream as the water only thirty feet in front of her exploded from the twisting action of the three-foot fish.

Louis hurled himself in a stampede towards the channel edge, arriving at the deeper cut a second before the bonefish. He stomped and thrashed along the trench spooking the trophy back up on the sugar sand of the left side flat. The fish continued to accelerate on his initial speed run, but away from the channel.

Louis looked liked a crazed Indian, sprinting and dancing in the knee deep water, driving the terrified fish toward even shallower depths to the west. Then Louis changed course to his right and ran ahead to position himself between the channel and the fish.

Sensing his retreat was leading to entrapment, the old bonefish veered off the skinny water, and now directed his course more to Louis. Louis screamed for Cami to come running as she cranked up the slack. When the bone had neared to within thirty yards, he again stomped the sand and ran into the deep channel driving the fish back towards the girl.

For the next ten minutes he guarded the access to the deep channel and deterred the trophy from entering the comforts of the preferred water. Louis knew that such a scenario would greatly tip the scales in favor of the fish. There, he could pull steady drag, and a snag would be far easier to find than on the clear white sugar sand to where he had recently been exiled.

Whether by confusion, shock, exhaustion or all three, the fish relented and allowed himself to be cradled in Louis' arms ten minutes later.

"Look at him, Louie, he is a monster!"

"You have got yourself a ten-pounder, lady," a hugely happy Louis beamed, barely holding the upside down yard long specimen.

"Not something you get a crack at every day." He looked to the blue sky and towering clouds above and said another happy thank you.

"You were unreal. Between fear and laughter I thought I was going to fall over and lose him. You looked like a wild man out there."

"Something an old friend from Cuba showed me, it worked many times for us. We better put him back in the water. These older specimens don't bounce back as good as the small ones."

Louis laid the trophy fish back in the water and righted him gently, immediately moving him back and forth to respirate him. When the fish caught his tail he found the deep water right away, and headed back out in the direction from whence he came.

Louis gleefully waded over to the four-foot-deep channel, and threw himself in staying under for a few seconds as he rolled around. He perked up and sat down on the side of the drop, rinsing his hands and forearms well, to rid them of the fishes' protective slime. The girl walked over to extend her hand to help him up.

"Need a hand getting up, you must be pretty tired after all that running and stomping around?"

"Sure," he replied as he extended his hand.

When they had grasped one another, Louie quickly tugged at the poor girl dunking her completely into the water. He picked up his rod, and hers, stepped up and walked on out.

"Hey, what do you think you're doin'?" She was playful.

"Gonna help me out? Here." She offered her hand.

Louis reached down and grabbed her firmly, leaning back to lift her up and out. But she took a little lunge at Louis. Catching her balance somewhat, she threw her arms around Louis' neck for a brace, pressing her length fully up against him. He felt paralyzed, unable to move. Well, not completely.

She smiled gently. Tightening her hold, she fitted herself against him, her eyes inviting him in.

Louis did not resist the magnetic pull and fell right into her in a long kiss. He slowly pulled away and smiled, looking warmly into those deep blues for the longest time. He was completely disarmed. Then he sensed he might be gaining an understanding, and the words surfaced from within.

"I have fond feelings for you, Cami, but as you can see, I am nearly twice your age." She did not release her grip on him in any way.

"Is that right. You don't look or act it."

"Thank you for that, but we both know it's true."

"From where I'm standin', everything seems to be in good working order."

Louis laughed loudly, and relaxed a little. "Yeah, you've gotten hold of me and definitely stirred things up inside."

"Go with it."

"Can't. At least not right now . . . When did your dad pass away?"

"Last January, how did you know?"

"A guess, had a sense that's all."

"That has nothing to do with my feelings, Louie."

"All right, Cami, but now is not the time. You're here with another, and I'm not gonna devalue what I feel by doing the wrong thing by him and us."

"Frank? . . . Louie, I owe my life to him, but it's not what you think. He picked me up when I was low on the street, cleaned me out and gave me my world back. It's been a hell of a

137

long time since he's even come to me." The blonde started shaking out her long hair. "I'm a whole lot more than you bargained for Captain."

"No doubt there, Cami. It's hard for me to imagine his lack of interest in you."

"He needs me around, yes, but Frankie is actually . . . rather asexual. Really, I could go on about dancing and . . . "

Louis gently put his hand on her mouth, "Come visit me back home, you and my daughter would be very good friends."

"I would like that. I am not giving up on you."

Louis pulled her back against him, and they remained in an embrace for a little while longer. Under blue skies and high cottony tropical clouds, they were caught up in a warm eddy, bathed in constant tradewinds. Surrounded by coral sea and miles from others, it was a beautifully simple moment they both needed. They did not let go of one another until the sound of the returning outboard brought them back down.

Louis reached down into the water, and gathered up the two spinning outfits and shook them off. The skiff was within a few hundred yards now, and the voices of its occupants could be heard laughing.

Crafty slowed the boat down to an idle and eased his way in, until he just cut the motor and drifted right into their position.

"Tell me a fish story."

And she did with prodigious enthusiasm, going over every little detail to the delight of the other two. Louis didn't even bother to comment, he was so captivated by her. He was at peace in his decision not to act on his feelings, rather than take advantage of hers. But she had such heart. If there was time, there would be another time.

"Anybody hungry, I'm starved," Cheryl polled the group, "We got a whole basket full of wine and sandwiches. Think there's some conch salad in here, and a beer for you, Louie."

"I'm ready, let's break it out. Hey, why don't we beach the

boat over there under the shade of them pines, be nice and cool for eatin' lunch."

"Les go."

The four had a friendly and hearty lunch hour. Cheryl displayed a few of the shells she had collected, Crafty quizzed Louis once again on the sub-details of the bonefishing expedition. When they were done, they all lay back on the beach and took a short nap. An hour later when Louis stirred and awoke, he looked down the beach to see Cheryl and Crafty heading his way. He looked over to Cami who was still asleep and nudged her.

"Let's go for a swim on a beautiful little reef around the corner from the point. It's got staghorn coral all over it. What'd ya say?"

"I'd like that," she responded simply grabbing Louis' hand, "I'm ready to cool off. You two ready to do a little snorkeling?"

"That would feel pretty good."

"You're drivin', Crafty. You know the place right around the point on the south side, that little patch reef?"

"Gotcha. I too, am ready to get wet."

When they made the turn around Chub Point, the light tan of the shallow reef a quarter mile ahead was unmistakable against the surrounding aquamarine water. There was another small boat anchored there and they had put out a small diving flag on a float.

Crafty maneuvered the skiff to within twenty yards of the visible coral and dropped his hook. He walked to the bow and checked his bite to be sure it was holding and cleated the line off, before finally shutting down the engine.

Louis had emptied the diving bag on the deck, and was sizing fins, mask, and snorkel for the girls. As soon as they were outfitted, they were over the side. It was warm in the open boat under the afternoon sun.

The four leisurely swam the short distance to the reef, where they regrouped to make fitting adjustments and clean their masks. They then paired off once again to explore the small but dramatic reef.

Tropical fish of all kinds continually darted in and out of their holes. These might be blue wrasses, clown fish, red banded shrimp, tangs or sergeant majors. Yellowtail, mangrove, and schoolmaster snappers were continually schooling around the high reef formations. Less frequently, a grouper would enter the divers' perimeter for a curious inspection, and the ever present barracudas were always on the move. Louis pointed out a spiny lobster and one spotted moray that would occasionally stick his head out and smile.

After forty-five minutes they were ready to get out. They slowly made their way back to the little boat where, one by one, they removed their fins and slung them into the skiff. Louis was the first one in, and he proceeded to gently lift the ladies up and over the gunwhale.

"Toss me the sling, Cap, I'm gonna take a quick look over at that pinnacle out there."

Louis knew the one but replied, "I forgot to pack one ol' boy, it's back at the boat."

"What? How do you expect us to eat tonight?"

"We'll make do."

"Under the seat, old man."

Louis lifted the mahogany board and found the Hawaiian sling laying in the compartment. "Well, well." He reached in and picked up the double arbalete.

Crafty cleaned his mask a final time, took the natural powered speargun from Louis and paddled on the surface in the opposite direction a little offshore. They had both dived on this little hump before, as it often held many snapper in its fifty-foot depth.

Crafty took a long look down as he repeatedly blew small amounts of water from the snorkeling tube as he stayed just under the surface. He then rolled and went straight down, his fins kicking on their entry into the water. He was down for almost a minute, until he popped up on the surface and pulled out the mouthpiece, "Be right back, one minute."

Back down he went for well over a minute this time, and the girls got a little edgy. "Is he all right, Louie?" Cheryl questioned, leaning over the side staring down into the clear water.

"He's a good diver, with a good breath. I've seen him do two minutes before," replied Louis, nonetheless starting to don his own fins.

"Yes!" It was him, yelling as he corked up about twenty-feet away from the boat. Still flapping on the end of his spear was about 15 pounds of hog snapper, run right through just behind its cheeks.

"I tell ya, Louis, there were plenty of mutts down there [snapper], but this hogger just swam right by and let me stroke him, a no-brainer." Crafty slowly kicked his way to the side of the skiff.

"That's a different looking fish with all those streamers and long fins, and teeth and stuff, a snapper, huh?" Cheryl touched the fins lightly, "doesn't look very pretty."

"A big old wrasse really, but one of the finest eatin' fish out here." Louis started smacking his lips before flashing her a grin. "Time to go."

He reached down and gave his mate a hand and big heave ho to get him in the boat. In the process, Crafty's trunks had slid down exposing his own 'cheeks,' and a butt redder than a cooked lobster. Louis' premonitions had been realized.

"Thank you, Cap," Crafty said gamely pulling up his trunks as he quickly winked his eye at Louis. The Captain just stood there for a moment eyeballing his friend. He relented and sat down. "You're the captain, get us home would you please."

"Not a problem." They were gone.

Crafty didn't pull the power off until they were well inside of the cut and twenty yards off the marina opening. It was rather quiet at three in the afternoon; the docklines hung on the pilings of a majority of the slips.

When they pulled alongside the big boat, they could hear the loud voices of the pair within, each apparently talking to a different party. So involved were they, that the crew was able to hoist, cradle and clean the skiff and equipment without attracting any attention from the occupants inside. They were both relieved.

As the girls had made their way up the hill, Louis and Crafty decided it was a good time to head for the showers at the end of the dock. The mate could contain himself no longer.

"Louis, what could I do? It was all her idea, she practically rendered me naked."

"Hey, it's none of my business really, it's more his I guess. I'm not the man to judge you or anyone else, but we are workin' for a living here."

"I know, I know. It's just that she told me there was nothing between them, literally. She said she felt like a possession, and hey, we both know what that can be like." He grinned at Louis tentatively.

"Depends on who is taking possession. Look, Crafty, we're good friends and always will be. This is completely your business, something to be reconciled between you and God. Okay?"

"Yeah, man."

Louis turned to his long-time friend and put his hands on his shoulders, gripping them firmly before giving in to a chuckle. "It's history. I'm in need of a shower."

"Done. Look, I ain't ready to jump in yet, I'm gonna filet that hogfish for dinner, and stick it in the bait cooler. I'll get up with 'ya in an hour or so."

"Sounds good, Crafty."

13

The crew had set the small grill up on the finger pier because they liked grilled fish and neither of them felt like making a mess in the galley. Throw in a little leftover conch salad and a baked potato, and they had the business.

Louis had already fired off the gas canister, and was wrapping the spuds in tin foil as Crafty arrived back from his soaking. He stopped by the bait cooler and picked out the fish he had bagged. He quickly made a check of his baits, and closed the lid.

"Whatcha think, Louie, some of my custom seasoning?"

"You shot it, whatever ya want to do. Talk to any of the guys over at the fishhouse, what went on out there today?"

"There was some fish caught out there, most of it from where we were yesterday on down to the pocket. That boy on the *Reel Job* got him one about five off the north end of Joulter's in about fifteen hundred feet. Saw another, and put a hurtin' on some big dolphin. All right there. Ah . . . let me see, Brian on that 61 Davis boat caught a double header white between the yellow bar and Rum Cay, and another boat got into the tuna pretty good off Morgan's Bluff. He had six or seven out of a few flurries. Didn't sound too bad for the coverage."

"I should say so. Probably be another right weather day tomorrow, sure is a pretty evening."

"Looks like it's gonna hold, Cap. Some guy at the bar last night said another late front was headed our way at the end of the week, though.

"Heard that. That's what they were saying on the weather channel last night. Anyway."

Crafty headed below for the spice rack and five minutes later returned with a platter of seasoned hogfish filet, covered with plastic wrap. He went back to the cooler, lifted the lid and stuck the tray inside.

"They're ready when you are. How 'bout a Becks?"

"Sure."

Crafty picked a pair out of the drink cooler and stuck them in wrappers. Jumping back up on the dock to where Louis had set up a couple of folding chairs, he handed his Captain one.

"Louis?"

"Yessir."

"Why did 'ya drop out. I mean . . . quit fishin' the kill tournaments? Some of the boys been askin', and I don't know quite what to tell 'em."

"Well . . . it just started not feelin' right."

"What didn't?"

"Crafty, what could you say about a man's life by staring at his corpse all nice and clean laid out on a stainless steel slab?"

"Not that much, Louis, not much at all. I want to know what he can't tell me."

"Well, then?"

"I gotcha good, Louis, but it's one fish. It wouldn't be scratch compared to the tonnage of the longliners."

"It ain't a relative thing anymore, Crafty. It's a black and white issue with me. Killin' is for eatin'. Look, man, you hate seeing plastic and garbage in the sea about as much as I do. Correct?"

"That's right."

"We both know the cruise ships are the biggest polluters out here, so that makes it okay for us to put our two or three bags over the side every day."

"No . . . it doesn't. I'm with you on that, Louis. I gotcha fine, Louis. So tell me, other than your successful bonefishing, how was your day?"

144

"One of a kind. Something very nice."

"You should talk."

"Not that way, man. It worked out for the best, and I somehow managed to avoid getting myself in trouble."

"I know you like her you old fart, you're not hiding it too well."

"Whole lot better than your ass." The laughter was mutual. "She's a sweetheart all right, with probably too much on her mind right now."

"Louis, did you catch that act with Wendt last night?"

"Which one?"

"Yeah . . . Where I returned his 'medications' to him in front of Whitman."

"Not really, what was that all about?"

"Evidently, the man didn't want Frank to know he had a scrip for prozac. He copped a real attitude with me, said I should have been more discreet with it. Can you imagine? There was also a few vicodin and some assorted others in that vial too."

"I didn't realize you still had such familiarity with those things."

"I can read, Louis."

"Yeah, well . . . there isn't anything necessarily bad on its own out there, it's what happens to us when we mix with it."

"Huh?"

"A poor man in possession is labeled a criminal, a rich man able to afford the legal scrip from a $150/hr psychiatrist is merely being assisted. One pusher, one user, one doctor, one patient. Same pill. The bad is not in the pill, it's in the person."

"The drunk is not in the bottle. "

"Yeah. We all have to deal with that same game eventually, don't ya think? You and I, we've both laid a pile of the old baggage aside, ain't we?"

"Yeah, that's right, but 'splain me what Wendt's problem was truly all about?"

"I guess he didn't want Frank to know, that even he needed a little outside help."

"That's right . . . What do you charge anyway, Louis?"

"Whatever the market will bear. I'm hungry."

"Do it to it."

So Louis waited on the potatoes about eight minutes, and then loaded the grill to the max with the hogfish. Crafty had prepared a couple of place settings on a nearby picnic table setting out the salad and a couple of backup beers. It was quiet on the dock, it appeared as though they were the only diners in their area this evening. In solitude, they ate quietly, much to their preference. But there was still plenty of filet left when the crew finally pushed away from the table.

The four from the hill could now be seen walking down the path to the marina. They had been refreshed and appeared dressed for dinner out. As they hit the dock, they remained in tight formation as they strolled down the impressive row of sportfishing machines. Occasionally, Frank would pause at the back of a particular boat, where he would do a little shtick or provide some history as to the boat, its owner, or some other form of notoriety.

When the party got within two boatslips, Cami broke off and headed for the crew.

"I think you two have the right idea tonight, it's pretty out right now. How was the hogfish?"

"Here, grab a piece. There's more than we can eat, and we're done." Crafty forced the tray upon her to back up his words. She snagged a fat piece and went right into it most indelicately. Louis passed her up a napkin.

"Now that's good," the lady said with a mouth still full of fish. "Think they serve this up at the restaurant?"

"They might, but I doubt it." Louis passed her a napkin holding another piece.

"Sounds like everyone had a great day, Louie," came Whit-

146

man's resonance as he was almost to the forefront. "Cami has not stopped talking about her fish. We must give the bonefish a try sometime, eh Captain?"

"I'm always ready for something like that, Frank."

"You two blew it by locking yourselves up in a business meeting all day, you know that," Cheryl teased her host as she lightly slapped his shoulder. "It was a lot of fun, the guys showed us a great time."

In the small pause that followed, Louis glanced over at Adam who was conspicuously distant behind the stern of the next boat over. He was leaning back against a dock piling and staring out at the setting sun. Louis understood that he wouldn't be disposed to much gaiety at the moment. Showing no affect he returned his attention to his boss.

"How does tomorrow look for fishing, Frank? You and Mr. Wendt take care of business today?"

"I'll be ready at the crack of dawn, but how does 8:00 sound?"

"Great."

"See you boys at eight." Whitman then provided closure on the meeting, taking Cami by the arm and heading her in the opposite direction down to the club. Wendt hopped into step alongside his host as he passed by, letting Cheryl trail the trio all the way down the dock.

"Nice fella, isn't he Louis."

"Who ?"

"My buddy, Adam."

"Oh, yeah. Let it go. Are we rigged and ready for mañana?"

"We are. Say, where's our gaff man been hangin' out? He's been Mr. Invisible around here lately."

"Byrd's around. Let's see if we can give him a chance to tag a grown-up tomorrow."

"Put me on 'em, Louis. You wanna pull all big baits?"

"Not necessary. Stick with your spread, it's been doin' the

147

job. If ya feel like it, maybe a big mack on the long right."

"All right. Let's clean this mess up and I'll buy 'ya a toddy at the bar."

"I don't think so, Crafty, I'm just gonna do a little readin' tonight. I'll get this, go on ahead."

"Thanks, Louis." Crafty stood up and stretched.

"For what?"

Louis watched as his mate started down the dock until he got a few slips away and turned to face him, "Everything," he kept on walking.

Crafty was into his third rum and coke as he sat alone at the bar. There were a few people in the joint, but it was a little early for any peak activity. He looked over at a corner table where a group of diners were getting up and making their exit. He knew the owners in the party, and the crew had been friends of his for years. Apparently, the captain and mate were remaining behind to take care of the bill and have a few after dinner pops.

The younger of the two men began waving and directing him over to the table. Feeling his years of seniority, he got up off his barstool and walked over to the pair in the corner.

"Sit down, Crafty, and tell us a lie about that woman, or a fish if ya have to."

"What's up, boys, how are y'all makin it tonight?"

"Huh! Not like you, Rad. Ain't tried a little of that, have ya?"

"Nope, nope. Stayin' clear."

"Not like you to do that, Crafty."

"Years go by, and . . . ah . . ."

"Nice goin on your slam, prickhead, you're makin' us all look bad."

"Big luck, Shortstuff. It'll be you and Deepwater's turn tomorrow. You know how it works."

"Tell you what, ol' Louie can still drive over 'em, can't he."

"He'll be out fishin' us when he's on the other side of the grass."

"Speaking of which," the younger mate replied, "I got a fat one in me pocket here. Let's get one to go, and take a walk over the hill."

The three rose and made a quick stop by the bar, "How 'bout three anejo and cokes in cups, Bradley, just stick it on the boss' bill, eh."

"Done, Cop," the young Bahamian answered with a big grin, "evry'ting gon be ret?"

"We're rigged, thanks Bradley."

"Okay 'den."

The trio walked out into the warm evening around to the rear of the restaurant, where they hiked up a hill trail that led to the south beach of the island. As they made it to the top and then down to the dune line, Crafty caught sight of a pair of men that appeared to be having an animated conversation a good distance away down the beach. He nodded to the others, and they turned to walk in the opposite direction.

Shortstuff fired up the bomber, took a deep hit, and passed it over to Crafty. He took the lefty, bringing it to his lips, and paused for a second. His attention remained fixed on the two down the beach, and for the moment, he believed that he recognized one of the pair. Crafty offered the lefty to Deepwater, "You g'head, I'll pass for now."

"Don't worry bout them, they ain't gonna do nuthin, Crafty".

But he was unable to take his eyes off the strangers. He was positioned with a perfect view of the pair 100 yards away. As his night blindness was steadily leaving him under the bright moon, he thought he might have recognized Scott Byrd as one of the two men. "What the . . . " now a third man emerged from the tree line and joined the other two on the beach edge.

"George, by what strange coincidence are we graced by

your presence on this little island?"

"Business, Adam. I fish for a livin'. Remember?"

The three men shared a brief laugh.

"How many marlin have you caught, George?"

"Haven't seen a damn fish all week."

"I see. Well, now that we are all here, I would ask if there are any questions or problems that might surface between here and Havana. This will be our last meeting together for a while."

"None from my end. Scoot just gave me a brief but much needed tour of the vessel. I've found some solutions."

"That's good, George, thank you for your efforts in this matter. I trust your people are ready and well briefed."

"They know only what they need to know, Adam. They're the best I've got in the Caribbean. The printer has completed all his work."

"Splendid. Give him our itinerary as we know it, Scott. Where do you want your first draw sent, George?"

"Tegucigalpa. Here," replied the fat Texan as handed Byrd a small slip of paper.

"Good-bye, Captain George, we'll be in touch. Please, no more surprises."

A minute later, Crafty saw the third man accept something from the man he thought to be Byrd, before the stranger departed in the opposite direction.

It appeared as though the conversation was over, and the remaining two men retreated up the dune and back down the path. The other man never gave Crafty much of a view.

"Here man, go for it," Deepwater nudged him on his shoulder.

Crafty shook his head, "No, you guys go ahead, it's cool. I appreciate the offer, but I got to go check out somethin' for the boss. Sees ya."

The two shrugged their shoulders, shook hands with the

worldly mate, and continued on.

Crafty picked up the tail, following the pair back down towards the bar, keeping far enough behind them just off the path. He was quite surprised to see Adam Wendt's face emerge in the glow of the overhead light in front of the bar. Could be social he thought, but things did not appear very jovial. They were not smiling at all. *Man, if I could read lips*, the mate thought to himself. And then they were gone, each going their own way.

Crafty considered the nature of his luck in stumbling onto the chance encounter. It did not ease the growing discomfort in his gut.

14

It had been a good ten days of practice. Frank and the crew had consistently enjoyed better than good fishing, averaging four shots at marlin every day they were out. Whitman's hooking success was definitely on the rise, even though he still managed an occasional skull, winding in only bare hook. Some fish jumped off, some hooks pulled, that's fishing. More importantly, Frank had gone from not having a clue, to batting around .400 on the hookups.

It was their final day's fishing at Chub, and it seemed that everyone out of the marina was on the hunt today. It was another patterned day in paradise, one that usually spelled a good bite from the fish. The ocean was kicked up a touch from eighteen knots of southeast winds, and there was much promise for activity above and below its surface.

There were boats ahead and behind Louis as he navigated the ranged channel leading past the point and out to sea. Indeed, a large fleet was headed out today, each boat hoping to get its shots before the predicted weather change hit them in the next day or two.

As they separated and powered up one by one, most of the boats had elected to head across to Joulter's, where the majority of the action had taken place in the last two days. *Reasonable*, Louis thought to himself as throttled his own rig up and started running, a couple of hundred yards distant from boats both ahead and behind him.

The line of widely separated boats stretched out before him all the way to the visible pines off Joulter's Cay, on the other side.

Louis casually made a turn to the north northwest, veering off the line most of the boats had taken. He was headed for a submerged point just off Rum Cay, a few miles up the line on the eastern side. Louis was fishing according to his own clock, hoping to meet up with that immense school of dolphin he had encountered two days earlier.

Down below, the four Penn 50W Internationals sat in their rod holders at each side of the fighting chair. Their rod tips trembled under the vibration of the two powerful diesel engines straining from the bowels of the boat. Crafty leaned back against the salon window as he sat atop the cockpit freezer, fully enjoying and anticipating the morning. He was completely ready and prepared to meet the day, with plenty of rigged bait and fully inspected, retied terminal tackle.

So the mate meditated as he sat in that corner, staring out at the eternal wake leaving the boat from the stern. He was soon mesmerized by the surging brilliant blue water, its wave pattern ascending upward into white foams of toppling surf. In the propwash itself, repeated clumps of flying fish leaped from the screw currents, some cut and disabled. The many trailing diving birds traveling along with the boat and would then make their swoop down and snatch their meal from the sea.

He noticed a pair of small porpoises surfing down the wake three waves back. They would swerve and dart down the face of the wave and then leap in the air, only to reunite with it a few feet ahead. He smelled the steam exhaust of the engines as they exhaled the waste gases of their cylinders. It was an old friendly smell, and wherever he was when he noticed diesel, it always brought him back to this very place and moment.

Crafty allowed the small bit of vibration against the side of his head to further set him into a trance in sync with all the other senses. It did not deaden him, it readied him for what was to come. It was a bridge between the defined, cumbersome world ashore, and the liberated free-flowing world out here.

Time, the mate thought, *must have been created for us. There was so much living going on in there for a gnawing past and a dreaded future. Out here, the moment was everything, and its beauty and joy overwhelming.*

"Where's your captain off to? All the other boats seem to be heading straight across," Adam drilled the mate.

"Probably up to Rum." Crafty answered as he thumbed in a direction about 2:00 off the boat's bow.

Wendt walked over to the starboard side of the cockpit and looked ahead to spot the little uninhabited cay.

"Right there?" Adam pointed to the little clump of pines.

"That's it." Crafty replied without even looking, as he knew it was the only land in that direction for miles.

"You would think he would at least try his hotspot of two days ago where everyone else is headed."

"I'spose you would. I'm quite sure he has his reasons, Louis isn't much on fleet fishing."

"You and the captain don't really converse and compare notes very often on where to fish."

Crafty hopped off his perch and began to clean his sunglasses with his T-shirt, "Never. I don't tell him where to go, and he doesn't tell me what to pull."

"Why is that?"

"It works best that way. Ever caught a billfish before, Mr. Wendt?"

"A sailfish or two off Florida. I did catch a small blue marlin off Kona, in Hawaii."

"Good. I hope you can remember the gist of our conversation the other night. I'll try and help you any way I can."

"I think I've pretty much got it, I'll give it a good shot."

Hearing a change in the pitch of the engines, Crafty walked to the rear of the pit and looked up to see Louis beginning to spread and deploy the outriggers. He pulled out his bait selections and clipped them to their appropriate rods, making one final tension check of all four release pins. He unraveled the daisy chain of squid, selected a dolphin colored 'bowling pin' for the other teaser, and clipped them onto the teaser lines on each side of the boat. All was ready.

They were into the dolphin as soon as they set down. Flying fish were showering out of the water everywhere, pursued by the yellow and green predators pushing water as they gave chase. Overhead, a pair of frigate birds competed with the many smaller terns, hovering and diving at the baitfish and fish scraps rendered by the marauding dolphin below.

By the time Crafty had finished putting the number four right rigger bait into position, they were covered up by a slug of twelve- to fifteen-pound dolphin. They wound up catching a pair of four in the air, and then went back to work with a fresh spread. Within a minute they were gang-tackled a second time, four jumping on the hook, with a fish or two at each teaser. A large bull of nearly sixty pounds was threatening to create the ultimate tangle.

Louis chuckled to himself, well I found the dolphin I wanted alright. Poor mate, ten minutes into the game and they burned up about thirty minutes of work. You couldn't keep a spread in the water for any longer than a minute before they nailed you.

"*Byte Her*, y'on there, Captain Louie, channel 71. *Reel Job*."

"74, Jimmy.

"74."

"On here?"

"Back to ya."

"That you runnin up from the southeast?"

"That's me. Gettin a late start here this morning, saw you make a right turn after runnin a bit. Thought I might pick a few of your scraps."

"Come on, can't keep a bait in the water for the dolphin up here off Rum. I mean they're thick."

"Gotcha good, I see ya up there."

"We should have it to ourselves, unless somebody followed us over to this channel."

"That's right. I'll see ya in a minute or two, I'm gone."

Louis turned the boat offshore away from the school of dolphin, if for nothing else, to give his mate a breather in which to get caught up and cleaned up. The dolphin bonanza had left the cockpit bathed in bright red, and they certainly didn't need to take any more for dinner.

He continued to troll the boat just offshore the feeding activity, allowing his fishing buddy to work into the area and provide a little action for his people. Ten minutes later, the frenzied feeding ceased as fast it had started. The two frigate birds remained, ascending to higher and wider circles, while all the smaller chicks and terns disappeared. The heavy silence provided a false sense of tranquillity.

"Sorry, Louie, I guess I brought the flowers for the funeral. Shut it right down for ya. Figures," came the glum transmission from the *Reel Job*.

"No, you didn't, Jimmy. Besides, we got more than we need. Those frigates are on something over there; those circles are getting tighter. I believe we have some new players in the game. Good luck, let me know if you do somethin'."

"Count on it."

Louis worked his way back in to the edge, and marked tremendous wads of bait right along, as well as some larger blue checks, characteristic of larger predatory fish. The intense, widespread feeding of the large school of dolphin had left the ocean's surface covered with fish oil slicks, casting off a rich primal odor that was Mother Nature herself. *Sweet as watermelon, like concentrated ocean*, Louis thought, *when ye smell land where there is none*. Right out of the legend of the great white whale.

"Behind the squids," Louis bellowed, "blue marlin!"

Frank rocketed out of the chair, snatching the short left rigger rod on his way. He immediately snapped the line from its outrigger clip, and began to reel up the Spanish mackerel even before it became tight. In two seconds he had it alongside the teaser, rod poised over his head, out of gear ready to feed the fish should it make a move.

Louis liked seeing his angler on his feet, for he was a large man who held the big game reel like a bait casting rod used for bass. He was quite sure that standing would be comfortable for him and greatly improve his hooking chances.

"I see him down there, Louie, he's black as the ace of spades, what's he doing.?"

"I'm not sure," Louis shouted back, "he ain't ready to do business. Just making a stroke now and then. Got your clicker on, Frank?"

"No."

"Put it on."

"All right." He reached below the right side of the reel casing and threw the small lever in a clockwise motion. He pulled off a foot of line and heard the spool respond with the familiar clanking of the spring ball hitting the punched plate on the inner spool. It would reduce the chances of a reel overide or snarl as in 'birds nest.'

Louis eased the boat into the fish's track with a slight turn to starboard. The maneuver led the trolled squids away from the boat, but did little in changing the mood of the trailing marlin.

"Give your mackerel a couple of jigs, Frank," Crafty prodded from behind the angler's right side. "Be prepared to drop it back to him if he gives you the chance. Are you open?"

"I'm ready when he is."

Louis caught sight of a jumping billfish behind the transom of Jimmy's boat, about the time the transmission came over the VHF, "Go over, Louie."

"Back to ya."

"Got a nice white on over here, out of a pair."

"I got ya, see him jumpin' over there. Got a blue one up over here. Been trailin' my teaser for a few minutes, won't eat, won't move off, won't do nothin'."

"You got him, Cap, hang in there!"

"I'll let ya know, thanks for that, Jimmy."

"Go get him."

"What do you think, Captain?" Frank was edgy, his hands shaking.

"I think he needs a nudge. Frank, when I close haul this teaser to the boat, all he'll have left to look at will be your mackerel. Whatever you do, make it believable."

"How's that?"

"If you were that mackerel, how would you feel being six feet from the mouth of a creature that could kill you or swallow you whole effortlessly?" Louis was smiling now.

As the Captain snatched his skipping squid chain from the sea, Whitman jerked at his bait twice. Sticking the rod tip in the water, he tugged hard a third time, as the black silhouette subtlety moved behind and a little to the side of the swimming mackerel.

Louis could see the tips of the marlin's pectoral fins begin to glow a deep sapphire. "He's likin' it, Frank, he's comin' on ya." The Captain was easily heard.

Then Whitman popped the mackerel from the water, out ahead of the fish just beyond the predator's blind zone. The fish responded immediately with a powerful kick of his great tail, and nailed the skipping mackerel from the side. Frank's relaxed hands let the weight of the fish pull his rod tip down till it was pointing directly at the marlin. At the bottom of the arc, he released his firm thumb hold on the spool and lightly guided the free spooling line out towards his fish.

He watched as the marlin swam lazily away from the spread, fish side to, the reel's clicker making a steady unhurried sound. As he continued to follow the fish he saw its outline pivot

158

and streak dead astern screaming the clicker with a tremendous acceleration. He put the reel in gear, throwing the drag lever up to its strike position.

There was no immediate rod bend, but a loop of line breaking water could be seen moving left to right over the surface, throwing water droplets as it tightened against the fish, which it did in the next second, pulling the rod tip down and knocking the tall man off balance.

Frank half-stumbled, but caught his fall on the covering board, quickly righting himself. He stuck the butt of the rod in his belt gimbal and leaned back on the rod bend twice, to drive the hook in deep enough to bury the barb. His fish was now on the surface, jumping away from the boat, the shape of his head and bill outlined against the morning sun.

This fish proved to be a magnificent jumper, making leap after leap dead astern, carving each one as artfully as the last. Nothing too frantic, no reversals of direction, no dives. Just one beautifully executed leap after another. Louis was backing moderately, keeping good pace with the fish. He watched in awe and admiration as the magnificent fish continued to leap clear of the water, throwing huge sheets of spray in all directions. He just kept on booking it dead astern, jumping over thirty times.

After initially losing about 400 yards on him, they were now keeping an even pace with him. In forty-five minutes the marlin had been worked to within 100 feet of the boat. The fish was clearly exhausted, displaying a dull copper coloration along the length of its lateral line.

In another minute, Louis perfectly presented the leader to his mate off the starboard quarter. Crafty easily gathered his mono until he held the fish off the side with a double wrap of leader in his right hand. He aided the tired marlin's efforts to swim by leading the fish at the head, forcing the water to plane the fish and flow through the mouth and gills.

"Byrd, put the tag in his shoulder meat just below the dorsal."

Byrd was standing to Crafty's immediate left, but hesitated for a moment when he realized he picked up the tagstick that wasn't loaded, "Just a second, Crafty," he turned to Cami and requested the other stick. Suddenly, the marlin came alive, getting up on his tail as he kicked hard under the restraint of the held leader. The stout fish made a lunge in Byrd's direction, as the young man had turned his back to the fish's slashing bill. Crafty raised a clenched left fist up his left side and then out to block the coarse bill with his free left forearm, knocking the fish's head into the covering board until it slid back down into the water.

"Now that was plenty stupid now, Byrd! Don't ever turn your back on a wired fish when you're in that position. Now put it in there!" He did on the second try, tag and release one blue marlin.

The hooting began once again, but Crafty was not all smiles as he surveyed the three-inch open scrape on his left arm.

"Byrd, go down below and get me some peroxide and neosporin, right now."

"All right, I'm sorry." When he returned, Crafty grabbed the bottle and liberally doused the entire area with a generous amount of the chemical. It foamed heavily.

"You okay?" Cheryl asked.

"Oh yea," Crafty paused, "billfish just have unbelievably powerful bacteria on that club of theirs. A little preventative maintenance."

He buried his arm into the ocean one time, gave the wound another purge with the peroxide, and gave it a final coating of neosporin. Everything settled back to normal.

Louis continued to work the area, but neither he nor Jimmy had another opportunity that morning. There had been a few bites up in the 'pocket' and a few coming from an area known as the 'yellow bar.' Mostly, sailfish seen there.

That afternoon the tide switched around 2:30, and with it the dolphins, second feeding of the day. For some reason, they were not getting the bites in this go round, yet Louis could observe selective feeding by some fish though not on a par with the morning's intensity.

They did catch one small dolphin around a seven pounder, though it appeared to be gut hooked and bleeding profusely. Crafty cut the leader and immediately went to work in rigging him as a trolling bait, using a pre-made 'tandem-rig' with a pair of large 14/0 hooks. He made a few adjustments to the fish's anatomy via the de-boner, and pinned him up in the 'hot' short left rigger. As a final gesture, he swapped out the teasers with the dolphin-like bowling pin leading the rigged dolphin on the left side. The dolphin pulled perfectly, frapping away, slapping the water as it skipped along at six-and-a-half knots. Once in a while, the rigged dolphin would dig his head, make a few kicks before resuming his surface antics.

"Go over to that one we been talkin' on, Louie."

"Gone." Louis switched over to channel 74.

"Forgot all about it. Get your fish, Louie?"

"Yes, we did, Jimmy, we let him go. Probably around 450 or so."

"Good deal. I haven't seen a thing for quite some time, I think I'll work on up to the corner. They seen a few there in the pocket the last half hour."

Louis had heard little on channel 71, the channel he was monitoring, and assumed Jimmy had been jumpin around the VHF and single sideband during the slowness of the last two hours. "I got ya fine, Jimmy, good luck."

"Think you might head that way?"

"I don't 'magine. I can't feel that they're done here. I'll probably stick it out right here for the rest of the afternoon."

"You're probably right, Cap, but the boss is giving me that

161

'do something even if it's wrong' look."

"I gotcha. Well good luck, see ya. *Hopefully, he'll grow out of that*, the veteran captain thought to himself. He watched his fishing partner pick up and run to the northwest as he placed the mic in its holder, turning his own radio back to 71.

He reached over the helm station and grabbed the ham and cheese sandwich that Cami had recently tossed up to him, pulling it from its ziplock bag. Louis took a good bite and returned his attention to his bait spread. As he inhaled the remaining bite, he spotted the dark form moving in for the kill beneath the dolphin they were trolling.

"On the dolphin, blue marlin!" came the shout from up top, "He's there underneath it!" Louis looked down at his shirt, and at the bits and pieces of sandwich all over it. He took the last of his Coke so he could talk and be understood.

"Be ready, Frank, although I've lost him for the moment," shouted Louie as he scanned the entire spread rapidly back and forth. He put the boat in a hard left turn, which served to speed up and spank the skipping dolphin all the more. Out from under the right rigger came the charging marlin at 50mph, steadily pushing water through the propwash. He caught the dolphin in full kick, and knocked the bait twenty feet in the air over the left long rigger line.

Crafty leaped at the line working out to the tip of the rigger and the release pin. When the dolphin hit the water, the marlin was on it in the blink of an eye, and inhaled the thirty-inch bait in the next second. Crafty cut the long rigger off, as the hooked marlin, feeling pressure for the first time, began to make a mess of the ocean.

It was indeed a grownup, at least 600 pounds. The big Blue on its belly shaking from side to side, throwing spray sixty feet in all directions. It lit up like a neon sign, taking out a couple of hundred yards in a matter of seconds. He stopped and did a 360-degree gyration on his tail windshield wiping all the way around in a full circle. Now he was off again in a another quick 150-yard spurt.

Louis pushed the boat into a hard reverse, blowing black smoke all over the place. Down below, Crafty had selectively cleared the pit depending on which way the fish had chosen to go. Now he was charging the boat on his belly, twitching and shaking his head, thrusting the gill plates outward to rid himself of the hooks. *The only thing he hadn't done*, Louis thought, *was take a deep run. He might be do-able early, if he kept this up.*

The huge predator was right in back of the boat now, showing classic leaps, getting as much height as his great weight would allow. He would clear the water on long lateral jumps, but not get all the way out if it was more a vertical up and down. He was getting closer to the transom with each new leap, so close you could count the remoras freeloading on his back.

"You up to it, Crafty?"

"I'm here. Byrd, load both those sticks this time and be ready, and be there!" Crafty was donning his third pair of cotton gloves.

Frank, who had been yelling and enjoying himself since this creature had jumped on the line, suddenly turned to his mate, "There are some welders gloves in there, too."

"Thanks, but no, Frank, these won't snag."

Whitman went back to work and back to yelling. It appeared as though the great fish had his heart set on jumping in the boat. Louis continued rotating the stern right to left with the crazy blue, trailing the telltale black clouds of smoke as water poured into the cockpit over the stern. The snap swivel emerged from the indigo sea one time, and then went back down with the marlin's spectacular glowing silhouette. Just a few kicks of its great tail propelled it more than fifty yards.

Louis dug in with both engines hard, going directly back at the fish's new position. With seas breaking over the stern, the snap swivel emerged from the water a second time, and the leader suddenly appeared within a few feet. It was that window of opportunity once again, as the huge billfish got on its tail not twenty-five feet from the boat.

As the captain was moving the boat laterally with the leaping marlin, starboard ahead, port going in reverse, he momentarily pegged the port engine so the leader might come within reach the next jump. Crafty was there and ready. The white-gloved hands began to move with the speed and grace of a slight-of-hand magician. There was a flurry of rhythmical wraps and twists, and unwindings, and more wraps and twists, until in just a few seconds, he was holding onto 600+ pounds of jumping blue marlin, each hand in a double wrap of the 500-pound test leader.

He had locked his knees under the overhang of the covering board in the corner of the cockpit on the starboard side. The fish again came up jumping against the pressure applied by the mate, and it caused the creature to turn in the opposite direction. It immediately snatched Crafty to the other side of the cockpit, a distance the mate covered in two lateral sidesteps. The fish came up and went the other way back to the other corner, again snatching up the man, shaking him like a stuffed toy animal. Somebody screamed through the black smoke.

But this time the big blue came up thrashing and shaking his head from side to side leaning away from the side of the boat, presenting a clear shot for the tag [gaff].

"Now, Byrd, stick him! Byrd, where are you, you mutha!"

Crafty dug in all the more with his legs and strained with all he had left against the fish, and its desire to be rid of the unnatural imprisonment. "Byrd!" he cried out a final time. He had not noticed that the young man had simply frozen and was immobile in the corner of the cockpit, a vacant stare on his face.

The huge marlin lay barely subsurface now. His entire length showing bright lateral bars of dayglow turquoise for he had much strength left within him. His scythe-like tail, nearly four-feet tall was swirling and propelling the water behind him. The large black bill was continually beating the water's surface, drenching all of the cockpit inhabitants. As the fish was veering off from the boat and the man who held him for the moment, the 500-pound test leader was nearing its breaking point. The fish settled his head back in the water and made a huge tail kick. On a straight pull, the monofilament leader snapped with a loud crack.

Frank broke the silence with a war cry his face all lit up in gladness. He set the rod in the holder and leaped right over to Crafty. He gave the mate, still holding the broken leader, a giant bear hug.

"Well done, man, best I ever saw!"

"Thank you, sir," replied Crafty, a little out of sync with Frank's genuine show of affection. "Pretty work yourself. I was just gettin' ready to dump the leader. Kinda' surprised it broke, Boss."

Louis came down from the bridge and walked over to his angler placing his left hand on his shoulder and offered the right to shake his hand. "Finest kind, Frank, you did everything that you had to."

"Thanks, Cap, couldn't have done it without you guys. Let's see if we can scrape up one more for Adam," Whitman continued to hoot.

"Let's do it." Louis returned to his station and put the boat in gear.

Frank motioned for Wendt to take a seat in the chair, "All yours, Adam, good luck." He then looked over at Byrd and motioned him inside into the salon, closing the door behind them.

"Look, Scott, I'm not going to jump all over your case, because you had somewhat of an event out there. Everyone has their own abilities, and weaknesses. But you have men counting on you, and if this makes you uncomfortable, say so now."

"Frank, I don't need this lecture, the man was unclear as to what he wanted me to do. I was just enjoying the fish's craziness that's all. I'm in it for the duration."

"Okay, Scoot, but you're out of second chances. You had better not come up short up again. No more screwups!"

Byrd paused briefly and then smiled thinly at his boss, "Not to worry, Mr. Whitman, I don't intend to."

It was late afternoon and Adam Wendt had nodded out in the chair, his head bobbing in rhythm with the rocking of the boat. Louis' fishing partner of the morning had rejoined him, along with about twenty other boats. The pair had drawn sufficient attention early on, outdistancing the fleet catch with their own smaller coverage just off Rum Cay. The few sightings since the morning bite all had things pushing this way, and the fleet's 'collective decision' had them positioned off Rum, should the fish pop up one more time.

Louis had visually acknowledged the growing crowd, but continued his fishing as if they had been invisible. In fact, he had left a bulk of the zig-zagging boats inshore, positioning himself in far deeper water than he had been fishing in that morning. For it was here that Louis recovered those conditions he found during the dolphins' voracious morning feeding. GPS and LORAN numbers held reflective value for the old fisherman but were secondary to the dynamics of a constantly changing ocean. This afternoon the sea conditions, tides, and bait movement were shifting rapidly from moment to moment and the static numbers of his nav aids were not able to keep pace as reference points. The old man was fishing with his eyes and his heart.

Louis reached down to change the scale on his color machine to the deeper offshore depths, taking his eyes off the spread. Down below, Crafty had moved to the side of the boat to begin a long scan of the horizon offshore. The breeze that the boat had been blocking felt cool on his face. No one on board saw the final bite of the day.

Wendt had been rudely snatched from his daydream by the sound of the screaming clicker to his right. Crafty spun around and flashed on the right flat line and the rod that was nearly bent over. Where the swimming ballyhoo had once been set, there was a large circle of foam ringing an area of turbulence in the ocean's surface. *Now that was a huge hole in the water,* he thought, as he aided Wendt in setting the rod into the gimbal of the fighting chair. The tip action and accelerating reel gave evidence of great speed from whatever creature had jumped on the line.

Louis had retrieved his two teasers about the time his mate had removed the other flat line from the water and was already proceeding back hard in the face of the sustained high speed run.

But it wasn't too long before Crafty waved his right hand to Louis in a gesture aimed at having him slow his backing down, until in another moment he was more frantic with his halting signal.

"Hold up, Cap, we're right over the top of him . . . he's goin' straight down."

Louis could see the line descending nearly perpendicular down into the water, and considered briefly that the fish might have put a huge loop in it. He might even come up jumping in front of the boat. The mystery fish was still pulling drag at a good clip but had slowed his speed slightly. *Perhaps the added drag of the line in the water had accounted for this*, the old man thought. That would not be as much a factor, however, if they were straight to and directly over the top of the creature.

Louis pulled away from the line where it entered the water, and initiated a slow circling of it. If slack was found in any portion of an arc in that circle, then the case could be made that the fish might have put a loop in the line down below. But no matter which direction the boat ventured away from the line, it maintained the same distance from the transom, as if it were following them around. It appeared as though the fish had indeed taken a straight run for the deep and they were parked right over the top of him.

The fleet had taken quick notice of Louis' backing down and now stationary position in the water. Many of them had overtaken him in his new location, and were circling him to get a better view of what was to unfold. Perhaps they might get a chance of their own.

"What do you want me to do, Captain Gladding?"

"What you're doin'. Just hold your rod high, let the fish do his thing."

"We can't reverse and go get him like all the others?"

"We could, right over your line if that's what you want."

"There must be something!"

"Still takin' it, Louie, . . . only not quite as fast. He's got to have three-quarters of the spool out," Crafty cautioned.

"Yeah, I got ya. We're sittin' in about 3,000 feet of water, and I gotta believe he's gettin' lonesome for the bottom."

Wendt was beginning to feel very conspicuous in that chair, a man alone and in the middle, who was being scrutinized by the many crews driving by. "I feel stupid sitting here, . . . give me something I can do! I'm going to push the drag up."

"Don't do that, you'll bust him off! It's increasing all the time," Crafty warned, "You got more line in the water creating more drag and a smaller spool diameter increasing torque. Just do what you are told."

Wendt screamed a steady stream of obscenities at the fish as he rocked back and forth in the chair against the tension, a pointless and ineffectual reaction. The line continued to pour off the spool, which was now beginning to show some gold anodizing between the wraps of monofilament that were left.

An International 50W might hold a half mile of line at full

capacity, but something told Louis that this time it would not be enough. Everybody waited silently, afraid to speak, fearful they might be the final stroke of bad luck.

There were only a few yards left now, and Wendt continued to feel contempt for whatever it was that he was tied to. How he hated that sound of that clicker as well, as it gave its impersonal account of the sand slipping away in the hourglass. When he came down to the spool knot, he was at first lifted up in the chair. But as Crafty grabbed for his angler, and the rod, the crack of the parting line signaled the final gun. Wendt slumped back in his seat, the silence magnified by the wind. No one on board uttered a sound for a long half minute.

Crafty turned to the man light-heartedly, "Good swimmer, huh."

"Whatever." Adam stared into the deep blue, a scowl across his face.

"I have no idea, Louis, never saw the bite. Did you?"

"Nope."

"Impressive nonetheless, Mr. Wendt, they always are when you never turn 'em around."

"Does this happen a lot? I can't believe nobody saw it."

"It happens. I believe that's what our captain was referring to when he said the big ones often get away, if ya know what I mean." Crafty winked at the man before starting his clean-up routine, he could definitely see it was time to go.

When all answered 'ready,' Louis put her up on a plane and began the twenty-minute run down to Chub. The girls joined him on the bridge to catch a little of the breeze, and they were quick to add their congratulations for another fine day on the blue water. Louis looked back once to see the fleet still working the area two miles behind.

"It's been a bitchin' break, Louie, I've really enjoyed this week."

"I'm glad, Cheryl, that's what it's all about. Crafty and I, well, we have certainly had the best of times with you and Cami."

"I feel a little sorry for Adam, though. He didn't get his fish and he seems extremely pissed off."

"He'll get over it. He shouldn't be taking this personally, anyway."

"Why?"

"Well...that fish, whatever it was, couldn't care less who Adam Wendt is, or whether the man is smart, successful or otherwise. It's way beyond his control, he doesn't begin to hold all of the cards."

"Somehow I don't think that's going to make him feel any better."

"Neither do I."

Cami put her hand on Louis' shoulder while she pointed off the bow about 2:00. "Louie, check that out over there, there's something breaking the water. See it?"

"Yeah, I see some sharks...hold on a minute." Louis squinted a bit harder, thinking he might have seen the dorsal of a different fish, but now it was gone. "No...there it is." He headed straight for it and powered off only when he closed to within a tenth of a mile of the surface activity. As he idled the boat in, no more than fifty yards from the cutting shark fins, the situation became readily apparent to him.

About half a dozen very large, bull sharks were circling and feeding on a very noble specimen of swordfish. Louis guessed the fish's weight to be around 800 pounds, and by the appearance of the chewed and dangling flesh, he reasoned that the fish had been dead long enough to gas him up to the surface. Just a trace of blood was still spilling from the once magnificent creature as it was being tugged and carried around by the 13-foot-long sharks.

"It's sad," Cami observed, "I never knew they had such long flat bills like that, and you can still see a little gold and purple on his back."

"They're a pretty picture when they first take to jumpin'.

170

Never know what killed that one, might have gotten free off a longline or somethin'."

Louis parked the boat a little distance away, with the transom facing the frenzy. He walked to the rear of the bridge and leaned over to fill Frank and the others in on what they were seeing from up top.

The sharks were marginally cooperating with one another as they alternately took hold of the corpse, getting their jaws on a big mouthful, and then writhing it off in ecstasy. Louis walked back to the console and just shut the engines off as they drifted with the scene.

Louis heard the crack of a carbine, and even he was startled as it pierced the silence of the natural feeding before them. Another crack, and he saw the trace of the round as it missed its mark entering the water a foot to the right of one of the bull sharks.

"What's that?" Cami was concerned and put her hand to her mouth.

"They're playin' with guns downstairs, that's all."

Another crack, and a swing and a miss. Then came a succession of reports, as the clip was now being emptied. White streaks dotted around the nearest shark until one found its target. The carnivore went into an irregular kicking on the surface, and was now suddenly swimming upside down, pushing the water as it went into a tight circle. More than likely he would be the next course. Louis shook his head as he scanned the entire horizon for other vessels. There were none.

Louis went down the ladder and into the cockpit, where he found Byrd laughing, holding the Ruger mini-14 pointed down at the deck.

"There's one less shit-eater you won't have to worry about, Cap!"

"How 'bout that. What are you doing, Scoot?"

"Adam felt like killing one of those sharks feeding on that

171

fish. I was merely giving him a little instruction. Got a problem with that?"

Louis walked over to the man and stripped him of the semi-automatic rifle, pulling out the two tape-wrapped banana clips to turn them around. He inserted the live clip, and levered the first round into the chamber.

"Here, Mr. Wendt." Louis handed him the rifle across his chest. "If you want any killing done for entertainment on this rig, you'll do it on your own. Why not start by finishing off that wounded one."

Adam poured out the entire clip on the twitching half dead shark, never getting one round into it. When all was quiet, he slowly lowered the rifle to his hip and stared out to sea.

"Just as I thought. Do you feel purged now?" Louis reclaimed the gun.

The man stared back at Louis, then at his host, before darting between them and storming inside the boat. Louis locked eyes with Whitman and shook his head before handing the Ruger back to Byrd. He slowly climbed the bridge ladder to finish the job of getting the boat back to her slip. It had been a good day so far.

He felt himself relax a little as he made his entrance into the marina. Once again, they were back to the dock before most of the fleet, and Louis could see that the fuel dock was clear. He instructed his mate that they would top her off now, and to grab a couple of lines. He brought her alongside quietly, shutting down all but the generator. He was most thankful for the day.

When they were all seated at dinner at the club that evening, Frank offered a toast to the week's fishing, and another on the prospect of having a good tournament in Cuba. Things had thawed for the most part and Adam provided his own apologies to the party for his behavior that afternoon, hoping he hadn't alarmed anyone.

"Forget it, Mr. Wendt, what's over is over. Let's try to better communicate in such matters in the future." Louis offered, being one not to cop an attitude. He believed one of the worst things you can do is to go to bed with unfinished business, begrudging someone or some thing. It wasn't right.

"What do you know about this cold front we're to get day after tomorrow, Louie?"

"They're talkin' Saturday, but it's movin' on us pretty quick. May blow on through Friday evenin', Frank."

"I see. I would like to spend a day just relaxing before we leave. Our first fishing day next week is Wednesday, and I want to take a practice day Tuesday, if you think it makes sense."

"Certainly."

"That would mean arriving in Havana Monday evening. How far a run is it from Miami to Havana?"

"Why Miami? I thought you wanted to make it to the lower keys before headin' down."

"I did. It's just that Adam has to take care of some personal business in Miami before he can leave. He needs a day, right Adam?"

"That's fine, Frank. I can be done by Saturday afternoon. We could even plan on heading down bright and early Sunday morning, so there's no crunch on time."

"Splendid, then we're all set. We'll fly out Saturday morning. Louie, . . . you and Crafty will be taking the boat to Ocean Reef—I am a member there. We can regroup either Saturday night or Sunday morning at our convenience for the trip down. Questions?" Frank quickly canvassed the table. "Jeremy, I'm ringing the bell! Get everyone in the house a drink, will you please."

"Yessah, Mr. Whitman."

"Oh yeah, and we're all starved to death over here, when you have the time." Frank was fully enjoying himself.

15

Louis awakened at his usual hour the following morning, and proceeded to make himself a stout pot of coffee. He had been stirred earlier from his sleep about 2:00 when the cold front passed through in the form of a pretty respectable squall line. The rain had long since quit, but the wind had swung around to the north blowing a steady 25 knots, with gusts. It would be anything but a flat ride back to Florida.

With mug in hand, Louis slid open the salon door and was greeted with a blast of the cooler, drier air. He checked the flags and could see they were well starched. *Miami*, he thought. *At least they would have the sea on the beam.*

The old captain decided to bring Whitman's own weather-fax on line for an update on the late spring storm. He climbed up to the bridge and hit the power on the satellite feed's computer head. In five minutes, he had the most recent satellite photo and surface map of the area. He tore off the paper, taking it back down below to study for a bit.

Crafty came up the steps behind him, and made his move for the coffee pot. "Blowin' good out there ain't it, Louis."

"Yeah it is. Big low pressure system blew right over the top of us last night and is centered somewhere nor'east of us on the other bank. Lots of packed isobars, Crafty. It'll be sporty, but doable—it's not tropical in nature according to the weatherfax. Let's get outta here as soon as we can. The longer we hang around the rougher that 'Stream' is gonna be."

"I'm with you. Another cup, and a trip to the head, and we can start loadin' her up. Glad we topped off last night."

"Yeah, didn't think there was gonna be a run to the fuel dock today, just wanted to get goin' as soon as possible."

The two men began to repack the boat with all its traveling gear, dockside accessories, and dock box. Everything in the cockpit had to be tied down firmly, some to fixed points such as cleats and ladder bases, the remainder of items around the stanchion of the fighting chair. It was a crowded mess when done, with half inch nylon roaming everywhere.

While Crafty was putting the finishing touches on his gift-wrapping down below, Louis was hanging two extra panels of isinglass on the starboard side of the bridge, extending the wrap-around tent to the rear of the flybridge. When he had zipped up the last panel he glanced at the sunrise. He did not like what he saw. Rather than the clear high wisps of wind-driven cirrus clouds usually accompanying a front's passage, he saw a large, cottony cloud mass of rich pink. At the horizon a low grey cloud bank was rapidly making its approach. Suddenly it was warmer and windier, and then it was cool once again. In another twenty minutes it was solid overcast with a very low ceiling, and the winds had freshened another ten knots. *Not too comforting,* Louis thought to himself.

In the distance, the sound of jet engines could barely be heard over the wind and generator. The jet engine noise began to intensify until Louis picked up the aircraft heading right at them. It buzzed the marina at no more than 300 feet, making a slight tip roll as it passed. It was Frank's signature gesture of good-bye. It is doubtful that anyone up or soon to be awake was awestruck by the moment, at seven in the morning.

Louis fired up his main engines. Once again the starboard side required more time in rolling over and the cooler air kept her smoking blue for a longer period of time. In five minutes they had retrieved their final dockline and were idling out of the Crown Colony Club on their way to Key Largo.

Once running, Louis punched in Northwest Providence

Light, giving him a waypoint bearing of around 280 degrees. The course to Key Largo made Great Isaacs an unsuitable waypoint for leaving the Great Bahamian Bank, as it would have taken him too far north, nearly forty miles north of Bimini. A more direct route was to approach to the western end of the shallows via the cut at Gun Cay. It was a small but high island a few miles to the north of Cat Cay, home to a once-manned lighthouse.

Passage through the reef at Gun Cay, required the vessel to closely hug the southern tip of the island. The deep water channel that ran nearly under the cliffs was the only hole in the barrier reef between Gun and North Cat Cay. The water gets a little shallow on the eastern side of the island as you approach the cut, but they would be arriving there on a flood tide, so Louis did not consider that his boat's six-foot draft would be a factor.

As they cleared the remnants of the toppled Northwest Light in its position as the gateway out of the Tongue of the Ocean, Louis said farewell to their fishing hole, adding thanks for the good days they had received. A hollowness grew in Louis' abdomen as he suddenly felt that he might never see this spot again. His apprehension grew, until Crafty came up on the bridge and took a seat in the companion helm chair.

"Here man, I brought 'ya a bagel and cream cheese."

"'Preciate it, thanks."

"Makin' good time . . . so far. Being that it's already three foot in here, I suspect it will be a little sporty out in the middle."

"Yup. At least we got a good angle on her, and this heavy thing ought to run the trough and beam sea fairly well. I'm assumin' the farther west we get, the better it should get. What time we got?"

"Quarter to eight."

"Should put us at Gun around a little after 11."

Louis suddenly braced himself up and cocked his head to one side, as if to tune up his ear a little. "Dang, you hear that, Crafty?"

176

"Hear what?"

Louis bent over the console and put his left ear up against the housing box for the dual action starboard control lever. His eyes meandered around a bit as he listened intently to the mechanical noise sent up to the bridge via the gallery of wires working up from the engine room.

"Stick your ear on that lever box, and see if you notice anything different. Try the other one and then go back to this one. Anything?"

"Not really, 'ol boy." But he tended to doubt himself more than Louis.

"Take her for a minute."

Louis went down from the bridge into the cockpit and opened the engine room door and hatch cover. He reached for the headphones hanging on the side of the accessway, fitting them to his head before taking a look down below. He set himself down between the two engines on an old milk crate, and adjusted the headset for clarity.

Everything looks fine enough, he thought to himself, *but these engines don't seem to want sync very well considering the regular rhythm of the small sea they were in*. His mechanical gauges all remained unified with the electrical ones up top, and he could not find a leak of any kind save the oil drips. He crawled all the way around the starboard engine, hoping to see or hear something unusual. Nothing caught his eye or stood out here either, and he apologized to his two horses for having ever doubted their hearts.

It had been quite hot down in the hole, and Louis was glad to be back on the bridge. He settled down into the helm chair and looked at his GPS and LORAN. Both units showed the cut to be forty miles out, within two-hundredths of a nautical mile variance between the two nav aids.

"A couple of hours and we'll be at Gun."

"Anything unusual down there?"

"Found nothin'. Maybe the hallucinations of an aged captain."

Crafty chose not to answer and began to kill a little time studying the charts and the approaches to Gun Cay.

It was eleven straight up, and the old light could be seen clear as day a few miles to the west. On most days, the scenery would have been spectacular on the gin clear shoals. But today, the water was powdered and opaque, the sand bottom kicked up from the heavy winds now blowing over thirty knots.

It was a quaint little lighthouse of pink and white pastel, set upon the tiny little cay amidst a few palms and five small houses. It was in fact, the subject of many paintings and oils, the very essence of a tropical still life.

When the crew cleared the cliffs at the southern tip, they got their first glimpse of the rough water horizon to the west. The large swells from the north could be seen undulating south, standing up, releasing, building, and falling out again, in constant arhythmic fashion. They would enjoy only a brief respite in the lee of the cay, before entering more exposed waters and the Gulf Stream beyond. It was certain to be a whole lot rougher before it got any better.

"Time to make a check below."

"Sounds good, Crafty. Bring me a Coke when you come back up."

"Done."

Louis tried the weather channel on the VHF, to try to get an updated forecast. Of the four channels, number three was the only one audible, and it was fading in and out of static. He did make out a trailing off transmission, " . . . all marine interests should take safe shelter . . . system has signs of intens . . ." *Man*, he thought to himself. He demanded another update from Whitman's toy and received a duplicate report of the one sent to him earlier. Ain't going to blow up all at once, we can slide over the 'stream' in time. We are on a schedule. He paused for a moment and looked skyward. He held her heading to the west.

They were about ten miles off the bank and she was blowing a steady thirty-five + knots, with heavier gusts. They hadn't even found any real current yet and it was a twelve-to-fourteen-foot sea already. The large ocean swell heaved to the south underneath the boat at a right angle, at a ground speed approaching fifteen knots. Louis knew that ground swell would continually build as they moved farther off the bank to the west.

Up ahead a quarter of a mile, lay the unmistakable line of northerly current where the effects of the Gulf Stream would be felt for the first time. Like a cartoon, the ocean surface just grew twice as tall as the water they were now in. In a matter of only a few feet, a sharp line of demarcation separated moderate from extremely rough seas. The strong northerly current was pushing against the large swells, making them stand up higher and steeper. There was far less spacing between the large ocean waves now, and very little backside to them. The crests were toppling frequently, and there was plenty of white water everywhere you looked.

Within a mile, Louis had eighteen-foot seas directly hitting him on the starboard side. Actually, the wind had swung around to about thirty degrees north northeast, blowing across the large groundswell, taking some of the rhythm out of the ocean.

Louis had the bow of the sixty-five trimmed up, as he steered his rig laterally traversing the face of each wave whenever possible. When the nose would tend to dig at the bottom, he would quarter the wave by slightly guiding her up and over the large swell, letting it pass underneath the boat's keel. This was the plan, the best way to ride through the sloppy mess, although here were a couple of drawbacks to be considered.

There were times when exceptionally large waves would not care to release the surfing boat from their hold, or a wave might be reinforced from behind, by an even larger sea. These were dangerous situations providing two equally undesirable and dire consequences; burying the bow into the wave and under water, or lifting up the stern dramatically reducing rudder control.

Neither outcome was particularly desirable, but the remedy was the same. Pull the power back on the inside engine to dig her outside rear, let the boat pop up like a cork, and then freefall on the empty backside until she caught the bottom of the gaping trough. Then start the 'bonzai pipeline' all over again. After about three-and-a-half hours of 'tubing it,' they would hopefully be out of the current into more caring seas.

"Here's your Coke, Louis, or what's left of it."

"Thank ya buddy. Gettin' a might sloppy ain't it."

"Plenty sporty all right. How's she doin'?"

"Holdin' her own I reckon, she falls off a good one every once in a while. How's things down there?"

"The usual. Things all over the floor, coupla' busted drawers. You know."

"Yeah. Getting mixed reports on this storm. VHF says this thing is nor'east of us, with surface pressures dropping, getting more tropical all the time. Frank's toy here, seems to be behind the times a little. Might be in for more wind in awhile."

"What'd ya think, Cap?"

"I'm keepin' on, Crafty, we've been through worse."

"It can always be worse, eh, Louis?"

"It can always be worse," echoed the old salt as he nodded his head.

As expected, they found harder current the farther west they ran. Louis continually felt the need to pull the boat back 100 rpm or so, or by whatever amount that maintained responsive steerage for his vessel. He looked over at his shotgun rider and noticed he was smiling and bobbing his head as he was slapping the side of his thigh.

"You're all smiles and happy this morning," Louis evenly stated with a slight grin.

180

"Just thinkin' of an old Lightfoot song, it seemed to fit."

"Well . . . give us a little of it."

"Brooding cathedral organ, lap top Dobro guitar, goes something like this:

Triangle, triangle, m'sea and m'ship dangle,
we're bound for Bahama my friend.
Like lovers like dangers, like daddies like mangers,
but that's where my story begins.

Like soldiers of fortune, believers in God,
And all kings without crosses to bear.
All squeakers and cleaners, with no misdemeanors,
Shouldn't try the triangle down there.

It's a mighty hard way to come down,
But a mighty fine way to be found.

"That's all I know, Cap."

"That'll do."

Louis felt the bow digging and grabbing hold a little bit. He pulled the power back, and she still continued deeper into the trough on her own momentum. About the time he saw the bow with no place to go except into the wave itself, he buried his port engine and put her hard to starboard. She got slapped by the face of the wave and began her ascent all the way up to the top. When the thirty-footer was directly under the keel, Louis countered back into her to port, so as to minimalize the travel of the boat over the backside of the huge wave. Unfortunately, there was little backside to that one, and the boat acquired some hang-time in mid air before finding the next awaiting trough some feet below, pounding and shuddering on impact."

Louis straightened his Busch cap and turned to Crafty briefly, "No time for the autopilot, is it now 'ol boy."

"A nice hole in the water that one was."

The sea conditions continued to worsen as the vessel pushed west, into the stronger current velocities of the Gulf Stream's axis. Twenty-five to thirty footers had become the rule, and some larger than that. There was very little spacing between them as the hard northerly current pushed against the storm's wind-driven seas, standing up the opposing swells higher and closer together.

Louis could now see the trailing foam streaks break from the toppling wave crests, and he knew they were now in a full blown gale of 40 knot plus winds. Throw in the opposing current of the Gulf Stream, and the wave heights now approached a dangerous full storm category.

They were in the worst of it now, in the 'hump' as it is often called, the axis of the Gulf Stream where the current sets at its strongest. In a nor'easter like this, with the 'Stream' running strong, it can be sixty or so of the most treacherous nautical miles you'll ever want a piece of. And right now, they were crossing where the velocity of the great current was at its peak, getting their ass handed to them in their sixty-five-foot dinghy.

"Maybe once that tropical storm moves off of us a bit, the winds will lay some," stated Louis as he scanned the horizon in a momentary break. He braced, waiting for a rogue wave to have at him once more. Again, the old man got his steerage and maintained control of her, but she fell off the back mightily for what seemed like an eternity until she crashed into the upward side of the trough of the next wave. She had now dug in deep enough to severely brake the ride upward on the face of that wave, and the crest toppled and broke over the bridge showering them in white. But like a cork she came out of a near broach, and was back up and over. She was ready to take on the next one, when the starboard engine stalled out.

Louis immediately heard the engine fade down, and turned

her hard to starboard to quarter the now oncoming head sea while he had the chance to maneuver at all with the one engine. There he held her into it, a couple of points off to port on his best angle with the raging ocean and her thirty-foot seas. While the engine alarms wailed at him, he quickly scanned his gauges. There was obviously no oil pressure in the stricken engine, but it hadn't overheated, and that was good.

He tried it one time and the huge diesel lit for a second, then died. On the next attempt, the engine slowly sputtered to life, sounding as if she might have dropped her fuel prime. In the next moment, all sixteen cylinders were firing as if nothing had ever happened. He had good oil pressure and coolant temp, and the psi in the transmission was normal. "Thank you," Louis mumbled, as he put her in gear and went on.

One hour later, the Miami coast began to pop up from behind the western horizon. Louis dwelled on the irony that he could be in such clear sight of the urban skyline, and still be getting his butt kicked so severely. Things were lessening a little at a time, however, and he knew that in another six or seven miles, they would be out of the worst of it.

"Doin' all right, Cap?"

"Yessir, it's nice to see America as usual. Things holdin' together down there, Crafty?"

"Kind of. The fridge got knocked loose from its hole, walked the step and blew grits all over the salon floor. The teak table is upside down and it took a big chip out of the side panel. Some trim is working away, a few busted drawers, you could take a shower in the engine room—not too bad really."

"Gotta keep some steerage up here, man, this swinging wind is really confusin' the seas. It's a hob-gobbly mess!"

"Doin' fine, Louis. She can take more than you and me." The two men broke out in laughter.

Louis had been steadily pulling the power back, as the seas had continued to build. His tachs were hovering around 1300 rpm right now. But ahead of him a mile he could see the seas dramatically subside to an acceptable twelve to fourteen, with far more space between the crests. As he piloted his rig across the Gulf Stream current edge, he looked back a final time at the raging ocean as he straightened his cap. The great warm current was thankfully remaining behind, releasing his little toy boat from her winterlike grasp.

Then he heard the noise come to visit once more, only this time it was beginning to crescendo. The starboard engine was suddenly dropping off a few cylinders. Louis reached for the control as the boat made a major shudder on that side. He instinctively looked behind the transom as a wide dense bluish-white cloud of smoke and gases poured out of the starboard exhaust. The starboard tack fell flat to zero, and again there was that unsettling sound of a lone engine.

"What in the world, Louis?"

"I think our little gremlin has finally surfaced and showed his self. Got to have blown that engine big time. Take her, Crafty." And down he went, while Crafty held her into the sea.

Nothing really jumped out at Louis as he entered the engine room, other than it was soaking wet with sea water running down every overhead cross member. A quick preliminary inspection indicated a little more oil than before on the napkins in the engine bed, but nothing to indicate the consummate failing of the engine.

He pulled the dipstick and was soon overcome by a sickening sensation growing in the pit of his stomach. The engine oil had blended with coolant and looked more like butterscotch ice cream than clear lube. Up the stick, there were more water droplets and air bubbles. As far as Louis was concerned, the diesel had suffered a mortal wound. He was quite sure that a head was completely destroyed; valves most certainly ruined, maybe all the way down to the crankshaft, or even a cam blown—he'd seen that too. Bottom line, the engine would have to be rebuilt, and it could not possibly be done in time to leave tomorrow morning.

Louis had not prepared himself for the disappointment he was now experiencing. Admittedly, he had taken on the job with much reservation, and maybe he had not honestly prioritized finishing it to completion over the simple outcome of helping his daughter. In reflection, he saw himself as even being wrongfully cavalier about the whole project. Now he found himself in a general sense of 'owing' to Whitman.

They had grown in their understanding of one another—might even call it a friendship, Louis would concede. He hadn't foreseen the determination growing within him to see the job all the way through.

He left the stifling heat of the engine room and went back out to the cockpit for a breath of cool air. He needed a few moments to think, and let the dizziness in his head clear.

"What's our headin', Cap?"

"Oh . . . hold her due west, Crafty. No point in buckin' the tide now. Just let her slide up to Port Everglades, where we'll head for Will's place on the Dania Canal. I can trust him with this one, and I know he'll be there today, it's Saturday."

"Got 'ya fine, Louis."

The air did have a little chill to it, and the old man sought his blue windbreaker before going back up top. When he arrived at the helm, he picked up the VHF mike, switching to channel 16 before keying the transmit button.

"Diesel Engineering Systems . . . the *Byte Her*, WHY 4466."

"KYS 298, this is Diesel Engineering answering channel 16 . . . please switch channel 14, Captain."

"Switching channel 14."

The two parties made their move and Louis allowed the base to be the first to speak, "Diesel Engineering, what can we do for you *Byte Her*?"

185

"How 'ya doin', Sally, it's Louie Gladding. Would Sweet William be around the shop?"

"Louie how are you and where have you been keeping yourself? He is, I'll go get him. Stand by." A few minutes passed, and Crafty was peering over at Louis as they waited, "Lookin' bad, ain't it."

"Yup. I'm quite sure we blew that one up."

The intermittent static was suddenly punched through by a clear transmission.

"Louie, old buddy, old bean, you trash another one?"

"Willie, I gotta mess on my hands."

"I love boats, boats are so good to me. Where are you Captain Louis?"

"Eighteen miles southeast of your inlet, on my way back from Chub this morning."

"On your way back from Chub this morning? That's nice, Louis. Did you have a pleasant ride?"

"Not particularly, Will."

Laughter. "I got 'ya. On your way in to the shop, are we?"

"That's right. Probably be two-and-a-half-three-hours."

"Not to worry, I won't close up till you get here."

"Thanks, Will."

"See yah. You have a nice day, Louis."

Once inside Port Everglades at Ft. Lauderdale, Louis started up the starboard engine and was amazed to find it could run, and even deliver power to the gear at idle. He then shut it back down, saving what may be left of it for any docking trouble they might encounter at the diesel shop.

"That's nice to know, Crafty, thing can still work with all that wrong inside of her."

"We were lucky to lose her on this side of the 'Stream' instead of the other."

"Yes we were, thank you, Lord." Louis paused and looked skyward.

186

They proceeded south on the ICW for a mile past the commercial docks, before taking a right on the cut-off canal leading west for a good way. Their destination was all the way at the end of the canal on its southern side.

As they approached the service dock extending out from the hangar, a wiry, spectacled, balding man appeared grinning broadly at the crew. He grabbed the first line Crafty threw at him and made it fast to a cleat for a spring, and pulled the stern over with the second line he was tossed. It would do for now, it was actually quite peaceful in the back recesses of the industrial canal. Will motioned for quiet as he ran his hand across his throat, giving his old friend the OK sign.

"How are things, Louis?"

"You're lookin' at it."

"Yunno . . . I love boats. I gotta tell you, Louis, I really love boats."

"Yeah, well, this one's supposed to be leaving for Havana in the morning."

"That's nice, Louis. What do we have?"

"Got coolant in the oil pan, one bank of holes that work. All started with a bang and a big cloud of white, blue, and yellow-like smoke."

"She really had a bellyache, didn't she. Where?"

"Just this side of the 'Stream.'"

Will nodded quietly, maybe tiring a little from his own cynicism, "Well, that's good, got a break there. Me and the lads will tear into her for a couple of hours. Why don't you take the truck, go get yourselves a room and get cleaned up. Do what you have to do with the boss man, and give me a call at around 8:30. I'll let you know what I found. Go ahead." Will shook his hand, and reached into his pocket for the keys sticking them in Louis' hand. "I'm busy, I got work to do."

The boys got their gear and took off knowing the boat was in the best possible hands. A nicer guy than Will Brady would be difficult to find. Harder still, would be finding someone who was as capable at wrenching a diesel engine. The boys were a salt lick from head to boot, and they were long overdue for a hot wash-down.

16

Crafty beat Louis to the shower almost before his captain could start unpacking his seabag that he'd thrown on the bed. Louis reached into his billfold and pulled out the hard card with all of Whitman's phone accessing printed on it. The first number he dialed was Frank's condo in Palm Beach. On the second ring it was received. Louis did not recognize the voice.

"Please leave your voice mail at the end of the tone."

"Frank, Louie. I'm at the Marriott in Lauderdale, (305) 288-5000, room 220. Call me as soon as possible, it's important."

Louis picked up the phone again and rang the front desk.

"This is Louis Gladding in room 220, I would like ATT directory assistance."

"One moment."

"What city?"

"Key Largo."

"What listing."

"The Ocean Reef Club." He then pushed the number to have it dialed. "Ocean Reef Club, how may I direct your call?"

"My name is Louis Gladding, I'm trying to reach a Mr. Frank Whitman, he is due to arrive at the resort this evening."

"Ah, yes . . . Whitman. Mr. Whitman has not been in contact with us as yet, sir, may I leave a message?"

"Please. Have Mr. Whitman call Louis Gladding at the Marriot in Ft. Lauderdale. The number is (305) 288-5000 room 220. It's urgent."

"We'll be happy to relay the message."

"Thank you, good night."

Louis settled the phone in its cradle, thinking if there was anything else he could do. There wasn't. He wouldn't even have any new information for his boss either, at least not until 8:00. He was starving.

"Louis, I need to make a call."

"Go right ahead, I'm headed for the shower."

Crafty punched in for the outside line as he pulled a small piece of paper from his shirt pocket. *South Miami Beach*, he thought to himself, *ought to be long distance*. He went ahead with the long digit dialing, half smiling when it began ringing.

"Yes?"

"Cheryl . . . Crafty."

"What do you want?"

"Hey Cheryl . . . it's me, your spring break buddy from Chub."

"Is that right. What are you doing calling me here?"

Crafty was flaming out, his enthusiasm was fading fast. "Seemed like the right thing to do at the time, Cheryl. I, at least, remember having a good time."

Cheryl paused with long sigh, "I had a good time as well. But that was then, and now it's a done deal, okay."

"Cheryl . . . why go to the trouble of giving me your number if your game is to freeze up at the other end? You got some kind of personal problem?"

"You big dumb bastard! I was paid to do you, you understand me! Money, honey. That's all there was to it. Do yourself a favor and write me off."

"And if I don't? Y'know, Cheryl, somehow I can't believe you need the money that bad."

"I need to be able to continue with my career. There are some things better left unsaid, so listen up. Watch your backside and keep your eyes open. Don't ever call this number again. Never." Click.

"Man! Dammit, what a June Bug," Crafty yelled out loud.

"What was that all about?"

"Tried to reconnect with the poor woman, Louis, and all I got was teeth."

"Who, Crafty?"

"Cheryl. She led me to believe that there might have been more bright moments ahead. She lied."

"Crafty, let's go get us some dinner. There's no more to be done here right now. I would just as soon be a little invisible until I have something definite to tell Frank."

"I'm ready. What'd 'ya say we go over to Chuck's and grab a rib."

"Yeah, that'll work."

The two men were just about out the door, when the phone rang, "Louie, Byrd here, what the hell is going on? You dudes are supposed to be in Key Largo."

"Ran into a little snag, Scoot, we're up here in Lauderdale."

"No kidding. I called you remember."

"Where are you, where's Frank?"

"I'm down at Ocean Reef, Frank's on his way back from Charlotte. He dropped Wendt off in Miami early this morning, and evidently Adam suggested he retrieve some important documents from the home office. He is only now flying back down here, and would you please explain to me why you are not here, Gladding."

"Mechanical problems, I'll know more in a little while, all right."

"That's just great, Captain. Shit . . . no . . . that's not all right! Here we are—"

Louis hung up the phone. "Ready to go, I'm hungry."

"What was that all about, Cap?"

"Byrd frothing at the mouth for no reason. It wouldn't do any good to tell him anything, I'll fill in the boss man later, . . . let's get outta here."

The jet was just passing over Cape Canaveral when Frank

Whitman looked up from his notes to take in the view. His pilot was walking towards him down the cabin, a pad and pencil in hand.

"Mr. Whitman, call coming in for you from Mr. Byrd."

Frank rose out of his custom chair, stretched leisurely and walked up the cabin to the phone just behind the cockpit and lifted the handset, nodding and smiling at his pilot.

"Frank here, what is it Scoot?"

"That damn boat captain of yours is sitting in Ft. Lauderdale picking his feet. Says he had a bit of a mechanical problem this morning on his way back."

"Oh?" Frank wanted more.

"Then the bastard hung up on me."

"Calm down, Scoot, really. I trust Louie implicitly. If he said he had a problem, he had a problem. It's not the end of everything. Did he leave a number?"

"He's at the Marriot, 288-5000 room 220."

Whitman checked his watch, 7:45. "I'll contact him when I land, we're only a few minutes out. And Scott, get a handle on things will you."

"Yes, Mr. Whitman."

"I'll keep you informed." Whitman hung up the phone and immediately tried Louis in his hotel room, getting no answer.

"Mr. Whitman, we've been cleared into Miami, should be there in fifteen."

"Good." Whitman gave up on the phone and returned to his armchair, fastening his seat belt. He stared out into the clear cool evening and the south Florida urban sprawl below. But he soon was drawn to the brilliant white moon in the eastern sky that lit up and highlighted the texture of the ocean's rough surface.

As the jet made its final approach into Miami, its owner felt neither worried nor concerned, only curious as to the situation that was unraveling.

Whitman was met at the gate by his Florida driver who

immediately escorted him to the waiting limo. He set his luggage in the trunk and jumped in the back, firing up the telephone right away. Still busy.

When a tired Louis and Crafty returned to the hotel room at 7:30, they both kicked off their shoes and went horizontal on the beds. Chuck's did have the best prime rib in town, after all, and they were stuffed full of it.

Louis was in the bathroom when the phone rang a little while later, and he heard Crafty pick it up. "Got Will here, Louis."

"Whatcha got for me, Willie?"

"Louie, you ain't going nowhere tomorrow on that rig. For that matter, Monday, Tuesday or Wednesday either. That's the best I can do, Cap, what with parts availability etcetera. If we are really dumb lucky, we can have her bundled up late Wednesday night, set the injector rack on her, and kick your butt out of here Thursday some time in the morning. If, and it's a huge if, and it's going to be expensive. I truly love boats."

"I got 'ya, Will. Money's no problem really, but what actually failed? The boss will want to know."

"The camshaft bro', the cam. There might be some good news in all of this. It's in about three pieces, and judging from the way the thing is scored, it might have been planning to do this for some time. Might be able to slide some of this in on a warranty claim. Problem is, I can't get my hands on another one until late Monday afternoon. Sorry. We'll also need a head and a few kits as well. Man, do I love boats."

"Okay, Willie, go for it. I'll be there in the morning to sign the work order, it'll have to be tended to no matter what happens."

"That's correct. You have a nice evening, Louis."

Louis hung up the phone, laid back down and ran his hands through his hair as he stared blankly at the ceiling. "We're hurtin 'ol boy—blown cam, cracked head, scored cylinders, valves, man."

"When?"

"Thursday mornin' at the earliest." Louis' mind continued to roam around; substitute boat? one of Whitman's friends? maybe charter one? would the Cubans allow it? Another loud ring from the phone jarred Louis back to the room. He knew it was Frank.

"Hey, Captain Louie, Frank here. That ocean looked mighty rough on the way back this morning, how was your trip home?"

Louis appreciated the upbeat words from the other end, but he knew Frank was into some kind of denial. "Frank, the boat did very well, but we have hit a major snag in the form of a blown starboard engine. She's cooked."

"Oh no!" Well he sounded worried now, and a major silence followed which Louie had decided best not to interrupt. "How . . . when, can you give me any details?" He was not angry, just curious, which Louis greatly appreciated.

"Boss, we did get our butts kicked a little crossin' the Gulf Stream, but we were out of the current, lookin' right at Miami, when we felt and heard the explosion down below. There was a big cloud of white smoke and she died on the spot. Nothing else major on the boat was damaged, like I said."

"What could have caused it . . . what was the probable source, do you know?"

"Frank, I went to the best mechanic I know in Florida, over in Dania at the end of the cut-off canal. We were lucky that he could drop everything and tear into it at such short notice. Ever hear of Will Brady?"

"I've heard of him, go on."

"I just got off the phone with him. Evidently, we blew a camshaft, and the domino effect cracked the head and ate a few valves."

"I understand."

"Will is of the opinion that there was flawed machining on the part, and that some of it may be recoverable under warranty."

"I appreciate that, Louie, I really do, but it doesn't help us on the short term."

"That's right, boss."

"How soon can we be a boat again?"

"Thursday morning at the earliest, giving us at least the final two days."

"I know you're doing all that can be done. Sounds like you don't intend to give up."

"I don't, Frank," the old captain paused for a few seconds. "There may be another possibility, some things I'm lookin' into. I'll have to sign the work order for the mechanic in the morning, and drop his truck off to him. I'll rent a car and meet you at Ocean Reef as soon as I can get there. Maybe I'll have some news for you by then."

"All right, Louie," Frank sighed, "I'll do what I can from my end. See you tomorrow at Ocean Reef. Good night and good luck."

Scott Byrd sauntered into the lobby of the resort hotel, and took a seat adjacent a row of public telephones. He began reading about the numerous leisure activities of the Ocean Reef Club: fishing, diving, parasailing, golf, tennis, horseback riding, shooting, even hand feeding dolphins. *What a playpen*, he thought to himself.

When the telephone to his immediate right began ringing, he lumped the flyers into a stack and casually got up to answer it.

"It's me," Byrd replied. He listened for a good five minutes until he had the opportunity to speak again. "You realize, of course, that this really changes everything, it messes up the whole works."

"Not so," came the reply from the other end, "you make adjustments once in a while."

Byrd listened impassively for another few minutes before responding at his end. "I don't agree with your take on that at all, you know the man well enough by now. I've done exactly what I said I was going to do. Now, I will contact you when I know more," the young man stated coolly as he hung up the phone. It had been a long day and he needed a drink or two.

17

Louis and Crafty gathered up their overnight gear, and made their way down to the lobby. It was 7:30 Sunday morning, but Louis knew that Will would already be at the shop, turning wrenches for customers that had brought nautical emergencies to his doorstep.

Louis checked and itemized the bill before putting it on the boat's credit card, and asked the Director of Services where they could rent a car nearby. They were able to do it right there, and in a matter of minutes Crafty was tailing Louis over to the diesel shop to finish up their business there. They parked the rental car in the lot, and took the truck around to the side entrance where it usually stayed. The men jumped on the boat and retrieved everything they needed for the trip down, in the event they jumped to another boat—charts, LORAN numbers and notes, passports, the rest of their clothes, everything.

Louis started packing the rental car while Crafty removed all his bait and loaded it into two coolers out on the deck. They left the AC running as the boat was going to be attended, the mechanics would surely appreciate that. They carefully stepped around to the side of the salon going back and forth, for the deck had already been ripped up. A-frames and engine hoists were mounted where there had once been a floor. They jumped off the boat and said a temporary farewell, cramming the remainder of their things into the rental car.

Will walked up to them from behind, toting a clipboard with a blue sheet of paper fixed to it. He handed it over to Louie, "Don't go anywhere without signing this, Louis."

"Nope, wouldn't do that to 'ya Will." He quickly scratched his signature on the bottom of the work order, and handed it back to the master mechanic. "Gotta go."

"Where to?"

"Duck Key. Got to find another boat."

"Good luck, you guys, thanks for the business. We'll be cranking at this end."

"Thanks for everything, Willie." Louis shook the man's hand.

They hopped into the car and headed for the Homestead extension of the Florida turnpike. At its southern end they would link up with US1, the mainstreet of the Florida Keys. Being that it was early Sunday morning, they made surprisingly good time. It was 11:00 when they pulled up to the waterfront home of Alfredo Silva.

They walked through the gate to the Spanish-style home, which lay on a point of very beautiful real estate overlooking the Florida Straits. In size, it could not be called a mansion, but the home was beautifully maintained and landscaped. They passed through another flowered trellis and up the walk to a massive wooden front door. Louis pushed the entry button on a lighted panel. After a minute, a woman's voice answered.

"Yes, who is calling please?"

"Captain Louis Gladding. Is Mr. Silva available to receive visitors?"

"One moment, please."

A few minutes passed until the two men heard noises from behind the door, and the sound of many locks being unbolted from within.

The door swung open slowly, to reveal a middle-aged Hispanic lady who smiled silently, and made gestures for them to enter.

They followed her around through a dining area and porch, and out onto an open aired terrazzo. Beyond, Louis made out the

old man sitting in his rattan chair, staring out towards his homeland across the Straits of Florida.

They remained on the patio as the housekeeper went over
and whispered in the old man's ear. He reached for his cane
and began to rise right away as she waved for the men to come
over.

He was an old man just into his ninth decade of life. He
wore a loose flowered shirt, a straw cap with a long visor, white
slacks and a pair of deck sneakers. His once leathery dark skin
was now thin and gray, freckled with numerous moles and can-
cers, his grey hair dyed black. He stooped as he walked, but he
had clear blue eyes, and the shine in them had remained.

When he first spied Louis walking towards him a few feet
away, he raised up both his arms and the cane, and waited at that
spot to receive him in an embrace. Louis covered the distance and
warmly hugged his adopted father.

"Luis, ees so good to see you here. I like to look out in the
morning before the heat come, I am so homesick for my country.
And Señor Crafty, how j'ou able to stay so young?" They shook
hands.

"Please, Luis, two chairs, pull up, we sit out here." The old
man eased quite slowly back down into his seat, falling the last six
inches. He straightened his cap and set his cane on the arm of
the rattan throne.

Louis looked out to the dock where Alfie's 53 ft. Whiticar,
Nina Mia, lay in her slip. There was a young man working on her
bow, sanding away at the varnished toerail that ringed the outside of the foredeck where it joined the hull. The teak rail ran
from the bow on down the sheer line to nearly the aft end of the
'house' or cabin. She was in word and reputation, "classic elegance" where form met function in a perfectly crafted sportfisherman. The *Nina Mia* was austere, but magnificently built and
designed for one purpose, to catch fish. She was from a different
time.

"I see j'ou eyeing my girl, she is much beautiful as ever, eh Luis?"

"She is so, Alfie. *Muy bonita.*"

"You are going to Cuba, no? I thin' you might already have left."

"The boat I was to take down blew an engine yesterday morning on our way back from Chub."

"Aieee, ees no good! You go a Chub, j'ou see Remedy?"

"Yes we did, and he sends his best to you. He say you been gone too long this time."

Alfie laughed and rolled backward a little in his chair, "Oh Luis, he is doing so better than Alfie to say such a thin'. I might never can go again." The old man's eyes turned back to sea, and settled in their familiar spot. "I am a man with no too many days left. You catch big marlin for heffe?"

"Yes, Alfie, many."

"Then boss man happy." The old Cuban yelled to his young captain, as he motioned him to come over. After a few tries, he finally got the blond haired man's attention. The young captain laid his palm sander down on the remaining unused sheets of sandpaper, and proceeded to dust himself off. He walked on down the side of the boat and jumped on the dock to pay the trio a visit.

"Ricardo, this my old friend Luis, the finest fisherman in all Caribbean. He is going to take my *Nina* to Cuba for the tournament next week. He is really my second son, so j'ou help heem to get her ready. Luis will say what to do."

"Alfie . . . you haven't heard what I am to say," replied Louis.

The old man waved him off, "Ahh . . . Luis, I know what j'ou are to say, and my heart sings out gladly that j'ou will make love to my girl for awhile. She is my most precious, my others are all gone."

"We will charter the boat for $1200 a day and all her

expenses, if we are to take her at all."

"If that is what j'ou wish, my son." The old man arose one more time and stood directly before Louis now standing as well. With considerable effort, he placed his tremoring arms on Louis' shoulders. "I am man who lives in his dreams, son, and remembers his life as it was once lived long ago. J'ou are in my dreams many days, living with us and my son, bringing much joy to heem and my heart. You go take *Nina Mia* and bring much joy to her, and then to me when I welcome j'ou home, Luis."

Louis could see the tears well up in the old man, as he felt them run down his own cheek. They embraced a final time. Louis knew Alfie's strength would be leaving him in a few moments, and he would again lapse into more sleep as he stared out to sea. The Cuban's heart was far stronger than his mind.

The old man sat down once again, smiling up at Louis as he held his hand up to bid him farewell. He held that smile until his eyelids drooped and closed him off. He let his head lay back against the high backed chair.

"Louie, just let me know what you need me to do. Here is the boat number, and my home number in Marathon. Keep me posted, man."

"We will, Ricardo, thanks for everything, and for being here for Alfie."

"Ricky . . . and there ain't nothing to it, Cap. I'd do anything for this man. I'll be waitin' to hear from y'all."

And so the two men were lead out in silence. They began their drive back to Key Largo both revitalized but saddened by the visit with their old friend. Words were not coming easily at the moment. The traffic was still light as the masses were squeezing out their last afternoon of the weekend in the Keys. Crafty looked over at Louis fully aware that his heart was still laid open.

"Want me to drive, Cap?"

"Yea, g'head, Crafty," answered Louis, as he dabbed at his

right eye. He pulled off the side of US 1 somewhere around Lower Matecumbe Key, and exited his door. Crafty slid over into the driver's seat but Louis kept walking on down to the water's edge, where he sat on the small beach. He stared out at the turquoise waters of his homeland, no longer fighting his heavy heart as he wept.

Crafty had slumped down in the seat and was listening to the radio when Louis returned and opened the passenger side door. Once again, they were headed east.

"He's had a long and wonderfully rich life, Louis, in a magnificent time to be alive. Don't feel too sadly for him."

"No, I don't. I don't feel sorry for him at all. Well . . . maybe a little for his loneliness. I'm just grateful that he entered my life. Here's a man who's lost everything—his homeland, his wives, all his children, relatives, all gone. Yet, he is so giving, asking nothing, sharing the only precious memory he has left. No, Crafty, a man with that kind of spiritual wealth will never be alone and unhappy for very long."

"It gives him great joy to do it, he said as much."

"He is a blessed man, I owe him my life. He will surely be with God when this one is over."

The men spoke no more until they got out of the car at Ocean Reef, on Key Largo. "

18

"Yes, miss, we're trying to locate Mr. Frank Whitman. I know he is a member here, and I believe he has a condo not far from the marina."

The redhead behind the hotel reception desk leafed through a few files and then a roladex before answering, "Yes, sir, that listing would come under a different department. Your best bet is to go right to the dockmaster over at the marina. He has a directory of all yacht club members, and any residential information. This all came about at the members' request."

"Thanks a lot."

"My pleasure, sir."

Should have gone right there first, Louis concluded to himself, but we'll find him sooner or later. They hopped back in the car and drove to the dockmaster's office, overlooking the entrance channel to the marina at the resort's southern perimeter.

The marina was a huge facility with all the first class amenities. It was a village, actually, housing bars and raw bars, restaurants, game rooms and gym, a ship's store, an electronics shop and a bait and tackle supply. A promenade of specialty shops offered a gourmet deli, a grocery and package store, boutiques of all kinds, and a well stocked pharmacy.

"Whitman . . . Frank Whitman . . . Ah yes, MV *Byte Her* she's a '65 sportfish, I should say, . . . " the elderly dockmaster replied in a perfect uptown British accent, "apparently overdue. She was to be 'laying to' here by now."

"That's right, I'm the Captain. We blew an engine on the

203

way here from the Bahamas yesterday."

"Oh my, how ghastly," the Brit replied, eyeing the two men over his half-frame glasses.

"What I need, is the address of Mr. Whitman's condo, if that's not a lot of trouble."

"Yes, straight away," he picked up the yacht club registry, "that would be . . . E400. Come, I'll navigate you there."

The three men walked outside past the fuel dock and around the corner of the dock office, when the dockmaster pointed to a series of townhouses. The complex ringed an area of the marina that contained the largest slips available for docking, as well as a long bulkhead that moored vessels in excess of 110 feet, along its length.

"That's building E over there, mates. Mr. Whitman's residence would be the entire top floor."

"Thanks, Cap."

"You will need this security card to get you by the outside door. Gentlemen." The spry little Englishman gave them the coded card and briskly marched off.

They decided to hoof it and began walking. "I say, Louis, ol' boy," Crafty began doing a fair accent of his own, "these patricians find we Yanks a bit stodgy for this line of work. I suspect they have little application for the hoi polloi, don't you quite agree?"

"Quite. How very astute, Radford."

The men rode the elevator to the top floor, discovering that the cab's outer door was the entrance to the condo. When it came to a halt they pushed the entry button. "Yes?"

"Louis Gladding to see Mr. Whitman."

"Louie' hold on," the voice sounded excited through the speaker. The door slid open and there was Frank in his boxer shorts, cell phone in hand, cigar in mouth, "Come on in, Louie, everybody's here but you guys. I'll be off this thing in a minute."

It was a huge apartment, very ornate in glass, mirrors, and

tile. They walked around a partition at the entrance into a huge living room, where Adam Wendt and Scott Byrd were parked on the longest L-shaped suede couch Louis had ever seen.

"There they are," Wendt offered with a renewed sense of warmth. He stood and offered his hand, which each of the new arrivals shook.

"Hi guys, good to see 'ya," Byrd now rising in his own gesture of politeness. The four men then remained silent and went to sit back down, willing to let Frank finish up his phone call and cue the direction of the following discussion.

"Jack, what did you find out from your insurance man, is this thing something that can be worked out?" Whitman paused.

"I see . . . I would be perfectly happy to put up my plane as collateral . . . Can't be done, eh? . . . Sorry to hear that, Jack. I'll have to try elsewhere . . . Say 'hi' to Winnie for me, good day."

Whitman ended his conversation with the young Senator and met Louis' gaze for a few seconds. "I didn't really think it would be this tough, Captain."

"What's that, Frank?"

"Coming up with another boat. It's been one snafu after another. Either it's insurance and liability, their lawyers or mine, or their crews have to be in charge, or its an exposure thing, you know. These guys don't want their boats down in Cuba for some reason. I tell you, Louie, some friends when you really need one."

"I told you, Frank, I have already made all the arrangements at my end," Wendt clarified for the group "My people have found a top notch vessel for charter, complete with crew, ready to leave in the morning out of Key West. It's the least I can do to repay your kindness all this week. It's nearly as big and comfortable as yours, a 63-footer as I recall, $1,500 a day. It's a done deal with a phone call."

Great, Crafty thought to himself, *where does that leave us, Wendt? You haven't said anything about us.* He looked at Louis and thought he saw the old man shaking his head slightly. He remained quiet.

"Crew," Whitman paused, staring at Wendt with a look of question, "Louie and Crafty are my crew, they're the best around. I would assume that these other guys could take orders, because these men right here are in charge." Frank met both men's gaze equally, he was for real. He looked back at Adam, "If that's the plan, then I could be coerced."

"Of course, Frank, I didn't mean to imply that we were planning the trip without your crew. I'm sure all the details can be worked out." Wendt scrutinized the two journeymen with a thin smile and a cold stare, "That going to sit all right with you two?"

Louis took the man's gaze head on, and sent one right back at him. He held it for a good long while, and was genuinely uncomfortable in doing so.

"Well, Captain?"

"I'm not in favor of it, Mr. Wendt, I have a better way."

"I don't think there is one, Captain. Let's hear it."

It did not go unnoticed to Louis that Adam Wendt's beguiling nature had all but taken control of the discussion. This man did possess a personal power about him that got Louis' attention. It made him uncomfortable, perhaps even instilled a bit of fear. He looked away from the man and spoke directly to Whitman.

"Frank, I don't go along with Mr. Wendt's plan for a number of reasons. It might appear workable on the surface, but crew relations will, without question, be a problem down the line. The captain and mate on that Stryker will not give in easily to an outside crew coming in on their baby, taking over the operation. Besides, that's simply just too many people on the boat."

"Captain Gladding, it's not that big an issue, believe me," Wendt challenged.

Without looking away Louis went on. "That's inexperience talking, Mr. Wendt. Crafty and I . . . we wouldn't respect them if they did it any other way. Second, none of us are familiar with the boat, its layout, where things are, its mechanical condition, the way she fishes, and so on."

"Again I say, you'll get all the help you need," Wendt replied more forcefully.

"Another thing to be considered is the Cuban government, and their reaction to a last minute boat substitution. They are a people prone to their whims, Frank, perhaps they would turn away such a change in plans."

"Louie, you're hitting on some important considerations, but what do you suggest we do?"

"The good captain is just trying to look at all the angles, and I can appreciate that, Whit," Adam interrupted nodding his head as he looked over at Louis. "We thank you for your tireless efforts, Louie, but I am happy to have made all the arrangements. Frank and I will be most comfortable, and I really think we are complicating the issue here, don't you, Captain Louie?"

Louis never took his eyes off Frank, and proceeded to present his plan as if the question had never been asked. "I have been given and entrusted with a fine custom sportfisherman for our use next week in Cuba. Not only am I completely familiar with her, I can testify as to her perfect condition in operation and maintenance. She's rigged and tournament ready. More importantly, she is well known to the Cubans and has fished there many times over the years. She'll be ours for the week, and she will add to the team that we are currently abiding by."

"Way to go, Louie, what is she?" Frank was smiling now.

"A 53ft. Whiticar, built in '74."

"A 53ft. Whiticar," a stunned Whitman reflected, "where did you find someone to flip you the keys to a boat like that in such short notice?"

"An old friend, Frank, he adopted me."

"Louie, you're one lucky man to have a friend like that."

"Thank you for that, Frank. I know."

"I don't like it, Mr. Whitman."

"What don't you like, Scoot?"

"Hmm . . . it's older, smaller, might be a little cramped on board, I wouldn't know where anything was,"

"You won't have to," Crafty answered unemotionally, "Louis and I do."

"I agree with Mr. Byrd, Frank . . . it will lack the size and creature comforts of your vessel, I question what we are really gaining here."

"Adam, I have to disagree with you on that score. She's every bit as good . . . no, she's a better sea boat at her length than mine. You could buy two of my rigs for what's in her for value. We're going fishing, Adam, and that's her thing. When the day's over we're all going back to the hotel anyway. What's her name, Captain Louie?"

"*Nina Mia*, Frank, she presents as fine a bait spread as you'll ever see."

"Does anybody have any legitimate concerns here," Whitman stated passionately as he threw out his final query. No one stirred. "Good. By the way, Louie, we have flight clearance via Nassau, so we'll just do what we've been doing and meet you two at the boat in Havana. Where is she moored right now?"

"Duck Key, down there by Marathon. We'll just head back down and make ready to leave, immediately if necessary. Nothing has changed on our end."

"I hope this doesn't present a problem, Frank, but my business affairs still have some loose ends that need attending to. Would a Tuesday morning departure be out of the question?"

"Matters little to me, Adam, that would be fine. You could use a breather and a little extra time on your end, couldn't you Louie?"

"Okay by me. We'll get out of here tomorrow, probably no

later than nine. We'll be ready to fish when 'ya get there Tuesday whenever."

"Perfect, we'll shoot down bright and early, and we'll still get our practice day in."

"Frank, I think I'd like to ride down with the guys for a change."

"Don't bother, Scoot, take the plane ride, we can handle it," Louis countered.

"No, really, I need to get to know the boat more, and figure out what you dudes want out of me next week."

"Not a bad idea, Scoot, I vote yeah," Whitman insisted. "Plan on driving down there in the morning. Now if you and Adam will excuse me, I'll see the boys out and let them be on their way."

He walked around the partitions to the elevator door and pushed the button before turning to face his crew. "Now I am in your debt all over again. How can I repay you for giving me the chance to keep going . . . and sticking by me?" He offered his hand to Louis.

The old man shook it soundly. "I told my friend the charter rate would be $1,200 a day and all expenses. For her."

"For her then, a small price."

"See ya in Havana."

Whitman's gaze followed the two men into the elevator, until the closing door severed the moment. He returned to join the two others in the living room, "That man never ceases to amaze me."

"How much is he charging you for the boat," Wendt asked casually reaching for his Bloody Mary.

"$1,200 a day."

"Convenient how he didn't happen to mention that point," Byrd snapped back.

"He'd been wasting his time, Scoot."

"How's that, Frank?"

"He knew you'd have been too ignorant to understand the value in the plan."

"You're quite taken with this old salt, aren't you, Whit?" Adam observed before emptying his vodka eyeopener. "I mean he's experienced, yes, but he's not the only qualified captain around. George, my man in Key West, has helped me catch many marlin down in St. Thomas. He's as good a hired gun if there ever was one."

Whitman stared at Wendt for a few long seconds, "You never told me you've fished down there, Adam."

"Oh . . . I'm sorry. I was sure I had boasted of that."

"Adam, I was due for a fresh approach to all of this, and I feel as though I have learned a great deal this past week. I know excellence when I see it, always have, and these guys are the best. I value their loyalty, and I intend on being a man good for his word. So you see, Adam, the discussion is closed."

"Whit, I commend you. I'm sorry I let this little test of mine go on for so long. Let's go kill some blue marlin! Another Bloody?"

19

The crew were now on their way back to Duck Key, and they were glad to be on the quiet side of US-1. The traffic was nearly bumper to bumper heading east, a common Sunday afternoon malady in the Florida Keys. Crafty downed the remainder of his Coke and glanced over at his passenger, "Louis, can you tell me what the hell is going down here? I know we had a little bad luck with the engine, but do you sense that all is not what it appears to be?"

"That's right. Seems like a couple of people are overly concerned about their own program. This whole thing started out as a fishin' trip at one time, and got changed into a promo deal along the way. Now, it feels like something different, like a cold that just got into your system, before it begins to beat up on 'ya."

"I got 'ya fine there, Cappy. The Byrd man is completely wired, and totally unreliable from what I seen. I'll be honest with 'ya, I don't want to travel with the bastard. I wish he'd go back to the office, and make Frank some more money."

"We got him till the end of the line. Let's just try to make the best of a bad situation. You're gonna have to spend some time with that pup, and give him a gaff lesson or two."

"I heard that. There something else I've not told you either."

"Yeah . . . there's a lot you never told me, and it never got in the way of much."

"Check this out. Last Thursday night in Chub, I took a little bridge cruise with Shorty and Deepwater out to the south beach. No, I didn't do any, but guess who I saw in the moonlight having

211

a little private chat down the beach from us?"

"Wendt and Byrd?

"That's right."

"Sure?"

"I followed 'em back down the hill to the bar. It was Wendt all right, saw them in the overhead light. They were joined by another dude for a minute or two, and then he split down the beach in the opposite direction. "Bout queer isn't it?"

"Could be nothing. Chub ain't that big a place. Maybe they were makin' a connection, as you say."

"They weren't barkin' at the moon, Cap. They both looked too serious to me, and there's more. When sweet Cheryl dusted me on the phone the other night, she slipped me a warning."

Louis sighed deeply. "Lay it on me."

"She told me someone put her up to doin' me, ya know paid her or played her. Before she hung up, she told me to watch my ass and pay attention."

"You must have stolen her heart."

"I'm serious, Louis. There is something foul brewin' up here."

"I know. I agree with you. For right now, you had better check and inventory our weapons and rounds when we get back to the boat. Put the .357 in your personal stuff and the 12-gauge under my bunk in that cubby. You can keep the Mini-14 in the gun locker but keep it locked and hold on to the key yourself. I don't want anybody to know where that stuff is. Matter of fact, I don't want Byrd to know where anything is, unless you need him to know it."

"Gotcha."

"Maybe if we plan for a little trouble, we won't find it. If we don't, Crafty, it will surely find us."

"Understood."

"There isn't much more to do except stop by the tackle shop and provision a few groceries. We can take care of all that tomorrow, let's go get us a room over in Marathon and take a break. I know's a spot to grab dinner."

"Sounds good to me. Stop by the boat so I can off these coolers of bait into the cockpit freezer."

"Oky doke. See if you can do it without botherin' the old man."

Scott Byrd looked at his watch after he downed his first martini, 10:55. *The hotel cocktail lounge was doing a fair trade for a Sunday evening*, he thought, *but then people accustomed to so much leisure time rarely gave much weight to what day of the week it was.*

He ordered another drink before asking the bartender where the nearest pay phone could be found. He slid off the bar stool and casually surveyed the room before making his way back towards the men's room. He looked to both ends of the alcove before entering an outer door where he found the phone. He went all the way into the bathroom and checked every stall to be sure it was unoccupied, before going back and making his call.

"Yes," answered a voice at the other end.

"I'm almost ready to go here, although I can't give you any specifics until tomorrow evening," Byrd stated.

"Why is that?"

"There's more study and work to be done at this end if this project is to run smoothly without a glitch. There's no place for sloppiness. Besides, positioning and timing are the keys to all of this, as I have already explained to you."

"I need more, what's the problem?"

"You know what the problem is—new boat, new plan. I've got to figure a way to get my equipment on that rig undetected. They're nobody's fool, especially out there. I can tell you this, it's going to happen as soon as possible. That bastard always attracts a lot of attention wherever he goes, it won't work in a crowd."

"Who does?"

213

"Captain Nemo! Why sic the girl on the mate?"

"I have personal reasons and they don't concern you in the least. Let's just say she's my little Black Widow."

"Black Widow?"

"She's intimately aware of the perils of unsafe sex." The voice at the other end paused for a few seconds, "When's our next contact?"

"Ah . . . same time tomorrow night, on the other line," Byrd replied.

"Very good. Your birthday present is now in Geneva."

"Good night." Byrd listened to the disconnect at the other end and held the receiver to his ears a few seconds before hanging it up. He grabbed the back of his neck and stretched it, and then brought his hand down holding it in front of his face. He saw that it was shaking.

20

Scott Byrd called Louis at the boat about nine in the morning asking for final directions to the estate of Alfredo Silva. When he arrived ten minutes later, Louis met him out front and escorted him around the side of the house to the dock. He noted that Byrd was carrying a duffle bag and one attaché case.

"Just set your personal stuff inside the salon, Scott. You'll be going to the hotel when we get there, anyway."

"No room for me on board, eh?"

"Nope. As you can see she s designed for two crew comfortably without cluttering up other areas. You'll be far more comfortable at the El Mirador."

"Whatever," Byrd replied looking the boat over as he stood at the teak transom at her stern. *Kind of narrow*, he thought, *looks rather plain*. He hopped into the cockpit and took a look around to see all the finished teak cleared in numerous coats of awl-grip on the bulkhead, concealed freezer and fishing station, and external trim around the house. The decks and covering boards were all fine-sanded and oiled. *She was fairly much a museum piece, a work of art*, he thought. No hard corners, but contours everywhere, pieces of hardwood fitted together in perfect joinerwork, the seams as fine as a human hair.

Her white hull held a bit of ice blue tint, and her topsides were a bone white. He studied the double doors to the salon, and then released the handle to open them apart. Inside, he found the same recurring theme, simplicity and elegance in design. Headliner trimmed in teak, two chairs and a simple couch facing a teak charting table. A small galley down a little gangway with

215

adjoining dinette, one stateroom and a V-berth, a head on each side of the boat. Ample rods and reels were stowed in their racks below the headliner in the salon and over the V-berth. Between the two stowage areas, the amount of tackle dwarfed the inventory on Frank's boat.

There was no television, just a modest stereo, and a small microwave visible in the galley. But all about, the beautiful hand-rubbed wood. It reminded Byrd more of a den than a modern boat interior, compared with the conspicuous opulence of Whitman's craft. He began opening cupboards and drawers, pulling out their contents and any materials he stumbled onto.

"Mr. Byrd, you are a guest on this boat as far as the crew is concerned, and this is our home for the week. If you need somethin', you ask and I'll try to get it for you. Louie has asked me to be respectful of the owner, and not have people ransacking his boat. Got me?"

"No, aah . . . not a problem. I'm sorry, Crafty."

"Then we understand one another."

Crafty fired up the generator, and switched the boat over to ship's power. A moment later, Byrd heard the first, then second of the main engines as Louis fired them up from the bridge.

"They seem much quieter than Frank's."

"They are. The boat has been repowered with ten-cylinder four strokes."

"Oh, I see," replied Byrd not having the slightest idea of what Crafty was referring to. Scoot laid his attaché case on the floor and followed the mate out to get lines and be gone. Louis watched and clutched her around on the dual action controls to assist Crafty to each piling, while Byrd coiled the electrical cord and hose before finally throwing the dock ends of each stern line into the cockpit. He stepped from the dock onto the covering board as Crafty was pushing off the last piling and they were free and going ahead.

Louis followed the channel close to the bulkhead of the

canal before merging with a larger channel leading them south and out to the inshore shallows. Byrd looked back in the boat's wake and didn't see an ounce of whitewater, even though he guessed the speed to be five to six knots. The whole feel of this boat was tight, quiet, and smooth. He had to admit, it was impressive. More like riding in a Rolls than a Chevrolet; this vessel seemed finely tuned like a Swiss watch. He assumed she was also quite maneuverable.

Louis passed by a large red nun bouy, and proceeded to put the Whiticar up on a plane. He settled the boat down to about 1900 rpm, and she was still doing about 23 knots.

"Very nice craft you got here, Louie, I'm impressed."

"She's a good girl, Scott."

"What's her top end?"

"Depends on her fuel load, maybe 28 . . . 29 knots."

"Full?"

"Twenty-seven . . . maybe," answered Louis now looking over at Byrd.

"That's respectable. How far to Havana?"

"Havana is about 125 nautical miles at a course of 220 degrees, true. Be there in about five-and-a-half—six hours. You need to get up with Crafty and get your head screwed on about gaffin' these fish. We're gonna need you to be there and be ready."

"Not to worry, Cap. I'll be there when you need me. Check you later."

Louis scan of instruments and gauges told him all was doing well at this point. This series of the German diesels had acquired a good reputation, and this pair were just approaching a flawless 1,000 hours. He was starting to relax a little and pull away from his suspicions. He was going to enjoy his fishing down there this week, and be quite glad to return home when it was over. Hopefully, their efforts might be rewarded with some money in his pocket for his daughter's future.

Much of the wind of the last two days had fallen off to a light ten to twelve knots. He was glad for the moderating weather actually. Even though there was a little leftover ground swell, they had it right on their tail, and the ride was invigorating. The *Nina Mia* was eating up the following sea beautifully.

The forecast was for the weather to hold and remain out of the northeast for the next few days, and that would be just fine with Louis. Those were the best possible conditions for his little fishing hole, and they would check it out first thing tomorrow. Never being one to wait, Louis preferred to take his chances early, as calm weather could persist across the area the entire week.

The old captain turned on the autopilot and walked to the rear of the bridge as he stretched. He leaned over to see his mate twisting some more wire leaders and bait rigs, showing Byrd some of the things he expected him to remember. Part of the program was to catch fresh bait each morning in the 'bowl' itself. Louis knew others would be getting fresh needlefish and bone-fish, both Cuban favorites for marlin. He on the other hand, pre-ferred fresh cero mackerels, as they were usually abundant in the thriving bait chain inside the subsurface canyon.

When the ceros were located, he would have Crafty put out small spoons, sometimes with trolling leads, on medium spin-ning outfits. Slow trolling with a chum bag to boot, they were usually most cooperative in taking the beaded spoons. The mack attack, it was beauty in simplicity. Not only was the bait of fresh scent, firm and able to hold up longer, it required minimal sewing and preparation when rigged with a 'pin rig.' It was noth-ing more than a glorified ballyhoo rig, where the spur was extended through the head of the bait, out and around and retwisted to the wire leader ahead of the fishes nose. The bait skipped, slapped or frapped, and swam exceptionally for a much longer period of time. Replacements could be rerigged in a mat-ter of seconds, more bait could be fished for simultaneously at any time. It was a good system, and it had paid off for him and Crafty in this tournament twice before.

By 3:00 in the afternoon they approached within 15 miles of the largest island in the Caribbean, its mountains breaking out of the haze to the south. In spite of all the propaganda cranked out by the two governments, Louis knew that Customs and Immigration would be quite lax for the event, and expected the international spring tourism on the island to be in major motion. Canadians, Germans, the English, and many other Europeans would be crowding the hotels and streets, doing the usual things that tourists do.

They would enter Havana harbor, top off at the city dock, then take a right down a few miles of man-made canal, where the Hemingway Marina complex was located in the province of Santa Fe. Louis fully expected not to be able to recognize the place. He had heard much about its recent renovation.

There they would be assigned their dockage, 'side to' on the long bulkhead, along with the forty or so other boats entered in the tournament. For the first time, it was a fifty-pound line class tournament, everything to be killed and brought to the dock. The angling team would score a point per pound for every marlin and sailfish brought in, but the fish would be eaten and there would be no waste. The Cubans had a taste for the billfish.

It was not the time of the year for the big fish to be there. They usually arrived in August and September at the waning of the tradewinds' cycle before the continental weather started hitting the island from the northwest. There would be more fish during the spring, but of a smaller size class. However, fish taken on the lighter tackle might include a 400-500 pound fish on any given day. And always when speaking of blue marlin, the point has been made often that they could be anywhere, anytime. Home is where their tail end is.

In the few times that Louis had fished the event, he recalled that most boats usually worked west out of the harbor, rather than his easterly direction towards Matanzas. This time of year, nearly all the fishing was done in depths inside of 200 fathoms or within a few miles of the coast. This gave even more significance to unique structural peculiarities present on the immediate coastal edges.

He had been educated about his old honey hole years ago by Hemingway's old captain, Gregorio, who had described the undersea canyon as shaped like a horseshoe, with an average depth of fifty fathoms. About two square miles in area, the 'bowl' was a unique cut into the submerged coastline of continental shelf. Surrounded by bounteous reef structures and coralheads, the canyon's walls ascended straight up to the surface to depths as shallow as a few feet.

The only safe entrance into the canyon was on its offshore side. With the exception of its bending 100-yard wide channel, the entire length on its northern boundary was guarded by dangerous, unnavigable reef. Lining up two ranges at their intersecting points put you right at the front gate, where it was less than a quarter of a mile wide. At two other points, dangerous brown bars of rock and coral reef penetrated far into the narrow channel.

From the air it might have appeared as a blue hole or volcano, or perhaps a cup with a chip out of its side. Whatever may have formed it, is pure conjecture. Many have tried to find and fish it, some with great success. However, numerous boats have suffered damage in their search, some having been lost. It was without question, one great fish trap where many marlin came to gorge on the teeming schools of bait, stacked up within its cavernous undersea walls.

To the few that have successfully fished it, the confluence of currents in and around the structural feature required constant attention. Changing tidal conditions were constantly shifting the sea life around the inner structures. Water movement was affected by both inshore and offshore currents. The 'down' inshore current sets westerly, the offshore Gulf Stream to north-east. As rich a fishing ground as the 'bowl' is, it is often a tough area to get a good read on. An inattentive mariner could find himself on the rocks in seconds.

The *Nina Mia* had her yellow quarantine flag half masted on the right outrigger halyard, when she pulled in behind another U.S. documented sportfisherman from Key Biscayne, Florida. It was another 65-foot Hatteras with an enclosed bridge.

As the three men were tying her off, they were approached by a few uniformed soldiers who greeted them with wide smiles. Louis pointed to the cleats on the bulkhead, and shrugged his shoulders looking down at the soldiers, "*Hola.*"

They all responded with thumbs up signals, and yelled back, "Okay man, okay man." One man pointed to a fairly new power post, and pointed to himself as if to say, *give me your cord and I'll plug you in*. They did. They were not getting a full 240 volts, more like 215, but it would be all right for a short time.

Louis asked one of the soldiers in Spanish about clearing customs to which he replied, "You are here, no? Fine. They need you, they find you. We tell them you are here. Who is angler, please?"

"Senor Frank Whitman."

"*Si, por pesca, esta bien.* One of the soldiers made a motion as if lifting up a fishing rod, "*Sans cocho? Heffe sans cocho?*"

All the soldiers began to laugh.

"What in the world are they jabbering about," asked Byrd.

"It means 'without head'. Like in getting skulled by a fish, you know, when the bait comes back without a head," Louis explained.

"So that's it."

"That's it. *Una parada de taxis?*"

They pointed down the way about 100 yards.

"You'll find a cab down there, Scott. Why don't you grab your gear and get settled in your hotel. Make sure the reservations are all set for the boss."

"That works for me. Sure you don't need me around here?"

"We're fine. Louis called to the soldiers now walking away one last time, *"Puedo mirar,"* Louis spoke as he waved his arm in front of his chest.

"Si, you may go where you want, go where you want," they smiled and continued on their way.

"Pretty casual, Cap. Don't look like anyone's too worried about security around here. You ready to give her a squirt? I've got some riggin' to do."

"You go ahead and start twistin 'em up, I'll take care of the boat."

"Thanks, Louis, appreciate that."

"De nada, amigo."

21

In the early evening, Louis and Crafty had taken a taxi into downtown Havana in search of a restaurant they had come to love. It was still there, only bigger and more crowded than ever. They had pigged out on grouper in vanilla rum sauce and black beans and rice. Louis scanned the check briefly as they downed the rest of their beers.

"I need a walk bad ol' boy."

"Reckon I could use one too, Crafty. Might should just go down to Frank's hotel, and see what the latest is."

"Let's go."

They headed that way, along the beach promenade where young couples and tourists had congregated for decades. Many people were out and about, smiling and shopping in the early evening. The breeze was light, the air comfortable, and the light of the day fading fast in the western haze.

"I don't believe it's gonna blow tomorrow, she's layin' down all the time," Louis observed looking skyward. "We'll still head up in that direction and take a look at things anyway."

"Suits me. If its going to be fair and balmy all week, we might as well go up and see what your honey hole looks like. See if she's holdin' and all."

"Yeah. You know, Crafty, these people here don't look too stressed out for all the bad press the place gets. Things really ain't changed as much as I would have figured. Still, see the soldiers everywhere."

"Yeah ya do. You know what Louis, they got a few shortages of stuff here, but the tourons all look happy and nobody's botherin' them at all."

"That's what gets me. The military seems more interested in their own walkin' the streets, than the foreigners. It's like everybody's talkin' to one another and happy an' all, but the Cubans are talkin only to themselves. They just ain't mixin' with nobody."

"I heard that. The bad fruit of a dictator's paranoia."

"Something like that."

They entered the canopy and glass doors of the El Mirador Hotel, strolling up to the front desk where a uniformed man was talking on a house phone.

"*Señores.*"

"*Habla usted ingles?*"

"I speak English, sir, how may I help you?" He did very well.

"We're expecting the arrival of Mr. Frank Whitman in the morning, and just dropped by to see if there have been any messages either for or from him."

"Yes, of course." The well dressed Cuban began the paper search, through the register and room boxes to his rear, and then suddenly cocked his head a little with a puzzled look. "No, Mr. Whitman himself has not checked in, but I do show a Mr. Byrd has checked into one of the three rooms. Yes . . . Mr. Whitman has reserved 506, 507 and the penthouse suite 1001. Mr. Byrd is in room 506. Would you care to leave a message?"

"Could you try his room?"

"You may use the house phone over on that wall," replied the desk clerk, pointing across the lobby.

Louis walked over to the lone wall unit and dialed the room number, letting it ring ten or so times. "Nobody home," droned Louis as he hung up the receiver and started rubbing his sunburnt lips.

Louis turned to Crafty. Both men scanned each other's eyes, as they waited for the other one to first provide the answer. Louis grabbed his mate's arm and led him off away from the counter. "This is going nowhere, I think we need to get our butts

224

back to the boat right now."

The pair walked outside and immediately had the bell captain hail them a taxi. The driver dropped them off at the same cab stand from which they left earlier, and gave them a card to insure that he would be their personal driver for the week. There was nothing that he could not provide for them. Louis said thank you and good night. They quickly walked down to their slip.

Another boat had since pulled in behind them, a sixty-three-foot Stryker, hailing port, Galveston, Texas. The crew was on go, the Captain moving around down in the engine room, as the mate rigged his offerings under the blaze of four halogen spreader lights.

"Good evening, man," Louis opened, "you guys here for the tournament?"

"That's right," the mate replied from the cockpit as he continued on with his rigging, not looking up at the pair.

"Seen anybody hangin' round that Whiticar in front of you tonight?"

"There's a dude on there right now, just got on her a little bit ago."

"Thanks." Louis slowed himself down considerably, halting Crafty as he did at the arm. They walked up along side the *Nina Mia*, and saw Byrd enjoying a drink in the salon. He had spread the large sailing chart over the small teak table causing it to run over the sides. On the chart were a parallel rule and compass spreaders, the basic tools of navigation and plotting. The situation appeared harmless enough, and stalling outside would only give the man more privacy. The captain and mate jumped aboard their vessel.

Byrd beat them to the bulkhead, and opened the double doors. "Come on in boys. Frank and I have a bet going, that I'm quite sure only you two can solve."

Louis took a casual look around, "Yes, Scott."

"I say you'll be heading to the west Wednesday morning,

Frank feels you'll be on an eastern tack. Where's it going to be, Captain?"

"How did you find your way in, Scoot?"

"You guys know you always stick the boat key in the second tackle drawer. East or west, Cap?

"East, as far as I know right now, Scoot."

Byrd shook his head a little, and walked over to Louis and slapped him on the back with a big smile. "Louie, you just lost me a Ben Franklin. Would you show me where we're headed. You must have some secret numbers in that little black book of yours?"

"Aaah . . . right in here someplace, I reckon," Louis made a circle with his index finger covering an area of a hundred square miles.

"Not very precise now are we, Cap. Show me where we'll be fishing, Louie."

"Aw, Byrd, if you must know, right here, offshore this point of land that juts out a mile." Crafty took the spreaders and pinpointed a position about ten miles east of the 'bowl.'

"Thank you, mate, what would be the Lat-Lon there . . . let me see . . . 23 degrees—"

"Scoot, when did you start to care, I'm curious?"

"Oh, I don't know, Crafty. I feel like I let you boys down at Chub, for some reason, I'm only trying to learn something here. 81 degrees west . . . "

"Well, if you want to help, be there with the steel when he's jumpin' at the back of the boat. Louis and I will take care of the rest."

"Absolutely." Byrd finished his interpolations and entered them in a small black book of his own. He looked at the crew that was studying him and smiled, "I always see you guys keeping a log on your fishing, thought I might start doing the same. I want to be ready when the time comes. As ready as you maybe."

"You said Wednesday morning, Scoot. Has there been

another change in plans?"

"Yeah, Cap. Frank called me this afternoon to tell me he won't be in till late tomorrow evening. He sends his apologies for canceling out the practice day. Oh, and Mr. Wendt is going to miss the first two days."

"That's too bad, I guess," replied Louis looking over to a smiling Crafty. "What happened?"

"He twisted his knee falling in the shower, if you can believe that, Louie."

"Disappointed, Scoot? It seemed like you and old Wendt were gettin' to be pretty good friends," Crafty remarked, studying Byrd for some kind of reaction.

"What do mean, Crafty?"

"Oh, just runnin' and gunnin' around together over at Chub. What were you guys waiting on a couple of babes down at the beach Thursday night?" The mate flashed Byrd a wink of acknowledgment.

"Oh that. No . . . Adam's always picking my brains about Whitman. Part of his job to get to know the man better, that is what he does. Hell, I used to work for Adam, that's how I met Frank."

"Really."

"Frank made me an offer I couldn't refuse. Yeah, we've all known each other for some time."

"I hope everything is okay up there, and Mr. Whitman comes ready to fish," Louis offered with a big yawn.

"Nothing serious, Louie, he got derailed in Miami by his attorneys, he'll be here tomorrow night ready to fish out the week with us."

"Always the mouthpieces getting in the way, eh Scoot?"

"Crafty," Byrd chuckled, "they have a special talent for doing that."

Byrd left the salon to go outside into the cockpit, where he lifted the lid to the drink cooler. He retrieved a six pack of beer and returned, shutting the doors behind him.

"Man, it's hot tonight. Who's thirsty? I've managed to get my hands on a sixer of *Nacionale*; this is the kind."

"Break it out all around, Scoot, we'll hoist one to a good tournament," Louis ordered. One by one the young man uncapped one of the local brews, and handed a long neck to all present. "To the fish, may they like us this week!" Scoot took a big chug. Everyone followed suit.

"Very different from those clear Becks we've been working on, eh Louie," Crafty observed not letting the distinction get in the way of his drinking.

"Quite." Louis thought to himself. Louis had drunk many *Nacionales* in his youth here, and this was one thing that hadn't improved with the passage of time.

"Hey, Byrd."

"Yes, Crafty."

"What about the other man?"

"What other man would that be?"

"The third man in your meeting on the beach at Chub that night."

"Oh him. Fishing buddy of Adam's from St. Thomas, runs a big mother ship operation out of there. I guess he wanted to give Adam a calendar with his open dates this summer."

"In the middle of the night on an uncrowded beach?"

Byrd shrugged his shoulders and threw up his hands.

"Man, this place is alive, Louie, the women are everywhere and friendly as they could be. Adam and the boss are going to have a hard time choosing between amateurs and professionals."

"I suppose so, Scott. The place is rather well known for its nightlife."

"What about you guys, maybe you can show me around a little. What do you say? Crafty . . . the guys on the dock all say you have your way with the ladies. How was Cheryl by the way?"

Crafty winced as he stared at Byrd, "Nothin' to the story,

Scoot. Nothing at all."

Louis looked over at Crafty and shook his head, "Nah, not me Mr. Byrd. I kind of laid that down years ago, not really into it anymore. Maybe, Crafty will put you on a couple."

"Sorry, Cap, too much at stake here. It's gonna be all work and no play for this dog all week. Scoot, you're hawkin' on your own."

"Whatever. I need to rig Frank up with a first-class cigar connection. Got any ideas, Louie?"

"Here, take this card. He was our hack for the evening, said he could find you the best cigars around."

"Thanks, man, I appreciate that," replied Byrd stuffing the card in his shirt pocket. The three men made small talk for a few minutes as they discussed the better restaurants of Havana and its wide ranging nightlife. Louis briefly touched upon some of the fishing strategy they were going to implement the first day, before the yawns began to get the better of the three men.

"Well, guys it's time I returned to the hotel, the night is young, but it's been a long day for this guy." The younger man rose up and made his way out the salon into the cockpit, taking a slow step up to the covering board. He walked towards the bow before stepping on the dock at the breast cleat, where the vessel was level with the bulkhead. He walked at a brisk pace as he headed for the cab stand.

Louis stretched out in his chair for a good long time, and finished the last of his brew. "Crafty, could be we're makin' a big deal out of nothing here. All he's doing is what anybody would do before a fishing tournament. You know, where are we going, Cap? What are we pulling, what are the numbers? Pretty typical stuff."

"Maybe so, Louis, but somethin' just don't feel right to me. It's nothing I can see or reach out and touch. It's a feeling I just can't shake. I don't believe the Byrd's act."

"I'm glad you said that, Crafty, because that about sums it

up for me. I just wanted your gut reaction to all of this. It ain't the boss man either."

"Agreed. He's been level on the level, and a man of his word."

"Yup." Louis yawned again. "Long day for this old man as well. It's me and the Book and the bunk. We all ready for the day, Rad, in the event the plans change one more time," Louis quizzed his mate as he stared at the chart over the top of his reading glasses. "Crafty?" He looked over to see his mate slumped down in the chair, beginning to snore heavily.

I guess we both could stand to sleep in a little, Louis said to himself with a huge yawn. He could hardly make his way down to the vee berth.

It was about 1:00 A.M., when the man walked down the dimly lit bulkhead that docked the line of sportfishing boats alongside. He had on a dark pair of shorts and T-shirt, and wore a black baseball cap. He carried a black knapsack slung over his shoulder as he walked quickly past the line of boats.

All that could be heard was the constant overboard pumping of cooling sea water that circulated through the air conditioning system of each vessel. The man walked around any direct light and found all the vessels' interiors dark and turned down for the evening, that is until he arrived at the stern of the *Nina Mia.*

The man looked inside the boat to find a well-lit salon, and a man sound asleep in a chair. Wearing soft neoprene diving booties, he silently boarded the boat, and carefully stepped into her cockpit. He ever so slowly eased the two unlocked double doors open, just wide enough for him to slide through holding his pack bag behind him. He pulled a pen light from the satchel, stuck it into his mouth, and immediately killed the interior lights.

Grabbing the headliner rail for support he slowly stepped over the sleeping man's legs, and eased down the gangway in the direction of the crew's stateroom. He stole a glance at the for'd vee berth to find the door closed, but assumed the man inside was also quite indisposed.

He opened the door to the crew's cabin and set his bag down on the carpet as he went to his knees. Carefully, he lifted the bedding and mattress, bracing it up against the side of the hull with his shoulder. His hands and arms were now free to remove the access hatch on the frame of the bunk itself. Once lifted up and out, he set it aside, leaning it up against the closet door.

The small light now revealed the maze of machinery and tubular containers mounted within the bunk frame, that he knew were the guts of the watermaking system. The feed and high pressure pumps were mounted in the engine room, but the plumbing and membrane systems were chosen to be mounted here, out of the way, and immediately over the other equipment.

The intruder reached into his backpack and pulled out three different elongated boxes, marked *membranes, fragile*. All three containers bore the watermaker brand name and logo on the outside. He carefully laid and wedged the three containers behind the four long tubes, where they were somewhat hidden and out of view.

He set hatch, mattress and bedding back in place, straightening up everything, exactly as he had found it. He killed the pen light as he retraced his steps back through the salon, the dock lights providing just enough light to direct him around the sleeping man's legs. He carefully closed the double doors to the salon behind him.

Once off the boat, the man quickened his pace down the dock, checking all around for any sign of another that might be out. He saw no one. About 100 feet down the dark dock he chucked his backpack into the basin, and watched as it sank. He could start to relax now.

22

What a beautiful mornin', Louis says to himself as he slowly wades along his favorite flat. He looks down at his brown feet as they churn up the sugar sand as he quietly wades along in soft steps.

The mountains are like blue slate when the air is so clear, he says. Behind their crests, the clouds over the warmer Gulf Stream waters ascend upward forever into the royal blue. They drop their moisture like silver dust that might never reach the sea's surface.

It is so quiet here this morning, the blood rushing through my ears is like a roar. Except for the laughing gulls that is—they are complaining more than they are happy. Why is that, when they have all that they need given to them.

There is life everywhere from sea bottom to high flight. From within the sand he sees at his feet, he kicks up the numerous crabs for others. Many are on the flat this morning, and once again they must swim on their sides to eat at times.

"Where is my Bonefish?" he asks, as he gazes out across the brilliant pearl and aquamarine shallows. *If he comes, he comes.* No, he will come because the day is especially beautiful, and the color of the sea under the white birds' wings is even more brilliant than ever.

"See, offshore to the south where the sea is still warmer, the Man-o-war bird circles endlessly over the purple waters beyond the white curtain of the reef. He is happy for the free flight as he is being lifted up from the heating air currents."

The man raises his deep brown hands before his eyes and

sees that they are strong and youthful, and he is grateful that he has used them well and often in the fisherman's life. He looks to the island when he hears the young man's voice. He is there in front of the green hills, far away, but only for a moment. For now he is only a short distance before the man, and his father is there also. The teeth so white in the brown face of the smiling man.

His older brother is holding a glimmering fish still kicking in his grasp. The light and water dancing off its form as it struggles to be free. They are both waving and smiling at Louis now, but he sees that they are waving farewell. It hurts him in his chest so that he looks away.

His eyes lead him once more to the beautiful beach out on the point. She is there with the small girl he sees eagerly, playing under the palms at the water's edge. His heart fills with warmth and energy and he begins to wade towards her.

She is standing and waving him to come in, as the little girl teases and runs from the breaking surf before him. She is so beautiful, she has been his for all time. Her long brown hair whipping in the wind as always, in a rhythm with the palms. The sound of the gentle sea pulses softly around him, and is carrying him easily to her.

He is feeling so strong this morning, and his feet are quickening him through the lapping surf. He can see her clearly now, and his heart is pounding with such force he can hear it with his ears. No, she is not ebbing away, but entering the water smiling as she nears. She raises her arms to receive him in an embrace, and they are locked together in warmth and light.

From her eyes rays of light shoot out in all directions, from behind her beautiful face a glow emanates in a gold corona. She is speaking and he understands her, but her lips do not move. He hears her, she is saying to him, "All is well, everything is good." She embraces him once again, and turns to walk out from the sapphire water. He reaches for her, but she is too far away now, high up on the white beach. She waves back to him as she softly steps to the trees. She is not so bright now, and her form is shimmering, dissolving. She slips behind the shaded palms and is instantly gone.

Louis makes steps toward the beach, but his legs are heavy and he is gaining no ground. "Why is the beach farther away now," he shouts to himself. He is becoming very weak, and the deeper water is wanting to overtake him. Why not let it he asks, it is warm and inviting.

Why must I fight so. He flails his arms to stay afloat, but he is being pulled under, he will surely drown. He struggles harder this time, and he is shaken. He wrestles with the blackness and the points of blue and red lights flashing within it, as he tries to keep himself from tumbling out of control.

"Louis, Louis! Easy ol' boy, hey! Louis Gladding wake your ass up! It's Crafty, Louis, come on now!"

The old man sat up on the floor of the V–berth, and opened his eyes. Double visions of Crafty kneeling down before him, moved ever so slightly in a slow circle. He drew in a couple of deep breaths and things began to settle down a little. He had cottonmouth like he'd never had it so bad, "Grab me a Coke, will ya, Crafty."

"Here, Louis, I thought you might be needin' one."

The old man took a big swig, and then proceeded to rub his eyes to get them focusing again.

"Louie, it's almost 9:00. You ain't never overslept a day in your life since I've known 'ya."

"Yeah, well what time did you get up?"

"I just woke up fifteen minutes ago, I thought you'd be gettin' me up like always."

"We have been drugged, ol' boy, I'll guarantee 'ya."

"You think?"

"Strange dream I had . . . Crafty, my alarm clock is as good as a Timex. I know we've been drugged."

"How, when?"

"The beer, must have been the beer. I've drunk more *Nacionales* than ten men, and it had a funny taste to it. I don't know why, but it was done. Right now, Byrd looks like the prime suspect."

"I'm checkin' all the guns and ammo."

"Definitely. And, Crafty, try and remember if everything appears exactly how you left it. Make sure nothing's been jimmied or messed with."

"I got a pot of coffee going, I'll tend to all of that when I've woken up a bit. What if the Byrd man comes down to the boat?"

"Throw him off. I don't want him settin' foot on this rig, unless he's with Frank, and we're both on the boat. I don't know, Crafty . . . in some ways I feel like untying the lines and heading this girl back to the Keys right now. But I need a little more to go on. Out there, I know you and I can handle the situation, but in here . . ."

"Still want to go fishin'?"

"Yeah, I do! We got a chance to nail this thing, and I can set Julie up with her little nest egg."

"I'm still in, Cap, in fact, I'm more interested than ever."

"Well, we're fishin' then, but don't let that youngster stay inside. Load him up with stuff to do in the cockpit, make him rig ballyhoo, whatever. But keep him out there.

"All right, Cappy, I'll be on my guard."

"You do that, and watch your own self. Do your best to keep 'em thinkin' that we don't know squat. It's just another days fishin'. Got me on that?"

"Gotcha fine."

At five o'clock that afternoon, a freshly showered Louis and Crafty patiently awaited the arrival of their angler and second mate as they nursed a couple of Becks in the cockpit of the *Nina Mia*. As the rigging and other boat preparations had all been done by noon, the afternoon had been a time of introductions and reuniting of old friends along the dock.

The tournament kickoff cocktail party was scheduled to start at 6:30 over at the Hemingway Marlin Club where it was rumored that the Premier might make a token appearance. To be sure, there would be much food and even more booze consumed as the competitors would be read the IGFA rules they already knew one more time. The purse would be set up for the competition, each boat providing their proration to round out the bonus round. The talk on the dock was that this year it could approach almost half a million, U.S.

"There they are comin' down the dock, Louie."

"Does he look happy, Whitman that is," Louis asked as he restocked the drink cooler.

"I would say, looks ready to party."

The tall man waived heartily, as he strode way ahead of his aide, "What's shakin' you guys, are we ready to do battle?"

"I feel like we are, Frank, welcome to Havana," Louis beamed as he stuck out his hand. "We're rigged and ready for the morning, and got a belly full of fuel."

"Let's go party, men. I'm looking forward to meeting some of these guys."

"Let's do it. Crafty, why don't you lock her up."

"Done' Louis."

The cab dropped the four off at the club a little before six thirty, but they were anything but early. The din was loud and boisterous, with many getting a jumpstart on the evening's drinking.

A buffet offered huge shrimp and grouper fingers, with an array of salads. Fresh bread and appetizers of chicken livers and bacon rounded out the finger food.

Frank was certainly in his element as, he circulated among the crews and anglers. He was not without his own reputation, and many of the internationals had sought to meet the famous computer icon.

Louis could see that his boss was enjoying himself as he lead a group of Brazilian businessman in animated conversation, undoubtedly presenting a picture of the very latest coming out of Whitman Technologies.

The old captain spotted his mate enjoying a hearty laugh with Mike Say, the All Pro Hall of Fame running back for the New York Giants. Louis remembered him as an angler hard to beat, he had fished here every year since its beginning. Louis flashed back to that first year when he and Crafty walked away with the event, with Alfie batting .1000 from the chair. He caught everything he saw behind the back of the boat.

Louis could see the line forming behind the registration desk, as crew members, acting as agents for their owners, waited in line to get in the bonus round. Each was holding $10,000 cash, in a field of forty plus boats. Louis could see that Byrd was right up towards the front, eager to be done with the task.

Louis continued to slowly circulate throughout the room, content to sip on his beer and exchange pleasantries every so often. He didn't know that many people here, and he truly felt his years with this next generation.

A short time later, the four men regrouped to discuss dinner plans, and share any tidbits of information that arose from the practice day's fishing reports. There had been a good bite to the west, the fifteen or so boats out accounted for more than twenty-five fish.

"Cami's here, Louie. She didn't feel like doing the party tonight. She specifically told me to tell you she'll be ready to go in the morning."

"That's great, Frank." Louis cracked a genuine smile. "How's Mr. Wendt's recovery doing?"

"What a dufus. I've called him enough on it. I'll send the plane for him tomorrow night," replied Frank shaking his head a little.

The noise of an incoming helicopter was now attracting a

large crowd outdoors to a large open knoll and grassy area. Across the canal on an isolated tarmac, the double rotored craft was just setting down.

When the aging Cuban leader emerged from the copter, he walked over to the P.A. that had been quickly set up for him, and proceeded to welcome all the participants in Spanish. Two minutes later he was airborne.

As the crowd returned inside to resume their partying, a well dressed civilian with two accompanying soldiers, approached the Whitman party.

"Capitano Luis?" The Cuban statesman scanned the four faces for some form of recognition.

"I'm Louis," answered the old captain stepping forward with outstretched hand.

"Ah . . . *hola*," the Cuban smiled and enthusiastically pumped Louis' hand.

"Please come with me, Premier wishes to see you briefly, this way." The trio led the four men out of the room and into the lobby, where the civilian put his arm around Louis and turned to face the other three. "Capitano only, sorry."

"I'll catch up with you later, Crafty, back at the boat."

Whitman cracked a big smile, and was not taken back at all at the request. "Now why didn't I just see that coming, Scoot."

"Beats me sir, go figure."

"What?"

"Nothing, Frank."

23

The crew ran through their usual routine of engine room check and tackle preparation. Terminal tackle had been rechecked and striking drags set by scale on the dock. The engines were running and the shore power disconnected, when Whitman, Byrd and Cami arrived at the back of the boat at 6:45 the following morning.

"Louie, I'm pumped," Frank stated gleefully as he rubbed his hands together storming around the cockpit. "Crafty, those spinning rods the ones for catching the bait?"

"They be the ones, sir. They'll produce a fresh-caught bait spread, provided that the ceros cooperate with us. It's easy, we just catch the bait as we go, replacing the frozen variety with the good stuff. You'll see."

"Sounds like a winning combination to me. Whatever you guys would have me do."

"Crafty, where's a good place to stash all this video stuff, where it'll be out of the way for the time being?"

"Ah . . . why not stick it up top with Louie, Scoot."

"I'd rather not, it might get banged around. It's nothing, I'll just shove it in the corner of the salon."

"Fine."

Whitman walked over to Louis and put his arm on the Captain's shoulder, "How was your visit with El Presidente last night?"

"Brief, but sociable, Frank." Louis cracked a big smile, "He wanted to know who I was fishing with, and I told him all about 'ya."

Whitman's face lit up in a big grin. "I just wanted to say one thing to the captain of this vessel before we got started."

"Yes . . ."

"Thanks for it all, Louie, I'm just glad to be here. There aren't many like you left in this world anymore. You're the one who made it happen, and I am forever grateful for that fact! I hope I don't let you down, and that I can do some good for the team. I promise to give it my all. But I'm a mighty happy man, even if we don't catch another one. I've learned an awful lot from you and Crafty, and I'm taking care of you two no matter what the outcome."

"Thanks, boss . . . we have come a long way. We've shown you a few things, but it's your love for the fish that's bringing out the best in 'ya. Now let's go find us a couple."

"I'm with you, Louis."

They pulled away from the dock five minutes later, and were soon cruising down the canal, heading east to Havana harbor. When they had cleared the harbor channel and made their turn to the east, Louis made a quick 360-degree scan of the inshore ocean. All the boats he was running out with had made a turn to the west. He did not have a boat within a mile of his position, although it gave him little comfort.

The sea was nearly flat this morning, with just a light wind rip on the surface. Even the swell had pretty much subsided, with only a gentle roll remaining. Louis took advantage of his privacy on the bridge and punched in his waypoint for the 'bowl,' on the LORAN C only. He knew Byrd had a better working knowledge of the GPS. *Why give the man any advantage,* Louis thought.

Then an idea tapped him on the shoulder. Ducking back down inside the helm station, he found the backside of the GPS receiver and loosened the threads on the coaxial cable connecting the antenna. He cracked a big smile to himself and went back out to scan and set the LORAN functions.

He watched as the LCDs blinked after pushing the customary route-enter, and the flashing 'aye-aye Captain' then appeared. Finally, the upper and lower windows came into view supplying the captain with the information he asked for from the compunav mode. The waypoint was 34.6 nautical miles, bearing 91 degrees. In the other window was a graphic representation of the rhumb line, and the cross track error of the boat's progress.

Louis took a quick look down in the pit and saw Byrd sitting on a cooler trying to sew a mackerel, apparently under some duress. Frank was in the chair, gazing out to sea, and his mate was nowhere in sight. He called down to Byrd, "When you get done there, make sure you take a file to those gaff hooks, understand me?"

"Yes, sir."

Louis didn't want to see Scott Byrd on the bridge all day. For the first time he could remember, he powered up the radar during his fishing time and watched as the unit counted itself down from two minutes of warmup. When it was at zero, he hit the transmit key, setting the range at 12 miles. Only one target came into view, a long blip representative of a large ship. It was offshore and northeast of him behind the horizon a little. He looked to the north and picked up the supertanker moving to the northeast with the Gulf Stream current. The unit was working well, and that was good.

"Morning, you." She was just peering at him over the deck from the side of the bridge. This boat had no ladder leading up top, just steps through-bolted on the port side of the superstructure.

"Hi, Cami, how's everything by you?"

"Okay," she sighed, "I'm just burnt out tired, Louie. I'll come up when the action begins to heat up. I'm planning on needing my rest till then. Good luck."

"Thanks. Take it easy for now, gonna be a long day." Louis

briefly thought about her statement, but soon waived himself off. He checked his progress to the waypoint, noting time of arrival in thirty minutes. Once there, he would dead reckon a course due south for one minute, before lining up on a range where an inshore rock stood directly beneath a dip in the ridgeline of a mountain. A quick jog to port was required for the last 100 feet at the western side of the cut. Louis had personally known of three vessels that had cleaned their bottoms on the subsurface coralheads and brown bar that extended southeast into the channel at that location.

Given good light conditions and light penetration, the darker blue water entrance could be easily 'read' against the reef shallows by the experienced mariner. However, under severe glare, or the zero contrast gray of flat light conditions, the cut was extremely treacherous, and not very forgiving. To not know the land ranges that marked the entrance, was to not know it at all.

The *Nina Mia* closed to within a quarter of a mile of her outer waypoint of the channel leading into the 'bowl'. Louis had decided to leave it on his starboard beam so as to approach it from due north. As he neared the coordinates, he scanned the inshore and all looked familiar to him.

Without warning, there was Byrd coming up the outside steps. He walked up to Louie's left, "Thought you might need some extra eyes up here, Captain. Hey, you forgot to turn on the GPS," noted the man as he bent over and hit the power button.

Unfortunately, the time of signal acquisition these days is brief due to the total network of satellites now available in the skies. In a matter of moments, the little box was spitting out Lat-Lons.

Louis felt like throwing the man off the bridge, but maintained his composure as best he could. He would now attempt to execute the rest of his plan. He watched as Byrd wrote down the coordinates in his log, entering a pair about every twenty seconds. The inshore bar and coralheads that protruded into the channel lay only a hundred yards ahead. The captain watched as Byrd dipped his head to enter the next longitude, and then Louis quickly hit the recall button. The LCD now flashed to indicate a recall mode had been selected, and a small lamp over the RCL had remained lit.

"Scott, go down into the helm and check our GPS antenna feed at the back of the unit, quick!"

Byrd looked at the flashing LCD of the GPS and dove quickly through the access door. Louis encountered his reef and made the subtle dodge to port and back to starboard.

"Got it, the coupler was loose," replied Byrd backing his way out of the small door. He looked over at the GPS screen to see the familiar steady numbers of Lat-Lon. He entered the first pair he saw in his notebook, and continued in like manner until Louis officially announced that they were all the way inside the canyon.

"Thanks for the help up here, Scott, I don't want that GPS actin' up on us. Better go down below and give Crafty a hand, we'll be fishing shortly."

"You got it, Cap."

Louis watched him descend into the cockpit from the steel steps on the side of the house. He observed the young man as he tapped Crafty on the shoulder, his inexperience around the cockpit readily apparent. But in Louis' mind, the jury was still out on who the real Scott Byrd was. Louis found him to be an increasingly 'hard read.' He did not intend to underestimate Whitman's lieutenant.

He returned his gaze to the radar screen for a few sweeps, and no targets appeared within its rings. It showed only the shoreline to the south within his selected twelve mile range.

Calm down Louis, he drilled into himself, *go fishing, nothing out of the ordinary has happened yet*. Rather than feeling completely apprehensive, he found himself to be waking up to the task at hand. It was downright stimulating, he hadn't felt quite like this since the war.

So Louis relaxed a little and laid down his outriggers, taking the teaser reels out of gear for his mate. He knew the area and how to fish it, how long and how far he could travel on any one trolling tack. Depending on the bottom contour itself, he could almost tell you his position, in what part of the interior structure you were, relative to the opening out to sea.

From the ambient currents he could usually pinpoint where the greatest concentrations of bait would be found. More importantly, how best to make a presentation into those areas. At times he felt at a disadvantage, because the great supply of bait often worked the mood of the fish against the angler. *Who fights for a seat on an empty bus*, he would say to himself. But there were particular constraints put upon the fish within the canyon structure that did restrict the fishes' ability to maneuver. Often it favored the fisherman to better work the fish once it was hooked up.

There was no experimenting today. Crafty had given him a bait spread of four Spanish mackerels. Louis could troll as slow as four knots, or as fast as eight, depending on the action he wanted to impart on his spread. For now, he was in a compromise at a little over six knots, with a wake nearly clear of white water.

Between and underneath the two flat lines, lay the weighted spoons designed to attract and hook the slightly larger cero mackerel. A dozen 'pin rigs' lay hanging on the side of the fish box ready to use when the Ceros came in over the side. Half the rigs had 12/0 hooks, the rest 10/0, all were rigged with #12 leader wire.

The mate knew piano wire was going out of fashion with many of the younger mates around the game, but he simply felt he was giving up nothing here. The density of the wire swam the baits far better, and allowed them to sink much quicker than the mono. But through it all, the mate would always argue to himself over the merits of evolutionary theory. Were all the fish that we used to catch on wire less savvy? I think not.

After an hour of trolling and hunting, Louis had found ample evidence as to the bait supply in his fishing hole. Good stands of the mackerels he was looking for lit the color machine up in the entire northeast section of the bowl. There were some balls of microbait subsurface in the same vicinity, probably glass minnows that would soon be the target of the feeding mackerel. Right now it just wasn't happening.

Louis checked his watch, 10:45. He guessed that when the tide turned and established itself on the flood stage, things would begin to get going. Louis was distracted by a subtle dimple on the calm surface off his port side, and made a turn into it with the sun at his back. It was a retreating school of juvenile blackfin tuna, no more than ten inches in length. Just then the right spinning rod bowed over, and Crafty sprung into view to retrieve the catch. It was one of the blackfins, not much larger than the outstretched hand of the mate. The eye of the young fish was oversized and larger than would be normal for an adult specimen.

"Cute little guy, Cappy," Crafty held the fish like a pack of cigarettes for his Captain to view, "should we be thinkin' live bait?"

"Not yet. If they were gettin' worked around by anything down there, I doubt if he would have bit. Let's give the tide a chance to push in here, I'd rather try trollin' for right now." He motioned for his mate to come to the bridge.

Crafty flipped the baby tuna back into the sea and reset the trolling spoon before resting the rod in the transom holder. He walked to the side of the wheelhouse and climbed up to the bridge.

"How's things lookin' down there, Crafty, everything where it's supposed to be?"

"Looks in order, Louis. The guns are in their regular spots, and are loaded. The ammo is there and checks out. I'll be dog bite if I can find anything out of the ordinary."

"Did 'ya check that stuff Byrd brought with him?"

"Yup. Looked straight up to me."

"All right. This is drivin' me crazy, maybe it ain't gonna happen. I still feel like takin' her home, but I can't talk myself into it without something more." Louis drew in a big breath and sighed. He scanned the radar for a few revolutions, and found no targets.

"How's it look down there, we got the bait under us, Louie?"

"Oh, yeah, plenty showin', of all kinds. I think they'll do business here in a little while. That kid stayin' out on the deck?"

Crafty walked to the rear of the flybridge, and peered over into the pit. "Yeah, he's been outside since we left. Sharpening the gaffs right now."

"Am I crazy, ol' boy?"

"No, Louis, just a scared old man." They both laughed.

"Well, Cap, at least we got Wendt out of our hair for a little while."

"Huh? You already backed into him once by accident, I wouldn't count him out for a second, Crafty. He could easily smell from 1,000 miles away."

"Ya think?"

"I know. All right, let me see if I can put ya' on one."

Crafty made his exit back to the cockpit, while Louis continued to troll his tight circles in and around the large stands of fish that filled the screen of his color sounder. Maybe the sea conditions are becoming too nice, Louis lamented quietly. There was just enough breeze to ripple the water's surface, and no more.

Then, as if someone threw the switch, the mackerels began to feed and push the glass minnows to the surface. There were rolling and flipping fish everywhere, darting around on the minnows. The terns and other shore birds had appeared out of nowhere, dipping and diving at vulnerable minnows and pieces left. The bite was on, except for the boys on the *Nina Mia*.

"Burn the cigar leads, Crafty, it's all on top."

"Right." In half a minute, the two spoons were now cutting a slight wake, streaming a hundred feet behind the boat. Crafty had pinned both flat lines into the short riggers to clear out the alley for the spoons. You couldn't keep the cero mackerel off the rigs now.

"Byrd, fill that bucket with sea water, and crank in these macks. Try not to hurt their mouths and cheeks when you dehook 'em, and slip 'em head down in the bucket. Get going!"

"Right. "

Crafty had the first bait up and in his hand, tossed it into the bucket and reset the spoon. It immediately bent over, and he cranked in a larger fish than before. "Got the program, Byrd?"

"Yeah, man." He was into it now, moving back and forth between rods, storing up a growing cache of fresh bait in a pair of five gallon buckets.

The mate reached for his first rig, and lined up the long spur with the point of entry on the fishes' nose. Where the bend of the hook lined up on the belly, he poked a hole right there. He ran the hook behind the gill and into the body cavity until the point could be cleared through the hole and out. He then straightened out the leader, and poked the spur through the top of the head in front of the eyes where he had originally lined up the spur. Creating a small loop, he brought the spur's tag end down the bait's nose and made a second twist of the wire to unite it with the rest of the leader.

The rig was now secure, but needed a little fine tuning. He grabbed a sewing needle, and a premade loop of dacron, and with one reef knot each, cinched the gill plates, sewed the fish's mouth shut, and poked the eye socket to complete the preparation of the bait. The complete process took less than a half minute.

Crafty knocked his left rigger out of' the pin and reeled it in,

247

replacing it with his fresh caught cero. "How many we got now?"

"Half dozen."

"Good, keep 'em comin'."

"I like it Mr. Crafty, I like it."

"It's worked before, Frank, let's hope the fish like it."

For the next few minutes things went at a quick, machine-like pace for the journeyman mate. He was now in the process of changing out the final right rigger mackerel, putting the finishing touch to his presentation. As in the previous three changes, Crafty flexed each fresh caught bait by hand back and forth at the tail, until he heard the unmistakable crack of their snapping spine. They would now swim flawlessly, and were ready for the ocean.

When he was satisfied with the placement and look of his brand new spread, Crafty returned his attention to rigging the rest of his pin rigs and placing the fifteen or so new baits on ice. *They looked good back there*, he thought to himself, satisfied. Had they had the cooler space to properly brine and prepare the bait for the next few days, they could have caught all they wanted. But they had already prepared bait. Fresh is fresh, and no other. So, when they had their fifteen fresh caught rigged baits on hand, they put the spinning rods away.

Louis moved off the center of the mackerel activity to its fringe on the northeast side, an area proximate to the entrance of the underwater cove. He would now proceed to troll laterally, across the opening's eastern side, in and out from the deeper center to the bottom that rose higher as you trolled to the east. He would always work in this manner at this location, at right angles to the fishes movement, in and out across the subsurface highway. Why? He didn't know. But that's when he saw the fish and got the bites. That much he knew.

Louis was peering into his color machine watching the ocean floor ascend upward, and was preparing to initiate another 180 degree turn back out, when the voice from behind startled him.

"This is cool," Byrd observed, once again paying Louis another visit up on the bridge. He could see that he might have caught Louis a little off guard. "I'm learning some good stuff here, Cap."

"That's inspiring, Scott. But what if we get jumped by the man in the blue suit right now, and you're up here out of position. I want you down below for the rest of the day, you've got a lot of ground to make up."

"You're right, Louie. Here I go again bothering the Captain, when I should be paying attention to Crafty's instructions. Now what's wrong with the GPS?"

"I tend to rely on my LORAN numbers when fishing in here, old habits die hard sometimes, Scott. I shut it down for awhile, we can live without it."

"I'm tracking our positions for Frank, I think he would prefer to have it on. Unless, of course, there is some reason for your not letting it run. Is there a problem with all of this, Captain Louie?"

Louis, seething underneath, turned the GPS back on, its functioning returned. Byrd made his way over to the side steps to go down, "I'm glad it's working all right. Wouldn't it be just like a boat to have that thing malfunction at just the wrong time."

"I reckon," Louie replied not looking up from his screen.

24

By Crafty's standards, each spread could be pulled for an hour and no longer. It was now 2:00 and they were just going into their third fresh changeout. They had not raised a marlin all day, in fact, had not had any kind of bite outside of the mackerels.

Crafty began putting out the spinning rods once again to try for a few more fresh macks at the feeding school's perimeter. Almost immediately, the ceros ceased their surface feeding. The terns and smaller shorebirds had vacated the scene, all that remained behind were a pair of man o-war birds circling high overhead.

"Be ready down there, Crafty, we have some company in here."

"See something, Louis?"

"Don't have to, he's around here somewhere."

Louis' eyes continued their roving scan from bait to bait, to the color machine, to the frigate birds in the sky, and back to the spread, looking unceasingly for something to connect with. The fisherman's eye, trained to scan and take in whole scenes and pictures, instantly seizing upon the disturbing element within those images, no matter how minute. That's what thousands of days at sea does for the senses.

Louis knew the currents and conditions were on the verge of changing, and the moment favorable for a shot. It was slack high tide, and the changing light conditions of the afternoon definitely favored the predator. Whitman had remained dedicated to his chair, leaving it only to void himself at the boat's transom.

When Louis had made his turn to work back out to the

deeper water, he engaged the autopilot briefly, and walked to the rear of the bridge. He looked down to see his mate standing directly behind the chair, scanning and squinting at his bait spread tracking across the clear indigo sea. He was searching for that silhouette of dark shadow, that color of bliss, the moment when the great fish come to visit you.

Byrd was sitting on the cockpit freezer, leaning against the corner where it joined the superstructure at the side of the house. He was on the nod, and not awake when the big blue one decided to stick its face up . . .

"On the right rigger, blue marlin! Louis bellowed as he ran to grab the boat back from the autopilot. There was precious little warning from the fish as it had moved nearly underneath the bait almost immediately, rising up from the depths rather than trailing the mackerel. The largest of the four baits at about six pounds, it was practically spanking the great fish on the nose.

As the huge marlin quivered and kicked its tail from side to side, the bill sliced and flailed away over the top of the bait and wire leader that it had managed to stay clear of so far. The marlin then cleared the water to his pectoral fins showing a monstrous girth, hued in platinum and deep blue slate. Only a hint of neon blue outlined the vertical bars on its side.

The Blue struck the cero with full force as it re-entered the sea, causing a tremendous lateral spray. The huge tail could now be seen swimming off to the right away from the spread. The force of the attack had knocked the fishing line from the outrigger clip but when the slack had been taken up, the broken mackerel twisted and spun as it once again was pulled along the surface.

Frank began to crank his destroyed bait faster back into the bait spread, striking the tip to pop the bait even more. The black submarine was suddenly back underneath the erratic bait.

"He's back on 'ya, Frank, but that bait is done!"

"I gotcha, Louie, I'm going to try and show him another one!"

Louis picked up on his cue and brought the boat to starboard, so as to allow Frank's maimed bait to pass on a line with the short right mackerel.

"Crafty, take this!" Whitman threw him the bad rod as he quickly charged over to the short right rod. He snatched it up in one motion, taking it out of gear and raising it over his head.

When Crafty had the mangled bait alongside the new bait, he reared back and launched it almost to the back of the boat, handling it up and over the transom. Frank studied the black form as it kept pace with his new bait, ten feet back and behind the now skipping, cero mackerel.

In the blink of an eye the great fish turned on the lights and freight-trained the mackerel on a dead run. Whitman had done well to anticipate, lowering the rod tip a split second before the marlin tore it from the short rigger in his strike. This time the fish inhaled the five-pound bait mackerel downtown, deep within its huge belly.

As the fish continued moving directly away from the boat, the reel's clicker was screaming and surging loudly from the kicks of the huge fishes tail.

"I know's he got it Crafty, what do you think!"

"Try him, boss, I agree with 'ya!"

Frank threw the drag lever up to strike and had immediate tension as the rod tip bent over. He leaned back against the rod bend in two deliberate motions to set the hook, driving the barb home wherever it had found flesh. Crafty put the belt on him from behind as Frank struggled to clip his shoulder harness to the two eyes on the reel.

Considering his great size and weight, the Blue was making one spectacular leap after another in the direction of the deeper water. He was clearing the water completely, windshield wiping with his head and bill as he landed, making an absolute mess out of the ocean.

"To the right and back!" Louis hollered down as he initiated a full bore reverse favoring the starboard engine that drove the vessel to the right. Crafty had managed to clear the left flat, and Byrd now had the left rigger coming in over the side.

The fish was still going crazy, kicking and thrashing away to the right of the boat's reversing track. *Perhaps he has ideas of finding the way out of here*, Louis thought, *I must talk him out of that.* He then pushed her stern around harder to the right by throttling up the reversing starboard engines near its maximum, while going ahead on his other engine. Once lined up on his intercept course, he resumed a straight line backing between the charging fish and front door.

Frank was gaining line in small amounts as the fish had not spent a great deal of time in the water and had been moving laterally with the boat since the fight started. The man was ecstatic, "What a fish! I've never seen a boat back down like this! It's outrageous, Crafty."

"Told 'ya, sir. Doin' fine on him, boss! Good goin' on that hookup."

But suddenly the 800-pound Blue made a sudden 180-degree turn of his own, reversing back across the boat's direction. Check that, he was now charging the boat on his belly, shaking violently and beating the ocean in his path into a white froth. His great high tail quivered frantically, now driving his dark form through the purple sea at 50 mph, his high brow pushing water like a torpedo.

"Crank! Crank! Crank on him Boss, he's comin'! Still comin'!"

The boat had since braked her backing at Louis' command, and was now trying her hardest to run off the fish to allow Frank to keep pace with the fish's charge. Even though the maneuver succeeded in eliminating most of the slack from the line, the sudden burst of acceleration from the great fish allowed it to overtake the boat's position.

"Still comin'! Still comin'," the mate yelled.

The fish came right into the back of the boat and rammed her transom with its three-foot bill. It was a glancing blow coming at an angle. The bill did not penetrate, and the fish tore off away from the boat in another burst of speed.

Crafty looked over the covering board at the transom, and studied the jagged two foot gash in its once perfect teak exterior. He started to laugh, "Oh, well. If I tell Alfie a fish did it he won't be nearly as mad. Stay with him, Boss, if he keeps this up we may get a chance at him early. You hear that, Byrd?"

"Yeah, mate. I heard you."

"Gaffs taped and loaded?"

"Yeah, buddy."

"Tether lines cinched to the rear cleats. Got your meat hook out?"

"Yeah."

Crafty left his post for a second and examined one of the fourteen-inch bite, double reinforced stainless steel gaffs, tucking the staff firmly under his armpit. "Like this, Byrd, this is your weapon. Get over his shoulder and deep," Crafty demonstrated in a violent lunge. "Understand where I'm comin' from?"

"You've covered that, Crafty."

Frank's reel started to scream once again as the huge marlin made another high speed run across the rim of the canyon. So fast was he taking line, that Louis had to spin the boat around and go after him in forward up on plane.

As they began to gain back line and pack some spool, Louis resumed an aggressive backing with the marlin, now headed for the deeper water out in the middle of the 'bowl'. Louis was backing down hard enough to slop water over the transom, for his maniacal maneuvering had created confused wakes all over the ocean's surface. But he was necessarily keeping pace with the line as it angled tautly down into the

Blue a hundred yards dead astern of the reversing boat. In an instant, the descending line went limp as the *Nina Mia* closed on the great fish.

"Crafty, be ready, he's put a big loop in it. I'm not sure . . ." Louis studied the line intensely for a moment as he started to slowly pull away from it. He began turning the boat to port in a semi-circle, when he saw the bowed line sliding past his stern. Louis' eyes were riveted to that line as far down into the water as he could follow it. In another moment he saw the line rise up imperceptably from the darker blue water.

"He's comin' boys . . . right at us!" The old man roared as he buried the throttles ahead. A second later, the blue one was up on top charging the boat, now almost up on plane once again. Frank was beginning to gain back his rodbend, but overall the boat was not able to outrun the huge marlin.

"Here he comes!" shouted Crafty, "Got his heart set on whackin' us again!" This time the 800-pounder rammed the transom with enough force to penetrate clear through the teak and the double planked hull. The fish shook so violently in the next moment, he broke off the last ten inches of his bill leaving it embedded in the stern as he swam off once again. A very wide-eyed Byrd stared at the black souvenir for some time.

For the next hour and forty-five minutes the blue marlin gave a true account of its strength, agility, and heart, putting up a sustained, courageous fight. It had done so much jumping that its air sacks were almost assuredly now jammed with air. If the fish took to making a deep run, it might in fact kill it.

The marlin was just below the surface now, fifty yards behind the boat. It's four-foot-high tail swirled the sea as it kicked back and forth in a slower, though no less deliberate motion. The fish had tried valiantly to outmaneuver its foes of angler, mate, captain, and boat, but had been unsuccessful in gaining any upperhand in the relatively shallow 300-foot depths of the canyon.

255

The big blue was being somewhat cooperative now, finning on the surface, showing considerable fatigue in dull coloration of dirty gun metal and dark bronze.

"Let's give it a try," Louis hollered down as he began again to back down into the fish to present his mate the leader.

"Let's do it right this time, Byrd!" Crafty spoke to the man behind him without looking. He was leaning over the corner of the boat at its starboard quarter to give him a little extra reach at the wire now just six feet from his outstretched arms. Wearing his customary three pairs of cotton gloves, he finally got the wire in his first single wrap.

The fish was still thrashing on the surface, but the experienced mate had a good measure of its strength and was steadily gathering leader. With each spinning off of the old wrap, Crafty would gather new leader and draw the fish closer, discarding taken coils back over the side.

Byrd stood behind and to the right of the mate this time, ready for his cue to deliver the stainless steel into the shoulder of the great fish at the front of his dorsal. Byrd stared down at the thick hook of reinforced steel and at the sharp two-inch point as it glistened in the afternoon sun. He followed the rope from the detachable gaffhead, to the cleat and made sure there were no loops or snag that would invite injury.

With only the opposite side engine ahead, Louis was presenting the big blue perfectly for his mate. He was easily guiding the bow slowly into the marlin's path, causing the fish to plane and swim easily in the water off the side of the boat. Were the creature to get into the propwash, it could lose buoyancy and began to sink into the vacuum of the propeller blades.

Now a mere eight feet off the starboard quarter of the boat, Crafty was within one last wrap of leader in presenting Byrd with a target. The gaff man looked down at the dark form in awe, as it was the biggest living creature in the wild he had ever been so close to. He was hypnotized by its beauty and grace, but he was keenly aware of the quaking and uneasiness in his legs as he supported himself against the side of the cockpit's covering board. He looked over at Crafty and could see that even his strong body was being jerked around by the slightest movement of the great fish.

"Ready," Crafty quietly warned his gaff man. When the mate had taken his last coil, he instantly made a double wrap of wire in his right hand, righting himself a little more erect to bring the marlin in the final foot. The fish lay like a puppy on its right side, its huge eye rotating around in the direction of the two men. Two remoras freeloading on its back still hadn't let go of their wild ride.

"Well! "

"Now?"

"Stroke him!"

Byrd led the giant hook into the face of the fish causing it to kick, and jerk Crafty from side to side. "Don't flash it in his face, come over his back from behind the eye!"

The young man tentatively leaned over the side one more time, bringing the staff forward of the high pointed dorsal, and began pricking the fish with its point. The point eventually found flesh high up on the shoulder.

Suddenly, the huge fish caught its second wind, lighting up from head to toe. He attempted to turn away from the side of the boat, straightening Crafty's arm to its maximum. In a split second decision the mate knew he would have to dump the leader, or wind up stretching and popping the wire. He spun his wrist counterclockwise, pointing all his digits in a straight line toward the fish. The leader unraveled and cleared his hand, but the mate caught it and guided the rapidly accelerating wire overboard with his hands raised high over his head.

Crafty watched the fired up marlin kick hard straight away from the stern, carrying the protruding gaff head in its back. When the half-inch tether line became taut, the hook only held for an instant as the blue continued to swim down into the dark cobalt water of the afternoon. Frank had the fish once again to the rod, holding on with his stick held high, as the creature made his blistering run to the bottom.

"That's it, Byrd, you're done!" Whitman was furious, "Get down below, and don't come out until I tell you. You'll just be in the way, . . . now move!"

Byrd dropped the staff on the deck, walked right by Cami, and slammed the salon doors shut.

"Give him a break, Frank, he's doing the best he can," Cami shouted from her perch on the cockpit freezer.

"There's a lot at stake here, Cami, and I don't want him hurt, either. Go check on him, would you please?"

Crafty watched the blonde hop off her seat as she opened the double doors and stuck her head inside. After a brief inaudible conversation, she closed the doors and started to climb up to the bridge.

"What's he doin', Cami?"

"Nothing, Crafty, just layin on the couch takin a nap."

The mate turned his attention back to the fish which was still heading for the bottom taking line. In a couple of hundred yards he had achieved his mission, and the reel went silent. After a few moments there was a hard tug at the other end and a few yards of line pulled off the reel. Again. One last time, a tug and a few more yards. The angler and mate stood in quiet vigil, as twenty long minutes passed and the fish had not budged, apparently content to remain in a standoff. Whitman himself could pull drag from the reel, but stationary to the fish, there was little happening at the other end. He might as well have been hooked to an old car.

"Got a bad feelin' about this one, Frank."

"What do you think, Crafty? What's happening down there?"

"Well, sir, if the dive didn't kill him, he might have gotten tail wrapped in the leader on that straight run down. It would, of course, have the same effect."

"What's that?"

"I'm quite sure he's hurtin, sir, maybe dead. Shock or asphyxiation, it really doesn't matter," the mate appeared sullen and disappointed. "I hate it when you kill 'em the wrong way . . . Frank . . . back the drag way off for a minute."

"Crafty?"

"Don't worry. Just try it for me, can't hurt at this point."

Whitman slid his drag lever back to the midpoint between strike and free spool, and the line started to go out immediately.

"Back a little more off, and let it run out for a way, Boss. Let him have a couple hunnert yards." The spool rpms were now gaining speed as the fifty-pound line tore off the reel. "Now go back up where you were, Boss." Whitman threw the drag back up to STRIKE, but it did not completely slow the movement of the fish. The pair in the cockpit watched the line begin to travel up and away from the stern as it gave a clear warning that the Blue was surfacing fast.

"He's comin' up again, Louis, real fast!"

"We'll go on him as soon as he lets us," Louis shouted from the bridge. "I'm startin' back easy on him right now before he takes to jumpin!"

The old man put both engines in a slow but sustained reverse, giving his angler time to repack the slackened line. When the fish broke the surface he was no more than 150 yards dead astern. The big blue jumped twice, unable to clear the water this time. Its great mass required huge amounts of oxygen but his prolonged captivity on the hook was now stealing it from him. In final desperation, the great marlin thrashed and pounded the surface with all he had left in him before laying over on his side finning ever so slowly.

"Let's go boys, we got to work fast, we don't want him sinkin' on us," Louis shouted as he literally steamed right back on the rolling creature. Crafty had picked up the other fly gaff, instructing Frank to pack the line on the reel as fast as he could.

When they neared the dying creature, Crafty raised the staff over his head before lowering it and driving it deep into the shoulder of the copper colored marlin, the point finally penetrating into its heart.

For one last moment, the fish returned to its spectacular neon blue, its death painting great beauty for the final time. The sea was still, and the intensely pure spirit within the noble creature departed. Crafty mounted the other gaff hook whose bite had been stretched open by the fleeing fish before it pulled loose, and stroked it into the same area of the fish's shoulder. "Did 'ya see that gaff, Frank, double reinforced steel and that fish opened it up over two inches!"

It was now quiet on the bridge. Louis' job was over for the present, and the moment returned to him the sadness he had come to feel whenever he killed these beautiful creatures. He would just as soon meet the fish in another ocean tomorrow.

Crafty was now hauling the dead marlin to the corner of the boat. He cinched the gaff ropes short to the cleats, put one last meat hook in the lower jaw of the fish, wrapping its rope leader around it's huge bill a few times. The mate unlatched the tuna door at the transom, folding it back against the stern before hooking it to another eye to hold it open. He looked up to his captain and smiled quietly.

"Well we got our pound of flesh didn't we, Cami?"

"Yes, we did, Louie," she answered him softly.

"We might all have to work on gettin' that one in the boat darlin'."

Whitman gently set his rod in the chair holder and walked over to his prize in awe, laying his hand on the side of the lifeless marlin's head. He surveyed the nearly thirteen-foot fish from bill to tail as he quietly spoke, "Nice work, Crafty, we got that brute with a peashooter."

"For your part of it, Boss, you done a nice job on that fish. That was a fine hookup, and you stayed right with him for the rest of it. Byrd, I'm gonna kill that guy, if he doesn't start comin' round, sir."

"Not to worry, Crafty, he's done on this one. I'm sending him home on the plane tonight when it goes to pick up Adam."

The double doors to the salon suddenly opened with a loud crash. There stood Scott Byrd with an automatic rifle leveled right at their heads.

"I don't think so, Frank," the armed man replied.

25

Crafty stepped away from the fighting chair and stared at the young man, the mate's face in total disbelief at the sudden turn of events. The calmness in demeanor and voice, the intensity of Byrd's stare dispelled any notion he was anything but serious.

"Scoot, you'll jolly well do what I tell you if you want to remain in my employ. Understand me!" Frank was still studying the huge marlin, examining the broken off portion of bill.

"Step away from the fish, Frank, and do exactly what I tell you, if you want to remain alive."

Crafty tapped the tall man's shoulder twice, "Better get to it, Boss, Mr. Byrd is the man holding a rifle to our heads."

Whitman reeled around to face his aide with a look of amazement, as if he couldn't believe Byrd was a man capable of such an act of betrayal. He backed away from his prize and took a couple of steps to the other corner, his lower jaw had gone completely slack. Then the angler's cheeks started to redden, the words exploding out of him.

"Listen to me you little shit. I don't know what you're up to, but it isn't going to work. You've got no chance at all out here! If you have anything left in that polyp brain head of yours, you'll put that toy away, and forget all this!"

Byrd remained quite calm, a departure from his usual hyperactivity. "Frank, you're really boring me, and you will do as I say. You are not to speak unless spoken to."

"You ungrateful little—"

Byrd squeezed off a few rounds into the tall man's upper thighs, knocking him back into the covering boards. "Frank, you're not being a good boy. Crafty, get your captain's attention from where you are standing, please."

"Louis, we got a bit of a problem down here."

The captain had a second to check the radar sweep when he heard the shots rip the silence of the peaceful afternoon. He grabbed Cami and practically hurled her onto the bench seat in front of the helm station. He now had a target eight miles out and closing, although he probably had ten or so minutes before he could make a visual on it. He walked to the rear of the bridge, and now saw Byrd standing behind the chair with his breakdown carbine drawn on the two men in the far corner.

He felt a brief second of pity for Byrd, but was shocked and quickly put on alert now that his worst fears had finally been realized. He knew the gun had sealed the young man's fate, there would be no time for forgiveness, or another chance at life. Hearts could change, but guns were cold and objective. He had been there once himself, a long time ago. Only by grace, was he shown his ways, and led out of his own prison of personal darkness.

"Howdy, Captain, surprised aren't you? Take the boat to these coordinates, I'll be checking you with my own GPS. Do anything squirrely, and your mate is lunch meat. You and Cami stay on that bridge, and don't be throttle-jockeying. Get to it."

Louis punched in the coordinates Byrd read to him from his black book, and set the boat in gear to the waypoint he recognized from the morning run in.

"Crafty, cut that fish off!"

"Byrd, reconsider man, that's a half-million dollars worth of blue marlin! You're losing it, bubba!"

The young man stepped to the rear of the cockpit, and shot up the face of the dead marlin. "Not any more it isn't, ol' boy," Byrd sneered, "I believe that just disqualified that animal, he ain't IGFA legal now," Byrd took time to laugh a little, his smile leaving quickly. "Cut it loose, now! Just uncleat everything and let it all sink to the bottom."

The mate slowly uncleated all three ropes holding the fish to the side of the boat and hurled them overboard. He pulled out his sidecutters and clipped the wire leader, finally releasing the lifeless marlin to its natural grave.

"There is a large box in the salon, Crafty. Fetch it up and drag it out on the deck, no tricks." The mate went inside and saw the boat's weapons, minus ammunition, stuffed into the box, along with the flare gun and all the kitchen knives. He should have known all along and seen it coming. He was quite angry with himself. But the thought of getting a chance to kill Byrd kept him going and kept him cool-headed. He must come up with something to use as a weapon.

Byrd watched as the mate dragged the box out from just inside the salon doors. "Now chuck all that crap overboard. Let's go!"

Crafty slowly hurled the contents over the side, and finally the empty box itself.

"Very good. Now all your fishing knives, ice picks, gaffs, those billy clubs and that bait knife in your holster. Now! Toss those sewing needles while you're at it. Byrd looked at his portable GPS, and satisfied they were on target, pulled another nondescript black box from his vest. "Q1 . . . .Q2 . . . "

"Go ahead 2."

"Secured here, moving towards inter position. Target A has been shot, but is alive."

"2 . . . we want it clean!"

"Roger . . . proceed visually after ID."

"Check."

Crafty knew they weren't talking on regular frequencies, he had seen those radios before in the war. He and Louis had sensed the danger building around them all along, but through reason and a masterful acting job on Byrd's part, had greatly underestimated that potential. *A weapon*, he thought to himself staring at Byrd, *I need a weapon!*

"How far to the numbers, Louie?"

"Two-tenths of a mile, Scott." The old man checked his radar noting the target to be five miles and closing. Not a speed merchant really, but a vessel that was definitely running at speed to their position.

"Scott, why are you doing this," a resolute Whitman continued to dog his attacker. "You had the world."

Byrd laughed slightly, "All I had was your dirty garbage, Frank. Pure shit. You were so taken with self and the need for control, that you couldn't see what was going on all around you. I almost blew it a couple of times, but I learned something valuable from our great captain. Humility. Never let the selfish wants of the moment override the big picture."

"You're not well, Scott, you're having some kind of reaction or psychotic break. Put down the gun while you have a chance. We can work this out."

Byrd let a couple more rounds, one found Whitman's shoulder.

"Workin' our way up, Frank," joked the Scoot. "The next one goes in your head. Crafty, clean up that blood that our leader of men is drooling all over our teak."

Crafty opened the side cubby, and pulled out some sudsy ammonia. Something told him to look up to the roof of the small compartment, and there he saw Alfie's old lip gaff used for the many tarpon they had released alive. *It could be a formidable weapon if used correctly,* he thought. A fifteen-inch gaff with a three-inch bite, and it was always kept quite sharp at the point. *But when, . . . how, . . . what kind of chance would he get?* Right now he had to figure how to get hold of it, undetected by Byrd.

Crafty knocked around the other chemicals a bit and closed the door to the compartment. He spread the sudsy ammonia around the reddened teak, letting the washdown hose run over the area where Frank was standing to prevent any further staining. He made a few passes with the deck brush.

"Very nice, Mate." Byrd picked up his GPS, giving it a scan. "Should be here by my calculations, Captain, is that what you are showing?"

Actually, they had been there for a minute or two, he just hadn't informed the man. "We're here, Mr. Byrd."

"You will keep the boat directly at this location, with your clutches as need be. I'll be verifying your position from here. Any deviation will result in your mate getting his head blown off. Do we understand each other?"

"Reckon we do," Louis slowly answered.

The current was setting Louis to the southwest and he would have to repeatedly put the boat ahead to maintain his coordinates. His radar showed the target four miles out and still closing. Louis squinted to the northeast and could now see the bow of the boat and a gray smoke trail. Louis had to admit one thing, the pup had set a nice trap. There was no place to go except right at the advancing boat.

Down below, Crafty opened the side compartment once more, and made noticeable noise in scattering the various chemicals about before jamming the gallon bottle and the mop back inside. *Now or never ol' boy,* he said to himself. He reached to his side for the bleach that had slid out and jammed it back into the stuffed compartment, grabbing the lip gaff from its holder in one motion. As he stood he turned to face his Byrd, shielding the gaff from view behind his body and huge forearm. "That good enough for 'ya?"

"That will do for now, Crafty. Now get back over to the other corner."

The mate picked up the door with his foot and slammed it shut sticking the gaff in his shorts behind him. He sidestepped his way a few feet over to the chair, not quite the distance to Whitman, and again turned to face his captor.

"I said go back over there by Whitman. Now, mate!

R1 . . . do you have a visual on us yet?"

"Roger R2 . . . we have you in sight, two miles 210 degrees."

"R1 . . . keep initial coordinates at constant bearing of 200 degrees, proceeding thereafter to current position.

"Confirmed R2."

Crafty began to quiz Byrd as he made the final two sidesteps over to Frank who was now holding himself erect with his long arms on the covering board. "What are you going to do with us, Byrd?"

"You, Mr. Whitman, Cami, and the good captain are going for a little boat ride. Then we are going to take your vessel in tow for awhile, and set it free inshore, somewhere southwest of here."

"What's that supposed to achieve?"

"Quite simple, really. The Cuban authorities will impound the vessel, if it's in one piece, go through it with a legion of ants, and discover many interesting things on board."

"Like?"

"Come now, mate, use your imagination. Like documents and governmental intelligence data and computer clearance codes, patent rights and future technical data held by Whitman Technologies. One might even suspect a bit of leakage was going on here. Frank, I'm so appreciative that you went to all that extra trouble fetching those important papers and materials at the last minute. A look at all those networks, supply lines and future product developments, should keep your competitors salivating for months to come."

"Scott, that material is all back in the penthouse safe at the hotel, you realize that don't you?"

"Yes, Frank, I'm sure it was all there at exactly 10:45 this morning as well. Of course, the Cubans will not find that material, as I have substituted useless, false, and outdated paper in its place. Rather creative don't you think, Frank? You have taught me extremely well, sir, how to play both ends against each other, for the good of the middle. Especially when you are fortunate to become that in between.

"You are not going to get away with this, Byrd! It's not going to happen!" Whitman appeared on the verge of a blind rage, the veins on his neck popping out and pulsating. His eyes were locked in a hardened squint, his whole body began to quiver uncontrollably. Crafty was sure that Whitman could see the gaff stuck in his shorts from where he was standing to the mate's left.

"Sorry, Crafty." The tall man uttered as he turned and extended his hand to his mate, rolling his eyes in the direction of the armed man. In a suicidal lunge, Whitman hurled his large anatomy directly at Byrd, momentarily smothering the rifle between their chests. Byrd let the clip go and lifted the taller man upward along with the top of his head. The momentum of the larger Whitman was carrying the pair towards the side of the boat pinning the weapon between them.

Crafty made a split second decision to immediately use his weapon rather than gamble in an attempt to wrestle the rifle away from Byrd. As he sprang toward Byrd, who was now trying to heave the heavy corpse off him to free his gun, Crafty reached for the lip gaff behind his back, grabbing the handle firmly. He made his target as he leaped across the rear of the cockpit. With arm held high, he brought the three-inch hook down on the side of Byrd's head with all the force he could summon.

In slow motion he watched the point enter the man's right temple and he felt hard resistance for only a brief moment. He twisted his hand again, and watched as the point of the gaff exited the Byrd's right eye. He could see the terror in the young man as his left eye rolled to the right, staring in total fear as the bloodied point with the eye on its tip squirmed and trumpeted the gravity of his own injury. Whitman continued on his silent track over the side, taking with him the rifle that Byrd had released in panic.

With his free left hand Byrd pulled a knife from the sheath attached to the left side of his belt and began to stab his assailant repeatedly. He was screaming in sheer agony and terror as he tried vainly to grab control of the gaff with his right hand.

Crafty remained welded to its handle with the powerful vice grip of a fisherman's hand. He led the mortally wounded man, like a big fish, hurling him to the edge of the rear covering board and over the stern into the peaceful blue sea. He watched the man twitch twice, and then lay still as he floated off behind the boat.

Louis understood that the power play had been taken when he first heard the shots ring out. What he didn't know was the outcome. He did know that if things went in their favor the approaching vessel would probably be unable to observe the activity in the cockpit. The current was pushing right on Louis' bow and he was nearly head-on with the oncoming boat that was a mile away and closing fast. The slight angle to starboard should have effectively shielded most of the cockpit to its right side.

"Louis, I'm here! Whitman and Byrd are dead, I got the little bastard. Hear me?"

"Gotcha, Crafty! We're just gonna slip with the current a little in behind the reef ledge a ways. I can't be makin' any wake or smoke! I'm sure they got us in good visual from their end. Hear me all right?"

"Yeah. I got pricked a couple of times, but I'm all right."

"If we get our chance it'll have to be quick and outta here blind, on ranges only. Understand?"

"I'm with you." Crafty saw the hand-held radio laying on the deck and picked it up. He took the squelch off momentarily causing the static to stab the silence. *Thank God it still worked*, he thought to himself. He picked up a boat towel out of the fishing station and began dabbing at his stab wounds.

"S2 we have you steady . . . confirm track."

Crafty keyed the transmit button, "Proceed on visual track S1," Crafty answered in his best Byrd.

There was a brief pause . . . "Confirmed."

269

Louis' experience had taught him years ago that there were really three mistakes made on this one, not a single miscalculation. Never run a reef blind looking directly into the glare of afternoon sun if you don't know the ranges from your own experience. Don't ever be afraid to second guess yourself or any aid to navigation. The third error was bound to follow, leading the approaching boat to its own "piece of the rock". It would soon find the reef.

"Cami, go lie flat on the deck to the right of the console, and don't be sticking your head up for any reason. Hurry!" The woman nodded at Louis and did exactly as she was told.

Louis waited patiently for the oncoming boat as it neared his position, now only a half mile away. He watched the numbers clicking off his LORAN, and he knew that he had slipped to the west of the submerged point at the opening's western edge. It was only a matter of seconds now.

The old captain now recognized the boat as the Stryker that had tied up behind them the night before. He wondered if the crew had met a similar fate, or if they had been good actors playing their roles last night. *It didn't matter*, he said to himself, as he pulled the autopilot's remote control from its holster on the door to the helm station. He uncoiled the fifteen feet of cable and handed it over to Cami laying prone on the deck next to the helm.

He turned his eyes back to the big Stryker running right at him. Should be any time now he said quietly. When she hit the first time, there was a light trail of black smoke, then it cleared for a brief moment. But on the second contact the sixty-three-footer reared up in her stern, throwing whitewater down the sides of her hull as she came to an abrupt stop. There was a big cloud of black smoke as her huge diesels went into an immediate stall. The crippled vessel then sank back in the water showing a near normal attitude, and Louis was uncertain as to the extent of her wounds. She could possibly free herself without using her engines with the help of the strong current around. Now was the time to run for it, when confusion was at its peak.

"We're gettin outta here, Crafty, take cover until I blow the horn. Don't go climbin' up here now."

"Go Louis!"

Louis buried the throttles to the max, making a course for the far right side of the opening. He left the wheel and hopped over the right side of the helm, where he laid atop Cami as he faced the stern. This provided as much of a shield as they were going to get.

He stuck his head up one last time, to get a position fix and saw armed men already scurrying out on the foredeck of the grounded Stryker. He would come to within a hundred yards of the vessel, overtaking her position port to port as he passed by. He fully expected a hail of automatic weapon fire, and quite possibly, something heavier than that. He again laid down over the blonde as low as he could, looking astern as he carved a long slow turn to port.

When his turn gave him a view to the southeast, he picked up on his first range, using the autopilot's course control to keep him steered properly on it. He looked at his watch. The second of the two ranges should be lining up soon. "There it is," Louis spoke out loud. He now corrected back to the north, and gritted his teeth waiting for the onslaught.

He saw the bullets before he heard the first shots, as they tore up the soft top overhead and canvas wrapping around the bridge. He also heard quite a few rounds deflecting off the tall aluminum tower. Now it was just a constant showering of noise and splinters, all around.

He looked back into the island and kept the boat on her range as shots penetrated the calm sea in his wake. Suddenly he heard the tandem whistles of incoming rockets, and buried his head in the neck of the blonde laying under him. The boat shuddered under the shockwave of an explosive column of water, a few yards short on the port side of the boat. They were two hundred yards from her now, and the fire they were drawing was becoming more random and less accurate all the time. Louis did not rise up until the boat passed well into his view, 400 yards off his stern. He did not stand until he had put another quarter mile between their positions.

Louis was on fire with adrenaline pumping all through his body. He could see that the boat had already maneuvered around somewhat, showing her bow in his direction. They could be clear of the reef in a matter of moments. But at least the gunfire had subsided.

He got on his feet long enough to read the compass, which indicated a course of ten degrees NNE. He sat back down on the deck and looked at his remote window, currently indicating six degrees NNE. He turned the course selector dial until the window showed 24 degrees, 28 mag., putting him on a line with Duck Key.

He looked back to the Stryker now over a mile back and was quite dismayed to see her attempting to get up on a plane. She was sucking down, however, throwing much wake. *Maybe she wouldn't be able to climb out*, Louis thought.

She was still laying back, and the *Nina Mia* had put almost another half mile between them. Then it was over. The wounded Stryker made a turn into the west, and limped her way back into the sun towards Havana.

Louis stood up and began to look around. Thank you Lord, for carrying us through. Thank you, Lord. "Okay, Cami?"

"Yeah, I'm fine, got lucky."

Louis was surprised at her being so calm. "Crafty, you all right?"

"Yeah, Cap. Just takin' a look around, doin' a little straightening up. Looks like we been bailin' dolphin down here."

There were chips and holes and dings everywhere along the side of the bridge. The radar had been taken out, along with the

272

GPS. They had the LORAN, AP and VHF radio still on line, some of the console had been shredded. Overall, she was running fine, but with considerable cosmetic damage to her topsides.

Louis walked over to the edge of the bridge, and looked down at his mate. The man looked up at him, in a broad smile, "Feelin' alive are we now, Cap? Just like the old days, a bit different."

Louis smiled back at him, "Don't move around, Crafty, Cami's comin' down to help you and take a look at those wounds. How's it look down below, the engines and all?"

"Louis, I have not found much cut-up below deck. Amateurs they were, they didn't even have the common sense to go for an engine block."

"Kill everything but the battery chargers on the AC circuits. I don't want genny pumpin' all throughout the ship with everything tore up."

Louis felt awful as he surveyed the once pristine Whiticar. "I'm so sorry darlin' to have dealt you this after all we've been through. But I thank you for bein' there to get us where we are. We'll take care of everything and get ya' painted up when we get home." He started patting her on the side of the disfigured helm.

"Louie, I'm going down to, . . . " Cami suddenly became quiet as she hopped up from the deck. She looked at the Captain and was not smiling now. "Louie, you took one. How do you feel?"

"Yeah, where?" The old man still pumped full of adrenaline started looking down his front, arms and legs.

"Right here," she answered as she pointed to a spot around his right kidney. A six-inch circle of red soaked his white T-shirt.

"I'll be. Don't hurt too much yet. Here, can you hold the wheel?"

"Sure I can, go down and check on your mate."

"Yeah . . . I need to know what's going on with him. She's set

273

on autopilot. If you need to change course, turn this dial to power, and you'll get the wheel back. When you get back on course just go over to auto here."

Louis was starting to get a little pain from his gunshot wound and he took some care getting down off the bridge. When he stepped into the cockpit, he found his mate leaning up against the corner holding a red towel to his side. "How are we doing, Crafty?"

"Frank . . . He gave his life for us, Louis. He threw himself at Byrd, burying the rifle and taking half the clip. I had found Alfie's old lip gaff up under the top of the cleaning locker, and slipped it in my shorts behind me. Frank . . . he . . . gave us the opening. I caught Byrd with the gaff square in his right temple, and twisted it back out through his eye. I felt him knifin' me in the side over here, and he stuck me in this shoulder a couple of times. I led him back to the transom and heaved him over the stern with the gaff still in him. Got lucky, Louis, we got real lucky. We'd better get back to Havana, and have that thing you got looked at."

"Not a chance. We ain't goin' back to that hornet's nest."

"Louis!"

"Now, Crafty, what have we got here? Two missing dead men, a tore up boat. You know they'll impound her, and Alfie won't ever see her again. We'll be sittin on ice till next year—if we're lucky and we get medical treatment. No, I'm headed home, Duck Key. Them boys in there don't even have a record of our bein' there. Maybe we never left."

"Cap, you need some attention."

"And you don't? Mine ain't that bad, Crafty. You look like you can hold on, you're not pumpin' out of any of them wounds. As long as I'm runnin' this rig we're headed for the Keys."

"All right, Louis, I'll respect that. But you keep me aware of what's happenin', know what I mean."

"I will, Crafty, you'll be the first to know," Louis replied with a slight grin. He picked his mate off the deck and helped him inside to lay out on the couch. He took a blanket from the crew's quarters and covered his mate with it. "You stay right here, take this pillow if you want. I'm headed back up."

"Louis, I'll be fine."

26

The man did not rise up out of his chair to answer the phone, now into its fifth ring. He stared out at the Atlantic Ocean from the balcony of his south Miami Beach penthouse, chugging the rest of his drink when the phone ceased its ringing. When it rang again in exactly fifteen seconds, he reached for the receiver, "Yes?"

"It's done, we have the material; we do not have the boat."

"Why?"

"The kid didn't come through; he must be history. I told you."

"Whitman?"

"Crab food. Found him floating, we cut him up with the props."

"We have what we need, that other was always secondary. As a pawn, Mr. Byrd served us well. You are tracking the vessel?"

"Of course."

"Finish it then, you have some cleaning up to do." The man hung up the phone, hopping out of his lounge chair to mix another drink. He viewed himself in the huge mirror hanging behind the bar, straightening his hair while studying his profile, before cracking a satisfied smile.

Louis checked his LORAN, and it put the red buoy offshore Duck Key at a distance of fifty-eight nautical miles. They were closer to home now, so he felt it was all right for Cami to spell him once again on the bridge. He tooted the horn twice.

She had spent some time taping Louis' side up, applying a

pressure bandage to the wound site. There was no exit wound, and they both figured the bullet was in there somewhere. Maybe a ricochet the captain said. At least it wasn't bleeding too bad at the surface.

"How are you doing, Louie, need a spell honey?"

"Yes, Cami, this thing's starting to pain me a little."

"I brought you a Coke."

"Thanks. 'Bout as pretty an evenin' as you would ever want. Good thing it ain't rough. If I go out Cami, there is something I got to show you. Crafty is not fit to drive the boat. How is he doing by the way?"

"Sleeping right now, I patched him up a little, too. He's pretty damn lucky to have all those stab wounds and have them miss anything vital. He's going to make it, Louie."

"You know how to work a LORAN?"

"Show me what to do."

"Can you drive and clutch this boat around?"

"That I can do. I used to help the old man all the time."

"Hey!" They both laughed for the first time all day. "The route into the dock is number 44, I'll key it up right now. There are four different waypoints to get you home. Louis made his keypad entries to bring up, enter, and reverse the route sequence. "See, there's the first leg of your trip. Just steer your course so that your COG, or course over ground, is lined up with your bearing to waypoint here in this window. It's that easy. When you pass each point, the next point will appear in the window automatically. You must clear each waypoint by passing it abeam on either side. Got it?"

"I think so."

"If you have a problem, just shake me hard till I wake up. I'm goin' down below where I can hear you and Crafty. I'd like to lay in the chair if ya' don't mind."

"Louie you just do that, I can take her from here." She watched the man strain as he carefully worked his way down the steps. At one point she saw him grimace in pain, and she leaped to the edge of the bridge.

"I'm fine, don't worry, I got it." He slowly stepped from the covering board into the cockpit and worked his way to the fighting chair. He swiveled the chair to face the port side and the setting sun in the west. After adjusting the cushions, he slowly helped himself into it before laying back.

He straightened his cap and closed his eyes for a few moments, letting the *Nina Mia* and her engines take him in her arms. The sound was comforting and narcotic. In a minute or two he opened his eyes once again and looked back at the wake running behind. A flying fish or two leaped from its surging waves.

He filled his lungs and nostrils with the fresh sea air, and it was sweeter than he had ever remembered in his thousands of days at sea. *Thank you Lord for all of this, for everything which you've given me in this life.*

He looked over to the fading sun now behind a line of dark clouds, the indirect rays were determined to remain bright. The old man remembered his Cuban father and brother, and the days long ago, in visions that were returning clear and strong before his eyes. He saw his daughter at home studying, knowing securely, that he would see her again.

From a distance, he heard Crafty call for him, and it reminded him of the time they first met on a dock at Cape Hatteras. The images were coming quite clearly now, and closing his eyes only made them stronger. He and Crafty had caught a winning fish, and the young captain had been talked into throwing his mate into the water at the Hatteras Marlin Club. Creekin' was an old custom of marlin fishermen. Louis had tried with all he had in him, but could not overcome the young man's strength. That is until he threw both of them in. He heard the shouts of all the fishermen standing around. He could see their smiling faces choked with laughter, and they all leaned over to him from the dock as they extended their arms.

Louis felt a sharp pain, and he brought himself back to the chair, "Cami."

"Yes, Louie."

"Put the AP on and come down here, please."

"On my way."

She left the bridge and hurried to the steps, before hitting the cockpit deck in a couple of jumps. "What's the matter, Hon? Louis? Feelin' okay?" She studied the captain's eyes, and they were clear, but without definition.

"Sorry, I'm gettin so tired, Cami, wish I could help you a little more. My day seems nearly gone."

"Louie, come on now, I'm not gonna let that happen," her eyes filling with tears.

"I tell you the truth, don't you dare feel bad for me. I know where I've been, and I know where I'm going. It is a far prettier place than even here. Listen," Louis pulled her down to his lips as his voice was suddenly becoming very weak, "you have no radar, there is a route into Alfie's dock stored in the LORAN. It's number 44, got that?"

"I got it, Louie, you told me."

"There may only be a little time for you. Look to the Lord, darlin', for where to go from here. There will be no warning, so you get your lamp lit and keep it lit. You need to be ready when He gets here."

"Louis, it's gettin' dark and stormy looking to the west, why don't you lay down inside. You shouldn't be talkin', just rest."

"You just keep your heart open, and you'll get it. He has been with you for awhile."

"What darling?"

"His gift for you will be made clear in his words. He gave you all of this, didn't He?" A smiling Louis motioned to the sea around them with his free arm. "You must be convinced of your offense before the living God. Ask the Lord, Him alone, for help.

For within you and of you, it is a complete impossibility. You can't reason for yourself, that which is so great and beyond your definition."

The old man turned to face the sea again, and his expression softened as he closed his eyes.

Cami was starting to lose it a little, now feeling very much alone. She searched for a pulse, it was very faint. *Could be getting a little shocky*. She was desperate. She ran into the salon and down the gangway into the first stateroom ripping a blanket off the lower bunk. She came back out and covered her captain carefully as she wiped the tears from her face. She checked his pulse again, and it was still there.

She hurried back up to the bridge, and made sure the throttles were buried. She noticed she was only a half mile from the first waypoint off her port side. She studied the window to see if the transition to the next point would be correct. There was some flashing of numbers, and then the message *Please Stand By* appeared. Finally, the second waypoint of the route into Alfie's dock appeared in the display windows along with other nav data. She moved the course selector dial on the autopilot, until the COG was the same as the Bearing to Waypoint on the LORAN.

Cami knew she was close enough to get weather on the VHF, so she selected the clearest of the four channels, even though it was still breaking up. The blonde quickly walked to the rear of the bridge and saw Louis laying comfortably in the chair. *Hang in there, Captain, we'll be home in an hour and a half*, she thought to herself.

The navigation lights, Louis awoke from his dream. The last thing he wanted to do was draw attention by coming in without running lights. The authorities would be on them like bloodhounds.

As he slowly got out of the fighting chair, he felt faint and the cockpit was spinning around. He leaned up against the bulkhead doors and took a couple of deep breaths. When his head cleared enough so that he could open them, he went inside over to the salon panel and switched the NAV light breaker to ON, bringing power to the switch on the bridge. On his way back out, he checked Crafty's pulse again, and was relieved to find he was still with him. The mate stirred, "Louis, I'm okay. Just conservin'. Let me know when you need me."

"I will." Out in the cockpit now, Louis called up to the new captain, "Cami, you hear me?" She came to the rear of the bridge and leaned over down at Louis. *She looks so good up there*, he thought. "Turn your Nav light switch on, and make sure you have your running lights," Louis instructed her as he nearly fell trying to get back in the chair. "We're not quite ready for customs or the marine patrol just yet."

She verified she had lights and was again skipping around the VHF, stopping at WX3, where the weather channel's transmission had cleared remarkably. The continuous loop tape was now spitting out a special marine warning for marine interests in the Florida Keys and adjacent coastal waters. The trailing edge of a powerful low pressure system was moving to the southeast at 45mph, bringing with it winds gusting to sixty, and the potential for hail. All small craft should seek port. "Yeah, yeah that's what we're tryin' to do, you . . . you tape!

She looked to the northwest, saw a little heat lightning, but that was it. Offshore it was dead calm with a light west wind, stars overhead. *A beautiful evening,* she thought, *or could be.* Cami scanned the LORAN, 25 miles out from the sea bouy. *Come on baby, get us all home, okay.*

But after putting a couple of more miles behind her, Cami was beginning to pick up something to the northwest. What could only be a line of dark clouds was blotting out the clear, starry night in a veil of black. Behind the dark curtain rapidly approaching from the northwest, the faint light of day's end separated clear air from the turbulence below. Occasionally, the entire line would be backlighted by lightning strikes, momentarily whitening the cloud tops.

The blonde could see the squall line was moving at great speed. The black drape was overtaking the clear night and ascending higher into the heavens as it rapidly approached.

She walked to the rear of the bridge one more time. Louis appeared comfortable in the chair and had not shifted in his position. *This thing is really movin'*, she said out loud. *No way I'm gonna beat that into the dock.* She walked to the side of the bridge to better view it, and to rid herself of the night blindness that staring at instruments and electronics had created.

"Damn nice lookin' squall," she said out loud taking a brief read of her compass. She made a bearing on the fast moving storm to be around 285 degrees. "I ain't gonna beat poor Louis to death when this thing hits. I'll have to slow down and put her nose right into it. It'll be the best ride for him." Cami was constantly talking out loud to herself now.

27

Something tapping on his shoulder woke Louis from his dream once again, forcing his eyes to slowly crack open. The moon had fully illuminated his boat's wake, as he stared back into the calm sea. He could see the wave pattern of toppling crests extending out almost 500 yards astern. And then far behind, another smaller point of white, and a dark form. He rubbed his eyes to clear and settle them, and gazed back once again. "Crafty," he yelled as loud as he could. Again he called out for his mate.

"Louis?"

"Come here quick, and bring the binocs." The old man heard his mate acknowledge his request, but it was a minute or so before he stood alongside Louis holding on to the chair for support.

Louis' apprehension had by now fully awakened him. He grabbed the binoculars from Crafty's hand, returning his attention to the boat's wake. After fifteen seconds, he handed them back to the other man, "Take a look, Crafty, and tell me I'm not losin' it. Back there in the wake, what d'ya see?"

The mate briefly scanned the moonlit sea astern, "I see a frickin' go fast boat, and she's closin' on us fast. Damn!"

"You thinkin what I'm thinkin'?"

"Somebody worried about covering up the trail."

Louis took the glasses back once more, "I see no radar, but I'll bet she's got an ADF. Take a look."

"Right on, cap. Must have known our course and destination."

"Cami, hear me?"

"Yeah, Louie," she answered.

"Turn off your course immediately, and head directly into that squall line." He settled back down in the fighting chair and turned to his mate, "Crafty, I wanted to sneak in there quietly so you two could jump ship with the rental car. But . . . I'm afraid we might have to hit the dock with bells and whistles, and you're gonna have to make it up top to help her out."

"Absolutely, old man! I'm up to it. What'd ya think I was gonna dump this whole thing in your lap and skip out. Just stay put now."

Crafty fought through the pain in getting himself up to the bridge with a final heave from the blonde pulling him up and over as she lay flat on her stomach. He went and collapsed into the captain's chair, instructing Cami to lay down in the front seat. *It would not be much longer for the weather*, he thought. He could smell the change in the atmosphere, the ozone, and then there was that eerie calm. What? He heard the whistling sound crescendo in the distance in the still air.

"Incoming!" Crafty screamed with all the effort he could summon. The rocket grenade exploded in a giant stand of water twenty yards off the starboard bow. The second blast nearly hit the fleeing boat dead center, blowing out the salon window on her starboard side.

When the wind did finally come up, it built to fifty knots in a matter of seconds, and got very cold. Crafty quickly checked the boat heading at 285 degrees, and continued to run full speed into the fierce winds as the rain with embedded hail intensified.

Once inside the fury of the squall line he pulled the power back to idle on both engines and shut off the running lights. He knew he had to kill the wake trail, for it was the only thing the closing boat had to verify their boat's track.

Crafty idled the boat to a new course of 230 degrees, knowing the torrential rain would sweep clean the screw currents and flatten any wake impulses at her stern. He was not running directly at his pursuer, but heading laterally against the boat's original course.

Two minutes later, Crafty was satisfied that the much faster attacker had most probably overtaken his own previous position. The mate theorized the pursuer would be committed to maintaining his original intercept course once he lost the wake trail he so desperately needed in the poor 100-foot visibility, spotlights or not. They had, after all, been fully aware of the *Nina Mia*'s travel plans.

Crafty again brought the power up, burying the throttles to the pins. He made course of 270 degrees, a compromise between the shortest distance to the coast, and a heading aimed at putting some distance between him and his attacker.

Cami had walked around from the front and was soaking wet as she took the companion seat next to Crafty. "I'm calling the cops," she said reaching for the VHF mike in its holder.

"Not yet, Cami, don't key that microphone!" Crafty warned her as he grabbed her by the arm. "They got an ADF on that boat, being the good smugglers they probably are."

"ADF?"

"Automatic Directional Finder. Hit that transmit key, and its sweep will pinpoint our location by tracing the radio waves of the transmission, painting our bearing for 'em on their set."

It was a deluge of unbelievably heavy rainfall. The winds held steady at least fifty, and Crafty was quite sure there were gusts to hurricane strength. He thought about his captain, laying in that fighting chair, exposed and out in the open in this mess. He was saddened and then became very angry.

"You should have moved him inside, Crafty, what were you thinking!" The mate began to berate himself out loud, "You covered him up, maybe it was better to have not moved him. Enough, will you quit!" He screamed out to the storm as loud as he could. "Please stop for my friend. He needs to get home."

The blonde quietly placed her hand on the man's arm and stroked it gently. Minutes later the squall passed on, its ferocity died down as quickly as it had overtaken them. He could see the line of weather moving off to the southeast now, looking for new territory to unleash its wrath. The charges of connective lightning made it appear white and rose colored, making it far more beautiful from this direction.

"Well, we're back out in the open now Cami, looks like a race to the sea bouy. You better go on down and check on Louis, and dry yourself off while you're at it."

She found Louis lying in the chair beneath the soaking wet blanket. She reached for a pulse and it was very weak, and his skin was ice cold. She threw off the blanket, picked him up out of the fighting chair, and literally dragged him into the salon, laying him on the couch. She stripped the Captain down to his skivies, removing everything from herself but her panties. She grabbed Crafty's dry blanket, covering the two of them in a cocoon of warmth as she kneaded and rubbed Louis' chilled body.

Crafty had the boat aimed right at the outer red bouy off Duck Key, showing it to be a distance of seven nautical miles. He set the boat on autopilot and left the helm to clear his own eyes of night blindness. *Sneaking into Alfie's dock unnoticed was still the preferred way to go,* he argued with himself, and he hoped he would have no need of any outside help.

The mate walked to the rear of the bridge and made a slow 360-degree scan. He repeated his lookout watch, this time using the binoculars. So far so good, he thought, but his realistic concerns started working on him. He had to believe that even as they were approaching the Silva dock from the west, his pursuer would almost certainly know it was their final destination.

What possible good could come by pulling into another dock. Questions would still be raised, and there was a chance others could be looking for him. It would only be a matter of time before the authorities would piece together the information and the Feds would come sticker and seize the boat anyway.

Confronting the truth head on, demonstrating their intentions to clarify the situation for all, was their only play. He only hoped it wouldn't finally do in the old man at the Silva house.

Five more miles. He rose again to take another look around the moonlit sea. His gut flip-flopped when he again saw the racing boat's form through the binoculars, porpoising towards them from the southeast, some distance away. "They must have infared on that rig," Crafty spoke loudly, "night eyes been keying in on our exhausts the whole time. Dammit! At least the squall line camouflaged the heat signature for a little while. Man . . ."

He hustled back to the helm and picked up the radio mike as he switched over to channel 22A, the Coast Guard working channel. He keyed the transmit button, "Wake up you lazy dogs, you gotta big hit goin' down right now! One carrier is probably half way into Duck Key by now, another smaller package is right behind him. Consider yourselves lucky, they ripped me off."

"This is the United States Coast Guard group seven Marathon, Florida, monitoring channel 22 alpha, could you repeat that last transmission."

"You heard me coastie boys, I gotta go!" The mate then switched over to thirteen and rang up the Florida Marine Patrol to invite them to the party. He could see their mouths drooling now. Finally, Crafty got hold of the marine operator and rang up the Silva house. He alerted Alfie's housekeeper that they were coming home with the boat early, and that they would be bringing lots of company with them. Everyone on board was okay, but he warned that there would be a wave of law enforcement assaulting their home. He suggested that she call the local police on 911 to report a robbery in progress at the home. Stay inside and cooperate.

Crafty took a look dead astern through his glasses and saw the boat in his wake. He laughed out loud. How many lobster pots could he grind up in his props running on plane all the way into the dock. He was in about 300 feet of water now, and knew he was only miles from the Sea Buoy. Then he heard that sound and just gritted his teeth as the rocket neared. Whooosh. And then another salvo.

The explosion of the second rocket attack blew more shards of glass into the salon from her right side window. An abruptly wakened Louis grabbed Cami, rolling the two of them, still wrapped in the blanket, off the couch onto the floor. He lay over the top of her, shielding her face and body as best he could. His returning consciousness had left him feeling a little better, and he knew right then that he was going to make it through another one.

Crafty remained at the helm as he covered his face and head with his arms, fully expecting another round. It was then that he heard the faint sound of the chopper. He looked back and saw the chase boat in the distance, probably headed back off-shore. As the sound grew louder, the mate continued to push his vessel at full speed.

As he passed the outer red bell buoy, he found himself in the spotlight, the star of the show. The chopper's huge 300,000 candlepower search light had the *Nina Mia* bathed in white light. He picked up the mike, "Anyone on channel 16?"

"Switch 22a."

"I'm here if you're there," the mate said with a big smile. "I'm right down here in your light, making way to a private dock four miles ahead. I have alerted the authorities, and will make no attempt to flee. I have two injured people on board, and require immediate medical attention. Acknowledge."

" . . . We got you, and will escort you to that dock along with the DEA vessel to your stern, and the Marine patrol vessel en route. Do not leave your vessel until U.S. Customs arrives on the scene."

"White hats on parade!" Crafty gave a loud hoot. "I love it."

A powerful roving search light was now streaking in and out

of the darkened cabin. Louis braced for another rocket as his mind raced for a plan if they were suddenly boarded. After listening to the chopper for a minute, he went to his feet slowly to sneak a look out of the empty window frame, and smiled when he saw the white and orange Coast Guard configuration, highlighted by the aircraft's running lights. This game was over.

He reached down and helped the blonde still in the blanket to her feet and over to the couch. He stroked her hair as he searched for pieces of glass. Occasionally, the roving beacon lit their faces and they smiled softly at one another. He spoke first.

"I'm so sorry about Frank. It was his decision to make the ultimate sacrifice, it was his finest hour. The Lord will surely have him in tow, Cami."

"Frank was mellowing to the point of becoming another person. He was learning so much at the end, Louie. You could see changes taking place everyday. We talked a lot more; there was excitement in his heart. He was a good father to me, Honey, I loved him very much. I must tell you that I'm not such a nice, friendly little thing. It's like I said—if Frank hadn't rescued me and cleaned me out, I'd still be hookin' and hittin' . . . "

"Been right there myself, Cami. We all have our own baggage as a reminder to convict us. We all need more than a little forgiveness, and then we got to move on." The old man closed his eyes and drew her to him.

Crafty had the dock in sight as he made his final turn into the canal, still lit up from the chopper's searchlight. He quietly brought the old girl along side her dock, and clutched her in reverse till she came to a dead stop. He took his time climbing down off the bridge, before putting a forward and aft spring line on her port side.

When the mate finally shut down the engines, all was quiet. The flashing blue lights were everywhere, and for as long as he could remember, this was the first time they had ever looked that good to him.

Epilogue

The heavy man was sweating profusely as he finally made his way inside the outer lobby of the South Beach condo. He set down the attaché case he was carrying and paused to dry himself off with a handkerchief. Entering a four-digit code, he then pushed the call button for the penthouse apartment. Within seconds he was buzzed inside the main foyer and the elevators. As he rode to the top, he continued dabbing at himself, most grateful to be in the AC.

When the doors parted he was greeted by his smiling host. "Capn' George, good to see you. Come in, come in!"

"What it is, Adam, been a long day."

"A drink, George?" Wendt offered as he led the way inside and over to bar.

"Definitely, sir, I'm in dire need," replied the fat Texan as he set his briefcase on the bar top.

"Help yourself, Capn' George, you know where everything is," Wendt replied, immediately going to the case. He was smiling from ear to ear as he rifled through its contents for a minute or two. He glanced over to his guest who had poured a near tumbler of Jack Daniels, and began to quietly nod his approval.

"All there isn't it, Adam?"

"Nice job, George. Call your banker, if you like. You'll find everything in order down in Honduras."

"Already done that, Adam, you ought to know my act by now."

"Excuse me for a minute, George," Wendt answered as he jumped off the barstool and made his way to the master bedroom where he kept his personal things in the safe. Before returning he took a detour to the bathroom for a quick refresher. He took a few Valiums from the pill case on the vanity as he began to wash up. He studied his reflection, smiling thinly, for there were still a few details left to contend with. The phone cut his grooming short.

Wendt briskly walked back to the living room bar, picking the phone up, only after the traditional second ringing fifteen seconds later.

"Yes?" Wendt passed the receiver over to his guest, "Your man."

"George here." The Texan listened for two minutes, showing Wendt nothing but an unreadable blank stare. "Okay," was all he said before hanging up. He started smiling and scratching his head as he continued to stare at Wendt.

"Out with it, George, where do we stand?" Suddenly, the world famous visage of the telegenic Wendt had lost a little of its color.

"Couldn't get 'em for you, sir, they slipped away from us. They had a little outside help from the weather and everything else for that matter. They got enough of their own troubles down there. You'll get your chance sooner or later."

"Not good enough! There's a trail that could lead to both of us!"

"Why Adam, you look like your getting a might seasick. What happened to all your color?" The Texan began to laugh hysterically, "Would you like me to put you out of your misery? They say when you're really seasick, you 'bout wish you were dead. Hey, Adam, you know what's worse than being seasick?"

"I fail to see the humor in this, George."

"Being seasick a second time!" Capn' George could hardly breathe he was laughing so hard. He reached for his Black Jack, and took a long pull as a pale Adam Wendt looked on. With his non-drinking hand the fat man produced a .45 from under the bar, leveling it at Wendt's head. George was not laughing anymore.

"It would seem, Adam, that our famous Cuban Louie and Boy Crafty, are proving to be an elusive catch. I can surely see that my job is finished here, I'm done. You can do what you want with them two. You see, Wendt, I got a whole lot more respect for them, than I ever could for you. People like you all measure out the same. You want the outcome, but you don't want the fight."

"You fool, George, this will turn on you and me!"

"AAh. This is how scum like you and me survive, Wendt. Checks and balances—a little paranoia is a necessary thing." Laughter again welled up from the belly of the Texan, "It's when you get too comfortable that the system breaks down, you know, ya' kinda drop your guard." Capn' George slid off the barstool and downed the rest of his sourmash, never taking his eyes off his host.

"I'm not comfortable with this, George!"

"Must be some kind of personal problem, 'cause, boy, you sacrificed comfort a long time ago. Forget you ever met me. You may have your people but I got mine . . . And, Adam, . . . I got more." The big man began to laugh once more as he let himself out, "See ya."

Adam Wendt again stared at his reflection in the huge mirror over the bar, turning his head from side to side. He saw that all color had left his face, and his eyes appeared dark and vacant.

You know, you could use some rest, he spoke out loud at his reflection. In a rage, he hurled the phone at the huge mirror, shattering it into bits and pieces.

Crafty was exhausted as he tried to lasso an outer piling for a bow line, but somehow completed the connection. He walked to the rear of the boat and put a line on her stern. The physically beaten mate was running on autopilot as he grabbed the shore cord and stepped back upon the dock. But for fear of electrical problems and fire, he chose not to plug the boat in.

There would be long hours of interrogation and days of investigation before this would all be laid to rest. But for now, he and Louis would be escorted to the ER to receive medical treatment.

Crafty watched as the ambulance crew lifted his captain off the boat on a stretcher and could see the paramedics already had him on a couple of IVs. He met the group at the end of the dock, halting them briefly so he might speak to his old friend. He softly grabbed Louis' hand and looked him in the eye.

"Wouldn't have missed this one for the world, Cap. Proud to have fished with you, the best I ever known. We got him didn't we, Louis? We caught the one we needed, the winning fish."

"Yeah . . . we got what was left of it, Crafty, but we didn't catch the spirit. Is that winnin'? I don't know. But, you were part of a much greater victory."

"Louis?"

"The reclaiming of a man's soul. Crafty . . . " Louis pulled his mate closer to speak quietly in his ear.

"Yeah, Louis."

"I feel like some of the vermin may be very close by."

"What's that?"

"The chase boat . . . I'm not totally sure, I don't think it ever veered off. Be careful now, ol' boy, I'll be seein' ya soon."

Crafty watched as the paramedics took Cami and Louis away into the awaiting ambulance. He felt good about those two, and he hoped things would continue on. His captain's warning had caused him to nervously scan all the players in his immediate vicinity on the dock. *Something this ambitious,* he thought to himself, would most certainly reach pretty high up.

He turned to the young Customs officer at his right, "I just want to secure the boat, and gather up a few personal things

293

before we go. That all right with you?"

"Not a problem. We're certainly not going anywhere. Be right here with you."

Crafty went back down into the salon and checked the panel a final time with a flashlight. He wanted to be sure that the boat was good to sit and the batteries were all right before gathering up his and Louis' things.

He found his captain's Bible on the nightstand beside his bunk, tattered and weather worn from its daily use. He reached for it, and held it in his hands. He instantly noticed a feeling of calm warming him from within his core, and the relief he felt was most welcome.

He thought of all the places and beautiful coral seas he and Louis had fished, and where his friend might have read from its pages. It was soothing to his nerves, his heart softened and release was welling up within him.

He began to weep in celebration for the unique life they had shared, for its closeness and joy. His mind reeled through the visions of all the times they had stared at death and cheated it. Even now, when its specter had come stealing, taking a certain happiness that would never be replaced. The truth was never more clear in the heart of the broken mate. He would always carry Louis with him wherever he went, for all his days.

He went up into the salon and sat down in the darkness, giving his mind a little more time before moving on. He leaned back and considered how this unreal adventure all got started. He and Louis had done it all, gone so many places and worked together in so many tournaments and cruises. It was really quite unbelievable, however, how they happened to get through this one.

It was as if . . . everything had been set into place at every turn, for things to progress in the timely manner that they did—like it was intended to happen.

But for who's gain? If all this was going to befall Louis anyway, he was grateful that he was to he along to the very end.

He stared at the gaping hole in the side of the cabin.

Someone had been watching over them.

"In time, Crafty, you might figure it out," the mate said aloud.

He put the Bible in the duffel bag, and carried everything out into the cockpit. He passed up the sea bags one by one, to the officers on the dock, again made aware of the sharp pain in his shoulder. Crafty closed the double doors a final time, taking one last look at her for him and the captain.

"Thanks, darlin', for everything. We'll always love you."

The now much older mate made his way off the dock to join up with his escort. It was dark in the early morning when they all headed out. The moon had just set.